# *A* Whisper *in* Darkness

# DARCY BURKE

USA TODAY BESTSELLING AUTHOR

OHB

*For my mom*

# CHAPTER 1

*London, June 1868*

$\mathcal{P}$rivate investigator Matilda Wren's pulse sped with anticipation as the coach rumbled on its way from Marylebone to Belgrave Square. As usual, she was riding with her partner, Hadrian Becket, the Earl of Ravenhurst, in his coach. She was seated next to him today on the forward-facing seat and imagined she'd sit there every day now that they were courting. Not that it was official yet. Or at least, public knowledge.

How Tilda wished it could remain private. However, Hadrian had, regrettably, informed her that wouldn't be possible given his position in Society. Tilda ought to have known that. He was an earl and couldn't marry just anyone, especially someone like her.

Tilda was not from the same social or economic class as he was, and she had a job reserved for men. Both those things would almost certainly earn her censure from the Polite Society in which Hadrian moved.

She glanced over at him, sensing he was as anxious as she was.

Her apprehension had nothing to do with their courtship, however. It was entirely due to their current case, for which they'd just been hired. A young Society miss had been kidnapped two days ago, and they were on their way to her family's home to investigate.

Her parents, the Chadwicks, had come to Tilda's earlier to hire her. The chilling ransom note they'd brought still echoed in her mind:

> We have your daughter. You will exchange twenty thousand pounds for her safe return. Another note with instructions will be delivered soon. Do not contact the police for assistance. If you do, Delia will die.
>
> Yours,
> Spring-heeled Jack

"We've scarcely had time to recover from our last case," Hadrian said, breaking into Tilda's thoughts. "And almost none to discuss our courtship," he added with a wry smile.

"I was thinking of that," Tilda replied. "There will be time to discuss our…attachment. For now, we must focus on the Chadwicks and their missing daughter."

"Agreed." Hadrian's tone held the faintest note of regret.

Tilda knew he was thrilled that she'd agreed to his courtship. Despite her many concerns about a future in which she became the Countess of Ravenhurst, she loved him fiercely, which was quite a shock to her, and he loved her. Hopefully, they could navigate a way to be together, even though it seemed—to Tilda in particular—challenging.

"Chadwick offered you an exceptionally large fee," Hadrian noted.

A staggering sum—two thousand pounds. Tilda could

scarcely imagine it. Chadwick had offered half when they arrived at the family residence in Belgrave Square, to which they were on their way, and half after their daughter, Miss Delia Chadwick, was found.

"How do you feel about that?" Hadrian asked.

"I'm not sure." Nor did she want to discuss it. Especially with a man for whom that was not a large sum. Hadrian would never understand what it meant to carefully budget a household to the last penny or to worry that he may not have enough funds to pay for his dear grandmother's medication, as Tilda had.

She'd managed her grandmother's household for eight years, since her own mother had remarried and relocated to Birmingham. Tilda had preferred to stay in London with her grandmother, not that Tilda's mother had extended an invitation for Tilda to live with her and her new husband.

Tilda straightened. "Let us review what we know before we arrive at the Chadwicks'. Miss Chadwick was discovered missing two days ago by her maid when she went to wake her. The maid found the bed empty and a ransom note on the pillow signed by Spring-heeled Jack." Tilda made a derogatory sound in her throat.

"You don't believe in Spring-heeled Jack?" Hadrian asked.

"A red-eyed demon who spits blue fire, leaps atop coaches, attacks young women, and has never been identified or caught?" Tilda shook her head. "No, I don't believe in him. Spring-heeled Jack is a story told to children to titillate and frighten. Speaking of the ransom note, you were going to apply some lavender for your headache."

"It has lessened a great deal, so I nearly forgot." Hadrian kept a small bottler of lavender oil in the coach for when he sustained headaches provoked by his highly unusual ability to see others' memories when he touched people or objects. Only *some* people, not all, for Hadrian did not see the memories of those closest to him, including Tilda.

There was some indication that Hadrian's emotions might influence what he was able to see. Following one of their investigations, he'd been struck in the head and lost the ability for a time. He'd only regained it after experiencing great fear for Tilda's safety. He'd saved her life and had realized in that moment how deeply he cared for her.

Today's headache was due to Hadrian touching the ransom note and experiencing a memory that carried a deep fear. He hadn't *seen* anything, just a flash of darkness, but he'd felt the emotion. He could also, on a rare occasion, smell something from a memory. He had not ever, however, heard anything.

After taking the small bottle of lavender oil from a compartment beneath the rear-facing seat, Hadrian dabbed a bit to his temples.

"It's odd that you have such a headache without having actually seen anything," Tilda noted. "I think you're correct that Miss Chadwick must have touched the note, and you were sensing her fright." They'd discussed the unlikelihood that the kidnapper would have felt that kind of fear. "It could also have been Mrs. Chadwick or Mr. Chadwick. They handled the note, and their fear was palpable."

Hadrian nodded. "That's very true."

"Back to Spring-heeled Jack." Tilda arched a brow at him. "You don't believe in him, do you?"

"No, but I admit I'm curious about the legend. I grew up hearing frightening stories about him." Spring-heeled Jack had terrorized London thirty years earlier with several attacks against young women. Hadrian's mother had told him and his siblings more than once how horrible that time had been. He replaced the vial of lavender beneath the rear-facing seat. "Whether he was real or not, I can't imagine this kidnapper claiming to be him is the same person."

"Nor can I," Tilda said. "From what I recall of stories about Spring-heeled Jack, he was not a kidnapper."

"I've never heard that he was either. Why do you think the kidnapper claims to be this notorious figure?" Hadrian asked.

Tilda lifted a shoulder. "Perhaps he merely hopes to provoke terror so that Mr. Chadwick will pay the ransom. It's an odd choice given the crime."

They arrived at number seven Belgrave Square. Leach, Hadrian's coachman and a vital member of their investigative team, opened the door. In his middle forties, Leach did not possess a great height, but he was barrel-chested and strong. Tilda would not want to tussle with him. He was also an excellent marksman, as evidenced just a few days ago when he'd saved Tilda from certain death at the hands of a thieving murderer.

Had that really only been this past week? And here they were in the throes of another investigation. Tilda didn't mind. In fact, this was what she'd dreamed of—a thriving business as a private detective. She hoped her father, a sergeant with the Metropolitan Police before he'd been murdered eleven years ago, would be proud.

Hadrian climbed out of the coach and helped Tilda to the pavement. They walked up the steps to the grand house. The glossy black door stood in sharp contrast to the cream stucco. Elegant pilasters framed the doorway, and neat, black wrought-iron railings enclosed the lower level.

An imposing, bespectacled butler opened the door. He had a stern face with thin lips and small, brown-green eyes. His gray hair was neatly combed back from his high forehead. "You must be Lord Ravenhurst and Miss Wren."

"Yes," Tilda replied.

The butler gestured for them to proceed into the entrance hall. "Come in."

Gleaming marble greeted them along with a statue of what appeared to be Hermes, given his winged hat. Looking into the lavishly decorated rooms on either side of the entrance hall, Tilda could see how Mr. Chadwick was easily able to pay her two thousand pounds. The furnishings appeared stately and expensive and were quite plentiful. Tilda wasn't sure she could be comfortable in such formal trappings.

"Mr. Chadwick said I should show you directly to Miss Chadwick's bedchamber. He and Mrs. Chadwick are waiting for you there." The butler turned sharply on his foot and led them into the immense staircase hall where a double set of stairs curved up to a landing. They took the left side, and Tilda tried not to gape at all the portraits covering the walls. She wondered if the Chadwicks were depriving some museum of its art.

As they neared the top of the stairs, Hadrian paused and leaned his head toward her. "I will endeavor to touch as much as I can in Miss Chadwick's chamber to see what I can detect. And I will be careful," he added with a knowing look, because he was undoubtedly aware—and rightly so—that Tilda would have cautioned him to be. Too many memories in succession could cause him to suffer a debilitating headache, and he already had one.

On the first floor, the butler led them to a small sitting room decorated with bright yellow floral wallpaper and pale oak furnishings. Mrs. Chadwick, a blonde who appeared paler than when they'd seen her at Tilda's a short while ago, sat in an ivory upholstered chair clutching a handkerchief.

Mr. Chadwick glowered into the fireplace, then turned his head as Tilda and Hadrian moved into the chamber. His heavy-lidded eyes fixed on them. "Thank you for coming so quickly." He spoke gruffly, and though he had a thick black and gray mustache, Tilda could see his mouth was drawn tight.

Tilda withdrew her notebook and a pencil from her reticule. "Can we begin with you providing a clear description of your daughter, including what she was wearing."

"We have a photograph." Mr. Chadwick swept a small, framed portrait from the mantel and handed it to Hadrian. Hopefully, he did that because Tilda was already holding her notebook and not because he saw Hadrian as in charge.

Hadrian moved closer to Tilda and held the photograph so they could both see it. Since he still wore his gloves, he would not experience a memory. Miss Chadwick was very pretty, with a heart-shaped face and the hint of a smile.

"What color is her hair?" Tilda asked.

"Light brown," Mrs. Chadwick answered. "She has a milky complexion—it's quite enviable. And beautiful rosebud cheeks." She sniffed. "Her eyes are a delightful brown, not blue like mine, nor are they lighter like Benjamin's. They have a golden sheen." She looked at her husband who nodded in response.

"They remind me of my favorite tawny port," Mr. Chadwick said with a faint smile that quickly disappeared. "Can't drink that just now," he added gruffly before coughing.

Mrs. Chadwick dabbed at her eyes. "She's of average height and is fortunate to have a very slender waist. The modiste loves to dress her."

Tilda recorded the description in her notebook and looked back at the Chadwicks with a serene expression. "Does she have any attributes or perhaps marks on her skin that stand out?"

"She has a dark mole on the back of her neck," Mrs. Chadwick replied. "I'd estimate it to be the size of the top of your pencil there."

"And what was she wearing when she went missing?" Tilda asked gently.

"Her nightclothes, I presume." Mrs. Chadwick pressed the handkerchief to her nose as she drew a stuttering breath. "I don't know precisely what she was wearing, but Bannet will." They'd mentioned Miss Chadwick's maid, Bannet, when they'd called at Tilda's earlier.

"We'd like to speak with the maid," Tilda said.

"Simpson, the butler, has gone to fetch her," Mr. Chadwick said. "She's resting upstairs. There's not much for her to do with

Delia gone." He twisted his face, pulling his mouth to the side as if he were trying not to succumb to emotion.

"May we go into the bedchamber to look around?" Tilda asked, glancing toward Hadrian.

Mr. Chadwick gestured toward the door leaning into the next chamber. "Please."

Mrs. Chadwick began to rise, but Tilda stepped toward her. "If you don't mind, his lordship and I would like a few moments to investigate without interference. We'll invite you in when we're ready to ask further questions." She gave the woman a warm, hopefully supportive smile before preceding Hadrian into Miss Chadwick's bedchamber.

The room was also decorated with yellow floral wallpaper and ivory furnishings. There were many touches of gilt—a lamp on the bedside table, the mirror hanging over the mantel, the decorations on the marble fireplace. As Tilda looked about the chamber, she realized there wasn't a thing out of place.

Frowning, she moved toward the bed, which was hung with golden velvet curtains. "They've made up the bed."

"They've disturbed any clues that might have been left," Hadrian noted.

"It's unlikely the state of the bedclothes would have told us much, but we'll never know." Tilda tamped down her mild disappointment as she turned her attention to the table beside the bed. In addition to the gilt lamp, there was a book, *The Woman in White*, and a silver filigree hairbrush. Tilda confirmed the color of Miss Chadwick's hair from the strands that clung to the bristles.

"May I?" Hadrian held out his hand—he'd removed his gloves—and Tilda gave the brush to him.

She glanced toward the doorway, hoping no one would walk in until they were invited. Tilda had specifically stated they wanted to be alone so that Hadrian could try to see Miss Chadwick's memories. If they were exceptionally lucky, he would see her memory of the abduction and be able to identify the kidnapper.

Hadrian's gaze went blank, as if he were asleep with his eyes open. The more skilled he'd become at using his ability, the more altered he appeared. Consequently, they endeavored to keep others from observing him in that state.

After several long moments, he blinked. "Nothing helpful." He pressed his lips together as he set the brush back on the table.

"I'm going to look at her dressing table," Tilda said. "Perhaps you should touch the bedclothes in case they haven't been entirely changed, just tidied."

"It's worth a try."

Tilda moved away. She didn't need to watch him employ his ability. Miss Chadwick's oak dressing table had several drawers and an oval mirror. Beginning with the center drawer, Tilda searched the contents of the table. She found all manner of beauty implements. Indeed, Miss Chadwick had multiples of many items, which seemed extravagant to Tilda. The drawers were quite full. Until she opened the fifth and final one, the lower drawer on the right side. It held a few letters and nothing else.

Tilda withdrew the three envelopes and perused the exterior. They were addressed to Miss Chadwick, but they had no return address. That wasn't terribly uncommon. Tilda removed the first letter. It was signed, "With love from Vin."

The letter revealed Vin to be her brother. Earlier, the Chadwicks said they had two sons—one who was traveling and one in the navy. Since this envelope had not originated with the navy, Tilda concluded the missive must be from the traveling brother.

Tilda read the other two letters. "These are from one of her brothers. They aren't very long as he appears to be concerned with just two things."

"What are those?" Hadrian asked as he joined her at the dressing table.

"Vin's gratitude for some favor his sister was performing and anger toward their parents. In the last one, Vin begged Miss Chadwick not to turn against him. He said he couldn't bear to lose her faith and assistance. Tilda tucked the letters back into the envelopes and returned them to the drawer before closing it.

"Should I touch them?" Hadrian asked.

"I don't want you to overwhelm yourself," she said with concern. "Did you learn anything from the bed?"

"Unfortunately, no." Hadrian shook his head, then winced.

"Has your headache worsened?" Tilda was now especially glad she'd returned the letters to the drawer without handing them to Hadrian.

"I'm not seeing anything noteworthy." His brow creased with frustration. "I see her parents. I see who is probably her maid. I see Hyde Park. I see a ball. I see the theatre. Everything is fleeting and benign. I don't feel any strong emotion whatsoever, and certainly not the fear I gleaned from the ransom note."

"Well, that's disappointing. But at least your ability hasn't disappeared." She smiled at him, but he shuddered.

"I don't like to think of that happening again. Not when we need it."

"I suppose we should invite the Chadwicks and the maid in." Tilda went to the doorway and saw that the Chadwicks had been joined by a woman around thirty years of age. She was dressed like a maid, in a dark blue gown and a stiff, white apron. Her sable hair was pinned up beneath a white cap.

"This is Bannet, Delia's maid," Mr. Chadwick said.

"Please come in so we may discuss what happened two days ago." Tilda pivoted away from the door to give them space to enter the bedchamber.

The Chadwicks came in first, followed by Bannet, whose hands were clasped tightly before her. Mrs. Chadwick immediately went to sit in a chair near the hearth, as if she didn't have the energy to stand. Mr. Chadwick stood beside her, his expression as dark as it had been since they'd arrived.

Tilda turned her attention to the maid. "I'm Miss Wren, and this is Lord Ravenhurst. We're investigating Miss Chadwick's disappearance."

"She didn't disappear," Mr. Chadwick said. "She was *taken*. We have a note stating there is a ransom."

"We know, Mr. Chadwick," Hadrian replied calmly. "Bannet, can you tell us about finding that note?"

"It was there." The maid pointed toward the pillows. "I came in to wake Miss Chadwick at nine, as always, and she wasn't in bed. I found the note instead."

Tilda moved to stand next to the bed. "I presume the bed wasn't in this state when you arrived that morning. Did you change the linens?"

"I did. It seemed wrong to leave them after they'd been touched by a villain." Bannet shuddered.

"Was there something on the bedclothes?" Tilda tried not to let her excitement show. Perhaps the maid had seen evidence of the kidnapper and that's what she meant by "touched."

"Not that I saw. I just imagined him stealing poor Miss Chadwick from the bed." Bannet bit back a sob, then composed herself before continuing. "The linens were tossed about, which was unlike her. Sometimes, the bed looked as if she hadn't even slept in it."

"I told you she was a tidy sleeper," Mrs. Chadwick said.

"So, two mornings ago, the bed looked different." How Tilda wished the maid had left things as she'd found them in order to preserve any evidence. "Can you tell me if anything else in the room seemed odd that morning?"

The maid gestured to the window that faced the back. "The lower sash was open the barest amount, but sometimes Miss Chadwick likes to take the morning air. It could be that she didn't close it entirely."

Tilda started toward the window, though Hadrian was already ahead of her. He kept his back to everyone as he touched the frame. Tilda eyed him expectantly, hoping this time he'd see something useful whilst also worrying he would suffer a greater headache.

To give him more time, she turned to face the maid and the Chadwicks. Before she could speak, Mr. Chadwick snapped at Bannet. "You didn't tell us about the window!"

"I forgot!" the maid cried, clearly agitated and perhaps defensive. Her cheeks flushed, and she chewed the inside of her mouth, twisting her lips. Her eyes flashed with heat. Was she angry?

"Did you notice anything out of place near the window?" Tilda asked. "Anything that may have suggested someone climbed in from outside?" She glanced out the window and didn't see a tree or anything that someone could have used to reach the window. *Perhaps Spring-heeled Jack had leapt from the ground,* she thought sardonically. She did not believe that.

Bannet shook her head.

"Are you certain?" Mr. Chadwick demanded. "Your memory seems unreliable."

Mrs. Chadwick touched her husband's arm. "Don't be cruel," she murmured before looking at the maid. "It's all right, Bannet. Please do your best to remember every detail. Anything at all could be helpful to Miss Wren." She turned her attention to Tilda. "Isn't that right?"

"Yes," Tilda replied. "Any detail—no matter how insignificant —could be of assistance to our investigation."

Finally, Hadrian turned from the window. His brow was creased and he brushed his fingers against his temple, which meant his head was still aching. She narrowed her eyes at him, hoping to wordlessly communicate that he mustn't try to use his power anymore.

Tilda fixed her attention on Bannet once more. "Mrs. Chadwick thinks Miss Chadwick was likely wearing her nightclothes when she was taken. Can you describe what she was wearing?"

"Just a simple night rail—ivory muslin with a bit of lace and blue ribbon around the neck and the ends of the long sleeves."

"Thank you." Tilda split her gaze between the Chadwicks and Bannet. "What does a typical day for Miss Chadwick entail? What appointments does she keep, particularly regular ones? What about social events?"

Mrs. Chadwick clasped her hands around her handkerchief. "She is in the midst of her first Season, so there are many social events. I would say we have engagements most days. We have one shopping day each week, usually Thursdays. She has riding lessons on Tuesdays and Saturdays, the pianoforte on Wednesdays, and watercolors on Mondays."

As Tilda recorded the young woman's schedule, she noted that she was busy nearly every day. Surely Sunday was reserved for church. That left Friday for her to be unencumbered. "What of Miss Chadwick's associates and your friends, particularly those who've visited here?"

"What do you mean by that question?" Mr. Chadwick asked brusquely. "Are you implying our friends had something to do with Delia's kidnapping?"

"Not at all. It's helpful for us to have an idea of who's been here. The kidnapper targeted your daughter—he knew she lived here and how to strike." Tilda paused. "It's odd that no one heard anything when Miss Chadwick was abducted. We must investigate the possibility that she knew her kidnapper, hence she didn't cause a ruckus."

"That doesn't make sense," Mrs. Chadwick said with great animation, her eyes widening and her cheeks flushing. "No one we know would do such a thing."

"And why would Delia allow herself to be quietly kidnapped?" Mr. Chadwick snapped as his thick brows drew together with irritation. "She is not a shrinking violet, Miss Wren."

Tilda made a note of that in her book. "I'm merely collecting information. The more I know, the better I can be of assistance.

Can you think of anyone who might have conceived of this scheme?"

"Of course not!" Mr. Chadwick nearly shouted. Mrs. Chadwick grabbed his hand and gave him an imploring look. He took a deep breath and exhaled before continuing in a more moderate tone. "My apologies. We're all upset. I hired *you* to find the person who conceived of this scheme."

Frustration buzzed through Tilda, but she maintained a placid expression. "It would be helpful if someone could provide me with a list of your daughter's tutors, friends, and anyone else you think would be helpful for us to speak with. This will allow us to determine if anyone from perhaps outside your circle was somehow inadvertently given information that may have led to this scheme. With an investigation like this, it's always wise to start at the center of the missing person's life and work outward." At least, that was what Tilda's father had said.

"That does make sense." Mrs. Chadwick sent her husband an encouraging look, then released his hand.

Hadrian stepped forward, his expression smoothed into an amenable almost-smile. "Chadwick, I wonder if we might have a glass of brandy or whatever you have on hand. You can tell me about your inner circle."

Tilda sent Hadrian a grateful glance. She wished she'd thought to pair him off with Chadwick. Besides Chadwick being unhelpful and even obstructive, it was likely he would feel more comfortable conversing with the Earl of Ravenhurst—or at least offer him a deference he didn't seem to want to give Tilda despite hiring her.

"That would be most welcome," Mr. Chadwick said wearily. He almost seemed relieved. "We'll go to my study." He looked at Tilda. "You may meet us there when you're finished to collect the first payment."

"Thank you." Tilda inclined her head, and Hadrian preceded Mr. Chadwick from the room.

"I must apologize for my husband." Mrs. Chadwick wrung the handkerchief in her hands. "This has been so difficult, especially for him. He blames himself."

"Why would he?" Tilda asked.

"He's frustrated with himself, and with the staff, for not noticing or hearing anything," Mrs. Chadwick replied.

"*I'm* to blame," Bannet said, as a sob shook her shoulders. "Miss Chadwick is my charge."

Mrs. Chadwick turned her gaze on the maid, her brow forming deep creases. "You mustn't think that. I suspect Delia was drugged or perhaps knocked unconscious, and that is why no one heard her." The woman's chin quivered as she appeared to fight a wave of tears. She blinked several times and sniffed.

Tilda regarded the woman with kindness and understanding. "That is certainly a possibility, but don't think of that now. I try never to move ahead of where the evidence takes me." She looked to the maid once more. "Did you tidy anything else in the chamber? I want to confirm there were no other signs of a struggle."

Bannet frowned. "Do you think the unkempt bedclothes mean Delia struggled?"

"It's a possibility, but I can't say for certain, of course. Was anything else out of place or unexpected?"

"No. Everything was as it should be, except the bed. And the window being open, which wasn't unusual." She flushed as she looked toward Mrs. Chadwick. "I won't blame you if you dismiss me for not recalling and mentioning that." Her gaze dipped to the floor.

"Nonsense," Mrs. Chadwick replied quickly. "It was a mistake anyone could have made. Of course we won't dismiss you."

"How was Miss Chadwick's temperament the night before she disappeared?" Tilda asked. "Was there anything odd about her behavior?"

"Not at all." Mrs. Chadwick frowned. "Why would she have

acted differently? It wasn't as if she knew she was going to be kidnapped from her bed. What a ridiculous question."

Tilda knew they were upset and did not blame them for being...vexing. "It may seem an odd query, but everything could be pertinent or nothing could be. For instance, what if your daughter was threatened and didn't tell you. She might have acted fearful or nervous. I'm not saying that's what happened, merely providing an example of why details that seem unimportant can actually be helpful during an investigation."

Mrs. Chadwick nodded, her features smoothing. "I see. I do apologize, Miss Wren. You seem very capable, which is why I wanted to hire you. I read about your brilliant role in the capture of the Levitation Killers."

That case in particular had earned Tilda a bit of notoriety and, with it, a steady stream of clients. "I'm going to do everything I can to ensure your daughter is found and safely returned to you."

"I'll write out a list of Delia's friends. I don't know how they could help you, but I believe you know what you're doing. I'll go to my desk and meet you downstairs." Mrs. Chadwick stood. "Bannet, please show Miss Wren to Mr. Chadwick's study."

"After you finish the list, I'd like to interview the rest of your staff," Tilda said.

"Certainly." Mrs. Chadwick departed.

Bannet led Tilda downstairs to the study where Hadrian and Mr. Chadwick were sipping brandy. They immediately stood as Tilda entered.

"I've a list of the Chadwicks' closest friends, as well as the names of Miss Chadwick's tutors," Hadrian said.

Bannet didn't linger. As the maid left, she passed the butler who went to speak with Mr. Chadwick. Tilda took the opportunity to go to Hadrian.

"Quickly, what did you see when you touched the window?" she asked.

"Nothing helpful. It was night, and I saw a reflection in the glass—it was only Miss Chadwick."

"Her memory then," Tilda said.

Hadrian nodded. "I had a brief sensation of excitement and happiness. I'm disappointed I couldn't see anything of use, but I do wonder if the kidnapper was wearing gloves. That would explain not seeing any of his memories."

"Good point." Before she could comment on the Chadwicks' agitation, Mr. Chadwick let out a gasp.

Tilda and Hadrian turned sharply toward where the man stood with the butler.

Mr. Chadwick held a piece of parchment, his hand shaking. He lifted his gaze to Tilda and Hadrian, his eyes wide. "This is from him—Spring-heeled Jack. I'm to deliver the twenty thousand pounds to Hampstead Heath at midnight."

# CHAPTER 2

"May I see that?" Tilda asked as she walked toward Chadwick with her hand extended. He placed the parchment onto her palm.

Hadrian moved to stand beside her so he could read the note over her shoulder.

*Deliver the twenty thousand pounds to the hollow oak off the Spaniards Road in Hampstead Heath by midnight tonight.*

*Yours,*
*Spring-heeled Jack*

"A man of few words," Hadrian murmured.

Tilda immediately handed him the note along with a grimace of apology. Clearly, she meant for him to see what he would detect from the parchment despite telling him he shouldn't use his power anymore that day.

As soon as he touched the paper, the room went dark. He saw

a small mahogany desk with a piece of blank parchment atop it. A hand belonging to a man gripped a quill and hovered above it. His nails were rough and a bit dirty, and his thumb and finger were dry and perhaps calloused. Hadrian tried to determine an identifying feature, such as a ring or a scar. All he managed to note was the edge of the man's sleeve, but it was a nondescript brown coat.

Though he tried to see more of the desk, Hadrian was forced to close his eyes because the pain in his head had become too strong to bear. Handing the paper back to Tilda, their gazes met, and he wordlessly communicated that he'd seen something. Curiosity and anticipation simmered in her eyes, but he could not tell her anything now.

"Where is the envelope?" Tilda asked.

The butler handed it to her. Again, Hadrian looked over Tilda's shoulder. The letter had originated from London WC. That wouldn't be helpful, as that was a very large area.

"I should go to Hampstead Heath and pay the ransom," Chadwick said.

"What's this about Hampstead Heath?" Mrs. Chadwick's voice came from the doorway.

Chadwick moved quickly to his wife and took her hand. "My darling, we've received a note about delivering the ransom."

"What's happened?" Mrs. Chadwick cried, her eyes moving wildly about.

Turning to Tilda, Chadwick held out his hand. She handed him the note, which he then showed to his wife. "This was just delivered with the post."

"I don't think it's wise for you to deliver the ransom alone," Tilda said as Mrs. Chadwick took and read the missive. "I think it would be far better if Lord Ravenhurst pretends to be you, and we organize a scheme in which we attempt to capture the kidnapper."

"No, it must be me," Chadwick argued.

"You should listen to them," Mrs. Chadwick said, her hand shaking.

"Why?" Chadwick asked sharply as he turned toward his wife. "I only hired them because we hadn't heard anything, and you were worried after waiting for two days. But now we know what to do. I'll pay the ransom, and Delia will come back to us."

Mrs. Chadwick clutched her husband's sleeve. "It's far too dangerous!" Her face was pale, and her eyes were wide. "How do we even know that Delia is all right, or that she'll be returned?" She released Chadwick and waved the note. "This doesn't say anything about how or when Delia will come back."

"No, it does not, and I find that concerning," Tilda said. "This is potentially quite dangerous. What if Spring-heeled Jack takes your money and you along with it? Or worse? Please allow his lordship and me to develop a plan that will ensure Delia's and your safety and that you keep your twenty thousand pounds. This will also give us the opportunity to capture the kidnapper."

Chadwick huffed. "How do you propose to do that?"

"As Miss Wren said, I will pose as you." Hadrian thought that was an excellent idea. They were of a similar height. "I'll deliver an empty bag to the hollow oak." He wasn't sure if that had been Tilda's plan, but she gave him a subtle nod.

"Someone will show up to retrieve the ransom," Tilda said. "That is when we'll attempt to capture him."

"*Attempt*? What if you fail?" Chadwick asked. "I *must* be there."

"I know you want to be. However, it isn't safe," Hadrian said firmly. "Furthermore, you're too emotionally involved. As you should be. You've hired Miss Wren to find your daughter. If you don't trust her to accomplish that objective, perhaps you should go to the police instead."

"Absolutely not!" Chadwick shouted, prompting his wife to flinch.

Once again, Mrs. Chadwick grasped her husband's arm, her expression beseeching. "Benjamin, you agreed that we needed help, and you refused to involve the police because of that horrid note. Please let Miss Wren and Lord Ravenhurst do what they must. You do *not* need to be there. I don't know what I would do if you were taken too. *Please.*"

Chadwick's frame shrank as he let out a long exhale. "What is your plan? You can't mean to catch him without help."

"We will have assistance," Tilda replied.

Hadrian knew they would have Leach, who had proven to be most helpful with their investigations. They could also bring Brian, Hadrian's burliest footman. Would that be enough? What if the kidnapper also had assistance? There could very well be more than one person responsible for Miss Chadwick's abduction.

Mrs. Chadwick regarded Tilda and Hadrian eagerly. "You must report back immediately. I won't be able to sleep until I know what transpired."

"Of course," Tilda assured her. "We will come directly here."

"Thank you." Mrs. Chadwick attempted a smile, but her features just looked strained.

"I'd still rather accompany you," Chadwick grumbled. "I have the twenty thousand pounds. You should take it with you."

"I don't think that's wise," Tilda said. "Now, you must excuse us whilst we make the necessary plans." She looked at Mrs. Chadwick with warmth, demonstrating the concern she always showed her clients and anyone who was in pain. "May I have the note? I want to keep it with the envelope and the first note. These are important pieces of evidence and will help with prosecuting the kidnapper."

Mrs. Chadwick handed it back to her. "What about interviewing the rest of the staff?"

"Hopefully that won't be necessary because Delia will be returned this evening," Tilda replied. "Our time will be best spent planning for tonight."

Mrs. Chadwick clutched her hands tightly and nodded.

"We'll be on our way then," Hadrian said.

Chadwick still appeared very frustrated. Deep grooves lined his features, and his brows were drawn. "We'll expect to see you tonight—with Delia."

Hadrian didn't want to point out that the ransom note made no mention of when or how Miss Chadwick would be returned. Did the kidnapper plan to leave her at the hollow tree?

Tilda preceded Hadrian from the study, and the butler followed them. When they reached the entrance hall, Simpson hastened to open the door.

Outside, Tilda slipped the letter and envelope into her reticule with her notebook. She looked over at Hadrian as they made their way to the coach.

"Do you really think we can capture the kidnapper?" Hadrian asked.

"I don't know, but after seeing that second note, I strongly believe we need to consult with Detective Inspector Teague. I didn't want to say that in front of Mr. Chadwick, of course."

Hadrian was surprised to hear her say that. "But the kidnapper instructed us not to speak to the police, and you promised Chadwick you wouldn't." She'd made that vow earlier when the Chadwicks had called at her grandmother's house to hire Tilda.

"We're not making a report or formally involving the Met," Tilda explained. "We're soliciting help from a friend, who happens to be a detective inspector with Scotland Yard. I don't think we can afford not to consult him. Mrs. Chadwick asked a very good question—we don't even know if Delia is all right. That second note offered no information as to her welfare or when or how she'll be returned. When I promised Mr. Chadwick that I wouldn't involve the police, I didn't know all the information, rather the lack of information."

"Your assessment makes good sense, as does you not wanting to tell Chadwick. I don't think he would have agreed with you."

"Probably not." Tilda's features wrinkled in a brief grimace. She exhaled. "I'd like Leach and Brian to accompany us in addition to Teague and whomever he designates, if you don't mind."

"Not at all. I'm sure they'll be amenable."

Leach waited for them at the coach and opened the door. "I hope your meeting was productive."

"To Scotland Yard with haste," Hadrian said to the coachman. "We have a plan to execute tonight, and it involves you."

Leach's eyes lit with interest. "Always happy to do my part. What will we be doing?"

"Catching a kidnapper," Tilda replied. "Specifically, Spring-heeled Jack. More accurately, someone claiming to be him."

"I read a penny dreadful about him," Leach said, his brows gathering. "I didn't think he was a kidnapper. I should think he'd more likely save the hostage."

"Why?" Hadrian asked.

"In the story, Spring-heeled Jack tormented the upper classes and rescued those in need. He was more of a hero than a villain."

"'Spring-heeled Jack' is a myth. Someone dressed up as him thirty years ago and attacked a few young women," Tilda said. "Since then, he's been memorialized in stories and on the stage. Whatever he was or is, there's a man—or woman—who kidnapped Miss Chadwick, not 'Spring-heeled Jack.'"

"I'm eager to help any way I can," Leach said holding the door of the coach.

"Thank you." Tilda smiled at him as she climbed inside.

As soon as Hadrian sat down next to Tilda and the door closed, she turned toward him. "What did you see when you touched the letter?"

Hadrian related the vision. "I had to stop because my head hurt. I'm disappointed I couldn't see anything more helpful. When my head is feeling better, I'll try again."

Her gaze shot to his forehead. "You had to stop on purpose?

You've never had to do that before, have you?" she asked with concern.

"No." In hindsight, he wished he'd endured the pain. What if he'd been about to see something important—such as Delia Chadwick?

Tilda moved to withdraw the lavender oil from beneath the other seat. "I'm not sure I want you to make another attempt. At least not today."

"I think I must," Hadrian argued. "We don't have the luxury of time if we're to catch this kidnapper. He's expecting the ransom tonight."

Tilda did not hand him the bottle of oil this time. She removed the top and poured a bit onto her fingertips, then gently massaged it into his temple.

The touch of her hand soothed him immediately, perhaps more than the lavender. He smiled and closed his eyes. "This is much better than doing it myself."

She moved her hand to his other temple and repeated her massage. Then she dashed her fingertips across his forehead.

When he opened his eyes, he found her regarding him intently. "Don't worry, Tilda," he whispered.

"We don't know the limits of this ability. What if you could do lasting damage to yourself?"

"Don't you think Captain Vale would have told me of that possibility?" Hadrian referred to the gentleman who also possessed the ability to see others' memories and who had shared his knowledge and experience with Hadrian. Until meeting him a few months ago, Hadrian had feared he was going mad. There was simply no explanation for what had happened to him after he'd hit his head on the pavement when he'd been stabbed back in January.

Vale had explained that the gift ran in families, seemed to come on after a trauma to the head, and generally caused a headache of varying degrees. The ability could be slightly different among those who possessed it, and Vale hadn't yet met a woman who could see others' memories.

"Not if he wasn't aware of it," Tilda replied to Hadrian's question.

"I would think that Thaddeus Vale would have tested the limits of this ability quite thoroughly with his fake conversations with the dead," Hadrian said with regard to Captain Vale's son, who'd masterminded a plot to defraud members of Polite Society with his "spiritualism society." He'd claimed to be a medium but had really been using his ability to see the members' memories to convince them he could speak to their deceased loved ones. Hadrian's mother had been among those taken in by Vale's scheme.

"Perhaps you should discuss this with Captain Vale when next you write to him."

"I sense it would soothe your concern?" Hadrian asked.

She smiled. "It would."

Hadrian tipped his head forward and brushed his lips over hers.

"Hadrian, we're working," she protested.

"You say that as if we haven't kissed in this coach before," he noted wryly.

"We need to focus on our plan for tonight, and I can't do that if you distract me."

"I'm very glad to hear I'm distracting." Hadrian held up his hand briefly. "Apologies. I didn't mean to flirt whilst we're working. I can't seem to help myself. Do you really think it's a good idea to inform Teague?"

"We must," Tilda said firmly. "I don't like that we have to hide that from Mr. Chadwick, but I didn't see another way. I will do whatever it takes to find Miss Chadwick and ensure her safety. I'll explain to Teague why we need to keep things quiet, and I expect he'll agree."

They arrived at Scotland Yard and made their way to Teague's office. He had just donned his hat. "Ravenhurst, Miss Wren," the detective inspector greeted them. "I was on my way out."

"I'm glad we caught you," Tilda said. "We've an urgent matter to discuss."

Detective Inspector Samuel Teague removed his hat to reveal his dark red hair. He tossed the accessory onto his desk and gestured to the seating area near the small hearth. "Let us sit."

Tilda perched on a chair and opened her reticule. "Sorry to keep you, but I think you'll agree that this situation is critical." She withdrew the letter they'd just obtained from the Chadwicks as well as the initial ransom note and handed them to Teague who sat across from her. "Mr. Benjamin Chadwick of Belgrave Square hired me this morning to find his missing daughter, Delia. She disappeared from her bedchamber two days ago."

Teague's brow furrowed as he read the notes. His frown deepened as he moved from one to the other. When he looked up at Tilda, his brown eyes were dark with alarm. "She was taken two days ago, and they only hired you today? Never mind that they didn't report this to the Met," he added.

"You can see why they didn't," Hadrian said. He'd taken the chair to Tilda's right.

Teague met their gazes. "I'm glad *you* did."

"The matter must be kept secret," Tilda explained. "We don't wish to endanger Miss Chadwick. We also had to persuade Mr. Chadwick not to come to Hampstead Heath tonight. He was rather insistent that he be there."

"That's the last thing he should do." Teague sent them a look of gratitude. "Thank you for talking him out of that. I agree this operation must be covert. I'll involve as few men as possible. We need to devise a plan."

"As it happens, Ravenhurst and I have an idea," Tilda said.

Teague flashed a faint smile. "Why doesn't that surprise me?"

"We propose that Ravenhurst assume the role of Mr. Chadwick and deposit an empty bag in the hollow oak whilst I and two of our investigative team, as well as you and your men, watch the area. When the kidnapper arrives to retrieve the bag, we will apprehend him."

"That is precisely what I was thinking, though I would prefer if Sergeant Wycombe acted as Chadwick." Teague looked at Hadrian. "I don't want to endanger a civilian."

"I understand," Hadrian said even if he was a trifle disappointed. He'd been looking forward to the role. It was shocking how much he'd come to love this work with Tilda. "Wycombe is also of a similar height to Chadwick."

"He will need the appropriate costume." Tilda looked to Hadrian. "Can you provide something?"

"Of course." Hadrian shifted his attention to Teague. "I'll send Leach back here with garments shortly."

"That is most appreciated." Teague glanced at the ransom notes he still held and shook his head in exasperation. "I'm troubled that Spring-heeled Jack—what a moniker to use—did not say how or when Miss Chadwick would be returned."

"I am too," Tilda replied. "We don't even know if Miss Chadwick is well—or alive."

Hadrian had a sudden thought. "Perhaps Wycombe should wait with the bag. Wouldn't a concerned father expect to see his daughter? The note didn't say Chadwick shouldn't stay."

"But what if the kidnapper doesn't approach the oak because Wycombe is there?" Tilda asked.

"That's a valid point." Teague fell quiet as he appeared to mull the options. "Still, I think we should take the risk. The kidnapper wants his money, and if it's just the one man, I imagine that won't be a deterrent. Besides, the kidnapper may have others working with him."

Tilda nodded. "I thought the same thing, which is why I thought it important to involve you. A couple of Ravenhurst's retainers will help, but I didn't think that was enough."

"I'll bring two constables in addition to Wycombe, who will

be armed and on high alert when the kidnapper approaches. I'll also station a van down the Spaniards Road with one or two constables. We'll make sure it isn't identifiable as a Met vehicle." He fixed his gaze on Tilda. "You should stay with the van."

"Absolutely not," Tilda replied with a touch of heat. "This is my case. I'll be on site at the oak." She sent a dark glance toward Hadrian, almost daring him to argue.

He knew better. Though he would feel better if she were away from the delivery, he knew she would never agree. Nor should she, because she was right. This *was* her case. And she was a brilliant and skilled detective. They'd both survived several dangerous situations.

"Fair enough," Teague said. "Would you mind picking me and Wycombe up at my house? That way Wycombe can arrive in a coach that looks like it belongs to someone who can afford a twenty-thousand-pound ransom."

"Happy to," Hadrian replied.

"We'll fetch you at eight o'clock this evening," Tilda said. "That will allow us to find our way to the hollow oak before full dark sets in."

Hadrian fixed his gaze on Teague. "What if Jack doesn't bring Miss Chadwick?"

"We'll ensure he takes us to her," Teague vowed, his dark eyes glinting with determination.

Tilda stood. "Good, because the safe return of Miss Chadwick is the only thing that matters."

# CHAPTER 3

Tilda surveyed herself in the mirror in her bedchamber that evening. She'd donned her father's old garments—from his youth—so she'd be able to move quickly. Her gowns would not allow such freedom. "Thank you for working so quickly, Mrs. Acorn."

"I'm pleased to help," the housekeeper, a lovely, supportive woman in her sixties, said as she picked up her sewing basket. Mrs. Acorn had just finished hemming the sleeves of the over-sized coat. "Now, be on your way. If you hurry, you may make it outside before your grandmother sees you," she added with a wink before departing.

Clara, Tilda's maid, had coiled and pinned her hair up tightly so that it would fit beneath the hat, which Tilda grabbed from the dressing table and pulled onto her head. It fit snugly because of her hair.

Tilda rotated her left shoulder. It was still stiff from her injury the other day when a piece of pottery had lodged into her flesh after the thief they'd been after had shot a large pot. She had a few stitches that would need to be removed in a couple of days.

Dr. Giles, who'd placed them, had offered to call on her here to complete the task, for which she was most grateful.

Hastening down the stairs, Tilda stopped short as her grandmother walked into the hall from the sitting room at the back of the house. In her seventies, Barbara Wren was petite with snow-white hair and bright-blue eyes. She regarded Tilda with a slight frown.

*Blast.* So much for avoiding her grandmother's almost certain disapproval of Tilda's costume.

"You can't go out dressed like that," her grandmother said. Thankfully, she couldn't see Tilda's father's pistol, which was tucked into a holster beneath the coat.

"I need to be able to move quickly tonight, Grandmama," Tilda explained. "My voluminous skirts would not allow that."

Grandmama pursed her lips. "Surely you could find something more feminine to wear."

Tilda quashed a smile. They weren't going to a Society event —her grandmother didn't even know that Tilda and Hadrian were now courting. Tilda needed to tell her, but she'd only just decided that afternoon, and today had moved at breakneck speed. "No one is going to see me, Grandmama."

"Lord Ravenhurst will. Isn't he fetching you for this investigative activity? I still don't understand what that means. It sounds dangerous, especially since you have to move fast." Her brow puckered. "What on earth is this new case about?"

Tilda often didn't reveal the specifics of her investigative duties to her grandmother because she would worry, but the truth was she *did* worry, as she was now. "It isn't dangerous." *Probably.* "I promise I'll explain everything tomorrow. Things are progressing quite rapidly with this matter, and I really must be on my way." Hadrian should have arrived by now.

In fact, Tilda walked into the entrance hall just as Vaughn, their exceptionally tall yet hunched butler, opened the door to admit Hadrian. Tilda's grandmother followed her and addressed Hadrian.

"Ravenhurst, do make sure my granddaughter is safe this evening," she pleaded.

"That is always my primary objective," he said warmly. His gaze swept over Tilda, and surprise flickered across his features. She hoped her grandmother hadn't caught it. The last thing she needed was the two of them finding common cause in questioning her costume. Though, Hadrian likely wouldn't take issue with it, since this was not the first time she'd dressed as a man in his presence.

Tilda bussed her grandmother's cheek. "Try not to worry, and don't wait up, as I will return very late." Or perhaps very early.

"You should understand by now, my dear, that you cannot order me about," her grandmother scolded gently. "I won't rest peacefully until I'm sure you're back home." She perused Tilda's costume—with a faint frown—once more. "Looking like yourself."

Tilda resisted the urge to roll her eyes as she smiled at her grandmother. "You're right. I can't order you about. Do as you must." She turned and preceded Hadrian from the house, hurrying to the coach.

Leach, to his credit, did not appear to register Tilda's clothing as he held the door for her. "Evening, Miss Wren."

"Are you ready for tonight?" Tilda asked. She and Hadrian had briefed Leach on the plan after leaving Scotland Yard. Hadrian had then shared the details with Brian, who, Tilda noted, was perched on the driver's seat.

The footman inclined his head toward Tilda. "Good evening, Miss Wren."

"Good evening, Brian," she replied. "Thank you for your help with this endeavor."

He smiled at her. "Pleased to be of assistance."

Tilda climbed into the coach. Hadrian sat beside her, and they were quickly on their way.

"It's been a while since you wore men's clothing," Hadrian said with the hint of a smile.

"I don't make a habit of it." Tilda glanced down at her father's garments. "This costume is not as attractive as what I wore on that one occasion," she added.

Hadrian grinned. "Our visit to a gentlemen's club with you dressed as a man was a memorable event."

Tilda cocked her head. "And yet you seemed surprised by my appearance tonight."

"I hadn't considered you would dress this way, but it makes perfect sense."

"I wasn't sure I'd be able to pull it together. Thankfully, Mrs. Acorn altered some of my father's old clothing."

Hadrian's brow arched as his gaze flicked over her again. "Those garments belonged to your father?"

"When he was younger." Recently, Tilda's mother had visited, and she'd found a box of items that had belonged to Tilda's father in the attic. Tilda had since gone up to look for more of his things and found a crate of old clothing and books that had belonged to him as a young man.

"It's probably best you aren't dressed as you were that other time. These garments are looser, and I will not be tempted to stare. Much." He slid her a heated look.

Tilda hadn't expected he would find her costume alluring. "Are you saying I look attractive in this ensemble?"

He regarded her once more, his gaze lingering on her legs. "I'm certainly not disappointed by it."

"I see," she murmured, aware of the charged current between them. They'd shared several kisses now and would again. She looked forward to that, she realized, as well as whatever might come after that, such as if their courtship led to marriage.

"How is your head?" Tilda asked, seeking to change the topic to something safer and more...pertinent.

"Much improved, thank you. I took a lavender bath, which is always the most helpful."

"I'm glad to hear it. You need to be more careful with overdoing things. And I need to stop asking you to try to see memories when you're already overtaxed."

Hadrian grinned.

"Why are you smiling like that?" Tilda asked.

"Because I like that you care so much about me," he replied, still grinning.

Was he flirting again? She'd told him they couldn't do that whilst they were working. And yet, she'd probably inadvertently flirted with him during the discussion about her costume.

She grasped for yet another topic. "We've talked before about my obtaining a smaller pistol. We must make that a priority."

"Don't you have your father's Adams with you?" he asked with alarm. Earlier, they'd discussed the need to bring weapons tonight.

"I do. It's beneath my coat," she said.

"We'll procure a new, smaller pistol for you as soon as possible," Hadrian said. "I'm armed with my Tranter. Leach and Brian also have revolvers."

Tilda hoped they wouldn't need them, particularly after assuring her grandmother that tonight wouldn't be dangerous. Hopefully, the kidnapper was only concerned with money. He would show up tonight, eager for his prize, only to be captured. They would recover Miss Chadwick, and all would be well.

The use of Spring-heeled Jack as a disguise still bothered Tilda. This kidnapper wasn't following the legend. Spring-heeled Jack was not known for kidnapping. He attacked young women and terrorized people with his strange physical attributes and abilities.

Apparently, the legend had recently undergone a revision.

Spring-heeled Jack could now also potentially be a hero of some kind. But what could possibly be heroic about taking a young woman from her family for ransom?

Tilda was curious to see if someone who looked like Spring-heeled Jack would even appear that evening.

They picked up Detective Inspector Teague at his house, along with Sergeant Wycombe and Constable Mercer. The constable had crammed himself onto the driver's seat with Brian and Leach, whilst Teague and Wycombe joined Tilda and Hadrian inside the coach. A van driven by two constables, which Teague had borrowed from a furniture remover, without explaining to them why, followed behind.

"You look very well," Hadrian said to Wycombe, who was garbed in Hadrian's clothing.

"It was kind of you to send your valet to make a few alterations," Wycombe said. "Mr. Sharp assured me the garments would be easily returned to their former state." The sergeant, who was a year or two older than Hadrian's thirty years, had a bit of color in his cheeks. "I will feel terrible if any damage comes to them."

Hadrian gave the sergeant a reassuring smile. "I'm not concerned about the condition when they're returned. Our goal is to catch Spring-heeled Jack, and if that results in a tear to the coat you're wearing…" Hadrian shrugged. "A small price to pay."

Wycombe appeared to relax and nodded. He didn't look like Chadwick, save their similar height, but the bespoke clothing would signal wealth and contribute to the disguise.

The sun had set shortly after they'd fetched Teague and the others, and now, as they reached Hampstead, the sky grew darker. They traveled along the Spaniards Road for a short while before the van behind the coach pulled off at an inn to wait.

After several more minutes, Leach stopped the coach before they reached the area with the hollow tree. He'd ridden out on horseback earlier that evening to determine the location of the tree and choose where to let everyone, except for him and Wycombe, out.

Tilda, Hadrian, Teague, Constable Mercer, and Brian departed the coach. In a few minutes, Leach would turn around and drive to a place where he could conceal the coach. They'd proceed to the oak in a couple of hours.

Creeping through the trees and shrubbery, Tilda and the others sought locations in which they would wait and watch for Spring-heeled Jack. Brian and Constable Mercer would take positions near the road, whilst Teague, Tilda, and Hadrian planned to observe the oak.

It would be easy to hear a vehicle approach, assuming the kidnapper brought a vehicle. Still, if he was on horseback, they ought to hear him. Tilda couldn't imagine he would come on foot, though she supposed he could do what they'd done—depart his mode of transport at some distance and walk the rest of the way.

The plan was for them to use the bit of light they had left in the sky to find their locations for surveillance. However, the moon would be bright, following last night's full moon, and they could have light even in the darkness—depending on the clouds. Currently, the moon was quite visible.

"I see the oak ahead," Teague whispered. "I'm going to climb this tree here. One of you should go past the tree and find a vantage point. The other should find a place somewhere between the road and the oak."

Hadrian glanced at Tilda as they moved way from Teague. "I was hoping we would stay together."

She shook her head. "We can't afford to lose a vantage point. I have my father's pistol, and I know how to use it. I can also climb trees very well."

"I'd like to see that," Hadrian said with the flash of a smile. "However, you should probably not climb a tree whilst your shoulder is still healing."

Tilda sighed with disappointment. "Alas, you are correct."

"At least let me walk you to where you'll be so I know how to find you," Hadrian said.

"What if I prefer that we walk to your location so I can be assured of *your* safety?" she countered with an arched brow.

He smiled. "I suppose we'll have to duel it out." Sobering, he held her gaze, and they paused briefly. "There is no one more important to me."

The warm, giddy feeling blooming inside Tilda was still so new. She'd never felt the power of this kind of love before. "We're going to be fine," she said confidently.

They reached the oak. "We're losing our light, and a cloud has moved over the moon." Tilda gestured to her left, toward the road. "That's a good cluster of hedges. I'll hide there."

Hadrian turned his head and pointed to the right, to another oak that wasn't hollow. "I'll climb that tree."

"Good. Now we know where each other is," she said.

Before she could turn, Hadrian snaked his arm around her waist and pulled her close. His gloved fingers touched her cheek as she tipped her head back and met his gaze once more.

"Please be safe," he whispered before kissing her.

It was brief but lovely. Exuberant joy spread through Tilda again.

He released her. "I know I'm not supposed to do that, since we're working."

Tilda wasn't going to complain. She hadn't thought she was anxious about their scheme, but he'd settled her nerves.

"You too," she said. "Be safe."

They parted and went to their hiding places. The sun set completely, and they waited. They heard a few coaches on the Spaniards Road, but then all grew quiet as darkness settled over the heath.

The hours passed as the clouds moved about the moon, plunging them into darkness and revealing a bright, shining light.

Finally, they heard a coach, which ought to be Wycombe arriving as Chadwick.

Tilda saw the light from the vehicle as it approached on the Spaniards Road. It stopped, and there was silence, followed by a lantern moving along the path from the road. That would be Wycombe. Tilda confirmed this as the sergeant moved into her line of sight.

Wycombe clutched the lantern with one hand and the empty ransom bag with the other. He plucked his way over the uneven ground to the hollow tree and deposited the bag inside. Setting the lantern on the ground, he began to pace.

Another hour or more went by before they finally heard another vehicle. Tilda's pulse quickened. The men positioned near the road knew not to make a move on the kidnapper, as did Leach who would watch from his perch in the seat of Hadrian's coach.

They all needed to make sure the kidnapper came to the tree —that way Tilda, Hadrian, and Teague could capture him, whilst the others apprehended anyone who might have remained with the coach, including—hopefully—Miss Chadwick.

Tilda strained her neck to see what was happening on the road, where the light from the coach gleamed, but couldn't discern anything. The moon had vanished again.

Suddenly, the sounds of yelling carried over the heath. Tilda couldn't distinguish what was being said, if anything. The sound of a pistol shot filled the air. Tilda gasped as her breath caught with fear.

For a brief moment, she wasn't sure what to do—because she couldn't see what was happening. But a pistol shot was bad. Then she saw Teague spring toward the road. Jolted from her uncertainty, she stepped from the hedge and turned her head to look toward Hadrian's tree. Hearing him hit the ground, she ran toward the light from the coach, Hadrian behind her. The deci-

sion to wear trousers instead of a gown had been an exceptionally good one.

When she arrived, Teague was already there, as were Brian
and Constable Mercer. Leach had joined them. A second coach
was parked behind Hadrian's.

The coachman from the second vehicle stood waving a pistol
over a supine body on the ground. Tilda crept forward cautiously
as Hadrian moved to her right. "Is that the kidnapper?"

"It's Mr. Chadwick," the coachman replied loudly, his voice
panicked as he brandished the weapon.

Teague approached him. "Put down the revolver. What
happened?"

The coachman lowered his arms. His eyes were wide in the
light from the lantern, and his skin was pale with fright. "We
came to deliver the ransom for Miss Chadwick."

Frustration rose in Tilda. Why hadn't the man listened?

A groan emanated from Chadwick. Tilda crouched down as
he opened his eyes.

"Have you been shot?" she asked.

"No," the coachman responded. "The beast hit him with his
horrible claws, then stole the bag and leapt away."

Indeed, Chadwick had a bloodied cut along his cheek. He put
his hand to his head as he struggled to sit. Brian moved to help
the man to his feet.

"Hit my head on the ground as I fell," Chadwick said,
sounding somewhat befuddled. "Where's Delia?" Chadwick
blinked, his eyes opening wider as he looked around wildly.

Tilda's stomach clenched, both with hope and fear. "Did you
see her?"

"No. The villain emerged from the shadows and jumped upon
me." Chadwick wiped his gloved hand across his cheek and winced.

"I fired my pistol at him," the coachman said. "But I must have
missed. I'm sorry, Mr. Chadwick."

Pivoting, Chadwick rushed to his coach and looked inside. "Did he get the ransom?"

The coachman paled even more. "I'm afraid so."

"The bastard has my money *and* my daughter." Chadwick's voice rose. Panic overtook his features.

"We'll find your daughter," Teague vowed.

Chadwick swung to face the inspector. "Who the bloody hell are you?"

"Detective Inspector Teague with Scotland Yard."

"*What?*" Chadwick turned a furious glare on Tilda. "You weren't supposed to involve the police. Now, my daughter hasn't been returned, and it's *your* fault, because we didn't follow the plan as Spring-heeled Jack instructed."

Tilda was taken aback by the man's vitriol, but she reminded herself that he was incredibly distraught, and understandably so. She also stood by the decision she'd made to seek Teague's assistance. It wasn't their fault that the plan had been spoiled by Chadwick's unexpected arrival.

"There's no way the kidnapper knows the police are here," Teague said calmly. "This was all planned with the utmost discretion. We're not identifiable as police, and the ransom note didn't say you had to come alone. I understand you're upset that your daughter is still missing, Mr. Chadwick. We're going to find her. In the meantime, you ought to go home and tend to the scratches on your face. They look rather deep."

Wycombe interrupted further discussion by returning with the fake ransom bag. "Nobody ever came to the tree."

"Do we think the kidnapper was watching since before the sun went down?" Hadrian asked.

Tilda glanced at Mr. Chadwick, who appeared anguished as well as angry. And Teague was right, the wounds on his cheek needed attention.

"That's possible," Teague replied. "We know the kidnapper

saw a second coach arrive when there was only supposed to be one."

"He saw Chadwick depart the coach," Leach said. "That's when he attacked."

Teague frowned. "Then it makes sense the kidnapper was watching. He saw the second coach, and Chadwick came out of it. Why wait for him to deliver the ransom to the tree?"

"We must presume he'll return Miss Chadwick now that he has the ransom." Tilda worked to keep her voice even, though her body was shaking. She'd never felt so powerless or ineffectual before. Yes, Chadwick's arrival had ruined their plan, but she ought to have planned for that. The man had been insistent that he deliver the ransom, and after he'd backed down, Tilda should have realized he might try to come anyway. "The kidnapper's note was frustratingly vague regarding her return."

That was something else Tilda had failed to do—prepare her client for the very real possibility that his daughter would not be returned immediately. In her haste to act on the ransom delivery plan, she'd neglected to think everything through.

"You *presume?*" Mr. Chadwick sneered. "I don't think you know a thing about what you're doing. How on earth you managed to gain a reputation for solving crimes is a mystery I doubt you could solve."

"There's no call to be insulting," Hadrian said sharply. "Miss Wren is highly qualified. I wholly endorsed her decision to seek assistance from the Met."

Tilda fixed a determined stare on Mr. Chadwick. "My primary goal is the return of your daughter, and I believed our best hope of doing so was the involvement of Detective Inspector Teague."

"But you *promised* me that you wouldn't involve the police," Chadwick snapped. "If you felt it was necessary, you should have said so."

"When I made that promise, I hadn't seen the second ransom

note asking for a payment with no information about when or where the kidnapper would return your daughter. I found it necessary to involve Detective Inspector Teague because of the risk of a ransom delivery about which we lacked important details."

"You didn't explain any of that to me," Mr. Chadwick snarled.

Tilda's heart raced, but she managed to keep an even tone. "No, and I should have. However, you were very upset—as you should be—and I made a judgment call to proceed in the safest and best way possible."

"I was there, Chadwick," Hadrian said. "I don't think you would have cooperated with our efforts with the Met, and that was the best course of action, even if you don't agree."

"It most certainly was," Teague added. "You should have informed us of your daughter's kidnapping immediately."

Mr. Chadwick didn't react to Hadrian or Teague. In fact, he didn't take his attention from Tilda. "I will make sure you never work again. If anything happens to my daughter, her blood will be on your hands."

Ice froze Tilda's veins, despite the heat of Chadwick's fury. Hadrian moved close to her side and tried to take her hand, but she wouldn't let him. Her avoidance wasn't about hiding their relationship whilst they were working. It was about her not wanting or deserving to be soothed. Mr. Chadwick was right that this was her fault.

Tilda managed to swallow. "We will find your daughter, and I will return your money."

Mr. Chadwick continued to regard her with fury and contempt. "I certainly hope so."

Teague looked to Mr. Chadwick and to his coachman. "I need a full description of the man who attacked you and took the money as well as a detailed account of what happened."

"It was Spring-heeled Jack," Mr. Chadwick announced coldly.

"He was immense, with waxy, pale skin, red eyes, devilish horns, and horrible sharp claws."

Leach cleared his throat. "I heard the coach approaching on the road. I thought it was just a traveler, until it stopped behind me. I turned my head, and that's when I saw a dark figure in the road next to the coach.

"The coachman jumped down on the other side and opened the door for Mr. Chadwick who climbed out. The dark figure circled around the back of the coach and leapt at Mr. Chadwick. That's when Mr. Chadwick began shouting, after which he fell to the ground. The coachman had fetched his pistol and faced the brigand who then breathed blue flame at him." Leach shook his head, his gaze darting toward Hadrian. "I can't explain what I saw, but it was as if he exhaled blue fire."

"Did you shoot at him?" Hadrian asked.

Leach's brows gathered. "I wasn't able to, for the coachman was blocking my aim. He shot at the brigand, however."

"The blue flame is why my shot went awry," the coachman explained, his eyes wide. "I was momentarily blinded."

"When did the brigand obtain the ransom?" Teague asked, looking toward Leach, as if he expected the better answer from him. Tilda found no fault with that since Leach seemed calmer and more reliable as a witness than the excited coachman.

"The beast must have grabbed it from the coach whilst I couldn't see," the coachman replied with distress.

As Teague shifted his gaze toward Leach once more, Hadrian's coachman nodded in response. "That's how it happened. I considered taking a shot at that moment, but I didn't want to risk injuring Mr. Chadwick's coachman. Furthermore, I didn't want to cause serious injury to the suspect since it seemed he did not have Miss Chadwick with him."

Tilda felt immense pride in Leach's quick—and excellent—assessment. It seemed Hadrian felt the same for he was looking at his coachman with keen admiration.

"You said he 'leapt' away," Teague noted to Mr. Chadwick's coachman as Wycombe wrote in a book. The sergeant had moved closer to the lantern so he could see better. "What exactly did you mean by that?"

The coachman nodded vehemently. "I saw him jump over that hedge." He pointed to the other side of the Spaniards Road.

"He didn't run along the road, but across it?" Teague asked, glancing at Leach who nodded.

"That's right," the coachman replied. "He disappeared into the trees over there."

"You must go after him!" Mr. Chadwick insisted.

Teague exhaled, and Tilda detected his frustration. "Not in the dark. We'll return as soon as it's light to conduct a thorough investigation of the area." He looked pointedly at Mr. Chadwick. "We *will* find your daughter. Go home now and tend to your wounds."

"How am I to tell my wife about this failure?" Mr. Chadwick appeared suddenly beleaguered, and Tilda felt a surge of sorrow for his situation.

"We don't know that it's a failure," Tilda said gently. "We have to believe the kidnapper will return her with haste."

"By providing the ransom, you have put your faith in the very man who stole your daughter," Teague said darkly. "But we *will* catch him."

Mr. Chadwick's throat worked, but he ultimately said nothing before turning and stalking to his coach whilst his coachman hurried to assist him.

Teague let out a weary sigh as he scrubbed his hand over his face. "How I wish Chadwick hadn't interrupted us tonight. He wouldn't have been injured, the ransom wouldn't have been taken, and we likely would have apprehended the kidnapper."

They all watched as Chadwick's coachman drove away.

Tilda voiced the fear that had worked its way up her throat since the kidnapper had disappeared with the ransom. "I'm afraid we must behave as though Miss Chadwick won't be returned. It's up to us to find her." She turned to Hadrian. "We have the lists of her friends and tutors. Let's start there."

Normally, this investigative work would excite and inspire Tilda, but she felt heavy and uncertain. She should have spent more time making inquiries and not relying on tonight's plan to return Miss Chadwick. She was still out there somewhere, frightened and alone, and they needed to rescue her as quickly as possible. Tilda doubted she would sleep tonight.

"I'd like those lists," Teague said. "I realize tomorrow is Sunday, but I'll be at Scotland Yard—after we come here to search at first light."

"Certainly," Tilda said. "We'll meet you here, and I'll bring them."

Teague inclined his head. "Thank you for your efforts this evening. I'm sorry things didn't turn out better. Get some rest. Tomorrow we'll find Miss Chadwick."

Hadrian escorted Tilda to the coach, along with Leach and Brian. He looked over at his coachman. "Well done, Leach."

"I should have pursued the brigand," Leach said harshly, his brow deeply furrowed.

They'd arrived at the coach, and Tilda turned to face Leach. "I'm glad you didn't. We've no idea what danger may have awaited you on the other side of the road, or what other tricks the kidnapper might have tried."

Leach's eyes narrowed. "I should like to know how he made it appear he was breathing blue flame."

"As would I," Hadrian agreed. "I intend to find out, along with why he's taken on this disguise. What purpose could he have?"

"You just said it yourself. It's a disguise," Leach suggested. "Why not Spring-heeled Jack?"

"There must be some reason for it," Tilda said. "Determining that might help us find him—and Miss Chadwick. That is our primary mission."

Tilda and Hadrian climbed into the coach, and they were quickly on their way. Exhaustion settled into Tilda's body though her mind was spinning. "We must make as many inquiries as possible tomorrow, despite it being Sunday."

"We will." Hadrian took her hand and looked into her eyes. "But promise me you will rest—as much as you can anyway."

She appreciated that he knew her so well. "I will try."

"I hope you won't let what Chadwick said in anger trouble you."

"He's entitled to his opinion. I broke the promise I made to him about involving the police. And now he's without his daughter and twenty thousand pounds."

"Neither of those things are your fault, Tilda. We *had* to inform Teague." Hadrian squeezed her hand and kept hold of her whilst he settled back against the squab. "Chadwick will come to his senses. He was merely venting his fury tonight."

Tilda hoped that was true, for if Mr. Chadwick set out to ruin her, she'd no doubt he could.

# CHAPTER 4

"*D*id you sleep?" Hadrian asked as he and Tilda traveled to Hampstead Heath the following morning at dawn.

Tilda grimaced faintly as she folded her gloved hands in her lap. "Very little."

"I'm not sure I slept at all." Hadrian leaned his head back against the squab and fought against exhaustion. "Do you think it's possible Miss Chadwick was returned to her parents sometime overnight?"

"Teague said he would place constables in Belgrave Square to watch the house. If Miss Chadwick had been returned, we would know." She sounded nervous.

"It's hard not to worry." He put his hand over hers.

"Impossible." She clasped his hand and held it on her lap. "I copied the lists we received from the Chadwicks and will give the originals to Teague. Miss Chadwick has several close friends. It will take us a few days to speak with all of them, as well as the watercolor and pianoforte tutors. Her riding lessons are with their head groom. We still need to interview the household staff since we didn't yesterday."

"The arrival of that second ransom note about the delivery

interrupted our typical investigation practice of making inquiries," Hadrian said. "Perhaps we should conduct the interviews with the Chadwick household today since it's Sunday. Then tomorrow we can work through the list of Miss Chadwick's tutors and friends."

Tilda smiled at him. "An excellent plan." She leaned her head back against the squab, and he sensed her fatigue.

Hadrian closed his eyes as he settled into the comfort of her touch. They spent the rest of the journey in silence. He presumed her mind was occupied with thoughts of Spring-heeled Jack and Miss Chadwick. Or perhaps she was battling unconsciousness as he was.

When the coach finally stopped, Hadrian jolted fully alert. Tilda released his hand and straightened in the seat. As Leach opened the door, gray early-morning light spilled into the coach.

Hadrian climbed down then helped Tilda to the Spaniards Road. Two coaches and several horses marked the area where they'd been last night. The oak was to the right side, but focus was on the left where Spring-heeled Jack had disappeared after jumping the hedge.

Detective Inspector Teague stood near that spot with Sergeant Wycombe. Tilda and Hadrian moved to join them.

"Morning," Teague said.

"Any word from Belgrave Square?" Tilda asked.

Teague shook his head. "If Miss Chadwick turns up, someone will ride out to tell us."

"What do you think the odds are of that happening?" Tilda asked, her expression somewhat bleak.

"I don't want to say there's no hope." Teague exhaled then frowned slightly. "However, in my experience, the longer she's gone, the less likely she'll return." He glanced at Wycombe, who nodded grimly.

Hadrian looked over at the wooded area beyond the hedge

where several men combed the landscape. "Have you found anything yet?"

"Nothing definitive," Teague replied.

Tilda moved closer to the five-foot-tall hedge. "This is where Spring-Heeled Jack jumped over. I thought we'd be able to tell exactly where, based on the foliage appearing disrupted, but it looks as though he cleared the hedge entirely."

"That's our conclusion." Teague jerked his head toward the hedge. "We found the indentation of his boots in the dirt on the other side. He has large feet, indicating Jack is taller than the average man, but not unnaturally so."

"Given how easily he cleared the hedge, I think it's safe to say he has long legs," Hadrian noted. "Let me determine how easy it is." He crossed to the other side of the road where he sprinted to the hedge. Hadrian wasn't able to leap over it, but he placed his hand on the top and swung his legs over.

"I don't think that's how Spring-heeled Jack managed it," Tilda said with a faint smile.

Hadrian peered at her over the top of the hedge. "Neither do I."

"How do you suppose he did it?" Wycombe asked. "He's supposed to have the ability to leap. Do you think that's how he got into the Chadwicks' house?"

"I've no idea how accomplished the feat," Tilda said. "However, Miss Chadwick's window is much higher than five feet from the ground. The exterior of the house bears closer investigation. Ravenhurst and I plan to return to Belgrave Square this afternoon to interview the Chadwicks' retainers, and we can do so."

Teague hesitated the barest moment. "Sergeant Wycombe and I discussed doing the same. I think it's best if the Met conducts these inquiries. Perhaps you could focus on Miss Chadwick's friends? Though, I'd still like the lists you mentioned."

"Certainly." Tilda removed the original lists from her reticule and handed the folded pieces of parchment to Teague. "We will also speak with Miss Chadwick's two tutors. I've been thinking we need to learn more about the history of Spring-heeled Jack. Perhaps that will help lead us to the kidnapper."

"We seem to be thinking the same things." Teague's words and accompanying smile gave Tilda a boost of confidence. "Yesterday, after you came to tell me about Miss Chadwick's kidnapping, I asked a clerk to find out what he could regarding Spring-heeled Jack from thirty years ago. He left a note for me, which I read this morning on the way here. He learned the names of the inspectors who investigated the attacks in 1838 but has not yet obtained the report books from the appropriate divisions. He'll do that tomorrow since today is Sunday."

Enthusiasm swept through Tilda, making her feel more like herself. "That's excellent, thank you."

Teague shook his head. "I should have recalled that James Lea investigated one of the attacks—he was rather famous for arresting the Red Barn Killer. Unfortunately, he passed away a few years ago. However, the man who investigated the other attack—on Miss Lucy Scales—Joseph Hopkins, is still alive and lives in Stepney."

"Detective Inspector," one of the men called from the wooded area. "I found evidence of a horse."

Teague and Wycombe strode to an opening in the hedge. Hadrian and Tilda followed after them.

Three constables stood near a tree. One gestured to the trunk. "A horse was tied here." He held out his hand to reveal several fibers. "These strands of rope were on the ground here, and there are hoof marks."

"I found a pile of manure just over there." Another constable pointed farther from the road.

Teague surveyed the rope pieces. "Excellent work. Now we know Jack came and departed on horseback. Not much, but it's better than nothing."

"I'm surprised to learn Spring-heeled Jack rides a horse," Tilda said sardonically. "I thought he leapt from place to place."

Everyone laughed, and even Tilda cracked a faint smile. Hadrian was glad to see it.

"Let's keep looking," Teague said. "I can't imagine Jack rode through these trees for too long before moving back to the path or even to the road. Let's try to follow the horse's trail."

Rather than split up, they all worked together to trace the hoofprints. Sure enough, the trail led back to a path and eventually to the road.

"Looks as though he was headed toward London," Hadrian said.

Teague nodded as he put his hands on his hips. "Agreed." He looked to the constables. "Trace your way back, lads, and see if you find any other clues," Teague said.

The constables moved to follow Teague's instructions.

Hadrian looked around at Tilda, Teague, and Wycombe. "What does the fact that the kidnapper rides a horse tell us?"

Tilda eyed him with pride, and Hadrian's chest swelled. "An excellent observation and question," she said. "It could indicate he's of a certain economic class, whether he owns the horse or paid to use it. Or he could have stolen it. The fact that he rode also points to a skill that not everyone possesses. I don't ride," she added with a faint shrug.

"These are good things to keep in mind." Turning to Wycombe, Teague instructed him to go to Belgrave Square to interview the staff and investigate the exterior of the Chadwicks' house, with particular attention to Miss Chadwick's window. "I'll join you there as soon as I can."

Wycombe nodded and started back up the road toward the vehicles and horses.

Teague then shifted his attention to Tilda as he took his hands from his hips and relaxed them at his sides. "Pardon me for saying so, but you seem exhausted. Why don't you go home? I'll let you know if we find anything."

Hadrian expected Tilda to argue, but she did not. "Thank you. Please send word if you find anything at all, and especially if Miss Chadwick returns."

"I will," Teague said firmly.

Hadrian inclined his head at the detective inspector, then escorted Tilda up the road toward the coach where Leach awaited them. "I'm a bit disappointed we aren't calling on the Chadwicks. If I could find a way to touch Chadwick, I might be able to see Spring-heeled Jack's memory."

"Because he touched Chadwick last night when he scratched him." Tilda's brow creased. "You might see Chadwick's memory of being attacked, which would also be helpful. But how would you ever find a reason to touch him? I don't think he'd shake your hand at this juncture," she added with an arched brow.

"Probably not," Hadrian said on a sigh.

"We don't even know if Jack actually scratched him," Tilda noted. "Those were awfully deep wounds for someone's finger-nails, and the kidnapper does *not* have claws."

"True. He may have used a tool or device of some kind, which would mean he didn't actually come into contact with Chad-wick's flesh. That would have prevented me from experiencing the kidnapper's memory."

They reached the coach, and Leach held the door whilst Hadrian helped Tilda inside. Hadrian directed Leach back to Marylebone.

They rode in silence again for a few moments. Hadrian did not feel as tired as he had on the trip to Hampstead Heath. His frustration was great. He would give anything to find a way to help their investigation. To help Tilda.

"You don't have Jack's ransom notes any longer, do you?" he asked.

"No, I gave them to Teague."

Hadrian had thought so, but frustration flashed through him anyway. "I wanted to try to see another memory."

Tilda blinked and pushed herself straighter against the squab. "I still have the envelope the second letter arrived in." She opened her reticule and withdrew it. "I don't want you to have another awful headache."

"It's a small price." Which Hadrian would eagerly pay. "We need all the help we can find right now."

Hadrian removed his glove before taking the envelope from Tilda.

As with the vision the day before, Hadrian saw a mahogany desk and a man's hand holding a quill above a piece of parchment. Focusing his mind, Hadrian attempted to ascertain a location or a time of day, any detail at all. His head began to pound. Why was this so hard?

At last, the scent of tobacco filled his nostrils, almost overwhelmingly so. He blinked, and the vision was gone.

"Did you see something?" Tilda asked eagerly.

"Nothing I haven't already, but I smelled something this time." That had only happened to him once or twice before, and it didn't occur for everyone with this ability. At least, that was Captain Vale's experience. He did not experience smells. "It was a strong scent of tobacco."

"What could that mean?" Tilda searched his face as if she could find the answer there.

"I saw the same memory as yesterday's—a man's hand about to write. I tried to discern other details about the location, but there was nothing beyond the desk. Perhaps he's in a tobacco shop or lives near one," Hadrian suggested.

"He could also be in a warehouse that stores tobacco." Tilda exhaled. "There are many options, almost too many to investigate. But we could try. On our own, of course, since we can't ask for help from Teague to investigate something we can't explain."

This was a problem they encountered often. It was difficult to share a lead from Hadrian's visions when they couldn't share how they'd obtained the information.

"Do you still want to go home?" Hadrian asked.

Tilda stifled a yawn. "I think I must. My grandmother will be going to church soon, so I can nap whilst she's gone. I'd like to call on Joseph Hopkins this afternoon. After, we can make inquiries of the tutors, then Miss Chadwick's friends tomorrow, as you suggested." She sent him an expectant look.

Hadrian smiled. Even if she hadn't appeared to want him to join her, he would've asked. "I'd be delighted to accompany you."

"You don't have tea with your mother this afternoon?" Tilda asked.

"Not today. In fact, our fortnightly Sunday teas have fallen out of habit, much to her chagrin. Our investigations have taken precedence, and I'm not always able to keep the appointment."

"That upsets her, I imagine," Tilda said with a faint smile. "She seems to rely on you."

She did. Hadrian was her only unmarried child and the heir. His three sisters were wed and had children. They were busy managing their own households. And Hadrian's younger brother had died several years earlier. Since his mother lived rather close to Ravenhurst House in Mayfair, Hadrian was naturally the child she depended upon most.

Hadrian straightened his waistcoat as he adjusted on the seat. "She understands I have other commitments."

Tilda slid him a sly look. "Does she know they're to do with our investigations?"

"More or less." Hadrian didn't meet her eyes.

She laughed softly. "I don't blame you for not telling her. I'm sure she finds it strange, if not unacceptable, that you, an earl, take time to investigate crimes with a private *woman* detective."

"She doesn't say *that*." She did occasionally voice her disappointment that he didn't give other matters the same attention he did his investigations with Tilda. Those matters mostly involved wife-hunting, which was of high importance to his mother.

"Then yes, I would appreciate your company this afternoon."

Silence fell again until they neared Marylebone. Tilda's dark whisper stole over him. "What if Miss Chadwick doesn't come back? Or worse, what if she's been harmed?"

Hadrian wanted to hold her, but he also didn't want to overstep. "My shoulder is here," he offered. "If you'd like to rest your head on it."

"Only if you put your arms around me too," she said, filling him with a deep and abiding warmth.

"Nothing would make me happier." He slid his arms around her, and she pressed against him, laying her head on his shoulder.

"Miss Chadwick *will* come back," he assured her, hoping so with all his heart.

"You don't know that."

No, he did not. And the truth was he feared Teague was right. The odds of Miss Chadwick returning lessened with each passing day.

# CHAPTER 5

That afternoon, Hadrian arrived at Tilda's grandmother's house and didn't even knock before Vaughn, their butler, opened the door.

"Good afternoon, my lord," the septuagenarian said as welcomed Hadrian inside. "It's always a pleasure to see you."

"Thank you, Vaughn. Likewise."

"Looks as if it's going to rain," the butler noted conversationally.

"Yes, perhaps sooner than later. I think I felt a drop as I walked to the door." Hadrian was just glad it hadn't rained on them that morning at Hampstead Heath.

"Miss Wren is awaiting you in the parlor." Vaughn gestured to the room to the left of the entrance hall.

"Thank you." Hadrian removed his hat, but not his gloves, since they would be leaving shortly. In fact, Hadrian wondered why he was going into the parlor at all.

"May I take that for you?" Vaughn asked, eyeing Hadrian's hat.

"No, thank you. I won't be staying long." He smiled at the butler before turning and going into the parlor.

Tilda stood with her hat and gloves already in place and her reticule in hand. He could see from her expression that she was eager to depart, but it was apparent why they were not already on their way. Her grandmother, Mrs. Wren, sat in her chair near the window.

She wore a bright smile and was clearly pleased to see Hadrian. "I'm delighted you came in to see me before you hurry off."

"It is my privilege," Hadrian said, walking toward Tilda's grandmother and giving her a courtly bow.

Mrs. Wren laughed softly. "You always know how to flatter me. I can't believe the two of you are working on another case so soon. Surely you should rest between your assignments." She glanced toward Tilda.

"We conduct investigations as we are needed, Grandmama," Tilda said with perhaps an edge of impatience. "I told you this is a very important and most urgent case."

"Well, I hope you'll be able to take a respite when you've concluded this one," her grandmother said with a note of disapproval. Whilst she supported her granddaughter's work, she also hoped to see Tilda pursue more traditional activities, such as marriage and motherhood. It was not a point of contention between them as far as Hadrian could see, but he suspected the news of their courtship would please Mrs. Wren. Unless she already knew. But Hadrian didn't think so. Tilda surely would have said something.

"I do think it's time that Lord Ravenhurst and perhaps his mother join us for dinner one evening," Mrs. Wren added.

"We can discuss that later," Tilda replied tightly. "However, now his lordship and I must be on our way."

"I know you've somewhere important to be." Mrs. Wren pursed her lips. "On a Sunday afternoon, of all times." She exhaled.

"We won't be gone terribly long," Tilda said before preceding Hadrian from the parlor into the entrance hall. Hadrian placed his hat back on his head and nodded toward Vaughn, who opened the door.

As Hadrian escorted Tilda to the coach, gentle drops of rain sprinkled upon them. Hadrian had already informed Leach of their destination. They climbed into the coach and were quickly on their way to Stepney.

Rather than ask Tilda about the case yet, Hadrian slid her a curious glance. "It appears your grandmother is not yet aware of our courtship."

"No," Tilda confirmed. "It hasn't seemed appropriate to discuss that amidst everything that's going on. I plan to tell her as soon as we find Miss Chadwick."

Hadrian studied her charming profile—her strong chin and pert nose that he'd come to know almost as well as his own. "You haven't had a change of heart, have you?"

She snapped her head toward him, her eyes widening slightly. "No, why would you think that?"

He shrugged. "Just asking a question."

She exhaled. "I have *not* changed my mind. I'm just incredibly distracted by this horrible case. I hate that Miss Chadwick has not been returned."

"I know, and I apologize if I made it seem as if our courtship should take precedence over finding and rescuing her." The simple fact was that Hadrian wanted the entire world to know how he felt about Tilda and that she was his—or would hopefully be. In his mind, he was already hers. "What do you expect to learn from Hopkins?"

"Anything he can tell us about Spring-heeled Jack and the investigation he conducted thirty years ago. I hope he has a good memory," she said wryly.

"If not, the clerk from Scotland Yard should be able to obtain the record books," Hadrian said.

"I hope so." Tilda fidgeted with her reticule during the ride to

Stepney. Hadrian had never noticed her do that before. She truly was agitated about this case, not that he blamed her.

Arriving at Hopkins's modest terrace on Salter Street, Hadrian was pleased to see the rain had stopped. They were greeted at the door by a woman in her late sixties. She surveyed them with a weary curiosity, her bright hazel gaze lingering on Hadrian.

"May I help you?" she asked tentatively.

"Good afternoon," Tilda said. "I'm Miss Wren, and this is Lord Ravenhurst. We've come to speak with Mr. Hopkins about a case he investigated thirty years ago."

The woman's expression changed dramatically. She was somehow seemingly both aghast and intimidated. "You can't be with the Metropolitan Police," the woman said to Tilda as she flicked a nervous glance toward Hadrian. "Why would you need to speak with my husband?"

"I am a *private* detective," Tilda replied. "Lord Ravenhurst is my associate. We're working on a case, and we hope Mr. Hopkins can be of assistance."

"I'm sure he'd like that." Mrs. Hopkins again glanced at Hadrian, her cheeks flushing slightly. She quickly adjusted her cap, which had been sitting a bit askew atop her white hair. "My husband has been retired for some time now, but he misses the work. Come in."

She showed them to a room at the back of the ground floor. It was something between a study and a sitting room.

"Joseph, you have guests." Mrs. Hopkins moved to the man dozing in a chair near the hearth and touched his arm.

Hopkins's head was mostly bald, save a band of gray hair that started above his ears and ringed his head. He jolted awake and sat up straight. "What's that?"

Mrs. Hopkins gestured toward Tilda and Hadrian. "Lord Ravenhurst and Miss Wren. They've come to speak to you about a case. They're private detectives, or at least, Miss Wren is. I'm not sure about his lordship." She sent Hadrian a fleeting smile, again displaying her nervousness.

It seemed Mrs. Hopkins found Hadrian's role both curious and perhaps strange, but that was understandable. He also realized it was possible she'd never met a peer, and here Hadrian was calling at her house.

"I'll fetch tea." Mrs. Hopkins gestured for Tilda and Hadrian to take a pair of chairs near where Hopkins was seated.

"That isn't necessary," Tilda said kindly, but Hadrian disagreed.

He didn't want to offend Mrs. Hopkins. "That would be welcome, thank you." He sent Tilda an apologetic glance. She responded with a quizzical stare, then gave a faint shrug before turning her attention to Hopkins.

Hadrian removed his gloves in anticipation of drinking the tea—and in shaking Hopkins's hand at some point. Perhaps he'd see something helpful. Hadrian always wanted to try.

"How can I help you?" Hopkins asked, glancing between Tilda and Hadrian.

Tilda clutched her reticule in her lap and sat ramrod straight. "We understand you were the primary investigator into an attack on Miss Lucy Scales in February 1838."

Hopkins snorted. "Are you really a detective?" His eyes narrowed with disbelief. "Or are you a writer or a journalist seeking to profit from the stories about Spring-heeled Jack? I can't believe someone's tried to make him into a hero," Hopkins scoffed.

"I'm here seeking the truth of what happened thirty years ago," Tilda replied. "I imagine you've had inquiries from plenty of people seeking to sensationalize Spring-heeled Jack, but I'm truly a private detective, and I've been hired to find a missing young woman. Her kidnapper claims to be Spring-heeled Jack."

Hopkins blinked at them in surprise. "A kidnapper, you say? Spring-heeled Jack didn't abduct anyone in my time. He attacked a couple of young women, which caused terrible hysteria, but he wasn't a kidnapper. We didn't catch the man—or men—behind those attacks or any of the other Spring-heeled Jacks who were sighted."

"You think there was more than one man?" Hadrian asked.

"Those of us working on the investigations thought it was possible, given the number of sightings in different places," Hopkins replied. "However, we believed the attacks here in London were committed by the same perpetrator. Still, he wasn't a kidnapper and that was decades ago. I'm not sure how I can help."

"Since this kidnapper has adopted the identity of Spring-heeled Jack, we hope details from your investigation might aid us in catching him." Tilda removed her notebook and pencil from her reticule. "Can you tell us about the incident with Miss Scales and your investigation? You worked for H Division?"

"I did. I was hired when the Met was formed." Hopkins rubbed his fingertips briefly against his forehead. "I still remember the investigation into Miss Scales's attack quite clearly. It's the most notorious case I ever investigated. As you mentioned, I have indeed been asked about it many times since, which has kept my memories fresh."

Hopkins's brow creased as he leaned forward slightly. "Spring-heeled Jack had been seen and talked about for several months before he appeared around here in February of 1838. Miss Alsop was attacked first, on the nineteenth. It caused a great fervor, and by the time Miss Scales was attacked on the twenty-eighth, people, especially young women, were very afraid to open their doors or walk about, particularly in the evening."

Tilda made notes in her book. "We understand the man who investigated Miss Alsop's attack has passed away."

"James Lea. The best inspector I ever knew," Hopkins said wistfully. "We worked closely together on these cases."

Mrs. Hopkins bustled in with a tea tray that she set on a table near the window facing a small back garden. She poured out three cups and asked how Hadrian and Tilda took their tea. Tilda indicated that she couldn't hold her tea and take notes, so Mrs. Hopkins left her cup on the tray.

Hadrian immediately sipped his and complimented Mrs. Hopkins on the blend. She smiled and seemed quite pleased as she departed.

Visions flitted through Hadrian's mind as he handled the cup, which happened when he touched items that were not familiar to him. He was exceedingly glad the things in his own home did not provoke him to see memories. The skill could be a hindrance when he was out, particularly because of the headaches caused by the visions.

Hadrian had been working on controlling his ability. It took focus and intention to keep his mind clear of others' memories when he didn't wish to see them, and he hadn't yet mastered that. Consequently, he balanced the teacup on the arm of his chair and touched it as slightly as possible.

"Can you tell us about Miss Alsop's attack as well as Miss Scales's?" Tilda asked.

Hopkins took a sip of his tea, then set his cup down on a small table beside his chair. It also held a newspaper and a pair of glasses. "I'll start with Miss Alsop since she was attacked first. She lived at Number One Bearbinder Lane. Around quarter to nine in the evening, a man claiming to be a policeman pounded on her door. He said they'd caught Spring-heeled Jack out in the lane, and he needed a light. Miss Alsop was eager to help, so she fetched a candle and opened the door. That was when the man threw off his cloak and revealed a white oilskin costume." Hopkins motioned as if he'd discarded an outer garment, then gestured to his head. "He also wore a tight helmet with a sinister, devil-like aspect with horns. She described his eyes as red balls of fire. He spat blue flames at her face, then seized her by the neck."

Splaying his hand across the front of his throat, Hopkins's voice climbed in volume.

"Holding Miss Alsop, Jack scratched at her with his claws, which she described as being like metal, tearing her dress and wounding her neck, shoulders, and arms." Hopkins made a slashing motion—it was as if he were conducting a performance. "When she tried to turn and retreat into the house, the phantom grabbed her by the hair, removing a significant amount. Fortunately, her sister was home and pulled Jane inside, then slammed the door closed. The man dressed as Spring-heeled Jack banged on the door, but then ran off, probably because a group from the John Bull over in Roman Road came running when they heard the girls screaming. They claimed to have passed a man in a long black cloak, and he told them Spring-heeled Jack was at the Alsop house."

"Clever rogue," Hadrian murmured. "Was Miss Alsop badly hurt?"

"Her gown was in tatters, and she suffered significant injury." Hopkins's expression dimmed. "It was very traumatic for her and her sister. Lea found a witness, a wheelwright called Smith. He said he saw a couple of men near the scene, so we brought them in for questioning—a carpenter named Millbank and a bricklayer named Payne."

Tilda wrote furiously in her notebook the entire time Hopkins spoke, missing most of the man's theatrical display. Now she fixed her gaze on Hopkins. "What happened with Millbank and Payne?"

Hopkins gestured to his clothing. "Millbank had been wearing white, and Lea believed that Miss Alsop had mistaken that for the oilskin coverall that Spring-heeled Jack was purported to wear. However, the men had an alibi. The publican at the White Hart said they'd been there, and Millbank, in particular, was quite drunk. Lea brought Miss Alsop in to identify at least one of them, but she couldn't say that either was the beast—that was her word

—who'd attacked her." The former inspector shook his head with an expression of regret.

Tilda frowned but gave a single nod. "I'm not surprised since it sounds as though the helmet Spring-heeled Jack wore may also have served as a mask. In any case, as you said, Miss Alsop was traumatized so it's not unusual that she may not recall what someone looked like. That is unfortunate."

"Was that the end of it?" Hadrian was quite caught up in Hopkins's retelling. The man had obviously narrated the tale countless times, and he was most engaging.

"We didn't see Spring-heeled Jack again for a few days, but people were thoroughly distressed, as you can imagine." Hopkins picked up his tea for a quick drink. "Everyone was waiting, breathless, for his next attack. He appeared a few days later, nearby on Turner Street at the Ashford residence. A female servant answered the door and again, a man in a dark cloak threw it off to reveal himself as Spring-heeled Jack. But when she screamed, he ran away. No one else saw anything, so we were unable to corroborate the young woman's report, unfortunately."

"Do you think she was lying?" Tilda asked.

"Everyone wanted to say they'd seen Spring-heeled Jack or knew someone who had." Hopkins's brow rippled with grave concern. "You must understand, there was a great deal of hysteria at the time. We received many reports, the majority of them filled with uncertainty and doubt. Of those, the servant at Turner Street seemed the most genuine."

Hadrian recalled the stories his mother had told him when he was younger. He'd been delightfully frightened, but she'd assured him that chaotic period had been awful. "Was no one ever prosecuted for Miss Alsop's attack?" He sipped his lukewarm tea as the former inspector replied.

Hopkins shook his head. "In the end, Millbank, who was the primary suspect, couldn't demonstrate an ability to breathe blue fire. The magistrate couldn't see a reason to keep him, especially without Miss Alsop being able to identify him as her attacker. There were a few reports later of a man in fancy clothing practicing fire breathing on Bow Fair Fields, but we never tracked him down."

Tilda finished writing and looked over at Hopkins once more. "Will you tell us about Lucy Scales next?"

"Miss Scales was just eighteen, same as Miss Alsop. Lucy and her sister were walking home from their brother's house in Limehouse and decided to cut through Green Dragon Alley. This was about the same time of night as when Miss Alsop was attacked. But in the Scales case, Spring-heeled Jack, a tall, thin figure in a large cloak carrying a bullseye lantern, stood in the alley and spat blue flames in Lucy's face as she passed. She claimed she was blinded, then dissolved into fits for several hours. Thankfully, the blindness was temporary."

Hadrian couldn't help thinking of Chadwick's coachman reporting that he'd also been blinded temporarily by blue flame.

"Miss Scales collapsed in the alley?" Tilda asked.

"Yes. She was screaming, as was her sister, and their brother came running. He picked Lucy up and carried her home." Hopkins pressed his lips together. "I'm ashamed to say the investigation into Miss Scales's attack was not as thorough as the one into Miss Alsop's. But Miss Alsop's family was of a higher rank, and, well, that matters sometimes when it comes to resources."

"I am aware of such inequity," Tilda said. "My father worked for A Division."

"I imagine he's proud of you," Hopkins said with a smile.

"I like to think so. Unfortunately, he is no longer with us."

Hopkins inclined his head at Tilda, his dark gaze earnest. "I'm sorry to hear that."

"He died doing what he loved." Tilda shared that information without so much as a crease in her brow. In fact, there was pride and even a hint of serenity in her features. Hadrian suspected it was because she'd recently discovered the truth of her father's murder, and he knew she was grateful for that.

"I gather no one was questioned before the magistrate regarding Miss Scales's attack?" Hadrian asked.

"That's right, though Lea and I still tried to determine what happened—for a short time anyway. Lea was soon busy with other work. He was a highly regarded inspector, and he was quite busy." Hopkins's gaze fell to Tilda's notebook. "I know he kept detailed notes about the investigation, but I've no idea where they might be."

Hadrian glanced at Tilda and noted the disappointment that flashed in her eyes. "Is there anything else you can tell us?" she asked.

"Lea and I concluded the attacker was the same man," Hopkins replied. "And that he likely wasn't the original creature who appeared in Barnes the previous autumn. We were also convinced that Millbank attacked Miss Alsop, but we didn't have solid proof."

Tilda regarded Hopkins intently. "What made you think it was him?"

Hopkins lifted a shoulder. "Just a feeling. Once you've done police work for a while, you come to recognize such things. Millbank spent a great deal of time at the White Hart and was known for drinking and showing off. It's not hard to believe he and Payne were drunk and decided to stir up mischief."

"I would argue that breathing blue flame and causing the bodily harm that was done to Miss Alsop was far more than mischief," Tilda said. "It was malevolent and premeditated. How else could they manage the trick with the blue flame?"

Hadrian inclined his head toward Tilda as he looked at Hopkins. "I agree. Did you have any notion as to how that trick was accomplished? What about the red eyes or Spring-heeled Jack's ability to leap great heights?"

"No one to do with the attacks we investigated reported

Spring-heeled Jack jumping, which is ironic given his name," Hopkins replied. "Lea had a few theories about the blue flame, but I don't recall what they were. I'm sure he wrote them in his notes. Perhaps you'll be able to find them."

Hadrian and Tilda exchanged a look. Hopefully, the clerk from Scotland Yard would find those tomorrow among the police records.

"The Alsop house is still standing in Bow if you want to speak with someone in the family," Hopkins added. "You may be able to obtain an account of what they saw."

"I might do that," Tilda said. "Thank you."

Hopkins settled back in his chair. "I thought this story had died out, at least around here. I know it's moved to other places, but Spring-heeled Jack mostly disappeared from London after that period of hysteria. He became a legend that has been sensationalized beyond recognition—penny dreadfuls and plays and the like. You can't trust that what you'll hear isn't a fanciful tale someone read and now thinks is a memory. I'm surprised to hear the legend has resurfaced in this way. You're smart to consider any ties this kidnapper might have to the Spring-heeled Jack of the past." Hopkins lifted a shoulder. "Your kidnapper could be someone who knew him or was related to him, or someone who's simply enthralled with the character. What a fascinating case." The former inspector sounded as though he envied them.

"The kidnapper is definitely doing his best to convince us that he's the Spring-heeled Jack of old. He was seen last night when he collected the ransom on Hampstead Heath. He wore white oilskin, had red eyes, breathed blue flame, and leapt over a five-foot hedge."

Leaning forward once more, Hopkins appeared most intrigued. "Since you're here, I gather he escaped?"

"Unfortunately," Hadrian replied.

Grimacing, Hopkins picked up his teacup. "Dare I hope the poor young woman was returned at least?"

Tilda's features tensed. "Not yet, which is why we're investigating the legend. We're desperate to find her."

"Certainly." Hopkins set his tea back down after taking a sip. "Once this news appears in the papers, I fear there will be another hysteria, perhaps even worse than before since a young woman is missing. If there's anything I can do to help, please don't hesitate to ask." He gave them a sad smile. "I miss my work."

"We will, thank you." Tilda slipped her notebook and pencil back into her reticule and rose.

Hopkins jumped to his feet, displaying a surprising agility for a man in his early seventies. "I'll walk you out."

Hadrian stood and followed behind Hopkins as he allowed Tilda to precede him to the entrance hall. When they arrived, Hopkins turned to face them.

"Please tell Mrs. Hopkins her tea was delicious," Hadrian said.

Tilda gave the former inspector a regretful smile. "I'm afraid I was too wrapped up in your story to drink mine, Mr. Hopkins."

"I'll go and drink your cup so she doesn't notice." Hopkins winked at Tilda, and Hadrian found himself hoping they'd have to consult with Hopkins again.

"You're too kind," Tilda said.

Now was the moment Hadrian had been waiting for. He extended his hand to Hopkins. "Thank you for your time today, Mr. Hopkins."

Handshakes were always a difficult way to see a memory, but sometimes it was all Hadrian could do. He focused his mind on Lucy Scales and her attack as he shook the man's hand. A man's face appeared. He was in his early thirties, with a mop of dark brown hair and rheumy eyes. His nose was red, and he appeared frightened. Unfortunately, as was often the case with short handshake visions, that was the extent of what Hadrian saw.

"I wish you the best of luck." Hopkins opened the door for them, and they departed after Tilda thanked him one last time. The skies had opened again whilst they were inside, so they hurried to the coach where Leach, wearing a wide-brimmed hat dripping with rain, opened the door.

"Leach, our next stop is number one Bearbinder Lane," Tilda said, surprising Hadrian as he helped her into the coach.

He nodded at Leach before sitting beside Tilda. "You want to visit the Alsop house?"

"I do. I just can't return home yet. Not without doing everything we can to find Miss Chadwick." She looked at him with hope, her eyes bright. "I don't suppose you glimpsed anything when you shook Mr. Hopkins's hand?"

Hadrian described the man he saw. "I've no idea who he could be. He could have nothing to do with Spring-heeled Jack at all."

Tilda exhaled. "Still, that was a helpful visit. I do hope the clerk finds Inspector Lea's notes. We may need to inform Teague that the clerk should look for those specifically."

"That's a good idea." He was eager to rescue Miss Chadwick too and was glad Tilda didn't want to conclude their inquiries yet.

"After we visit the Alsop house, would you mind if we called on the tutors?" Tilda asked. "I know we may not have much luck on a Sunday, but I'd feel better if we tried."

"I would too." He smiled at her and took her hand.

Tilda sent him a brief but grateful smile. "Thank you for coming with me."

Hadrian brushed his lips against her temple. "There is nowhere I would rather be."

# CHAPTER 6

Despite her anxiety over Miss Chadwick's continued absence, Tilda had managed to find sleep last night—likely only because she'd been so exhausted after rising so early the day before and making several inquiries in the afternoon. This morning, she felt rested and eager to do her utmost to find Miss Chadwick.

At the Alsop house, they'd spoken to one of Jane Alsop's sisters, but not the one who'd pulled her out of the doorway. Unfortunately, she did not reveal any information they hadn't already learned from Mr. Hopkins.

They'd also called on Miss Chadwick's tutors. Both were distressed to hear she'd been abducted. The pianoforte tutor, a gentleman in his late sixties, had just seen her last Wednesday, the day before Miss Chadwick was taken. He hadn't noticed anything odd about her behavior.

The watercolor tutor, a middle-aged married man with small children, had broken down sobbing upon hearing the news of her kidnapping. His wife had come in to console him whilst Tilda and Hadrian attempted to complete their inquiry.

Neither tutor had offered any helpful information. They

reported Miss Chadwick to be exuberant and delightful and said her abduction was a grave tragedy. Seeing their agitation hadn't eased Tilda's anxiety.

Tilda and Hadrian planned to call at Scotland Yard this morning to learn what Teague and Wycombe might have discovered with their inquiries, as well as share the information from their interview with Mr. Hopkins. Then they would begin to call on Miss Chadwick's friends. Tilda watched through the front window in the parlor as Hadrian's coach pulled up outside.

Pulling on her gloves, she turned and started toward the entrance hall but had to stop short as her grandmother walked into the parlor. "You're off again this morning with Lord Ravenhurst?"

"Yes." Last night, Tilda had told her grandmother a little about the case, that it was a kidnapping and the investigation wasn't going well.

"I hope today brings better results," her grandmother said with a kind smile. "I see the toll this is taking on you. The lines between your eyes have never been more pronounced."

Vaughn greeted Hadrian in the entrance hall. Tilda's grandmother pivoted so she could see the two men, then Hadrian appeared in the doorway to the parlor.

"I don't suppose you can stay for tea when you return later?" Grandmama asked Hadrian.

"We can try, but we don't know when we'll return," Tilda said. "If it's not possible, we'll have tea another day."

"All right." Her grandmother sounded disappointed. "You have to take a respite some time. You can't work constantly."

"We aren't working constantly," Tilda tried not to sound defensive and was fairly certain she'd failed. "This case is simply more urgent than the others."

"I understand," her grandmother said gently. "But you don't need to accept every investigation."

"I can't afford to turn them down," Tilda replied with perhaps too much frustration. "This is our livelihood, Grandmama." Without her work, their household would fall into financial ruin. She flicked a glance at Hadrian, wondering what he was thinking.

He was well aware of their financial state, and whilst it had improved over the last few months, due to her increasing work as a detective, their household had also expanded. When she'd met Hadrian, it had just been Tilda, her grandmother, and Mrs. Acorn, their housekeeper and cook. Since then, they had taken on Vaughn, her grandfather's cousin's butler, who'd found himself without a position, after his employer had died. And Clara, Tilda's maid, had become unemployed when her mistress had returned to the country following the murder of her husband.

Whilst Tilda hadn't really been able to afford additional retainers, she also hadn't wanted to turn Vaughn out, not when he was at an age when he should retire and had no means to do so. Clara was only supposed to join the household temporarily whilst looking for a new position, however Tilda's grandmother loved having her there. Though she was ostensibly Tilda's maid, she did much to aid Tilda's grandmother, and she lightened Mrs. Acorn's load. In the end, Tilda recognized she possessed a soft heart. She found ways to keep everyone employed, and she didn't regret it one bit. Though, that meant she had to ensure a steady stream of work.

Unless she wanted to marry an earl, which of late had become an actual possibility.

Perhaps that was why Tilda hadn't yet told her grandmother that she and Hadrian were courting. Grandmama would almost certainly say it was the answer to all their problems, including those Tilda didn't even think existed, such as her lack of a husband. Grandmama and those in her generation believed women needed a spouse to ensure a good position and security. However, Tilda desired her independence above all else. That was, in fact, a major obstacle to any future she might share with

Hadrian. That and the fact that Tilda did not come from the same class and didn't know the first thing about being a countess.

Another impediment to a marriage between them, and perhaps the primary one, was Tilda's occupation. She did not see how a woman could be a countess and a private detective at the same time. And Tilda was not willing to give up her dream, especially not when things were going so well.

Rather, they had been—until this difficult case and the possibility that Mr. Chadwick might ruin her reputation. She sincerely hoped it was only a threat.

"I didn't mean to cause any upset, my dear," her grandmother said quietly. "I suppose I find things to worry about when I don't need to."

"It's all right." Tilda bussed her grandmother's cheek before moving into the entrance hall. "I promise we'll invite his lordship for tea soon."

"Wonderful," Grandmama said with a wide smile.

Tilda turned toward the door, ready to leave, but when Vaughn opened it, Sergeant Wycombe stood on the threshold, poised to knock. Tilda's entire body tensed. She had a feeling this was very bad news, certainly because Wycombe wore a grim expression.

"Good morning," Wycombe said with a nod toward Tilda's grandmother.

"Good morning, Sergeant Wycombe," Tilda said. "I expect you have news to share. Please come in."

Sergeant Wycombe nodded, his features creasing into a grimace that did not bode well at all. "I'm afraid so."

A sick feeling spread through Tilda's belly. She pivoted and looked to her grandmother. "Would you mind excusing us, Grandmama?"

"Of course." She turned and retreated to the back of the house.

Tilda walked back into the parlor on wooden legs and was

followed by Sergeant Wycombe. Hadrian came in last, closing the door behind him. His features appeared as unsettled as she felt.

"It's bad news, isn't it?" Tilda braced herself.

Wycombe pressed his lips together. "I wish it wasn't. We've found a body. It's Miss Chadwick, I'm afraid. We identified the mole on the back of her neck, as described by her parents."

Tilda managed to take a breath, though it wasn't as deep as she'd hoped. She shook for a moment as horror and sadness raced through her. "Where did you find her?" The question scratched from her suddenly dry throat.

"Limehouse in Green Dragon Alley."

Gasping, Tilda exchanged a look with Hadrian. "Green Dragon Alley was the location of one of the attacks in 1838. Lucy Scales was walking home from her brother's when Spring-heeled Jack approached her and spat blue flame in her face. She was temporarily blinded and fell into a terrible fit. Her brother had to carry her home."

"Hell," Wycombe breathed. "I was not aware of that connection, and neither is Detective Inspector Teague, or he would have mentioned it. He's in Green Dragon Alley now and sent me to fetch you. You look as if you were already heading out."

Tilda nodded. "In fact, we were going to Scotland Yard."

"Let's be on our way," Hadrian said urgently as he returned to the door and opened it for Tilda and the sergeant. They returned to the entrance hall where Vaughn opened the front door as they made their way outside.

Sergeant Wycombe had come in a police vehicle. "You'll follow me?"

"Yes," Hadrian replied before going to Leach and providing their new destination. He then helped Tilda into the coach.

They were quiet, a tense silence blanketing the interior of the coach as they started moving. Tilda had feared this result. Now, faced with it, she felt an overwhelming sense of failure.

After a few moments, Hadrian put his hand over both of

Tilda's, which were clasped tightly in her lap. "I'm so sorry, Tilda."

"I failed her," Tilda whispered, hating that she felt so emotional. She ought to maintain a calm and unemotional demeanor.

"You didn't fail her. *We* didn't fail her," Hadrian said strongly. "The kidnapper received the ransom he requested and killed her despite that, which makes me think he never planned to return her. For all we know, she's been dead all this time."

Tilda tried to breathe deeply, to slow the rapid beat of her heart. "The Chadwicks will be devastated."

"This is not your fault, Tilda." Hadrian placed his hand on her shoulder, and she turned her head toward him. "Please don't try to comfort me. I don't deserve that. I mean, I don't want that right now."

Hadrian's brow darkened. "I heard what you said. You absolutely deserve to be comforted, regardless of what you say." He clasped one of her hands firmly and held it in her lap for the remainder of the ride.

Tilda was glad for his quiet support, but it didn't keep her from wondering what might have happened if she hadn't involved the police. As the coach slowed, she reminded herself that sometimes there was no good answer or path, that she could only do her best. She oughtn't doubt herself.

This case was making that difficult.

They departed the coach at the end of Green Dragon Alley. Sergeant Wycombe's gig was parked in front of them, and there was also a police van.

Sergeant Wycombe led them into the narrow alley, and Tilda saw Teague up ahead. She walked faster, both eager and dreading to see what they'd found.

Miss Chadwick's body lay supine between two doorways, next to an empty crate. She wore a simple gown of light blue and her feet were bare, though Tilda noted they were not very dirty.

Her dark hair was partially pinned up, but several strands lay flat against her cheek and neck. The bodice of her gown bore four long tears caked with blood, and her torn flesh was exposed beneath. Her face was red, almost as if she'd been burned. Tilda surmised that she had not been dead very long.

"A resident down the alley found her about an hour ago," Teague said. "I've constables interviewing people in the alley, and then they'll move to the surrounding neighborhood." He glanced over at Wycombe. "Check on their progress, please."

With a nod, Wycombe took himself off with haste.

"She's not wearing the nightgown the maid described," Tilda noted.

"Perhaps the kidnapper provided her with a gown," Teague suggested.

"One that fits her very well." Tilda's gaze flicked to Delia's bare feet. "But no shoes or boots. Despite that, her feet are surprisingly clean." Tilda surveyed the area. "Do you think she was killed here? Given the state of her feet, I doubt she walked along this alley."

"Agreed," Teague said. "It appears she was placed here after she was dead, but I don't know why."

"It may be because Lucy Scales was attacked here by Spring-heeled Jack in 1838. Lord Ravenhurst and I met with former Inspector Hopkins yesterday. He told us all about the investigations into the two attacks in February 1838."

Teague clenched his jaw. "Damn."

Tilda and Hadrian shared the other information they'd learned from Hopkins the day before.

"You say Spring-heeled Jack spat blue flames in Miss Scales's face, and she was temporarily blinded, as was Chadwick's coachman last night," Teague said. "I'd thought Miss Chadwick's face looks as if it may have been burned."

"I was thinking the same thing," Tilda said.

"We'll see what the coroner says." Teague gestured toward her mutilated chest. "I'd say this was definitely made to look as though Spring-heeled Jack killed her, especially knowing he scratched Miss Alsop in a similar way."

"There can be no mistaking that intention," Tilda said in agreement. "Mr. Chadwick was also scratched, though the wounds were on his face." She crouched down to closely investigate the body. The cuts on Miss Chadwick's chest were much deeper than her father's had been. She could have died from blood loss, but Tilda suspected that would have taken quite some time. She shuddered to think of the horrible death this young woman might have suffered. A lump caught in her throat, and she blinked away tears as she rose.

She needed to rein in her emotions. There could be nothing worse than gaining a reputation as a detective with an excess of sentiment.

Hadrian's eyes fixed on her as his brow furrowed. She was torn between wanting him to hold her and not wanting to show her vulnerability. The former was completely inappropriate in her current situation. She needed to behave in a competent—and stoic—manner.

Tilda glanced up at Teague. "Do you think she died from blood loss?"

"It would appear so, but I hope not." He seemed to have arrived at the same awful conclusion as Tilda. Teague lowered himself next to her and studied the body for a moment. "Actually, I think it's possible these wounds were made after she was killed."

"You could be right," Tilda said, narrowing her gaze. "I don't think there's enough blood here. It's also possible she was tidied before being moved."

Teague nodded. "The majority of the blood would be wherever she was killed. I didn't note any defensive wounds."

Tilda looked closely at Miss Chadwick's hands. They were not scratched, nor did any of her nails appear broken. "I don't see any marks that would indicate restraint on her wrists." She glanced at Miss Chadwick's ankles and could only see part of one beneath the hem of her gown. "Did you see any evidence of restraint on her ankles?"

"I did not." Teague rose. "But we'll see what the surgeon concludes after he performs the autopsy."

Hadrian offered his hand to Tilda as she straightened. "I don't understand why she was killed instead of returned to her parents," he said. "The kidnapper received the ransom. And it certainly seems as though she was killed *after* the money was received."

"That is what we must determine." Teague glowered at nothing in particular. "If we can."

Anger boiled up in Tilda. "If I were the kidnapper and received that much money, I would be well away from England by now."

Teague sent her a grim look. "I'm trying not to think about that. I can't fathom a reason why the kidnapper would wait a day after receiving the ransom before killing her and leaving her here."

Tilda couldn't either. "I think that's likely a clue."

"Agreed," Teague said with a nod. "As much as this has been made to look as if Spring-heeled Jack killed her, I can't believe this is related to the attacks thirty years ago. This kidnapper—and killer—has simply stolen the legend."

"Detective Inspector," Wycombe's voice carried down the alley.

"Excuse me for a moment," Teague said before hastening toward the sergeant.

Hadrian immediately dropped down next to the body. Tilda knew he'd been waiting for an opportunity to touch Miss Chadwick. He withdrew his glove and put his hand on hers. His gaze was fixed on the wall beyond the young woman, but his features were blank. He stared like that, still as a statue, for several moments, which gave Tilda hope. The longer the vision, the more likely it was he saw something helpful.

She turned to glance back down the alley and saw Teague and Wycombe part ways. Teague started toward them. Tilda turned back to Hadrian. "Teague is coming."

Hadrian blinked then removed his hand from Miss Chadwick's before rising.

"Quickly, what did you see?" Tilda asked, unable to contain her urgency.

"I had two visions. The first was Miss Chadwick in a drawing room or similar environment." Hadrian kept his voice low. "She wore a rose-pink colored day dress and stood in front of a large landscape painting. I felt a sense of anticipation. Since I saw Miss Chadwick, it wasn't her memory. I couldn't see anything that would lead me to guess whose memory I experienced."

"It could be anyone who touched her, including her family who most certainly would have seen her as you described," Tilda said. "And the second vision?"

"I refocused my mind on Miss Chadwick's kidnapping and death. That's when I saw a flash of her sitting on her bed. She did not appear alarmed or afraid. I was in the process of gathering more details within that vision when you interrupted me."

Tilda felt an immense wave of frustration. If only they could reveal Hadrian's ability to Teague. But would the detective inspector believe them? Or would he refer Hadrian to a lunatic asylum as his great-uncle had been?

"That could also have been the memory of one of her family members or even her maid," Tilda said just before Teague returned. Setting her disappointment aside, she turned to the detective inspector. "Did you learn anything helpful?"

"Wycombe spoke with a witness who said they walked by this spot two hours ago, and Miss Chadwick wasn't here."

"She was placed here in broad daylight?" Hadrian said.

Teague nodded. "Very recently, too."

"And nobody noticed who did it?" Tilda asked in disbelief.

"Nobody we've spoken to so far, but the constables have many more interviews to conduct." Teague blew out a breath and frowned deeply as his gaze dimmed. "I need to inform the Chadwicks that we've found their daughter."

Tilda's stomach clenched. "I need to return Mr. Chadwick's payment." She'd completely failed at the objective for which she'd been hired to complete.

"Now may not be the best time for that," Hadrian said gently.

"I'll leave it with the butler," Tilda replied. "I can't hide from the Chadwicks. I failed to accomplish what they hired me for." She turned to Teague. "Did you learn anything from your inquiries there yesterday?"

"The retainers are all incredibly distraught, but we couldn't discern any specific motives for kidnapping and certainly not for murder," Teague explained. "We could not determine how the kidnapper entered the house. The window was open, but to reach it, he would have had to climb the side of the house. I think we all agree he didn't jump," he added wryly. "He had to have found a way inside as well as the location of Miss Chadwick's bedchamber. It raises questions, frankly."

"How do you suppose the kidnapper left with Miss Chadwick without her waking the household?"

"That is another mystery, but I'm inclined to agree with Mrs. Chadwick, that her daughter was likely drugged." Teague met Tilda's gaze. "She indicated she'd said as much to you the other day."

"She did." Tilda brushed her hand along her jaw. "We should have taken time then to conduct these inquiries, but when the second ransom note arrived, I was distracted from gathering evidence. We instead focused on speaking with you."

"You mustn't doubt yourself," Teague advised. "I would have done the same thing upon receipt of the second ransom note. My focus would have been on planning for that as the best way to rescue the victim."

Tilda acknowledged to herself that she was overwhelmed by remorse and may not be thinking as clearly as she would like. She was aware of Hadrian watching her with concern but kept her focus on Teague. "Thank you."

"We concluded Miss Chadwick was likely unconscious when she was taken from the house," Teague continued. "Or that she was complicit." He frowned again. "We've since abandoned that theory, given what we found today."

"So, Spring-heeled Jack did something to make her unconscious and carried her from the house? Did he then toss her over his horse?" Hadrian's tone was sardonic and tinged with frustration.

Tilda well understood his sentiment. "We have many questions we can't answer. Including why Miss Chadwick isn't wearing the nightgown she was taken in."

"Do you mind if we accompany you to the Chadwicks?" Tilda asked. "Though I'm no longer being paid to investigate this case, I can't walk away."

Teague gave her an understanding smile, and Tilda was glad to see she wasn't the only detective with sentimentality. "I know you can't."

"We'll meet you at the Chadwicks' then." Tilda glanced at Hadrian who gave her a subtle nod in response.

The coroner, Graythorpe, arrived, and Tilda and Hadrian made their way to the coach. They would meet Teague in Belgrave Square when he finished speaking with Graythorpe.

Seated together in the coach as they moved through Limehouse, Hadrian looked over at her. "You don't need to go into the Chadwicks' house. I can return the bank note to the butler, and you can wait here."

Tilda turned toward him, and her emotions spilled over. "You can't spare me from my duty. I failed the Chadwicks, and I deserve their wrath. Whether it was right or not to contact the police, I did so without informing them, and that was a breach of trust."

"You absolutely do *not* deserve anyone's wrath," Hadrian said firmly and with a touch of heat. He exhaled. "I understand you're upset about Miss Chadwick. I am too, and I also feel as though I failed her. But none of this is our fault. I realize now we've had good fortune in solving our cases, including one to do with your father that went unsolved for over a decade. We were bound to have a case like this eventually."

"I won't accept that I can't solve every case." Tilda stiffened her spine. "You're right that I'm upset. However, I cannot allow myself to be this emotional."

"It's perfectly tolerable," Hadrian said softly.

"Not whilst I'm working, especially as a woman." She needed to be sensible and composed. "I confess it's difficult having you near in such moments. I find myself wanting your comfort when I should be focusing on the investigation. I'm afraid I'm going to have to rethink our courtship."

Tilda hadn't planned to say that, nor had she been thinking it. Her mind was whirling right now.

"You must do as you will." Hadrian moved his gaze from hers and fixed it straight ahead on the opposite side of the coach. "I hope you'll recognize this is a terrible situation, and that you've comported yourself extremely well, in spite of it. Just as you have during all our other investigations, which have also included difficult crimes and situations."

He was probably right, but Tilda was not of a mind to give herself any quarter. She did not, however, wish to take her emotions out on him. None of this was his fault.

She looked at his profile, the elegant sweep of his aristocratic nose and the soft outline of his lips above the masculine lines of his chin and jaw. He was so familiar to her and so very dear. This was surprisingly difficult—loving someone. Since her father had died, she really only actively loved her grandmother, and perhaps Mrs. Acorn. She supposed she felt some kind of love for her mother. But nothing she experienced came close to the vulnerability she felt with Hadrian. It wasn't just hard. It was terrifying.

"I only meant that we should rethink the timing of this courtship, not that we should abandon it," she said, trying to explain the tumult of her emotions without really explaining it. Because she couldn't.

"Good." His voice was firm and perhaps a bit brighter than it had been. He slid her a quick glance. "Because there's no way I'd allow you to abandon our courtship before it's even really started. I love you, Tilda, and you're worth fighting for. Don't ever forget that."

# CHAPTER 7

*H*adrian slept a bit later than usual the following morning. Worried about Tilda and how badly she'd taken Miss Chadwick's death, he'd tossed restlessly well into the night.

He understood Tilda didn't want to be emotional in her work and was concerned being so may reflect poorly on her. However, she could not let herself be immune to sensitivity. Hadn't she noticed that Teague had also been distraught? He'd probably become quite good at hiding how he felt, but there was no mistaking his distress over Miss Chadwick's murder. They all felt horribly.

Their visit to the Chadwicks had been agonizing. Mrs. Chadwick had been inconsolable, and understandably so. Mr. Chadwick had been devastated, but he'd quickly become furious. He'd railed at Teague and even more at Tilda, who hadn't so much as flinched in the face of his fury. She'd been the soul of calm and compassion throughout the entire encounter.

Hadrian had wanted to intervene on her behalf, but she'd sent him a decidedly steely stare, and he'd kept quiet. When they'd ridden home in the coach after, she'd allowed him to hold her in his arms, and he hoped that by the time they parted, she felt better. She'd seemed to.

After eating breakfast, Hadrian went to his study. His butler, Collier, typically set out a few newspapers atop his desk. One of the headlines on the front page of the *Daily News* caught his attention:

## *SPRING-HEELED JACK AND A LONDON TRAGEDY*

Pulse hammering, Hadrian snatched up the paper, his gaze moving rapidly over the article. Right away, he saw Tilda's name.

The story was a sensational account of Miss Chadwick's kidnapping by Spring-heeled Jack. It resurrected every piece of lore to do with the phantom legend. Hadrian's blood boiled when he reached the paragraph about Tilda.

Chadwick had been interviewed and stated that he'd hired Miss Wren to find his daughter. The article explained how she'd ignored Spring-heeled Jack's instructions and involved the Metropolitan Police. As a result, his daughter had been murdered despite Chadwick paying the ransom.

The article did *not* say that Chadwick had interfered with their plan to capture the kidnapper, nor did it explain the caution exercised by the Met and the near impossibility that the kidnapper could have been aware of their involvement. Chadwick's account made it look as if Tilda was entirely at fault and that the Met hadn't been able to prevent her incompetence.

Hadrian's anger spiked. The least the reporter could have done would have been to interview Tilda as well. He looked to see who'd written the offensive rubbish and became incensed: Ezra Clement!

They'd worked with Clement on several cases, sharing information and helping one another. Why would he do this to Tilda? Hadrian crumpled the paper and swore.

He swung toward the door, intent on going straight to Clement and demanding to know how he could do this without speaking to Tilda. He stopped and took a breath. He should see Tilda first and make sure she was all right. She would likely have read this, and it would not have improved her mood—or the guilt she'd been feeling over Miss Chadwick's death.

Hadrian continued toward the door, but Collier appeared on the other side of the threshold. "My lord, Lady Ravenhurst is here to see you. She's waiting in the front sitting room."

Hadrian's jaw twitched as a wave of frustration crested within him. As much as he wanted to ignore his mother and be on his way to Tilda, he ought to see what she needed since she typically didn't arrive unannounced.

"Thank you, Collier."

Hadrian strode past the butler and went to the sitting room, where his mother sat perched in a chair near the hearth. She still wore her hat and gloves, which made him think she did not intend to stay long. He was grateful for that at least.

"Good morning, Mother." He hoped he didn't sound as harried as he felt. "Is there some emergency?"

"Perhaps." She appeared flustered. Her cheeks were slightly pink, and her lips were pursed.

Hadrian set his impatience aside. "You've caught me as I was preparing to leave."

"Well, this is important. Do sit down." She used her most motherly tone, and Hadrian decided to sit—for now.

"What is it?" He tried not to convey his irritation.

"I read a disturbing article in the *Daily News* this morning. Perhaps you saw it?"

Hadrian clenched his jaw and flexed his hands against his thighs. "Yes."

His mother looked at him with wide, expectant eyes. "That's all you have to say?"

"I assume you're referring to the article about Miss Chadwick.

It's a terrible tragedy." Why did she want to speak to Hadrian about it? He could only think she was curious about Tilda's involvement and since they worked together, perhaps she wanted to know if Hadrian had also participated in the investigation.

"It's absolutely awful." She shook her head and closed her eyes briefly. "But I've come to speak with you regarding the part about Miss Wren. Please tell me you were not part of the investigation she conducted. I assume not, since I didn't see you mentioned, but I wanted to be sure."

Hadrian froze. Why *hadn't* Chadwick included him in his blame? Hadrian hadn't thought he could become angrier, but somehow he did. He suspected Chadwick had gone directly to the *Daily News* to tell them this story and besmirch Tilda. Chadwick had vowed to ensure she never worked again.

"In fact, I *was* part of the investigation," Hadrian replied coolly. "Please understand that the article left out some important facts. It's a sensational piece meant to stir people up."

"Was it really Spring-heeled Jack?" Her hand fluttered to her chest. "I hate to think he's returned and is doing more than just terrorizing young women. To think he would kidnap and kill is unconscionable."

"It is indeed." Hadrian's patience was stretched thread thin. "I was actually on my way out. We can discuss this another time." He started to rise, but she waved him back down.

"I haven't said what I came to say. I'm most concerned about Miss Wren. That newspaper article does not reflect well on her at all. Perhaps you ought to distance yourself from her, at least until the gossip dies down."

"What gossip?" Hadrian asked angrily. "The newspaper only came out this morning."

"I'm sure there *will* be gossip and plenty of it. The Chadwicks have a great many friends."

"I would never distance myself from Tilda." Hadrian noted the flare of his mother's nostrils as he used Tilda's given name.

"I'm not asking you to do so permanently, just for a little while," she said with a cajoling tone. "You certainly shouldn't be trailing around after Miss Wren whilst she conducts her investigations. I don't really understand why you do that."

"Yes, you do," he insisted, growing quite cross. "I'm helpful to her because of my special skill." He'd told his mother about his ability to experience others' memories very recently. He'd been afraid to do so for some time, but she'd been supportive and kind. Whereas today she was being condescending and superior.

"That is not the only reason I work with Tilda, however," Hadrian added. "I enjoy doing so. We have a wonderful partnership."

Deep pleats furrowed his mother's brow. "You keep calling her Tilda, and you should not be so familiar. Don't you care that she's going to be maligned for how she botched this investigation? It's apparently her fault Miss Chadwick was killed."

Hadrian bolted to his feet. "That's completely untrue!"

His mother's eyes rounded, and her jaw dropped briefly. He almost never raised his voice like that and certainly not to his mother. Clenching his hands into fists, he fought to take a deep breath. He straightened his hands and flexed his shoulders.

"Forgive me. I did not mean to react in that way, but it's not her fault that Miss Chadwick was killed. That article did not portray all the facts of the investigation. Chadwick blames Tilda, and he provided the fodder for that nonsense. I don't understand why he doesn't also blame me. I made it clear I supported her decision." As he said that, Hadrian realized he'd also made it clear that it had been her decision. He'd inadvertently helped direct the blame at her.

"Why weren't you mentioned?"

"Because this article has been written to hurt Tilda. Mother, please don't tell me you'd believe a biased article over what I, your son, is telling you happened. I helped with this investigation as well as in the creation and execution of a plan to rescue Miss

Chadwick. If Tilda is to be blamed for the failure of that scheme, then I and the Met must be too—along with Chadwick. He didn't follow the plan and was consequently injured. He also lost the ransom we advised him not to bring, and we were unable to apprehend the kidnapper. Tilda is *not* to blame."

"Your defense of her is both extraordinary and astonishing." His mother regarded him with slightly narrowed eyes. "I hope you don't speak of her like that to anyone else. They might misconstrue your feelings for her."

"There is nothing to misunderstand: I'm in love with her." He hadn't meant to tell his mother that today, and certainly not in this fashion when his emotions were elevated. "It's my greatest hope that she will someday soon become my countess."

The shock his mother had displayed when he'd shouted was nothing compared to the extreme dismay that captured her features now. She rose from her chair.

"You can't mean to marry Miss Wren. She lacks the necessary background and the ability to be Countess of Ravenhurst. Never mind that she works for a living, and now she's been shown to be incompetent."

"She is *not* incompetent," Hadrian snapped loudly, causing his mother to flinch.

"Everyone will think she is." Her features softened, and she gazed at him with great concern. "Your association with her will be a negative influence. I have always liked Miss Wren, and I'm sorry she's been disparaged so publicly—whether true or not. I also appreciate whatever...emotional entanglement you have with her." She held up her hand as Hadrian clenched his jaw, then opened his mouth to speak. "However, Miss Wren is not an appropriate choice for your countess, and you know that. You aren't betrothed, are you?"

"Not yet. We're conducting a private courtship. I prefer you not mention this to anyone." He wished he hadn't said anything to her at all, but he'd been unable to keep his own emotions in check.

"You can be assured I won't say a word," she said quickly. "We must discuss this before you do anything you regret."

Hadrian didn't want to lose his temper again. "Not right now. I need to see Tilda. This horrible article will have certainly upset her, and I want to be there for her."

"There's another reason that I wanted to speak with you. The Duke of Alnwick's daughter went missing yesterday."

"What?" Hadrian said, barely waiting for her to finish. "What do you mean she's gone missing? Has she been kidnapped? Why didn't you tell me this straightaway?"

"Because I was going to suggest to Alnwick that he hire Miss Wren to find Lady Priscilla, but after reading that article, I don't know if I can. I wanted to talk to you about that first."

Hadrian tamped down his frustration, which was growing increasingly difficult with each passing moment of this conversation. "What do you know about Lady Priscilla's disappearance?"

"Only that Alnwick said they received a note asking for money—a ransom, I suppose."

This sounded too much like Miss Chadwick's abduction. "Was it signed by Spring-heeled Jack?"

"That I don't know."

"Did they report this to the Met?" Hadrian asked, wondering if the note had also instructed the duke not to alert the police.

Her brow creased briefly. "I don't believe so. I heard all this from Hetty."

Henrietta York was a friend of his mother's and one of London's most feverish gossips. "And how on earth did she hear it?"

"Her housekeeper is the sister of the Alnwicks' housekeeper."

"You should know better than to listen to servants' gossip," Hadrian said shortly. Even so, given the abduction of Miss Chadwick, he would not discount the veracity of the rumor. It was better that Teague looked into the matter.

*Blast!* He realized Mrs. Chadwick had listed Lady Priscilla as one of Miss Chadwick's close friends. Hadrian needed to see Tilda as soon as possible. "I must go." He started toward the door.

"Promise me you won't do anything rash with Miss Wren," his mother called after him. "And will you please think about taking some time away from investigating? You've been woefully absent from social engagements this Season."

Turning his head to look back at his mother, he worked to keep his voice even. "I think what you're saying is that I should take some time away from *Tilda,* but I will not. I will stand with her. Always."

Hadrian stalked from the room, driven by anger and apprehension that Spring-heeled Jack might have kidnapped someone else.

Collier met him in the entrance hall with his hat and gloves. "Leach just pulled up with the coach."

"Good," Hadrian replied, quickly donning his accessories. "See if my mother wants tea before she leaves."

"I hope you don't mind my saying so, my lord, but please give Miss Wren my very best."

Hadrian didn't know if the butler had overheard any of the conversation with his mother, which wouldn't have been impossible given the volume of Hadrian's voice; or if the butler had read the newspaper. Either way, he appreciated Collier's support and thoughtfulness.

"I'll do that. Thank you."

Collier opened the door, and Hadrian hurried toward the coach. He never should have told his mother about his feelings for Tilda or their courtship, except that he couldn't keep it secret forever. The timing had just been exceedingly poor, and now another young woman might have been kidnapped.

He arrived at the coach, where Leach opened the door. "Make haste to Marylebone," Hadrian said sternly as he stepped inside. He turned his head and met his coachman's gaze. "*Great* haste."

~

Tilda had not thought she could feel any worse than after visiting with the Chadwicks the day before, but then she'd read the *Daily News* that morning.

Fortunately, she'd seen it before her grandmother and asked Mrs. Acorn to dispose of the newspaper. Tilda had also requested the housekeeper fib and say it wasn't delivered today. When Tilda had simply explained that it would spare her grandmother considerable worry, Mrs. Acorn had understood. The last thing Tilda needed was Grandmama fretting over what Clement had written about her.

It wasn't that Tilda wanted to hide anything from her grandmother. She'd already told her that Miss Chadwick had been found deceased, though she hadn't revealed the details. Her grandmother had embraced her tightly and soothed Tilda's raw emotions. Grandmama had then noted, with grave concern, that once again, the case that Tilda and Hadrian were working on had turned into a murder. How Tilda wished it hadn't.

They'd had a shopping excursion planned today to pick up several items for the household, but Tilda had received word from Dr. Giles that he planned to come by to remove her stitches. So, she'd remained at home whilst her grandmother and Clara went out.

Dr. Giles's visit had gone quickly, and the removal of the stitches caused only a mild discomfort. He'd advised her to continue to be cautious with her shoulder for another week or so.

After he'd gone, Tilda focused on what she could do next in

order to find Miss Chadwick's killer. All she could think was that this new "Spring-heeled Jack" was using information from prior Spring-heeled Jack attacks. Why else would he leave Miss Chadwick in Green Dragon Alley with what appeared to be burns on her face and scratches across her body? Tilda was anxious for the inquest, which was to be held Wednesday afternoon.

Vaughn came into the library at the back of the house where Tilda was seated at her grandfather's old desk and paused in the doorway. "Mr. Clement is here to see you."

Tilda leapt up. "Good." She strode quickly toward the door, prompting Vaughn to step backward.

"I hope you're going to berate him, Miss Wren," Vaughn said quietly as she passed.

Pausing, Tilda turned her head to look back at the butler. "You saw the newspaper this morning?"

"I confess I read it every morning," he said a bit sheepishly. "His article was unkind to you." His brow darkened. "I know Mr. Clement has been here before, and I believe you've worked together, but if you don't mind, I'd be happy to thrash him."

Tilda suppressed a smile as warmth spread through her chest. Vaughn had become such a dear member of their household—no, their family. "Thank you, but I shall verbally thrash him myself. I do appreciate the offer."

Grateful for the interlude with Vaughn, for it calmed her ire, Tilda walked more sedately to the entrance hall where Mr. Clement stood. He held his hat in his hands, and his thinning brown hair was tousled as if he'd run his hand through it. His brown eyes were wide with contrition as he regarded her. As usual, he wore impossibly outrageous trousers made of purple and yellow striped wool.

Though Tilda had calmed herself, she did not mask her irritation with him. "Have you come to apologize?"

"I have, actually. May we speak for a few moments?"

"Yes." Tilda exhaled and led him into the parlor where she

closed the door. It wasn't that Vaughn or Mrs. Acorn eavesdropped, but she didn't want them inadvertently hearing anything about the case, because it was frankly disturbing.

She faced Clement, crossing her arms over her chest. "That was quite an article you wrote. I should think you would have taken the effort to interview me, but perhaps you weren't interested in the full truth."

"You know I am," he said earnestly. "However, I didn't have any choice as to the scope of this article. One of the newspaper's proprietors is a close friend to Chadwick. He went directly to the proprietor's house to demand that an interview with him be published as soon as possible. The proprietor instructed my editor to assign the interview to his best reporter."

"You," Tilda concluded. She didn't doubt it, for Clement was very good at his job. "I'm sure you were thrilled to write the first report of Miss Chadwick's murder at the hands of the notorious Spring-heeled Jack."

"I was," he replied without guile. "Until Chadwick began to blame and disparage you. I want you to know that I defended your abilities."

"I appreciate that." She unfolded her arms, relieved to hear that Clement had verbally supported her at least. "Could you not have included some of that in your article?"

"I tried. However, the night editor was instructed to change the tone to be more…"

"Sensational?" Tilda suggested. This was Chadwick's anger seeking revenge against the one person he could publicly ruin. He wouldn't have been able to do that to Teague and certainly not to Hadrian. "Chadwick would like me to be held accountable for his daughter's death."

"As the editor put it, since there's no suspect at this time, the public's anger—and the blame—can be directed at you. He said those were the proprietor's words." He grimaced. "I'm sorry. You must know I value you as an associate—and as a friend."

"I appreciate the sentiment." She'd also thought they'd become friends. "Did you only come to apologize?"

"Actually, no. I'm going to write another article interviewing you about the case."

Tilda arched a brow at him. "Will you be allowed to write the truth?"

His eyes took on a defiant sheen. "That is all I will write. In this instance, my editor has not been ordered to produce—or suppress anything. Are you amenable?" he asked hopefully, a slight smile lifting his mouth.

"I suppose." Tilda was still skeptical about what would actually be printed, but she was glad for the chance to tell the full story. She gestured Clement toward the settee and sat opposite him in a chair.

He removed a notebook from his pocket. "I hate to say this, but the more dramatic you can make the tale sound, particularly with regard to the return of Spring-heeled Jack, the more likely I'll be able to publish everything as you say it."

"I see," Tilda murmured. "Before you begin taking notes, I hope you know me well enough to realize I would never willingly endanger anyone. I think Mr. Chadwick, in fact, endangered his daughter by not informing the Metropolitan Police as soon as he received the ransom note. I understand why he didn't, that he was afraid, but he should have done so."

"That seems perfectly reasonable to me," Clement said. "Mr. Chadwick did not seem to care much for reason when I spoke with him. He was, dare I say, consumed with bitterness and grief. He clearly stated that if not for your involving the police, his daughter would still be alive."

Hearing that pained Tilda something fierce. "He has a right to feel that way. However, there wasn't any other way for us to ensure we captured the kidnapper at the ransom delivery location. You must understand that delivering a ransom to Hampstead Heath after dark is a dangerous prospect. Furthermore, the kidnapper hadn't mentioned whether Miss Chadwick would be present. In the interest of everyone's safety, I thought it best to involve the police."

"I understand why you made the decision." Clement smiled apologetically. "When did that happen? Chadwick indicated that he'd only hired you because you'd promised not to inform the Met."

"I did promise him," Tilda said carefully. "That was before I knew all the details, however. The second ransom note was delivered to Mr. Chadwick whilst Ravenhurst and I were at his house. I realized we had a chance to rescue Miss Chadwick, but that we would require assistance. That's when I involved Detective Inspector Teague."

"Ravenhurst was involved with this?"

"Of course. He's my partner. I noticed he wasn't mentioned in the article." Tilda believed Chadwick truly was trying just to discredit Tilda.

"That's because Chadwick didn't mention him at all." Clement regarded Tilda with faint surprise. "Ravenhurst is your partner? I've always seen him as more of an assistant."

"That's how things began, but I rely on him greatly during our investigations, and we approach them as a partnership. However, I would appreciate you not mentioning him in the article you write after speaking with me. There are many who would find his work with me to be beneath him." Tilda did not wish to tarnish his reputation amongst his peers. "Perhaps you could just mention that I have an associate I work with."

Nodding, Clement wrote in his notebook. "I'll do that."

"*My associate* and I came up with a plan to capture this man posing as Spring-heeled Jack. We weren't going to bring the ransom, so there was no chance that the kidnapper would have been paid. We had to involve the police so that we would have plenty of men on the ground to apprehend him." Tilda pursed her lips faintly. "However, Mr. Chadwick arrived in the middle of the scheme and bungled everything. Spring-heeled Jack attacked Mr. Chadwick and escaped with the ransom he'd brought, despite everyone instructing Mr. Chadwick *not* to bring it. Unfortunately, Miss Chadwick was not there."

Clement had been writing notes and now looked up at her. "It seems Chadwick was duped by the kidnapper. No wonder he lied to me. I will do my utmost to make sure you're absolved."

They'd *all* been duped by the kidnapper. Tilda had arrogantly believed they could recover Miss Chadwick and keep from paying the ransom.

"What can you tell me about Spring-heeled Jack?" Clement asked.

"I didn't see him," Tilda replied. "But Ravenhurst's coachman did, and the description in your article was rather exaggerated. I don't recall anyone saying the kidnapper had 'dagger-like' claws."

"I suspected his descriptions weren't entirely accurate," Clement noted wryly. "And he left out the part where he wasn't supposed to be there. What do you suppose the connection is between this kidnapper and the Spring-heeled Jack of lore?"

"I've been trying to determine that," Tilda replied with frustration. "The kidnapper wore a costume much like what Spring-heeled Jack was purported to wear. He also had red eyes, breathed blue fire, and possessed sharp claws, which he used to scratch Mr. Chadwick just as Spring-heeled Jack did when he attacked a young woman named Miss Alsop in 1838. The kidnapper also leapt over a five-foot hedge as he fled. However, aside from the kidnapper's appearance at Hampstead Heath and signing the notes to the Chadwicks as Spring-heeled Jack, the kidnapper doesn't have much else in common with the Spring-heeled Jack who assaulted young women thirty years ago."

Clement leaned forward with interest. "In what ways?"

Tilda met his gaze. "Have you ever heard of Spring-heeled Jack kidnapping and killing anyone?"

"I have not," Clement said. "But he may have had the intent to kidnap one or more of the young women he attacked in the past and was interrupted or prevented from doing so."

"I suppose that's possible, however he didn't keep trying, did he? I think someone is merely borrowing Spring-heeled Jack's identity in order to provoke terror."

"Well, I'd say it's working," Clement said darkly. "Rather, it will, after people read the article published today." He sent her an apologetic look.

"Which is a shame, because you've sensationalized the tragic death of a young woman, and *that* is the truly terrorizing part. It isn't Spring-heeled Jack in his ridiculous costume and trickery; it's the fact that he killed this young woman. And we can't let him get away with it."

"So, your investigation will continue?"

Tilda clasped her hands in her lap and straightened her spine with determination. "Yes."

Clement eyed her dubiously. "Chadwick said you were no longer working for him. Are you working for the Met then?"

"No. I have a personal commitment to investigate the matter."

"I understand," Clement said softly, his gaze warming. "If I can be of any help, I hope you'll just ask."

"I'm not sure I dare, given the article you wrote," Tilda said sardonically.

"Please don't let that end our excellent relationship." His tone was sincere, almost pleading.

"I won't. However, next time, I would appreciate you giving me advance notice. It was fortunate I read the paper before my grandmother this morning and was able to keep it from her. I don't need her worrying about my reputation."

Clement grimaced again. "I am terribly sorry. Truly. But this new article will be a vindication. I promise."

Tilda wasn't sure she believed him, not when he had an editor to answer to, and the editor took direction from one of the proprietors who was apparently eager to listen to Chadwick.

The door opened without preamble. Tilda startled upon seeing Hadrian, and his face was a shade of red she'd never seen before. His gaze fell on Clement, and he strode to the settee where he reached for Clement's lapel. Clement lurched backward, avoiding Hadrian's grasp.

Tilda jumped up from the chair. "Hadrian, what are you doing?"

"I'd hoped to hunt this bastard down, and now I don't have to." His blue eyes looked as though they could spit fire like what Spring-heeled Jack breathed on his victims.

Clement also rose and moved around the settee to escape Hadrian's reach. "I understand why you're upset about the article I wrote, but I didn't have any choice."

"There's always a choice," Hadrian ground out.

Tilda had never seen or heard him so angry. There was something oddly attractive about it, likely because he was furious on her behalf. He'd swooped in like an avenging hero protecting his lady, and she was shocked to find that rather satisfying.

Perhaps she would keep that to herself. She was an independent woman and didn't need saving. Even so, that didn't mean she couldn't enjoy this.

"Not for those of us who have to worry about things like earning money." Clement's tone carried a hint of derision as he regarded Hadrian warily.

The two men had gotten off to a rocky start when they'd met, for Clement was a dogged reporter and made it clear his readers expected the sort of details that bordered on gossip. He'd pursued an interview with Hadrian's mother, and Hadrian had put a stop to it with irritation and firmness.

"Perhaps you should have thought of one's livelihood when you sought to ruin Tilda's reputation in such a public manner. Don't you respect the fact that she needs to earn money too?"

Clement went white, and Tilda felt a surge of pride and happiness that Hadrian would fight for her right to earn money as a detective. "I should have fought harder against my editor and the proprietor." Clement sounded and looked completely defeated. "I came here today to apologize to Miss Wren and to interview her so I can write a follow-up story with the truth of what happened."

"Good. If it doesn't, you'll hear from me," Hadrian warned. "As will your editor. In fact, I may even speak to the proprietors."

"That's what Chadwick did," Tilda said, drawing Hadrian to look at her. "He went directly to one of them, who instructed Clement's editor to have a reporter interview Chadwick and write his account."

Hadrian frowned as he returned his focus to Clement. "Which proprietor?"

"Labouchere, but you didn't hear that from me," Clement replied crisply. "I should be on my way."

Tilda moved to the door and opened it. "Thank you for coming."

Clement tucked his notebook back into his coat. "Thank *you* for sharing the truth of what happened." He glanced toward Hadrian but said nothing before ducking out of the parlor.

Tilda closed the door and faced Hadrian. "I've never seen you so angry."

"No, and why shouldn't I be?" His eyes were still ablaze, and his face was a darker complexion than normal. "That article was nothing but lies and innuendo. How dare Chadwick denigrate you like that? I'm even more troubled that Clement would be a party to it. I thought he was your associate, if not a friend."

"I know, and I was upset at first too," Tilda said. "However, I understand why he had to do it. It's his job."

Hadrian put his fingers to his chest. "*I* should have been included in it. Did you tell Clement about my role?"

"I did, but I told him not to write about you, because I didn't want it to reflect poorly on you, given your position."

"It's not fair that you should bear the brunt of Chadwick's

blame. You did not act alone." Hadrian pressed his lips together and turned slightly away from her so she could only see his profile.

"Damn it," he breathed, surprising her, for he didn't typically curse and that was the second time he'd done so since arriving. "I'm tired of hiding our work together. I love you, and I want to be with you. And I want everyone to know." He turned his head to look at her. "If we can't even be open to the world about the fact that we work together, how are we ever going to truly engage in a courtship?"

"I don't know," she replied softly. "This is part of why I haven't wanted to focus on…us. I'm asking you again to please be patient. I need to find this man who killed Miss Chadwick."

"You want to continue with that?" Hadrian waved his hand as he turned his body toward her. "Of course you do. But you won't be paid, and that's always been a chief concern for you."

"It is, but I'll manage." Tilda recognized the defensive note in her reply. "This is a matter of my professional reputation—my integrity. Regardless of how I feel, this newspaper article has blackened my reputation and will almost certainly affect my ability to earn money. People won't trust my skills. I must prove myself. I won't rest until I bring this villain to justice."

"I know. It's who you are. Even if your reputation were not at stake, you would not give up on Miss Chadwick." He exhaled, the fire in his gaze finally diminishing. "In fact, you *must* keep working on it, because there may have been another kidnapping."

"*What?*" Tilda exploded as she strode toward him.

"The Duke of Alnwick's daughter, Lady Priscilla, may be missing. It's gossip at this point, but we need to ascertain the truth." Hadrian explained how his mother had heard the information and what she knew. "I'm sure you've already recalled that Lady Priscilla was on the list of Miss Chadwick's close friends."

Indeed, Tilda had remembered that as he'd shared the details. "We don't know if it was Spring-heeled Jack."

"Agreed. Shall we call on the duke?" Hadrian asked. "I've no hesitation in doing so. I know him somewhat. We've worked together in the Lords."

"Yes, let's go at once." Tilda's brow furrowed. She could only pray that if another young woman *had* been kidnapped, it would not end in murder.

# CHAPTER 8

As the coach stopped in front of the Duke of Alnwick's house in Upper Brook Street, Hadrian pondered whether he ought to go in alone. Except he knew Tilda would want to be part of the interview. Furthermore, she needed to be. Whilst Hadrian had learned many investigative skills from her, she was still the professional with far more experience.

"You should conduct the interview," Tilda said. "I'll join in if necessary."

"Because of my title?" he asked as Leach opened the door.

She arched her brow in a sardonic fashion. "He's a duke. Don't you think he'll be more likely to speak with you?"

Hadrian smirked before climbing from the coach and helping Tilda to the pavement. She didn't take his arm for the short walk up the steps to the front door.

The late spring afternoon was particularly temperate and bright. It was hard to think that things such as murder and kidnapping could happen on a day like this. Hadrian dearly hoped that Lady Priscilla had not, in fact, been kidnapped. They would soon find out.

He knocked, and a moment later a short, austere butler with a small, sharp nose and dark, assessing eyes opened the door. The butler regarded them with a cool hauteur that some members of the peerage preferred their butlers project, particularly when greeting people.

Hadrian adopted an amiable tone and pleasant expression. "Good afternoon, I'm Ravenhurst, and this is my associate, Miss Wren. We've come to speak with the duke about an urgent issue."

The butler's gray brows dipped toward his nose in a perfect V. "I am not sure His Grace is receiving. Please step inside for a moment." After Tilda and Hadrian moved into the entrance hall, the butler closed the door and faced them. "May I tell His Grace what this is about, specifically?"

Hadrian hesitated. He wasn't sure what to say. What if the rumor his mother had heard was nothing but nonsense?

Fortunately, Tilda spoke up. "Please tell His Grace we have information about his daughter."

Surprise flashed unmistakably in the butler's gaze, but he quickly composed himself. He inclined his head, then turned on his heel and disappeared into the staircase hall.

Hadrian pivoted toward Tilda. "What do you suppose his reaction meant?"

Tilda lifted a shoulder. "It could be anything, but I'm inclined to think he was eager to tell His Grace that we're here."

"I am as well," Hadrian said. "Even if the duke's daughter hasn't been kidnapped, he'll want to know what sort of information we might have about her."

"That was my hope," Tilda said.

Hadrian regarded her with admiration. "This is why you are a brilliant investigator."

They waited only a few moments before the butler returned. "Come this way."

Hadrian and Tilda exchanged a glance and followed him through to the staircase hall, then to the left into a handsomely appointed study with mahogany bookcases. The chandelier hung from the center of a painting of Midas receiving his golden touch from Dionysus. Hadrian recalled that several of Alnwick House's ceilings had been painted a few years ago by an Italian artist. The scene here in his study was fitting for a man known for his investment acumen and wealth.

The duke was in his late forties with thick, dark sable hair, and wide features, particularly his nose and chin. He'd been athletic in his younger years, with a reputation for exceptional equestrian skill. However, he now sported a slight paunch. He sat in a red and gold chair near the hearth, clutching a nearly empty glass of what looked to be whiskey. His eyes narrowed at Hadrian.

"Ravenhurst, I can't imagine what's brought you here today, but my butler says you have information about my daughter." The duke's low voice rumbled toward them like an approaching carriage. "What does that mean?"

"We've heard she's missing and came to speak with you about that," Hadrian replied.

The duke bolted to his feet, his face twisting with fury. "Who told you that?" He tossed back the remainder of his drink and set the empty glass on the mantel next to a photograph of a young woman with large eyes and sculpted features. She was very pretty.

As the duke's gaze flicked to the photograph, Hadrian wondered if that was his daughter, Lady Priscilla.

"It's true then?" Hadrian asked.

"Nobody is supposed to know," the duke snapped. "You had to have heard it from someone in my household. No one else is aware."

Hadrian kept his expression neutral. "I can't say precisely how the information came to us." He wasn't going to reveal the duke's housekeeper as the origination of the leak.

The duke eyed them skeptically, his brows riding low over his eyes. "Why have you come here?"

"Miss Wren is a private detective," Hadrian replied. "I work with her, and we'd like to help you."

"You work with her? What the bloody hell for?" the duke asked, incredulous.

"I enjoy it," Hadrian said evenly. "And I like helping others."

"Did you say her name was Miss Wren? I recognize the name from that article about the other young woman who was kidnapped and *murdered*." The duke's angry stare moved to Tilda. "You must be the same person."

"I am." Tilda didn't flinch as she met the duke's gaze, and Hadrian felt a surge of pride—as well as a need to protect her.

"I don't know why you bothered coming here," the duke scoffed. "I wouldn't allow you to help if you were the last detective in London."

"She's not the last," Hadrian said. "But she *is* the best. That article in the paper didn't tell the entire story of what happened." He regarded the duke intently. "You've known me for some time. I would not align myself with anyone who wasn't completely competent and capable."

"I would expect that, yes." The duke pursed his lips. "Still, I'm not interested in hiring her. Now, be on your way."

Hadrian wondered if he'd have more luck with Lady Priscilla's mother. "Where is the duchess?"

"When Priscilla was discovered to be kidnapped, she took to her bed." Again, he glanced at the photograph, and Hadrian was certain it was Lady Priscilla. "I have kept the news about Miss Chadwick from her today, so she's not aware that our daughter is in mortal peril. I prefer to keep it that way. She cannot suffer more devastating news."

"I understand." Hadrian felt bad for the man despite his rudeness to Tilda. He truly wanted to help him. "You can trust us with this matter—and you wouldn't be hiring us, for we aren't asking for payment. We only want to help you bring your daughter home. We've already been investigating what happened with

Miss Chadwick, and we think we can help find Lady Priscilla. You must believe me when I say there is no one better than Miss Wren."

"Then why did she seek help from the police?" The duke demanded. "Or was that not true?"

Hadrian hurried to answer the man. He didn't want Tilda to have to defend herself. She'd done nothing wrong. "That newspaper article is not a true representation of what transpired. I prefer not to delve into the specifics, but Chadwick is distraught and under unimaginable stress. I fully support every action Miss Wren took."

"May I see the ransom note you received?" Tilda asked, surprising Hadrian by not contributing to her defense. Though, he should not have been. It was not only natural but expected for her to focus on the case.

The duke regarded her a long moment, his eyes narrowing. He abruptly turned and went to his desk where he plucked up a piece of parchment and handed it to Tilda.

Hadrian looked over at Tilda as she scanned the short note. She didn't give it to Hadrian quite yet.

"This letter reads verbatim to the one the Chadwicks received, including that you should not contact the police," Tilda said. "My advice, however, is that you must. When it comes to recovering someone who has been kidnapped, the Met has the resources to execute such an endeavor. Furthermore, this appears to be the same kidnapper, and if he behaves in the same manner as with Miss Chadwick, we can expect he'll demand the ransom be delivered at an unsafe place and time and that your daughter will *not* be returned." She handed the note to Hadrian.

The duke's lips flattened as he went to the mantel, where he plucked up his empty glass.

Hadrian focused on the note he held and instructed his mind to see the author's memory of when he wrote it. The Duke of Alnwick's study faded as Hadrian was transported to the same place of the memory he'd seen when he'd handled the other notes. A candle flickered on the corner of the mahogany desk, and the scent of tobacco lingered in the air. The hand with the rough fingernails was now frustratingly familiar.

Worry pulled at Hadrian from the memory along with a nervous anticipation. The kidnapper turned his head toward a doorway to another room. A flash of irritation streaked through him.

As the kidnapper returned his attention to the letter, Hadrian strained to see something else that might help them find the man's location. The desk also held a book and a small hand mirror beside it. Gold lettering on the green spine of the book lodged into Hadrian's mind: Enfield. The hand mirror was crafted of silver filigree and tickled Hadrian's memory.

Hadrian was immediately distracted by a sensation of fury—a deep bitterness that was nearly smothering in its strength. Excruciating pain exploded in his head. He winced as he tipped his head forward slightly. Blinking several times, he handed the note back to Tilda. The agony was too great to allow another vision just then.

Hadrian found Tilda's eyes. They conveyed that she was both anxious to hear whether he'd seen anything and worried he might be in pain. The latter typically happened when he experienced a longer memory. He gathered he'd been lost in the vision for several moments.

Tilda turned her attention to the duke, who'd filled his glass and returned to his chair. "If the kidnapper follows the same pattern as with Miss Chadwick, you can expect to receive a second note tomorrow that will provide instructions for the ransom. If you choose to accept assistance from us and the Met, you will notify us once you receive it."

The duke contemplated his whisky before responding. "I don't want the police involved."

"It's possible they already know," Hadrian said. "Since we

heard about Lady Priscilla's disappearance, it's not implausible to expect the police have been informed."

A rather vulgar curse spilled from the duke's mouth. Hadrian glanced at Tilda, but she didn't react.

"I just want my daughter back." The duke's hand shook as he lifted his glass. He managed a large gulp of whisky. "You think Priscilla and Miss Chadwick were kidnapped by the same man?"

"I don't like to make assumptions, but I'm inclined to think so," Tilda replied. "The note you received is identical to the one left at the Chadwicks. I suspect that when the two are compared side by side, the handwriting will match. Does Lady Priscilla have any suitors?"

"Lord Farnsworth. I called on him to make sure he and Priscilla hadn't run off, which I strongly doubted, and I was right. This was before I knew about Miss Chadwick being kidnapped. Farnsworth was distressed to hear Priscilla had been abducted."

"I'm curious why you thought they'd eloped when the note clearly indicated a ransom," Hadrian said.

The duke looked up at him, his eyes cloudy. In that moment, he appeared very much a father in agony. "I suppose I was hoping it was nothing worse than that." He sounded sad and disappointed.

"I'm sorry it wasn't," Hadrian said quietly.

Tilda tucked the ransom note into her reticule and withdrew her notebook along with a pencil. "It would be helpful to know Lady Priscilla's daily schedule—what activities she engaged in, where she went, who she saw, any events she attended recently. We'd also like to know who her close friends are."

"Why do you need to know all that?" the duke asked with irritation.

"It helps us identify potential suspects and motivations they might have for kidnapping your daughter and seeking a ransom," Hadrian replied.

The duke glowered. "I can't really tell you what her days are like. Her mother would have to do that, and she isn't currently able. I believe she's taken laudanum to help her sleep."

"Can you tell us how and when Lady Priscilla was discovered missing?" Tilda grasped her pencil, poising it above her notebook.

"Yesterday morning, her maid went to wake her as usual, and Priscilla wasn't there. The maid found the note and screamed the bloody house down."

"May we speak with the maid?" Tilda asked.

"If you must." The duke sounded resigned.

"We'd also like to look through Lady Priscilla's chamber for clues," Hadrian said. "Will you permit us to do that?"

The duke's eyes turned sad again. Standing, he sloshed a bit of whiskey over the rim of his glass onto the front of his coat. He moved, staggering slightly, to the bell pull. "I'll have the butler show you up to Priscilla's room, and he'll fetch her maid."

"Thank you, Your Grace." Tilda slipped her notebook and pencil back into her reticule.

Nodding faintly, the duke waved his hand at them as if to shoo them away, before collapsing back onto his chair where he nursed his drink once more.

The stern butler appeared and led them upstairs to the second floor, where Lady Priscilla's bedchamber was located. "I'll fetch her maid." He left Tilda and Hadrian alone in the room.

Tilda turned to Hadrian. "What did you see when you touched the note?"

"How do you know I saw something?"

"I can tell you're in pain." She reached up and smoothed her gloved fingertips along his brow. "We'll apply the lavender as soon as we're back in the coach."

Hadrian smiled. How he loved her care and attentiveness. "The vision was in the same place as before—with the man writing—but I was able to see more." Hadrian related every detail. "I just don't understand the tobacco. It's not overpowering, which it would be if someone were using it. Perhaps there's a tobacco warehouse or a shop nearby." He pulled his gloves on lest he be tempted to touch something else.

"That's a good clue, but I don't think we can use it to find this place," Tilda said. "I'm not familiar with the author you mentioned. Did you say it was Enfield?"

"That's right. I don't know the name either, and unfortunately, I didn't see a title. I'll check my library to see if I have anything by the author."

Tilda blinked at him. "Your library is large enough that it might contain a work by an author you've never heard of?"

Her wonder made Hadrian feel slightly self-conscious. Their backgrounds were so different, and yet he was more comfortable with her than anyone else of his acquaintance. "It is. You're welcome to visit it anytime."

"I may do that," she said. "You said the mirror was silver fili-gree. I recall that Miss Chadwick had a silver filigree brush. I don't suppose they matched?"

Hadrian sucked in a breath. "Now that you mention it, the mirror sparked something in my mind, but I was distracted by the sudden onslaught of fury. It's possible the silver filigree was the same, but I honestly can't say for sure." He was suddenly quite frustrated and wanted to handle the note again, except he knew that wouldn't be wise just now with the pain still throbbing in his head.

"Perhaps it will come to you," Tilda said encouragingly. "It's interesting you sensed irritation and anger as opposed to the fear you felt with the first note the Chadwicks received."

"The sentiments were completely different." Hadrian's shoulder twitched. "In fact, there was a distinction between the irritation, which I strongly believe was directed toward whatever was behind the doorway, and the subsequent rage, which seemed to have more to do with the note. It felt very personal and specific, but I don't know why."

"Perhaps Miss Chadwick was behind the doorway, and the kidnapper was irritated with her?" Tilda suggested. "And the note made him angry...he was irritated with one of his captives and felt fury toward another?"

"Don't those emotions make it seem as though these crimes weren't committed for money alone?"

"Exactly," Tilda said with a nod, her eyes narrowing slightly. "It's unfortunate we can't share these observations with Teague, but we can use them to inform our inquiries." Whilst his visions were helpful, they themselves were not evidence they could use. They either had to provoke someone to confess what Hadrian had seen or find other avenues of proof.

They turned their attention to Lady Priscilla's beautiful bedchamber, lavishly furnished with a gilded four-poster bed draped in pale pink silk damask. The walls were covered in richly patterned flocked paper, and as with the study, the ceiling had been painted, but it did not look as though it had been done by the same artist. The design was a feminine floral motif originating from and inspired by an ornate carved rose in the center of the room from which descended a cut-glass chandelier.

As Tilda moved toward the gilded dressing table, the maid entered, her expression tentative. She was in her early thirties, with light brown hair pulled up tightly beneath a white cap. Her eyes were wide with apprehension.

Changing course, Tilda turned and addressed the maid with a warm smile. "You're Lady Priscilla's maid?"

She nodded. "I'm Harper."

"Harper, I'm Miss Wren and this is Lord Ravenhurst." She turned her head briefly toward Hadrian before continuing to speak to the maid. "Can you tell us about when you discovered Lady Priscilla was missing?"

The maid clasped one of her hands with the other whilst she spoke. "I come in every morning between nine and ten, depending on how late Lady Priscilla was out the night before. I bring chocolate and toast with lemon curd." She paused, her features creasing. "However, yesterday, when I entered her room, I knew right away something was wrong. I went to the bed and saw she wasn't in it. There was a note on the pillow. I read the note, and I apparently screamed, though I don't remember doing so." She wrung her hands. "I'm terribly worried about Lady Priscilla. I heard her friend, Miss Chadwick, was kidnapped and that she's… I can't say it." Tears welled in her eyes.

"Were they close?" Tilda asked.

The maid blinked and dashed her hand over her eyes. "I would say so. They visited one another a few times a week, and they went on shopping excursions together. Lady Priscilla's stories about the events she attended often included Miss Chadwick. I can't believe she's gone."

"Is there anything you can tell us about the things the two of them did together?" Tilda asked. "Any particular activities they enjoyed or places they frequented?"

"They usually promenaded in the park once or twice a week with their mothers," the maid replied. "And, of course, they saw one another at Society events. Lady Priscilla felt a bit sorry for Miss Chadwick."

Tilda sent a curious glance toward Hadrian. "Why?"

"Because of her stutter. Lady Priscilla befriended her and has helped Miss Chadwick try to conquer the difficulty."

"That was kind of her," Tilda said. "His Grace told us Lady Priscilla has a suitor. Did Lord Farnsworth call here often?"

"Just once, so far. Their courtship was new. Lady Priscilla was reluctant to be courted again so soon."

"*Again?*" Tilda asked sharply.

The maid nodded. "She had a different suitor earlier in the Season, but His Grace did not approve of him. He wasn't even really a suitor—he called once, and His Grace made it clear he would not be considered."

Tilda's gaze narrowed slightly, and Hadrian knew her mind was working. "Why was Lady Priscilla reluctant?"

Harper glanced behind her before answering in a soft voice. "Because she'd developed a tendre for her previous suitor." Her eyes darted toward a corner of the room.

"Who was the suitor?" Tilda asked.

The maid fidgeted nervously, and her gaze kept sliding toward that same corner. "I shouldn't say. His Grace forbade his name from being spoken here. He was adamant that Lady Priscilla not see or speak of him ever again."

Hadrian had to assume the "suitor" was someone from a lower class. Why else would the duke be so opposed? Unless he was a fortune hunter or a young man with a scandalous reputation.

"We won't tell anyone," Hadrian said. "It's our job as private detectives to keep things secret. The word 'private' is right there in our name."

Once again, Harper looked at the corner, this time her attention lingering. Hadrian followed her gaze.

Tilda moved slowly in that direction. "Harper, is there something in the corner?"

The maid blushed profusely. "I think Lady Priscilla kept letters from her previous suitor, and they might be tucked behind the wallpaper. But you mustn't tell anyone."

"Of course not," Tilda assured her. "Thank you." She turned and walked toward the corner.

Hadrian followed Tilda but stopped short as a glint in the floral-patterned carpet near the bed caught his eye. He bent and picked up a thumb-sized brass cap of some kind. Placing it in his gloved palm, he studied it intently but couldn't determine its use.

"What's that?" Tilda asked.

Joining her, he handed her the cap. "I found this near the bed on the carpet. I can't identify its use."

Tilda held it toward the maid. "Harper, do you know what this is?"

Harper stepped forward and surveyed the brass cap in Tilda's palm. The maid shook her head. "I've never seen that before."

"Are you saying it doesn't belong to Lady Priscilla?" Tilda asked.

"Not that I'm aware of. She would never have anything so… plain."

Hadrian could understand that, given the extravagance of everything in Lady Priscilla's chamber.

"May I go now?" the maid asked.

"Yes," Tilda replied. "However, would you wait in the corridor in case we have more questions?" She met the young woman's gaze with a gentle, earnest smile. "We'll do our very best to find Lady Priscilla and ensure she's returned home safely."

Harper smiled weakly. "Thank you. I will pray for her every moment."

The maid left, and Tilda held up the cap once more. She narrowed her eyes and inspected it closely. "I'd say this fits onto something, but what?"

"Do you think it belongs to Spring-heeled Jack?" Hadrian's pulse thrummed at the possibility that they'd found a clue.

Tilda shrugged. "It's certainly curious. We should give it to Teague to retain as evidence." She tucked it into her reticule, then turned to the corner that had drawn the maid's attention.

Hadrian followed her. "Are you going to tear the wallpaper away?"

"I don't have to." Tilda crouched down and grasped a frayed edge corner. "This looks as though it's been pulled up often and recently." She peeled the paper back and withdrew a small stack of folded paper tied with a pink ribbon. She rose with a faint smile, her brows arching briefly. "Shall we see what we've found?"

Tilda went to the bed and unfolded the papers, laying out each piece by date. There were eight letters in all.

Together, they perused the missives. The first one revealed the secret suitor, and he was astonished by the man's identity. *"Vincent Chadwick?"*

"Apparently," Tilda murmured as she surveyed the letters. They were quiet as they read.

At length, Tilda said, "Mr. Chadwick doesn't like having to live away from her in Richmond."

"But he likes his view of the Thames," Hadrian noted. He kept reading. "There's a tobacconist on the corner." He recalled the tobacco scent from the memory he'd experienced from the other letter.

Tilda turned her head toward Hadrian, her green eyes glimmering with excitement. "Where he purchases his favorite blend. I can't help thinking of the tobacco you smelled in your vision."

He shared her excitement. "Do we finally have a clue?"

"Perhaps. The connection between Lady Priscilla, who has been kidnapped by Spring-heeled Jack, and her friend Delia Chadwick, who was also kidnapped by Spring-heeled Jack, is unmistakable given that you saw both notes written in the same place. The tobacco smell could implicate Vincent Chadwick, who we could easily argue would have a motive to abduct the woman he'd been denied. However, *why* would he kidnap—and kill—his own sister?" Tilda's brow creased as she once again focused on the letters.

She gestured to one of the papers. "In this letter, Chadwick is glad for his sister Delia acting as the go-between." She met Hadrian's gaze. "It seems she mailed Lady Priscilla's letters to her brother, then received her brother's letters to Lady Priscilla and delivered them to her. I would say that's the opposite of a motive for him to kill his sister. She was helping him."

A moment later, Tilda sucked in a breath as she snatched up

the last of the missives. "This says he was overjoyed that Lady Priscilla wanted to elope because he was thinking the same." She turned toward Hadrian with the letter in her hand.

"I was just reading that," he said.

"I can't ask you to touch this," Tilda said. "Your head already hurts, and multiple memories can worsen things to an unbearable degree." Deep furrows marred her brow.

"Yes, but it's lessened since we came upstairs. This is important. I'll be quick."

She held the paper toward him. "I'll take it away from you if I think you're gone too long."

Hadrian arched a brow at her. "*Gone?*"

"You disappear into the memory," Tilda explained.

He hadn't thought of himself as going anywhere, but that was exactly what he did, at least in his mind. "I suppose that's true." Hadrian took the paper.

He was abruptly seated at a small, simple oak desk. The window above it offered a sweeping view of a river he was certain had to be the Thames. But this wasn't a familiar vantage point to Hadrian. He felt love and a passionate sense of longing. Those emotions were quickly eclipsed by a rush of anxiety and fear. The clashing sentiments warred within him.

Suddenly, Hadrian saw the papers on the bed once more. The ache in his head intensified so that he closed his eyes with a grimace. He realized he was no longer holding the note, and his hand was at his temple.

Peeling one eye open, he looked over at Tilda. "Did you take the letter away?" He rubbed at his throbbing head.

"I was concerned." She looked it too, her forehead creased and her eyes dark. "You began to clutch your head whilst you were gone."

"I'm not at all sure I like being 'gone,' though I know why you use that word. I'm beginning to think the stronger the emotions I feel, the more agonizing the pain." The ache finally began to ease, but only a very little. "I hate to admit it, but it's good you took the letter. I don't think I should try to see anything again until later today." He lowered his arm to his side.

"Or until tomorrow even." Tilda gave his arm a quick pat then she gathered up the papers. "We'll take them with us, and you can try again tomorrow when you're recovered." She tucked them into her reticule.

"Why did the Chadwicks tell us their son Vincent was traveling when he's actually lodging in Richmond?"

"Do you suppose they lied to us about that?" Tilda mused. "Or has Vincent been lying to *them* about where he is?"

"We should ask the Chadwicks," Hadrian said. "Though, I'm not sure the Chadwicks will speak to us."

"Probably not." Tilda exhaled with disappointment. "But I suppose it doesn't matter, because Vincent isn't a suspect. He has no motive to kill his sister. He does, however, have a motive to elope with the woman he was courting. Except Lady Priscilla's abduction matches Miss Chadwick's perfectly, right down to the way the ransom note was written."

"Perhaps he copied what happened to his sister," Hadrian suggested.

"How would he have known about what happened to his sister? Her kidnapping wasn't publicized until today." Tilda's eyes widened briefly. "Unless the Chadwicks did lie and knew he was in Richmond. Perhaps they sent him a letter apprising him of his sister's kidnapping."

"And he grasped the chance to copy Spring-heeled Jack and 'kidnap' Lady Priscilla. He didn't have time to warn or plan with her, which would explain her surprise."

Tilda was quiet a long moment. "That is possible, but I'm not convinced. We need to go to Richmond tomorrow and speak with Vincent Chadwick. I'd go today, but I don't think we have enough time to get there and back before dinner, and I'd rather not abandon my grandmother."

"Tomorrow morning then," Hadrian said.

They shortly departed Alnwick House and barely made it to the pavement before they encountered Detective Inspector Teague and Sergeant Wycombe. Teague startled when he saw them.

"Can I presume you're here about Lady Priscilla's disappearance?" Teague asked.

"Yes," Hadrian replied. "My mother heard a rumor, and we came to confirm it."

Teague pressed his lips together in a near frown. "I've heard the same rumor. Did you learn anything?"

"I'm afraid it's the same situation as Miss Chadwick," Tilda said. "Lady Priscilla was taken from her bed, and the kidnapper left a note identical to the one found on Miss Chadwick's pillow."

"Spring-heeled bloody Jack?" Teague made a sound in his throat.

"You should be warned that His Grace doesn't want the police involved. He didn't particularly want us sticking our nose in either, but Ravenhurst persuaded him." Tilda glanced over at Hadrian.

"What did he persuade him to allow you to do?" Teague asked.

"He showed us the ransom note, the handwriting on which will almost certainly match the others in your evidence drawer," Tilda said before opening her reticule to retrieve the letter. She held it toward Teague. "The wording is precisely the same."

"Blast," Teague breathed as he took the parchment and quickly skimmed it.

Tilda continued. "His Grace also permitted us, somewhat reluctantly, to speak with Lady Priscilla's maid and to survey her bedchamber. We found something that could be important—or not." She reached back into her reticule, and Hadrian knew she meant to give Vincent Chadwick's letters to Teague.

Withdrawing the papers, she handed them to the detective inspector, then sent Hadrian a look of apology. Though he acknowledged she had to do it, he was still annoyed. He'd wanted to see what other memories he might experience from handling them.

"Those are from Lady Priscilla's former suitor," Tilda explained as Teague glanced over the first letter.

He lifted his gaze, his eyes round. *"Vincent Chadwick?"*

Tilda nodded. "He was supposedly traveling, but you'll see that he's actually lodging in Richmond. Ravenhurst and I plan to find him tomorrow." She dug through her reticule once more and withdrew the brass cap Hadrian had found in Lady Priscilla's bedchamber. "We found one other item, but it may not pertain to the case. You should keep it with the evidence for now, however."

Teague handed the letters to Wycombe and asked him to keep custody of them whilst Teague accepted the cap. "Can't imagine what this has to do with the kidnapper, but I'll lock it in the evidence drawer as soon as I return to Scotland Yard."

Hadrian tamped down another wave of disappointment upon losing access to the mysterious cap as well.

The detective inspector tucked the cap into his pocket. "I appreciate this very much. Dare I hope you'll continue sharing information with me? I realize this case is a bit different than those we've worked on together in the past since you aren't actually working for a client."

"Nor am I working for Scotland Yard," Tilda pointed out.

Hadrian wished the Met would hire her to assist with certain cases. The police employed women in various roles. In fact, the City of London Police *had* hired Tilda, and she'd been very successful.

"Not at this time," Teague said ruefully. "But I'm keen to share information if you're committed to finding Lady Priscilla and apprehending this kidnapper."

"I'm completely dedicated to both causes, and I would appreciate us working together, even if I'm not being compensated," Tilda replied.

"Which is a crime of its own," Hadrian remarked none too quietly.

"You know it's not up to me." Teague lifted his hands briefly. "If it were, I would engage Miss Wren's services permanently."

"Ravenhurst and I will see you tomorrow at the inquest," Tilda said. "And we'll provide our report from interviewing Vincent Chadwick."

"I'll share whatever I learn here." Teague inclined his head toward the house.

Hadrian and Tilda continued to the coach where Leach greeted them. When they were seated inside and on their way to Marylebone, Hadrian allowed himself to frown.

Tilda turned toward him on the seat. "You're disappointed I gave the letters and cap to Teague."

"How well you know me." Hadrian's frown lifted into a half-smile.

"We had to share those things." She looked at him earnestly. "It's imperative we find Lady Priscilla, and I simply cannot with-hold information."

"Of course you can't," he assured her. "I'm not angry. I may yet have a chance to handle the letters and the cap. It does sound as if we'll be working with Teague, though I *am* irritated that he can't pay you."

"I know, and I love you for that." She smiled, and his heart somersaulted. But then her features darkened, and Hadrian's chest tightened.

"What is it?"

"I'm afraid Lady Priscilla won't be returned, that she'll meet the same end as Miss Chadwick."

Hadrian took her hand. "We will do everything in our power to keep that from happening."

"I tried to do everything to rescue Miss Chadwick," she whispered. "I can't help feeling frightened."

Hadrian scooted closer to her and pulled her to his chest. She snaked her arms around him. "I understand. But the Tilda I know isn't driven by fear. She's brilliant and measured. We'll find Lady Priscilla."

"I hope so." She squeezed him tightly. "Before it's too late."

# CHAPTER 9

The following morning, Tilda waited in the parlor and watched for Hadrian's coach. As soon as she saw Leach, she dashed to the entrance hall.

Vaughn shuffled to open the door for her. "What time shall we expect you back?"

"I'm not certain." After their errand in Richmond, they would attend the inquest regarding Delia Chadwick's murder. "It could be late this afternoon."

"Very good," Vaughn said with a nod.

"Thank you, Vaughn." Tilda sailed through the door, clutching her reticule.

Hadrian had just stepped out of the coach as she quickly approached. "You're in a hurry."

"I'm keen to interview Vincent Chadwick." She smiled at the coachman. "Good morning, Leach."

"Good morning, Miss Wren. His lordship has directed me on what to look for in Richmond." The coachman regarded her with resolve. "I'll find the tobacconist with a view of the Thames."

Tilda thanked him as he helped her into the coach. Hadrian climbed in after her, and Leach closed the door.

"Did you sleep well?" Hadrian asked after he was settled beside her.

"Better than some of the most recent nights," she replied, adjusting her skirts and setting her reticule in her lap. "I confess I'm anxious to find Vincent Chadwick. I spent far too much time trying to determine how he fits into the kidnapping and murder of his sister, as well as the kidnapping of his secret paramour. I still have no idea."

"Well, I plan to shake his hand the moment we meet him," Hadrian said.

"Your head is recovered then?"

"Indeed. I took a lavender bath last night, and that helped immensely. My valet has noted my sudden penchant for lavender. He found it an odd choice for a gentleman—unless I'm trying to eradicate lice, which he assures me I don't have."

Tilda had met Sharp. He possessed a wry sense of humor. "I'm glad to hear you're not infested. Did you give him a reason for your newfound love of lavender?"

"I told him I liked it, and he was not to scold me about it. He also asked if it was, by chance, the scent that you wear." He rushed to add. "I have not told him much about us. However, as my valet, he knows me rather intimately and was perhaps aware of my emotional attachment to you—or to someone—before I was."

She laughed softly. "I can't decide if that's wonderful or horrifying. Are you not able to hide anything from him? How is he unaware of your ability to experience others' memories?"

"Only because it doesn't happen much at home, which is convenient since, yes, it's challenging to hide things from him, not that I need to. I've never had much to hide."

They fell silent for a few minutes before Tilda realized Hadrian was watching her somewhat apprehensively. "Is there something wrong?" she asked.

He grimaced faintly. "I need to confess something, and I'm

rather upset with myself about it. I may have revealed our private courtship to my mother."

Tilda's eyes rounded, and her jaw tightened. "You *may* have?"

"I *did*. But it was an accident," he assured her quickly. "We were discussing Clement's idiotic newspaper article, and I became rather passionate in my defense of you. That's when I blurted that I was in love with you and hoped— Well, that's what I said."

She wasn't sure what he'd been going to say after "hoped," but decided she didn't want to ask. She could guess, and that wasn't a conversation she was ready to have.

"Why did you have to defend me about the article?" Now Tilda felt apprehensive.

Hadrian hesitated the barest amount, as if he had to choose his words carefully, which did not soothe her anxiety. "My mother called because she was concerned after reading the article. You know she thinks you're an excellent detective, and she didn't care to see your reputation maligned."

"How nice," Tilda said softly. "What was her reaction to what you said?"

"She was happy for me—and for you too."

Tilda wasn't entirely sure she believed him. Again, he'd hesitated, and she had to think that, as much as Lady Ravenhurst believed in her as an investigator, she likely wouldn't want someone like her as a daughter-in-law. Tilda was simply not countess material.

"I'd like to host a dinner in a few days for you and your grandmother and my mother," Hadrian proposed. "One of my sisters will be visiting, and I want you to meet her."

Tilda's brows arched briefly. "The timing of that will be dependent on our case."

"You can't work around the clock," Hadrian noted.

Irritation rose rapidly in Tilda. "I absolutely will, if I must, in order to save Lady Priscilla. She was kidnapped in the identical manner as Miss Chadwick, and we *cannot* allow the same result."

"Of course, you're right." Hadrian's tone was contrite. "I apologize. If it's *possible*, I would like you to come to dinner."

"I will try."

"If you can't, I'll be with you. I'm not going to have dinner with my family whilst you're out investigating alone."

Tilda gave him a sardonic look. "I did that for some time before we met."

"Isn't this better?" His tone was mildly flirtatious, but she didn't call him out. Investigating with him *was* better.

Tilda turned her mind to theorizing about the case again. They reviewed what they knew and their outstanding questions until they arrived in Richmond, at which point both she and Hadrian were looking out the windows, trying to see a tobacconist on a corner.

After perhaps half an hour of driving about, Hadrian pointed to the window. "There it is. I knew Leach would find it."

Tilda craned her neck to see out his side. "Excellent." She turned her head, which brought her face quite close to Hadrian's. He was an attractive man, and at this proximity she couldn't help admiring the silvery outline at the edge of his blue irises as well as the lush thickness of his black lashes. He was also wealthy and powerful. She could scarcely believe he would want someone like her as a countess, but with each passing day, she became more certain he did. And whilst that was thrilling, it was perhaps even more terrifying.

The coach came to a stop, and Tilda settled back against the squab. Hadrian sighed, and she had the sense he was disappointed she hadn't kissed him. In truth, the idea had stolen into her thoughts, but she'd worked—almost successfully—to ignore it.

Leach opened the door and helped Tilda to the pavement. Hadrian followed, then escorted her into the tobacconist's shop.

The scent of various kinds of tobacco from all over the world was overwhelming.

A long oak counter stretched along the left side of the shop. Windows at the front and on the right side offered milky light.

They walked to the counter behind which a shopkeeper stood. He was of middling height with nearly black hair and darker skin.

"May I help you?" he asked in a distinctly Welsh accent.

"I'm Lord Ravenhurst, and this is my associate, Miss Wren. We're looking for one of your clients, Mr. Vincent Chadwick."

"Chadwick comes in often, sometimes just to chat. He seems a bit lonely." The shopkeeper smiled at them. "Have you come to visit him? I think he'd like that. He says he has to stay here for a few months and he's eager to go home, though I don't know where that is."

"We *are* here to visit," Hadrian confirmed with a smile. "However, I forgot the exact building he's lodging in. Can you direct us to the right place?"

"Three houses down, my lord. Boarding house run by Mrs. Block."

"Excellent. Thank you," Hadrian said kindly as he offered Tilda his arm, then escorted her from the shop. He informed Leach of their destination, and they continued along the pavement to Mrs. Block's boarding house where Hadrian knocked.

A few moments later, a woman opened the door. She was petite and plump and wore a white apron and cap.

Hadrian smiled pleasantly. "Good afternoon. I'm Lord Ravenhurst. This is my associate, Miss Wren. We're looking for one of your lodgers, Mr. Vincent Chadwick."

"He's not here," she replied.

Tilda suffered a wave of disappointment. "When do you expect him to return?"

The woman shrugged. "Don't know. I think my husband saw him leave with a valise."

"So, he could be gone for a few days?" Hadrian asked.

"I wouldn't know," the landlady replied.

"Did you see him with anyone else—a young woman, perhaps?" Tilda was hopeful for any information that might help them.

"Why would he be with a young woman? He lived alone. He's a good lodger. He doesn't stay out late. He's not a drunkard. He pays on time."

"How long has he lived here?" Tilda asked. "And does he regularly leave with a valise for periods of time?"

"Close to two months, I'd say. And no, he hasn't left with a valise before." The landlady's eyes narrowed. "Why are you asking all these questions about Mr. Chadwick?"

"We've an urgent matter to speak with him about," Hadrian replied. "Do you know when he might return?"

"I don't. But I'll tell him you were inquiring about him."

Hadrian inclined his head with another smile. "Thank you for your time."

She closed the door, and Tilda turned toward the street with a frown.

"That was an unfortunate result," Hadrian said. "But perhaps Chadwick did, in fact, elope with Lady Priscilla. She could have been waiting somewhere whilst he fetched his things."

Tilda's frown deepened. "I'm disappointed we couldn't access his room for you to touch anything, but I didn't think it was even worth asking."

"I agree the landlady would have told us no if we had." Hadrian escorted Tilda to the coach.

"You were awfully quick," Leach said.

"Chadwick's gone," Hadrian replied. "With a valise, so who knows when he'll return."

Leach's features creased with sympathy. "That's too bad. You'll be a bit early to the inquest, but that's all right."

Since they had time, Tilda preferred another destination.

"Actually, I'd like to speak with Lord Farnsworth." She turned to Hadrian. "Do you know where he lives?"

"He rents rooms on Jermyn Street, along with several of the young men he runs with. I believe he lives over a wine shop. Either way, we'll find him just as we found Chadwick, or at least where Chadwick was living." His mouth flattened, and Tilda could see he was as disappointed as she was.

"Jermyn Street then," Leach said.

"Yes, thank you." Hadrian helped Tilda into the coach, then climbed in after her.

As they returned to London, Tilda leaned her head back against the squab. She stared at the roof of the coach as if she could discern the answers she sought in the blue-patterned damask.

"We're missing something," she said again. "I think we need to find what Miss Chadwick and Lady Priscilla had in common, if anything, besides just being friends."

"Well, they have Vincent Chadwick in common," Hadrian replied. "One is his sister and the other is his former paramour, or current paramour, since they're continuing to write letters to one another."

"Yes, but we can't come up with a motive for him to kill his sister. Without that, he's a weak suspect." Tilda crossed her arms tightly over her chest. "Hopefully, Lord Farnsworth will tell us something helpful. We need a break if we're to find Lady Priscilla and bring this kidnapper and murderer to justice."

~

*H*adrian confirmed with the owner of the wine shop that Farnsworth did indeed live upstairs on the first floor. He and Tilda ascended to the landing where Hadrian rapped on the door.

A manservant dressed simply in austere black answered the

summons. In his early thirties, he surveyed them with small, assessing eyes that bordered on judgmental—at least when they fixed on Tilda. Hadrian disliked him immediately.

"Good afternoon," Hadrian said coolly. "I'm Ravenhurst, and this is my dear friend, Miss Wren. We've important business to discuss with Farnsworth regarding Lady Priscilla."

"Certainly, my lord," the manservant said crisply. "Do come in." He held the door wide for them to enter into a compact vestibule with doors leading to the right and left. "Wait here." The manservant walked through the left doorway, and Hadrian could see it was an exceptionally appointed sitting room.

A moment later, the manservant returned. "Please follow me." He led them into the masculine space, which was decorated with elegant furnishings, including several paintings by Millais. Marble surrounded a coal fire burning behind a highly polished fender, and thick blue velvet curtains cloaked the tall windows facing Jermyn Street.

Lord Farnsworth, the twenty-six-year-old heir to the Earl of Bolton, stood from a small round table upon which sat a cup of tea and a newspaper. He was of average height with dark-blond hair and rather flat brown eyes. He wore a plum velvet dressing gown over a pair of dark gray trousers and a white shirt.

"Afternoon, Ravenhurst. Your arrival is unexpected. I can't imagine what you have to do with Lady Priscilla." He flicked a glance at Tilda, but his attention didn't linger on her, as if she were unaccountable. "Has she been found?"

"No," Hadrian replied. "We're investigating her disappearance and would like to ask you some questions."

Farnsworth's brows drew together, and he appeared confused. "You're investigating? Is that because the note instructed the duke not to report her disappearance to the police?"

"Yes." Hadrian didn't care to explain that the police were already involved. He lifted his hand and darted a look toward

Tilda. He was trying to silently communicate his intent to remove his gloves and touch something. Hopefully, Tilda would distract Farnsworth with questioning.

"Do you mind if I sit?" Tilda asked, clearly understanding Hadrian. She moved to perch on a dark blue damask settee.

Farnsworth seemed reluctant to join her but ultimately did, lowering himself into a buttoned leather chair opposite the settee. "I'm not sure I can answer many questions for you."

Hadrian surreptitiously removed his right glove and wandered toward the table where Farnsworth had been sitting.

"How long have you and Lady Priscilla been courting?" Tilda asked.

"Only about a fortnight," Farnsworth replied. "Though, I do expect our courtship will lead to marriage. That is my hope, anyway."

Tilda flashed a smile, but Hadrian could tell it was for show. "Does she feel the same way?"

Farnsworth didn't hesitate to reply with clear confidence. "Of course."

"Didn't Lady Priscilla have another suitor?" Tilda probed.

Farnsworth snorted. "Some second son without even a title to his family name. I can't recall who he was."

"Did you have any reason to believe that Lady Priscilla might still have feelings for that man?" Tilda continued.

Hadrian touched the table, flattening his palm against the polished wood until the room around him faded away. Music filled the air and candlelight glittered in a crowded ballroom. He was waltzing with Lady Priscilla, whom he recognized from the portrait he'd seen in Alnwick's study.

Lady Priscilla was smiling, then she laughed at something Farnsworth said. Hadrian had the sense he was trying to be amusing, but underneath, the man felt a distinct disgust toward the woman in his arms. Hadrian then felt a rush of anticipation for the social status and dowry that marriage to her would bring Farnsworth.

"The rapscallion!"

Farnsworth's declaration interrupted Hadrian's vision, and he was suddenly back in Farnsworth's sitting room, blinking. A sharp ache spread from his temples to his scalp as he took his hand from the table and looked to see what was happening with the viscount and Tilda.

"Do you think this former suitor kidnapped my Priscilla?" Farnsworth asked, aghast.

The vision—rather, Farnsworth's emotions within the memory—prompted Hadrian to dislike the viscount. And given the man's reaction to her, Hadrian was annoyed that he considered Lady Priscilla, whom he was merely courting, to be his. Then again, Hadrian thought of Tilda, whom he was *barely* courting, as his.

Except Hadrian loved Tilda. He wasn't disgusted by her in any way, and he didn't care what advantages she might offer him beyond those of a helpmate and partner who would share his life.

"Now I remember who that suitor was," Farnsworth said angrily. "Vincent Chadwick."

Hadrian and Tilda exchanged glances as Hadrian drew on his glove.

Farnsworth bolted from his chair. "I'm going to Belgrave Square to confront the scoundrel."

"He's apparently travelling," Hadrian said, repeating the lie the Chadwicks had told him.

"Bah," Farnsworth said with another snort. "I saw him at a gaming hell in Leicester Square just last week."

Hadrian and Tilda exchanged another look.

"Did you speak with him?" Tilda asked.

"Why would I?" Farnsworth's nose wrinkled with disgust. "Judson," he called. "I'm going out."

"You really shouldn't," Hadrian cautioned. "The Chadwicks are grieving right now because of the death of their daughter."

Farnsworth snapped his attention to them, his eyes widening. "What?"

"Their daughter was kidnapped in the same manner as Lady Priscilla several days before Lady Priscilla disappeared, and she was murdered."

Farnsworth paled.

"You see why now is not the best time to call on them," Tilda said softly. "Furthermore, they may be at Miss Chadwick's inquest, which is to begin soon."

"Now is the *perfect* time to speak with them," Farnsworth insisted. "We must save Lady Priscilla from the same fate." He walked through the vestibule, likely to his bedchamber to change his clothing.

Tilda stood and moved to stand close to Hadrian. "What did you see when you touched the table?" she whispered.

"That if anyone is a scoundrel, it's Farnsworth." Hadrian sneered toward the bedchamber. "He was dancing with Lady Priscilla, but he was filled with disgust towards her, as well as anticipation for being associated with her father's title and obtaining her dowry."

"How awful," Tilda said. "I wonder if Lady Priscilla knows."

"She seemed rather happy dancing with him, but I wonder if that was fake, given her ongoing epistolary relationship with Vincent Chadwick."

Tilda's brow creased. "We can't let him barge in on the Chadwicks like this."

"Agreed. We should try to go with him to soften the intrusion. Also to possibly learn where Vincent has gone."

"I was thinking the same thing. What of the inquest?" Hadrian asked.

"I don't want to miss it, but I think we really must accompany

Lord Farnsworth," Tilda said. "Teague can tell us about the inquest if necessary."

A few minutes later, Farnsworth rejoined them, fully dressed. "You're still here."

"Would you care for a ride to Belgrave Square?" Hadrian asked. "We don't mind accompanying you. In fact, it may be beneficial."

Farnsworth inclined his head. "That saves me time, thank you."

They left his apartments and went to Hadrian's coach where he instructed Leach to take them to Chadwick's house. Hadrian helped Tilda into the coach then climbed in after her. That left the rear-facing seat for Farnsworth. He pursed his lips in a near-pout, appearing a bit offended.

"What do you plan to do at the Chadwicks?" Hadrian asked once they were moving.

"I shall demand to know where Vincent is." Farnsworth's brows drew together in anger. "If he knows anything about Lady Priscilla's disappearance, he must say so. Don't you think he must be held accountable?"

"If he's involved, certainly," Hadrian said.

The Chadwick house was bedecked in black, with a large mourning wreath centered on the door. Hadrian and Tilda had encountered many of those since they'd met.

The butler answered the door. His gaze flickered with surprise and then anger as he saw Tilda and even Hadrian. Hadrian was happy to let Farnsworth speak.

"I'm Farnsworth, and I'm here to speak with Mr. Chadwick about Vincent Chadwick. Whom I understand is *traveling*," Farnsworth added sardonically.

"Mr. Vincent Chadwick is here, my lord," the butler replied.

"He is?" Hadrian blurted.

"I must speak with him immediately." Farnsworth pushed

himself inside. The butler had no choice but to open the door wider and let them all in.

"I'm afraid no one is receiving," the butler said. "We are a house in deep mourning."

It seemed the Chadwicks were not at the inquest then. Hadrian wasn't surprised. A man of Chadwick's status would have been able to avoid being there in person. He'd likely sent testimony via a solicitor. He may also have sent their physician to speak about Miss Chadwick as well as a retainer from the household to recount the morning Miss Chadwick was discovered missing.

"I'm sorry for their loss, but another young woman, to whom I am nearly betrothed, is missing." Farnsworth glared at the butler. "Either you fetch Vincent, or I'll search the house until I find him."

"Very well." The butler disappeared into the staircase hall.

Hadrian had the sense that Farnsworth was used to getting his way. He watched as the viscount paced, his face puckered with irritation.

A few minutes later, Mr. Chadwick appeared in the entrance hall. "What the devil are you two doing here?" He fixed his furious gaze on Tilda and Hadrian.

"They're with me. I'm here to speak to your rapscallion of a son."

Chadwick turned his glare on Farnsworth. "What business would you have with him?"

"The woman I'm courting, Lady Priscilla, has been kidnapped, and she had a past flirtation with your son. If he had something to do with her disappearance, we must find out."

"He would never kidnap anyone!" Chadwick raged.

A young man who had to be Vincent Chadwick walked into the entrance hall. He looked a bit like his father around the mouth and chin and was perhaps a year or so younger than Tilda's twenty-five years.

Farnsworth strode to where Vincent stood and sneered in the taller man's face. "I demand to know what you've done with Lady Priscilla!"

# CHAPTER 10

$T$ilda stiffened due to the thick tension in the hall, and she realized she was holding her breath.

"What do you mean?" Vincent Chadwick appeared genuinely confused, his brow deeply furrowed.

"She's been kidnapped," Farnsworth spat. "I know you begged the Duke of Alnwick to reconsider your suit after he refused you. And that you became such a nuisance, you were banished to Richmond."

Tilda exchanged a glance with Hadrian. That was good information to know. It perhaps explained why the Chadwicks indicated their son was "traveling."

"Priscilla has been kidnapped?" Vincent had gone ashen at the news. In fact, for a moment, Tilda worried he might collapse.

"I'm so sorry," Tilda said softly.

The senior Chadwick's gaze burned into Tilda. "Another young woman has been kidnapped, and you have somehow involved yourself."

"Yes, another woman has been taken in the same manner as your daughter by someone claiming to be Spring-heeled Jack."

Tilda wasn't going to respond to his snide comment about how she was involved.

"What have you done with my Priscilla?" Farnsworth shouted in Vincent's face. He whipped his gloves off and tossed them aside. "Tell me now," he growled.

Vincent took a step back, his eyes rounding and his face still pale. "I've done nothing. And she isn't *your* Priscilla." He said the last with a bit of heat.

"I'm sure she's waiting for you somewhere so the two of you can elope," Farnsworth accused.

"She's not. I swear. I've lost my sister, and now the woman I love is missing." Vincent put his hand to his forehead. "I can't even think straight just now."

"So, you admit you still love Lady Priscilla," Farnsworth said. "The woman *I* am planning to wed. That is unconscionable!"

Farnsworth advanced, driving Vincent back. Hadrian moved quickly and grabbed Farnsworth's hand, pulling him to a stop. Tilda's gaze focused on where Hadrian touched Farnsworth and hoped he was seeing something. She looked at Hadrian's face. His gaze did indeed appear unfocused. But then Farnsworth jerked his hand away, and whatever connection Hadrian might have had was gone.

Chadwick quickly moved between Farnsworth and his son. "Back away, Farnsworth. This is a house in mourning. You've no right to come here and act in this manner. Vincent had nothing to do with Lady Priscilla's disappearance." He shifted his gaze to Tilda. "When was she kidnapped?"

"Two days ago," Tilda replied as Hadrian moved to fetch Farnsworth's gloves from where he'd thrown them. Tilda gathered what he was doing. He planned to use the gloves to try and see a memory.

"Her father can't have hired you to find her," Chadwick said to Tilda with disdain.

Tilda stepped forward to distract from Hadrian. "No, he has not. Though, Ravenhurst and I did offer to help."

Chadwick's dark eyes glowed with rage. "You'd best not bungle it the way you did with Delia."

Tilda was not going to debate him about what had or hadn't ruined their scheme to rescue Miss Chadwick. "I'm incredibly sorry for the loss of your daughter. I think we may be dealing with someone who is not entirely sane. The kidnapper's actions make no sense. He received the ransom, and that should have been the end of it. Your daughter should have been returned unharmed."

"You're damn right she should have." Chadwick's chin quivered, and Tilda felt a wave of sorrow tinged with guilt. She hated that her actions may have led to Miss Chadwick's death.

Vincent stepped toward his father and clasped his shoulder.

Chadwick cleared his throat. "Farnsworth, you must go."

Glowering at Vincent, Farnsworth bared his teeth briefly. "If I find you've had anything to do with this, I will call you out. There will be nowhere you can hide." Spinning on his heel, he stalked to Hadrian and snatched his gloves before departing the house.

Tilda wasn't sure if Farnsworth had interrupted Hadrian's vision or not. She hadn't looked at him whilst working to keep everyone's attention on her.

Now, however, she watched him press his fingertips to his forehead and assumed he'd seen something. Unless his head was simply paining him from earlier.

"You must go too," Chadwick said coldly to Hadrian and Tilda.

"We apologize for the intrusion," Hadrian said. "We were interviewing Farnsworth about Lady Priscilla's disappearance, and when he recalled that your son had been Lady Priscilla's prior suitor, Farnsworth insisted on confronting him. We attempted to persuade him not to, but he was unmoved. I decided we ought to accompany him to try to mitigate the situation."

Chadwick narrowed his eyes at Hadrian. "What are you even doing with her?" He jerked his head toward Tilda, and she stiffened again.

"I'm assisting her in the pursuit of justice," Hadrian said simply and earnestly. He'd moved to stand in such a way that he was partially blocking Tilda from Chadwick. It was a posture of protection, and she appreciated it. Whilst she understood Chadwick's fury, entangled as it was with his grief, it was still somewhat frightening.

Tilda looked at Vincent, who remained pale, and met his gaze. "We're sorry about this, Mr. Chadwick."

"Can you tell me about Lady Priscilla's kidnapping?" Vincent asked desperately. "Please."

"She was discovered missing two mornings ago," Tilda replied. "The kidnapper left a note identical to the one that was found when your sister disappeared. May I ask you a question?" At his nod, she went on. "Your parents told us you were traveling, but we learned you've been lodging in Richmond and have been seen in London. Why lie?" Tilda wanted to know if Farnsworth's accusation had been true.

Vincent looked at the floor. "His Grace did not approve of my suit."

"Yet, you kept trying to see her," Mr. Chadwick said angrily. "We sent you to Richmond to regain your senses. Indeed, His Grace asked that I ensure you remain gone until Lady Priscilla was wed."

Eyes darkening with betrayal, Vincent gasped.

Tilda felt awful for him. "The two of you continued to correspond?" she asked gently.

Vincent nodded. "We love each other."

"So much that you mentioned elopement," Hadrian pointed out.

"Blast it all, Vincent!" Chadwick thundered. "I told you to leave Lady Priscilla be. She's too far above you." The man's expression dampened, and he wiped his hand over his brow. "Our wealth is great, but our position is not exalted enough for some people, my boy. We cannot afford for His Grace to malign our family." There was regret and sadness in his tone. Tilda felt horrible for him too.

Vincent looked to Tilda and Hadrian with worry. "Priscilla and I didn't elope—obviously—nor did we have plans to."

Chadwick waved his hand at Tilda and Hadrian, but the movement lacked conviction. "I insist you cease upsetting us."

Vincent regarded his father briefly. "Father, I must know what's happening with Priscilla." He looked back to Hadrian and Tilda with an eager desperation. "Has there been a note yet about the ransom delivery?"

"You know about that?" Tilda asked suspiciously, wondering if they were witnessing a brilliant theatrical display and whether Priscilla might be waiting somewhere for Vincent.

"My father explained all that happened. I arrived home yesterday afternoon after receiving word about Delia." Vincent croaked his sister's name. His seemed genuinely upset.

"There has not yet been a note about delivering the ransom," Hadrian responded. "We expect that today—if the kidnapper follows the same timeline as before."

"I must warn His Grace not to inform you of its arrival," Chadwick said sharply, regaining some of his earlier emotion.

Tilda's heart pounded.

Hadrian gave Chadwick a look of superiority that Tilda wasn't sure she'd seen before. "I wish you wouldn't."

Chadwick's eyes darkened, and his brows pitched low into a V. "You won't persuade me otherwise."

Tilda reached forward and grasped Hadrian's sleeve. "Let's go," she murmured.

Hadrian inclined his head toward Chadwick, then turned and escorted Tilda from the house. Outside, Tilda glanced around the square. "I don't see Farnsworth."

"He's not in the coach or with Leach," Hadrian noted.

The coachman stood waiting outside the vehicle.

"Did you see where Farnsworth went?" Hadrian asked as they approached Leach.

Leach gestured to the right. "Stormed off that way, muttering. To the inquest now?"

Hadrian consulted his pocket watch. "We're late, but yes." He glanced at Tilda, and she nodded in response.

Hadrian and Tilda climbed into the coach, and right away she turned to face him. "Did you see something?"

His eyes gleamed with anticipation, and she knew he had.

"When I grabbed Farnsworth's hand, I had a very quick vision of him at a ball. I recognized it as the Marquess of Asquith's ballroom. I know they hosted a ball this past Sunday because I received an invitation. I didn't attend, but I've been there before, so I recognized the surroundings. Farnsworth stood with a woman with pale blonde hair in a red gown with rubies at her throat and her ears. I believe it was Mrs. Bankes, but I can't be certain. I couldn't see anything more because Farnsworth pulled his hand away."

"That's why you went and fetched his gloves, so you could try again," Tilda said.

"Yes. I appreciate you distracting everyone so I could take time to do so," he added with a smile. "I saw the same woman, and she was in a bed next to Farnsworth. I could tell it was dark outside due to the candlelight in the room. I was able to see the same red dress she was wearing draped over a chair, and she still wore the rubies. I'm all but certain this was the same night—Sunday night."

"He's having an affair?" Tilda asked.

"Or an assignation," Hadrian replied. "Either way, I'm confident Farnsworth isn't emotionally attached to Lady Priscilla. His anger over her disappearance seems to stem from his loss of the bride he was hoping to win."

"It also tells us Farnsworth has an alibi for when Lady Priscilla was kidnapped. If that ball took place on Sunday night, and what you saw was happening overnight, he couldn't have kidnapped her."

"It does seem that way," Hadrian agreed. "Though, he could have hired someone."

Tilda had no trouble believing Farnsworth had the resources to do that. "But why kidnap a woman he expected to marry?"

"What if he knew Lady Priscilla still loved Vincent? He may have wanted to compromise her so they would have to marry."

That was actually a decent motive for abducting Lady Priscilla. "What was his motive for kidnapping Miss Chadwick, let alone killing her?"

Hadrian frowned. "No idea. Does this mean Farnsworth is not a suspect?"

"He has an alibi for one of the kidnappings and no motive for the other. I don't think he's a suspect." Tilda blew out a frustrated breath. "We need to determine if there's a connection between Miss Chadwick and Lady Priscilla, besides the fact that they were friends. The kidnapper targeted them because of their families' wealth. And why all the Spring-heeled Jack nonsense?"

A long moment passed before Hadrian sent Tilda a tentative glance. "What if the only thing they have in common is that they were randomly targeted by Spring-heeled Jack as wealthy young women?"

"Then this will be a difficult case to solve. But we *will* solve it," Tilda said loudly, her eyes flashing with resolve. "I wish Chadwick wasn't going to speak to His Grace. I'm concerned the duke won't tell us when he receives the second note."

"Perhaps we should call on him now, before Chadwick can get to him," Hadrian said. "Though, I'm sure you want to get to the inquest."

"I do, but I think calling on His Grace is more important."

"Agreed." Hadrian knocked on the roof, and the coach quickly stopped. When Leach opened the door, Hadrian directed him to Alnwick House instead.

"I wonder if you shouldn't stay in the coach when we arrive," Hadrian suggested.

"That's probably wise."

When they arrived at the duke's house, Hadrian went inside whilst Tilda tapped her fingers on her reticule. As she waited, she tried to make sense of what meager clues they'd gathered about these crimes.

Finally, she saw Hadrian coming back toward the coach. Her pulse quickened. However, when he climbed inside, his face told her all she needed to know.

"It didn't go well, did it?" Tilda asked.

Hadrian shook his head. "The duke insists he has not received a second note."

"Do you believe him?"

"I couldn't read him, and I didn't have an opportunity to shake his hand, nor could I touch anything."

"Damn," Tilda breathed. She glanced at Hadrian. "Pardon me."

"I don't know that I've ever heard you swear," Hadrian said with a faint smirk.

"I only do so when it's necessary."

"I asked him to promise that he'd notify me, you, or Detective Inspector Teague when he receives the second note. He refused." Hadrian pressed his lips into a grim line.

"We shouldn't even assume he'll receive a second note," Tilda said. "Honestly, I don't want this abduction to follow the same pattern as Miss Chadwick's."

"It *won't*." Hadrian spoke with a firm confidence that Tilda didn't share.

Right or wrong, she felt responsible, in part, for Miss Chadwick's death. And she was going to do everything in her power to ensure Lady Priscilla didn't suffer the same end.

he coach stopped near The Waterman in Limehouse, not too far from where Miss Chadwick had been discovered. Tilda and Hadrian quickly departed the vehicle and hastened to the pub. However, the stream of gentlemen leaving seemed to indicate the inquest had concluded.

Tilda stepped inside the common room just as Detective Inspector Teague entered from a doorway in the right corner. "I think we missed the inquest," she turned to say to Hadrian as he walked in behind her.

They met Teague, and he confirmed Tilda's presumption. "The inquest just ended. You won't be surprised to learn that Delia Chadwick was murdered." He gestured to the doorway. "Let's move outside."

A few reporters stood around the entrance to the pub. Tilda hadn't paid them notice in her haste before, but now, she looked for Ezra Clement. He didn't appear to be there.

Teague glowered toward the journalists. "I'd rather not speak where any of them can hear us."

Hadrian gestured to his coach. "We can sit in my coach if that would suffice."

Teague nodded, and they made their way to the vehicle. Leach moved to open the door for them. As she climbed inside, Tilda glanced at the pub once more and saw Clement leaving.

When they were settled in the coach, she looked at Teague. "Was Ezra Clement at the inquest?"

"He was." Teague scowled. "I confess I told him afterward that I found his article about his interview with Mr. Chadwick to be misleading. I suggested he obtain both sides of a story before publishing."

"Good," Hadrian said with zeal. "He had the nerve to call on Miss Wren yesterday with the intention of writing an article from her perspective, only I saw no such thing in today's *Daily News*."

Tilda had noticed that as well. "One of the proprietors is friendly with Mr. Chadwick. I don't think Mr. Clement is being permitted to write or publish what he'd prefer."

"Then he should find another paper to write for," Teague said. "One must maintain their integrity." He waved his hand. "Enough of that. Let me tell you about the inquest. The surgeon who completed the autopsy determined Miss Chadwick's cause of death to be suffocation."

Tilda leaned forward slightly. "That's surprising. What of the wounds she suffered?"

"The coroner said they were inflicted post-mortem. She was killed a few hours before she was found—between six and seven."

"Do you have any theories as to why she was suffocated and then disfigured after she was dead?" Tilda asked.

"I believe the killer tried to make it look like Spring-heeled Jack committed the murder with his claws. However, she was already dead." Teague crossed his arms as he leaned back against the rear-facing squab. "To me, this is further proof that the Spring-heeled Jack act is pure nonsense. The killer is dressing up his kidnapping and murder in a decades-old legend meant to terrorize the populace. And thanks to Clement and the *Daily News*, Spring-heeled Jack—whoever he is—is succeeding. We had far too many people show up before the inquest who wanted to observe. Graythorpe sent several dozen away."

"Who provided the testimony regarding Miss Chadwick's disappearance?" Hadrian asked. "Was Chadwick not called to testify?"

"He was not, and it seems you knew that."

"Yes, we came from seeing him in Belgrave Square, so we knew he wasn't at the inquest."

Teague uncrossed his arms. "I'm surprised he allowed you in."

"He didn't, really. We went with Lord Farnsworth who, frankly, forced himself inside." Tilda shared the details of their disappointing visit to Richmond and their subsequent visit with Lord Farnsworth. She concluded by telling him about accompanying Farnsworth to Belgrave Square and finding Vincent Chadwick in residence.

"It certainly seems as though Farnsworth didn't kidnap Lady Priscilla," Teague said when she'd finished.

"That was our determination as well," Tilda said. They couldn't reveal how they knew Farnsworth had an alibi, but even without it, he was a weak suspect. "Farnsworth appeared to truly believe that Vincent may have kidnapped her to elope. However, that doesn't make sense as he's at home and Lady Priscilla is still missing."

Teague blew out a breath and slapped one hand on his thigh. "It's most frustrating not to have a suspect." He cocked his head. "His Grace should have received a second ransom note today—if the kidnapper is repeating what he did with Miss Chadwick. I'll go to Alnwick House now."

"I called on him before we came here and asked exactly that," Hadrian said. "The duke replied that he hasn't received anything, but I don't know whether to believe him."

Teague's mouth twisted with distaste. "I must interview him. With any luck, which I think we are due, we'll be able to catch the kidnapper when he tries to retrieve his second ransom. *If* I can persuade His Grace to cooperate."

"And if you can't?" Hadrian asked.

"We'll determine that when, and if, it happens. I don't suppose you'd drive me to his house now? For expediency's sake. Furthermore, you can wait in the coach whilst I interview him."

"I'd be happy to convey you. I'll just inform Leach." Hadrian opened the door and spoke with the coachman.

They were shortly on their way to Upper Brook Street. For the second time that day, Tilda waited in the coach whilst someone else went to speak with the Duke of Alnwick. But this time, she wasn't alone.

She rose up on the seat and pressed a kiss to Hadrian's cheek whilst they were waiting.

He turned his head sharply, surprise softening his features. "What was that for?"

Shrugging, she smiled. "No reason. Actually, that's not true. Every reason. They are simply too numerous to name."

"Careful, Tilda. We've no idea when Teague will return, and you're encouraging me to take you in my arms and behave in a most inappropriate manner."

Tilda could imagine what that might be, though she had no experience with such things. She'd never thought much about them. But now, with Hadrian, she found her curiosity had grown to encompass more than solving puzzles.

"You're flirting again," she said without a trace of heat. In fact, her tone might have been just the tiniest bit flirtatious.

Hadrian laughed. "You started it." He met her gaze with warmth and love. "I'm glad to see you in good humor."

It had been a very trying several days. His words had a sobering effect, which was probably not what he'd intended. Fortunately, Teague returned, and that was a welcome distraction.

"I hope you don't mind, but I asked your coachman to deliver me to Scotland Yard," Teague said as he settled on the seat opposite Tilda and Hadrian.

"I don't mind at all," Hadrian replied. "Did you have more luck with the duke?"

"He was none too pleased to see me. When I asked about a second ransom note, he wouldn't look me in the eye. I informed him that the best chance to recover his daughter was to allow the Met to help him and cautioned him not to pay the ransom under any circumstances. I then reminded him what happened to Miss Chadwick when her ransom was paid. That was when he lost his temper and threw me out. It was also the moment I became certain he'd received a note and is concealing it."

"How did that reveal his deception?" Hadrian asked.

"He wasn't just angry," Teague explained. "He was afraid. I know fear when I see it, and my warnings made the duke wonder if he might have made a mistake."

Tilda pressed her lips together briefly. "But he didn't admit a second note was delivered."

Hadrian shook his head. "He wouldn't, not after he'd insisted he hadn't. He's far too stubborn. What do we do now?"

Teague narrowed his eyes with intent. "We come back after dark and watch the house to see if someone leaves to pay the ransom. I'll post a constable to watch the back of the house, and I'll put Wycombe and another constable on the Woods Mews. If you'd like to join me, we'll watch the front of the house."

"Thank you for inviting us," Tilda said. "I know you don't have to."

"I value your investigative talent and appreciate you contributing it to this case. Let's meet at the corner of Park Street in front of the Danish Embassy at dusk."

# CHAPTER 11

As Hadrian helped Tilda into his coach that evening, he sent a concerned glance back toward her grandmother's house. "What did your grandmother say about you going out so late with me for our investigation?" He climbed into the coach beside her, and Leach closed the door.

"She was concerned. Not that I blame her, since I was kidnapped not so long ago." Tilda didn't have to remind him. Hadrian was all too aware she'd been abducted near this very spot. He'd found her by using his ability to experience a memory of the man who'd taken her. But she'd been in mortal danger. Thankfully, Leach had killed the man, else Hadrian would have hunted him down.

"I said she needn't worry about anything happening. Not to me anyway," Tilda said.

"I will ensure it doesn't." Hadrian met her gaze with steely promise. "I confess, since that happened, I sometimes don't want to let you out of my sight. It's silly, I know, but I hate that I wasn't here to protect you that night." In fact, he'd only left for a short while, during which time she'd been abducted.

Tilda put her hand on his and gave him a gentle smile. "You

returned very quickly and were able to find and save me—with Leach's help. That is all that matters." She looked toward the basket on the opposite seat. "What have you brought?"

Hadrian chuckled. "Mrs. Rowe insisted on sending cake and biscuits in case we grow hungry this evening."

"Your cook is always so thoughtful," Tilda murmured.

"Will there come a time when we decide nobody is going to deliver a ransom payment tonight?" Hadrian asked. "I'm only curious how long we may be waiting."

"I've no idea." She withdrew her hand from his and sent him a determined look. "I'm prepared to watch all night if we have to."

They arrived at the Danish Embassy and met Teague, who was accompanied by Sergeant Wycombe and three constables.

The detective inspector gestured for everyone to come close. "You all know the assignment. We're looking to see if anyone leaves the house or the mews. If so, we'll follow them. We have a cab stationed just there." He gestured across the street to an unremarkable vehicle. "And we've another constable in uniform patrolling the area who will act as a messenger between us in the front and those in the back and mews if one of us sees someone leaving."

"It occurs to me that we can position my coach on the corner," Hadrian suggested. "Leach can easily watch the house from his seat."

"Excellent idea." Teague looked to Tilda and Hadrian. "I recommend you both take various positions on the opposite side of the street. I'll be patrolling the side on which Alnwick House sits. You don't want to loiter anywhere too long, as you'll draw notice." He looked around. "Any questions?"

When there were none, he dismissed everyone to assume their places. Hadrian went to inform Leach of the new plan to have him watch from the corner. Leach was, predictably, thrilled to participate.

Hadrian joined Teague and Tilda. "Are we prepared to stay out all night?"

"I am, but you needn't do so," Teague replied.

"I've dressed warmly," Tilda said. "And Ravenhurst's cook sent sustenance. We aren't leaving." She looked over at Teague. "You're welcome to cake and biscuits in Ravenhurst's coach."

Teague smiled. "Most thoughtful of you, my lord."

"It's entirely due to my cook. I will pass along your appreciation."

Hadrian escorted Tilda to the opposite side of the street whilst Teague moved along the other toward the park. "I don't know why I didn't think of watching from Leach's seat on the coach. He has the prime perspective."

They stopped on the pavement not far from the corner where they'd crossed. Alnwick House was in view on the other side of the street, a pair of houses away from where they stood.

Tilda's left arm was curled through his, and she placed her gloved right hand atop his sleeve. "I like that Leach has something to do. It almost makes me think we're superfluous."

"It's good there are so many of us. We're far less likely to miss anything." Hadrian felt a tremor move through Tilda.

"I hope not," she said. "I don't know how I'll bear it if something happens to Lady Priscilla."

"You can't think like that. You've done all you can in the face of the duke's resistance. If things end badly, it won't be your fault." He stopped and angled toward her. "I know I keep saying this, but you really mustn't blame yourself for Miss Chadwick. You said we're dealing with someone who is mentally unstable, and I agree. Her death was a tragedy, and you did everything you could to find her."

Her lips lifted briefly as she looked up him. "I know that. This case just has me confounded, and I don't like it one bit." She focused her gaze on Alnwick House. "What do you suppose is going on in there?"

Hadrian noted the drawing room on the first floor was brightly illuminated. "No idea, but if the ransom delivery is the same as it was for Miss Chadwick, we've some time to wait until they leave."

"I can't imagine the kidnapper would use the same ransom delivery location," Tilda said. "In fact, he may have changed the time as well." She gripped Hadrian's arm more tightly, prompting him to look at her. "What if he arranged the ransom to be delivered earlier? What if we've missed his departure?"

Hadrian moved to stand in front of her. There was true panic in her eyes. He caressed her cheek. "Don't cause yourself upset. We're here now, and we'll be vigilant."

She stepped back and peered around him. "I can't if you stand in front of me." She brushed her hands down her skirt from her waist. "I ought to have considered that the kidnapper might have done things differently with Lady Priscilla to avoid detection. The observation of the duke's house should have started immediately following Teague's visit earlier."

Hadrian heard the agony in her tone. "Tilda, please don't torture yourself like this."

The sound of wheels on the granite street drew them to look toward Park Street as a cab turned onto Upper Brook Street.

"That's not the cab Teague stationed, is it?" Hadrian asked.

"I don't think so." Tilda exhaled, as if she'd held her breath.

The cab stopped in front of Alnwick House, and Hadrian held *his* breath. Tilda grasped his hand.

They watched as a woman stepped out of the hack. She stood in the pool of light cast by a nearby gas lamp. Hadrian made out medium-dark hair that hung down her back, and she wore a dark cloak. She tipped her head up and seemed to be looking toward the drawing room. In that moment, Hadrian was able to make out her features.

Tilda started across the street, pulling Hadrian with her. *"That's Lady Priscilla."*

The cab started moving forward as they reached the other side of the street. Lady Priscilla had already walked to the front door. Tilda saw Teague leap toward the hack, waving his hands. The vehicle stopped, and Tilda focused her attention on Lady Priscilla.

She'd just stepped into the house. Tilda took her hand from Hadrian's and dashed up the steps, but Hadrian moved faster and placed his palm against the door to keep it open.

The butler appeared, holding the door from the other side. He frowned upon seeing Hadrian.

"You must allow us inside," Hadrian commanded, pushing at the door and forcing the butler to step back.

Hadrian inserted himself into the house and took control of the door from the butler so Tilda could walk inside. Whilst Hadrian stared down the butler, Lady Priscilla moved out of the entrance hall. Tilda hurried after her.

"You can't come into the house!" the butler cried.

"We're already here," Hadrian said firmly. "We must speak with Lady Priscilla. Detective Inspector Teague will be here presently."

Tilda registered Hadrian's reply as she caught up to Lady Priscilla at the base of the stairs. The poor young woman looked dazed. Her auburn hair hung lank about her shoulders, and her green-blue eyes were wide with a mix of fear and confusion. Her porcelain skin was nearly translucent, appearing as if it might shatter like a fine teacup dropped upon a marble floor. The dark gray cloak covered a nightgown, and she wore black boots that buttoned up the sides.

"It's all right," Tilda said softly. "I'm Miss Wren. I'm so glad you've been returned. How did you find your way home?"

"I woke up with—" She shook her head. "I want to see my mother."

"Of course." Tilda didn't want to upset the young woman. She'd already survived a terrible ordeal. "May I escort you upstairs to find her?"

The butler had come into the staircase hall, as had Hadrian, and strode to where they stood. "You cannot just barge into this house." The butler glowered at them.

"Please fetch Lady Priscilla's father," Tilda said evenly. "His Grace will want to know she's returned. I'm going to help Lady Priscilla up to her chamber. She would like to see her mother."

Sputtering, the butler looked as if he wanted to rail at Tilda. Instead, he turned on his heel and hurried away.

Hadrian moved to join them as Tilda put her arm around Lady Priscilla. "I'll stay down here and let Teague in after he's done speaking with the driver of the cab," he whispered.

Tilda nodded at him, then aided Lady Priscilla as they ascended. "How did you pay for the cab?" Perhaps a simple question of what had happened most recently might be easier for the young woman to answer.

"I awakened earlier this evening in the yard of a coaching inn with a coin in my hand." She sent Tilda a bewildered look. "I used that."

"How fortuitous." Tilda gave her an encouraging smile. "Were you alone in the yard?"

Lady Priscilla nodded. "There were others about, but I didn't know anyone. I don't know how I came to be there. I've been locked in a cupboard since I was taken." She began to shake.

As they reached the top of the stairs, the duke's thundering voice carried up to them from the hall below. "Priscilla!"

The young woman turned. Tilda feared she would lose her balance, for she was rather unsteady. Keeping a grip on Lady Priscilla, Tilda ensured she was safe and didn't tumble down the stairs.

Her father raced up and swept the young woman into his

arms. "My poor girl." He didn't even look at Tilda as he carried her up another flight of stairs.

"I want to see Mama," Lady Priscilla said, sounding like a small child.

"And you shall," the duke said kindly. As difficult as he'd been, Tilda knew he was driven by fear. She was exceptionally glad his daughter had been delivered safely. Indeed, Tilda felt slightly unsteady herself. She'd been so worried this wouldn't happen and now that it had, relief ran through her like a torrent.

Tilda followed them to Lady Priscilla's chamber and stood just inside the door. A moment later, Hadrian and Teague joined her, so she had to move farther into the room.

"Were you able to speak to the driver?" Tilda whispered as the duke set his daughter down on her bed.

"Yes," Teague replied in an equally soft tone. "He picked Lady Priscilla up at The Galloping Goat, a coaching house off the Strand. She approached him looking just as she does now: confused and terrified, wearing a cloak over her nightgown, her hair in disarray. He could tell she was Quality and was glad to help her."

"I don't suppose there was anyone with her?" Tilda asked even though Lady Priscilla had said she was alone and didn't know anyone.

Teague frowned and shook his head.

The duke turned and came toward them, his expression taut. "You must leave at once."

"Please, Your Grace, it's imperative we speak with your daughter," Teague said earnestly. "I understand you're worried about her welfare. We are too. However, time is of the essence if we're to ensure Spring-heeled Jack doesn't claim another victim."

"We're relieved Priscilla has been returned," Alnwick said, his voice cracking. "I paid the ransom. I followed the instructions. We just want to put this behind us."

"What if this happens to someone else?" Teague asked. "What

of that young woman's family? Are we to let this villain continue to abduct young women and demand a ransom?"

Alnwick clenched his jaw. "Why must it be now? Can't you come back tomorrow? Priscilla needs a bath and to rest."

*And her mother,* Tilda thought. "Because things are fresh in her mind. She may forget something between now and tomorrow. Please, Your Grace, we implore you. Put yourself in the place of the next victim's father."

"Papa, I don't want anyone to suffer what I did," Lady Priscilla said from the bed, her voice small but stronger than it had been a few moments ago.

The duke hesitated, and Hadrian stepped forward, his expression full of sympathy and kindness. "You know me, and you can trust Miss Wren and Detective Inspector Teague. We won't tax Lady Priscilla."

"Very well." The creases in the duke's brow deepened as he returned to the bed and spoke softly to his daughter. Tilda could not hear what he said.

"My girl!" A woman raced into the bedchamber, passing Tilda, Hadrian, and Teague. She wore a dressing gown and a cap on her head. A sob escaped her when she reached the bedside, and the duke stepped back as she cast herself over Lady Priscilla.

The duke walked toward them, his expression weary. "You will allow them a few minutes."

"Of course," Tilda said deferentially.

As Lady Priscilla and her mother cried together, Tilda had a horrible feeling in the pit of her stomach. Why had this kidnapping played out differently than Miss Chadwick's? Was it really because the duke had followed the directions he'd received, and the police had not been involved with the ransom delivery?

What if the duke had shared that he'd received a second note, and allowed them to execute a plan to capture Spring-heeled Jack instead of leaving a ransom, as they'd tried to do with Chadwick? Would Lady Priscilla have been killed too?

Tilda struggled to draw a deep breath.

After several minutes, the duchess stood and faced Tilda. "You may speak with my daughter for as long as I allow, and not a moment more."

"Thank you, Your Grace." Tilda approached the bedside as Lady Priscilla moved to perch on the edge of the mattress.

The duchess sat beside her and put her arm around her daughter. Tilda wondered if the woman would ever let her go again and wouldn't blame her if she didn't.

Tilda started with a kind smile. "Thank you for speaking with us, Lady Priscilla. I won't take too much of your time. You are exceedingly brave and strong."

Lady Priscilla's eyes were red from crying, but she was still rather pale. Tilda truly hated having to interview her now, but it was necessary.

"Are you wearing the clothes you were taken in?" Tilda asked.

"The nightgown is mine," she replied softly. "I don't know where the cloak or the boots came from. It's strange, but these boots remind me of a pair that belong to a friend of mine."

Tilda tensed upon hearing that and stored the information away for later. She looked to the duchess. "I'm sure Detective Inspector Teague would like to have these garments and the boots as evidence. They will help us catch the man who did this. Will you set them aside for him?"

The duchess nodded. Tilda glanced toward Teague who sent her a look of appreciation.

Tilda found it odd that Miss Chadwick had been found in a simple day dress, which was not the garment she'd been taken in, whereas Lady Priscilla still wore her nightgown. And someone else's boots whilst Miss Chadwick's feet had been bare.

Fixing her gaze on Lady Priscilla once more, Tilda gently asked, "Can you tell us what happened when you were taken from your chamber?"

"I don't remember much, only that I was awakened when

someone grabbed my arm. All I saw was a dark figure standing over me, then a flash of blue before he put a cloth over my mouth and nose. I smelled something sweet, almost unbearably so, and the next thing I knew, I woke up on a pallet in a small, window-less room. It was more a cupboard, really."

Tilda was certain the kidnapper had used chloroform to render Lady Priscilla unconscious. "Do you have any idea how long you were asleep?"

Lady Priscilla shook her head. "When I awoke, I called for help. The door opened the barest amount, just wide enough so someone could push in a candle and a plate of bread and cheese. There was also hot milk with sugar."

The duchess gasped. "Your favorite. How did he know that?"

"I don't know, Mama. He didn't ever speak to me. But he gave me hot milk with sugar whenever I woke up. It was a small comfort." She leaned her head on the duchess's shoulder.

It sounded as if Lady Priscilla had slept a great deal. Tilda suspected the sugar in the milk may have been used to mask laudanum, which, if dosed properly, would have kept her uncon-scious during her captivity. "What happened after you ate?"

"I fell asleep again. I slept most of the time."

"You said the kidnapper never spoke to you. Did you ever see them?"

"No."

That was unfortunate, but smart of the kidnapper. He'd been very thorough.

"Did you ever hear anyone talking?" Tilda asked.

"No."

"Did you ever see Miss Delia Chadwick?" Teague asked, inter-rupting Tilda's questioning.

Lady Priscilla lifted her head and blinked at Teague who'd stepped closer to the bed. "No, why would I have seen Delia? It's funny you would mention her, because I had a dream that I heard her scream. But I dreamt many strange things whilst I was in that cupboard. It was horrible. Also, these boots remind me of a pair Delia had." She lifted her feet briefly to display them.

"Do you recall when you dreamed of Miss Chadwick's scream?" Tilda asked. "Was it soon after you were kidnapped?"

"I think so—the first day anyway."

Tilda exchanged looks with both Hadrian and Teague. She wondered if Lady Priscilla had *actually* heard Delia scream. She turned her attention back to Lady Priscilla. "Have you any idea who abducted you?"

"Not at all. I can't imagine who would do this to me." Tears welled in Lady Priscilla's crystal-blue eyes.

"We're almost finished," Tilda said. "Can you think of anything about your captor—the way they smelled, the size of them, anything at all?"

"I smelled tobacco, but it wasn't smoke." Lady Priscilla wrinkled her nose. "I heard him mutter something once. But it may have been a dream. I don't know."

Tilda held her breath, eager for the slightest clue, though the tobacco scent was a helpful confirmation of Hadrian's visions. They could now investigate that with Teague without having to come up with a reason why. "What did he say?"

"Something about 'just one more.' I thought maybe they were eating biscuits." She looked at her mother with a faint smile. "Like Cook's lemon ones. When I was a child, I always asked if I could have just one more."

Her mother smiled and stroked her daughter's smudged cheek. "You may have all the lemon biscuits in the world, my dear. We'll have Cook make some immediately." She looked at Tilda. "Is there anything else?"

Tilda glanced at Teague who gave his head a slight shake. She gave the duchess and Lady Priscilla a grateful smile. "No. We just need the clothing and boots. Do you mind if we wait downstairs for them?" Tilda desperately wanted Hadrian to touch the items, especially the boots. She also wanted to determine if a pair of Miss Chadwick's boots—or any other items—had gone missing.

"I'll send a maid down with them shortly," the duchess replied.

"Thank you very much for allowing us to speak with your daughter," Tilda said warmly. "And thank you, Lady Priscilla. Will you please send word to Scotland Yard, or to me if you'd prefer, if you remember anything else?"

"I will," Lady Priscilla said.

Tilda removed one of her cards from her reticule and set it on the table next to Lady Priscilla's bed. "This is how you may reach me." She smiled at Lady Priscilla before turning to rejoin Hadrian and Teague, who'd also retreated toward the doorway. The duke stood at the foot of the bed.

"Come, let's get you in the bath now," the duchess said to her daughter. "You weren't hurt, were you?"

"Just my hands, Mama. The few times I was awake, I pounded on the door and asked where I was and why I was there, but nobody ever answered." She turned her wide eyes to her father. "Why would someone do this to me? Just for money?"

"My dearest, some people are not fit to walk this earth," the duke growled. He turned and moved closer to Tilda, Hadrian, and Teague, his gaze darting toward the door in a silent but clear communication that they ought to leave.

Teague addressed the duke, speaking softly. "May I return in the morning to ask a few more questions and see how Lady Priscilla is doing?"

The duke did not appear pleased. "If you must."

"Thank you," Teague said. "One last thing, you *did* receive a ransom note, and you lied about it?"

"Of course I did." The duke's eyes dared any of them to find fault with that. "I followed Spring-heeled Jack's instructions to the letter." He lowered his voice to barely above a whisper. "Seeing as how Priscilla came home to us, unlike Delia Chadwick, it's a damn good thing I did."

Teague pressed his lips together, then turned and left the bedchamber. Tilda and Hadrian followed him. They didn't speak until they were downstairs in the entrance hall.

"I suppose we'll wait here for the garments," Teague said.

"Actually, why doesn't Ravenhurst wait in the staircase hall? He seems to offend the duke and his household the least."

Teague nodded. "Excellent observation."

Hadrian met Tilda's gaze, silently communicating that he understood her intent for him to see if the garments and boots gave him any memories. "What did you think of Lady Priscilla's comments regarding Delia Chadwick?" he asked.

"I wonder if she may have actually heard Miss Chadwick scream," Tilda said. "The timing could match since Lady Priscilla was taken early on Monday, and Miss Chadwick was killed that same morning."

"That would mean they were kidnapped by the same person, which I think we all agree on." Teague frowned contemplatively. "Miss Chadwick was suffocated. I'm trying to think what would have prompted her to scream preceding that manner of death. Did she anticipate what was coming?"

Tilda voiced her other thought. "I'm also curious about the boots. We must determine if they are missing from Miss Chadwick's things and ask if anything else is absent."

"I'll speak with Chadwick," Teague said. He frowned and rubbed his fingertips briefly against his forehead. "I'm certain he'll be shocked to learn Lady Priscilla is home."

"If you'd like me to accompany you to call on him, I'd be glad to," Hadrian said before moving back into the staircase hall.

"What about the tobacco smell?" Teague asked. "That could be a clue."

"Perhaps the garments have a scent," Tilda suggested. She dearly hoped Hadrian would be able to see something when he touched them.

Cocking her head, she looked past Teague into the staircase

hall and saw a maid deliver the items into Hadrian's arms. The boots sat atop the nightgown which was folded on the cloak. Hadrian's hands were on the cloak as the maid went back up the stairs. His eyes became unfocused, and it seemed to Tilda that he was experiencing a memory.

"I don't know how we narrow down a tobacco scent to find where a kidnapping victim was held," Teague mused. "But it's something at least."

"I'm curious as to why Miss Chadwick was found wearing a day gown instead of the night clothes she was taken in," Tilda said.

"It seems these two victims were treated very differently." Teague's eyes narrowed with contemplation. "It's bloody curious."

Hadrian came back to the entrance hall. The lines between his eyebrows told Tilda he had a headache. "The garments smell like tobacco," he said as he handed everything to Teague.

Teague's nostrils flared. "Vincent Chadwick was lodging near a tobacconist in Richmond according to his letters to Lady Priscilla. Though after what you told me earlier, what would be his motive to kidnap Lady Priscilla and keep her locked in a cupboard? It's one thing to think they eloped, but that isn't what happened."

Tilda firmly agreed. "No, and there's no motive for him to kill his sister, who was, in fact, aiding Chadwick's secret romance with Lady Priscilla."

"I wanted to question her about their relationship," Teague said. "But not in front of her parents. I hope I can speak with her alone tomorrow."

"I'll come with you, if you think it may help," Tilda said.

Teague nodded. "Yes, thank you."

"May we accompany you to Scotland Yard now to assess the clothing and boots?" Tilda asked.

"Certainly. I need to relieve Wycombe and the constables

from their positions. Meet me in my office." Teague gave Tilda a wry look. "I'd say you can wait until morning, but something tells me you won't."

She smiled. "Absolutely not."

Hadrian held up his hand. "Before you go, what did you think of what Lady Priscilla heard, 'just one more?' Do you think that was a dream?"

"I don't know, particularly since it appears she was drugged, but I'm concerned it means there'll be one more kidnapping." Teague's gaze moved to Tilda. "That's what you're thinking, isn't it?"

"Yes, and we must be ready for that to happen tomorrow." Tilda felt the weight of another potential kidnapping of a poor young woman.

"I think we ought to publish a notice in the paper warning people to be on guard," Teague said. "But then again, I'm loathe to cause another Spring-heeled Jack hysteria."

"Judging from the crowd that gathered at Delia Chadwick's inquest, it may be too late for that," Hadrian noted.

"You're likely right." Teague's mouth dipped into a grim frown.

"I believe Mr. Clement often works late at the *Daily News*," Tilda said. "If we go there now, we may be able to ensure the notice is published in tomorrow morning's edition."

"That would be best." Teague gestured with the items he held. "Do I need to accompany you, or can I meet you at Scotland Yard? I'd like to apprise Wycombe of what occurred."

"We can manage it," Tilda said, glancing at Hadrian who gave her a slight nod.

They parted ways, and Hadrian escorted Tilda to the coach where Leach was waiting for them.

"Is Lady Priscilla all right?" the coachman asked.

"She seems to be," Hadrian replied. "It's a wonder she was returned when Miss Chadwick was not. We must go to the *Daily*

*News* and ask that a notice be published, warning people to beware of Spring-heeled Jack, as he may attempt to kidnap another young woman. After that, we'll continue to Scotland Yard."

Leach opened the door of the coach. "Busy night." He helped Tilda inside.

Hadrian followed, and Tilda barely waited for the door to close before turning to face him. "What did you see?" Her pulse thundered with anticipation.

Hadrian rubbed his temple. "Lavender first please, if I may."

"Sorry." Tilda should have offered that immediately. Leaning forward, she fetched the lavender from the compartment beneath the other seat, then held it out to hm.

"I like it better when you smooth it on," he said with a hopeful smile.

That was the least she could do after callously asking about his visions before ascertaining his well-being. She removed the stopper and gently applied the oil to his temples. "That must have been quite a vision. I'm sorry I neglected to ask about you first."

"I understand. You're eager to know what I saw." His brow furrowed. "When I touched the boots, I experienced a memory of removing them from someone's feet."

"Do you know who either of them were—the person having the memory or the person wearing the boots?"

"Unfortunately, no, but I recognized the hem of the gown. I'm almost positive it was the one Miss Chadwick was found wearing."

Tilda sucked in a breath. "So those *were* her boots."

"I believe so, but Teague should still confirm that with the Chadwicks. Actually, he must, since it's not as if I can share what I just saw." Hadrian's eyes narrowed slightly. "The cloak was perhaps more interesting. I had a memory of taking it from a peg on a wall where many other garments hung. I smelled tallow, but not like a candle. It was more like…greasepaint. I recall the smell from Mrs. Longbotham's dressing chamber at the Hen and Chicken." He referred to a gentleman who preferred to garb himself as a woman and went by the name of Mrs. Longbotham. They had provided assistance to Tilda and Hadrian with disguises on more than one occasion.

Tilda slumped against the squab. "You could be describing Mrs. Longbotham's dressing room—or anyone else's."

"So, that memory isn't helpful at all?" Hadrian's expression dampened.

"Not yet, but I hope it will be," she said earnestly. "You experienced *two* memories. I'm so sorry I didn't take care of you before jumping into the case." She shook her head with regret.

He angled toward her. "Do *not* worry yourself. I'm fine."

She slanted her gaze toward him. "You're certain?"

"Quite." His brows drew together. "Why don't you look relieved?"

"This case is most aggravating. We *must* make progress. If we don't, another young woman could go missing."

"I know." Hadrian caressed her cheek. "You'll puzzle it out. You're the most brilliant investigator I know."

Tilda worked to keep her frustration and fear at bay. "Then why don't I feel like it?"

# CHAPTER 12

Hadrian held the door open to the offices of the *Daily News* for Tilda, then followed her into the compact entrance hall. An elderly porter, whom Hadrian estimated to be at least seventy, rose from behind the small desk situated between the base of a staircase and a closed door that, judging from the noise behind it, led to the printing room.

"Evening, how may I help you?" His voice was surprisingly strong and loud, but then he had to compete with the sound of the presses.

"We're here to see Mr. Ezra Clement," Hadrian replied.

"Rather late, isn't it?" the porter noted, though he didn't wait for a response before moving to the speaking tube mounted on the wall behind his desk. "Mr. Clement, you have visitors."

The porter sat back down, and a few moments later, Clement walked down the stairs. His eyes flashed with surprise as he saw them. "Ravenhurst, Miss Wren, this is unexpected. Please, come upstairs." He turned and led them back the way he'd come.

They stepped into the long editorial room where several desks were still occupied by journalists writing by gaslight. A few stood together at one desk talking animatedly. This was Hadrian and Tilda's first time here. They'd previously met with Clement at his favorite coffee shop on Fleet Street.

Clement stopped at a desk next to the wall where a gas bracket illuminated his working space. It appeared as though he'd been in the middle of writing something when they'd arrived. He moved to drag a chair toward his desk, but Tilda held up her hand. "We aren't staying long."

Releasing the chair, Clement faced them. "What's brought you here so late?"

"There has been a second kidnapping," Tilda replied without preamble. Clement gasped as she went on. "The victim has been returned to her home this evening, so all is well. Except her father is out a large sum."

"Can you start at the beginning?" Clement reached for a notebook on the corner of his desk.

"We're not providing a statement or information to you about the kidnapping," Tilda said. "We've come to ask you to place a short paragraph warning that the kidnapper may strike again."

Clement blinked, his attention riveted. "Is that expected?"

"It must be," Tilda replied simply, and Hadrian concluded she wasn't going to disclose the reason behind their concern—what Lady Priscilla had overheard during captivity about there being "just one more."

"I can only provide about ten or twelve lines, but that should suffice." Clement sat at his desk and plucked a new piece of parchment from a pile. He poised his quill above the paper. "Tell me what you'd like it to say."

Tilda spoke softly but clearly. "The police caution the public about the potential for another kidnapping by someone purporting to be Spring-heeled Jack. A second young lady was abducted and has been returned after the ransom was paid. If you learn of a young lady who has gone missing, please contact the Metropolitan Police immediately."

Clement looked up at her. "This will likely lead to many

reports of missing young women, none of whom have been kidnapped."

"That's better than if another woman is kidnapped and nothing is said at all," Tilda said.

Nodding, Clement finished writing. "This is coming from Scotland Yard?" He raised his gaze once more. "I ask because neither of you is from the Met, and I can't tell the night editor that I've learned this information from Miss Wren." He sent Tilda an apologetic look. "I'm afraid your credibility is rather strained."

The comment pricked Hadrian's ire. He narrowed his eyes at Clement. "Inform the editor that the Earl of Ravenhurst is delivering this message on behalf of Detective Inspector Teague from the Detective Branch who asked us to come here."

Clement cleared his throat. "Yes, of course." He looked at Tilda. "I'm sorry for your situation. In fact, I was just working on the article from our conversation the other day."

"You were supposed to have published that already," Hadrian said coldly.

"I haven't been given the space yet." Clement's face flushed slightly.

Tilda's gaze turned a bit haughty, which Hadrian found oddly alluring. "I don't wish to be mentioned or quoted in this article that will be published in the morning, nor in anything you write about this second abduction. Do you agree?"

"Absolutely," Clement said. "It's frustrating to me that people don't remember how instrumental you were in the capture of the Levitation Killers. I'm reminding them of that fact in this article that I'm writing about you."

Tilda didn't say anything, and Hadrian couldn't discern how she felt about that.

"Are you going to tell me the identity of the second kidnapping victim or any other details?" Clement asked hopefully.

"It was Lady Priscilla, the Duke of Alnwick's daughter."

Clement's eyes rounded. "And was it Spring-heeled Jack?"

"The ransom note they received when she was taken was exactly the same as the one left for Miss Chadwick," Tilda replied.

"How has this been kept quiet?" Clement asked.

"The duke wished to follow the instructions of the kidnapper," Hadrian said.

"That seemed to have worked out for him, since his daughter was returned." Clement sent a regretful glance toward Tilda. "I don't mean anything by that."

Hadrian again tried to gauge her reaction. Her face was impassive, but he had to think the comment rankled her.

"I'm sure you could call at Alnwick House tomorrow if you wish to try to obtain an interview," Tilda said. "I only ask you don't mention me or Ravenhurst. Just say you heard a rumor. In fact, a rumor is how we learned of the kidnapping, but you can't print that either."

"Thank you." Clement inclined his head. "Truly. I appreciate you bringing this to me. You could have sought any other journalist."

Tilda inclined her head. "Yes, but I know you, and I was fairly certain you'd be here. Time is of the essence."

"So, this was more of a convenience?" Clement asked wryly.

Tilda did not respond to his question. "You're certain this will be published tomorrow morning?"

"I'll do my best," Clement said.

"It must be in tomorrow morning's edition," Hadrian insisted. "Where is the night editor? I will demand it."

"I'll fetch him." Clement rose and hurried into an office that likely overlooked Bouverie Street.

Hadrian glowered after Clement. "I can't help thinking no one would question your character or credibility if you were my countess."

Tilda turned toward him, her cheeks flushing. "I disagree. Even if I was your countess, I would always be from a different class and the daughter of a policeman. No one is ever going to forget that, no matter what I become." She turned her gaze from his. "It's too soon to speak of such things. In fact, I don't want to speak of it at all. We must focus on the case."

Was her agitation because he'd mentioned marriage, or because of how this case had affected her reputation?

Clement returned with the night editor, a long-nosed man of about fifty with curly gray hair and spectacles. Tilda stood mute, her hands clasped in front of her, a blank expression on her face as the editor questioned Hadrian about the police warning.

"As I told Clement, this comes from Detective Inspector Teague, from the Detective Branch of the Metropolitan Police," Hadrian explained. "He would have come himself, but he is busy working on this case, which is, I'm sure you understand, of urgent importance. We're all committed to ensuring a third victim isn't claimed."

"Of course," the night editor replied. "I'll make sure it's in tomorrow morning's edition. Thank you for bringing this to us." He glanced at Tilda but didn't say anything.

Hadrian escorted her from the building and back to the coach, where they were quickly on their way to Scotland Yard.

"I didn't mean to upset you," he said.

"You didn't." She kept her gaze trained on the opposite side of the coach, and her tone was crisp.

"You seem bothered."

"I am, but only because we need to stop Spring-heeled Jack before he kidnaps another young woman."

Hadrian hoped that was all that was troubling her. "I should think he would have enough money to make his escape, and if he was smart, he would."

"I'm not sure we're dealing with a particularly smart person. Rather, I'm concerned he may be unhinged. I can't say for certain he'll strike again, but we must be prepared."

She was right. They needed to focus entirely on this right

now. It seemed easier for her to do that, however, whilst he kept thinking of their courtship and future. Perhaps that was something he should consider.

~

When Hadrian and Tilda arrived at Teague's office, they found a table had been moved into the center of the room. A few additional lanterns had also been added to provide more illumination.

"There you are," Teague said as they walked in.

Tilda took in the table and smiled. "You started without us."

"Not yet," Teague assured her. "I just finished laying the evidence out and decided we needed one more lantern. Wycombe's gone to fetch it. How did it go at the *Daily News?*"

"Fine." Tilda set her reticule on a chair, then removed her hat and gloves, which she placed next to it.

Teague arched a brow and looked to Hadrian in curiosity.

"We spoke with the night editor," Hadrian explained. "The warning will appear in tomorrow morning's edition."

"Excellent." Teague turned toward the table, and Hadrian removed his gloves, then tucked them into his coat pocket.

The nightgown and cloak were spread across the table, and the boots sat on one end, toe to heel.

"I've already recorded the evidence, and I've started a report." Teague inclined his head toward his desk.

Tilda gestured to the bodice. "There's a stain on the nightgown here, a brown ring." She went to her reticle and removed a magnifying glass, which she used to closely inspect the garment.

"How have I never known you carried that?" Hadrian asked in bemusement.

Tilda twitched her shoulder. "I haven't had cause to use it in any of our other investigations." After a moment's scrutiny, she straightened. "I don't think this is just the sugared milk she was drinking. This brown ring seems to indicate something else."

"I suspect she was being drugged with laudanum," Teague said. "May I?" He held his hand out, and she gave him the glass. He bent over the table and studied the nightgown. "This looks like a laudanum stain to me."

"What's that on the neckline?" Tilda asked. She pointed to the fine lace edge at the top of Lady Priscilla's gown. "Is that singed?"

Teague moved the glass to examine the lace. "It does appear to be burned." He returned the glass to her, and Tilda bent to survey it.

"Lady Priscilla said her kidnapper breathed blue flame before he covered her mouth with what I suspect was chloroform," Tilda said. "I wonder if the flame singed her nightgown."

Hadrian wanted to look but preferred to do so when attention would not be directly on him.

Tilda handed him the glass and gave him a meaningful look as she moved toward the cloak with Inspector Teague. "We need Inspector Lea's notes from the Spring-heeled Jack attacks thirty years ago. Did the clerk find them?"

"Honestly, I've been distracted with Miss Chadwick's murder and then Lady Priscilla's kidnapping. I'll make sure we have them tomorrow." Teague looked toward the doorway. "Ah, here's Wycombe."

The sergeant set the lamp on the table between the nightgown and boots. As Teague explained what they'd observed with the nightgown, Hadrian took the opportunity to examine the stain on the bodice. As he held the glass close to the garment, he allowed his fingers to graze the fabric.

He suddenly found himself in a dark space. There was just a single taper for light, but it was enough to register he was in some kind of cupboard. He felt certain he was seeing Lady Priscilla's memory.

She lifted a cup and drank. Hadrian tasted sugared milk and

perhaps something else. Was that the laudanum? He'd never tasted anything in a memory before, but then he'd never put anything in his mouth during one either.

A door slammed in the vision, and the person—presumably Lady Priscilla—holding the cup jolted, splashing the drink onto her chest. He looked down and saw where the stain now was on the bodice of Lady Priscilla's gown. She brushed at it with her fingers, and Hadrian noted their distinct femininity.

The memory faded, and he straightened, his head pounding. He handed the magnifying glass to Wycombe so the sergeant could take his turn examining the garment.

Hadrian edged toward the cloak and surreptitiously placed his hand on the dark gray wool. He'd already touched the garment at Alnwick House, but he wouldn't pass up the opportunity to do it again. He was desperate for Tilda to feel as though she was making progress with this case.

He pivoted away from the others as Miss Chadwick's face appeared in his mind. A masculine hand stroked her cheek. Hadrian felt an overwhelming sense of love. *Love?* Was this not the kidnapper? He tried to focus on the hand to see if it was the same as the one he'd seen before, but the vision faded, only to be replaced by another.

Miss Chadwick was before him again. However, this time she lay on a wooden floor. Her face was pale, her eyes open and unseeing. Her lips were parted, and she was deathly still. Blood pooled along the scratches that marred her chest. He had the sense they'd just been made, but by whom? He wanted to look around, only the person could not look away from Miss Chadwick. Hadrian suffered a wave of debilitating horror and grief, as if the terrible emotions were his own.

Pain exploded from his temple to his nape. The agony was all-encompassing in a way it had never been before. Hadrian suddenly felt weak, and the room tilted sideways. Which room? The one in the memory or Teague's office? He couldn't tell. The memory and his present blurred together until his vision narrowed.

Feeling as though he might fall, Hadrian grasped the edge of the table. His sight disappeared completely, and he was engulfed in blackness.

The pain in his head intensified. He hit the floor.

Then everything was gone.

# CHAPTER 13

*W*hilst Hadrian had conducted his mental inquiries with the evidence, Tilda kept one eye on him as she engaged Teague and Wycombe in conversation to keep them distracted. She watched as Hadrian moved from the nightgown to the cloak and noted his furrowed brow and unfocused gaze. He was clearly lost in a memory that was not his own. After several moments, he flinched. Deep lines creased his face just before he went pale. He grabbed at the table but fell to the floor.

Tilda gasped as she dashed to kneel beside him. His eyes were closed, and his breathing was fast.

"Good heavens, what happened?" Teague hurried to join her. He crouched down on Hadrian's other side. Wycombe came to stand over them.

"Fetch some cold water," Teague said to the sergeant. "And smelling salts. We should have some downstairs."

Tilda cupped Hadrian's cheek and stroked her thumb along his cheekbone. "Hadrian," she whispered. "Are you all right? Can you hear me?"

His lids fluttered open. His eyes were dazed. He appeared confused, his brow furrowing, but then he sucked in a breath and clenched his jaw. Tilda could see he was in terrible pain. She moved her hand to his forehead and gently massaged him. "Let's get you home."

"Do you know what's wrong?" Teague asked.

Tilda looked over at him. "Sometimes he experiences headaches that are quite painful." That wasn't a lie. But she certainly couldn't tell him the reason behind them. "He needs rest and some lavender."

Teague frowned. "I don't believe we have any of that."

"There's some in my reticule, if you wouldn't mind handing it to me."

Teague quickly stood and fetched her reticule. "I don't want to look through your private things," he said awkwardly as he handed it to her.

"That's quite all right." Tilda gave him a reassuring smile. She took her hand from Hadrian as she rummaged in her reticule to find the vial of lavender.

Hadrian watched her, his expression strained. She poured a generous amount of lavender onto her right fingers and massaged it as softly as she could into his brow and temples. Hadrian closed his eyes and finally began to breathe more easily.

After a few moments, Wycombe returned with a pitcher of water and a cup. "Couldn't find the smelling salts, unfortunately."

"We don't need them," Teague replied. "Pour some water, if you would."

Teague knelt on Hadrian's other side. "Are you ready to sit up?" he asked Hadrian.

"I suppose I must." But Hadrian did not immediately open his eyes.

Tilda replaced the vial of lavender into her reticule. She and Teague clasped Hadrian's arms which finally prompted him to open his eyes. They supported his back as they pulled him to sit up. He grimaced and groaned faintly.

"That must be a horrible headache." Teague's brows gathered with concern.

"I explained to him that you suffer these from time to time," Tilda said, meeting Hadrian's gaze intently.

"Yes," Hadrian said in agreement. "I'm not sure what triggers them, but the lavender helps."

"Is it a migraine?" Wycombe asked after he'd poured the glass of water. "My mother suffers those from time to time. They can be quite enervating." He looked at Hadrian with sympathy as he held out the glass.

Tilda took it from the sergeant and held it up to Hadrian's lips. "Drink some water, then I need to see you home."

Hadrian glanced toward the table. "We don't need to leave right away. You can't be done with your investigation of Lady Priscilla's things."

"I am for now. You need to go home, and I'm making sure you get there." She used a firm tone, for she was not going to brook an argument from him.

He drank quite a bit of water, then closed his eyes briefly again as Tilda handed the almost empty glass back to Wycombe. She watched him for a long moment before asking if he was ready to rise. He didn't really look as though he could. "Can you stand?"

He opened his eyes and fixed on her. The lines carved along his brow revealed his pain. "I think so."

Wycombe came forward. "Allow me."

Tilda stood and moved to the side whilst Teague and Wycombe hoisted Hadrian to his feet.

"I can walk to the coach alone," Hadrian insisted.

"Absolutely not," Tilda said. "Please let Teague and Wycombe help you."

"I'm fine." Hadrian tried to take a step toward the door and had to reach for the table to keep his balance. Teague caught him, and Hadrian summoned a weak smile. "On second thought, I will gladly accept the assistance."

"Good." Tilda was glad her voice was steady for she was very worried. Retrieving the magnifying glass from the table, she dropped it into her reticule. She quickly grabbed her gloves and hat. "I'm going to rush ahead to prepare Leach to assist us."

Hastening from the office, Tilda donned her accessories as she hurried down the stairs. She dashed outside, and Leach immediately jumped to the pavement from his seat on the coach.

Tilda held up her hand. "Don't be alarmed, but his lordship collapsed in Detective Inspector Teague's office. He has a monstrous headache, and we need to take him home directly."

Leach's eyes widened briefly, and he nodded. "Of course."

Teague and Wycombe departed the station with Hadrian between them and walked him to the coach. Hadrian grasped the side of the doorway into the vehicle with his left hand. Leach took his right and the coachman used his other hand to boost him inside.

"Will he be all right by tomorrow?" Teague asked. "We'd planned for him to join me when I question Mr. Chadwick."

Tilda wasn't going to promise anything. "That depends on how he's feeling. We'll send a message in the morning if he's not able to accompany you. Why don't you and I plan to meet at Alnwick House first," she suggested. "That will give Hadrian more time to recover."

Teague nodded. "I can pick you up just before eleven. I don't want to arrive too early, since I'm sure Lady Priscilla is recovering from her ordeal. That also gives me time to obtain Inspector Lea's records from K Division."

"Excellent," Tilda said, eager to review them too. "I'll see you then."

Leach helped her into the coach, and she settled herself on the forward-facing seat. Hadrian was in the corner, his head resting against the side of the coach and his eyes closed.

"We can drop you off at home first," he said without opening his eyes.

"Absolutely not," she repeated. "Leach is taking us to Ravenhurst House." She moved closer to him as the coach moved at a faster than usual pace. "What happened? Why did you swoon?"

"I saw a series of visions. The first was with the nightgown. I can confirm Lady Priscilla spilled her cup of milk on the bodice of the garment. Someone slammed a door and it startled her, which made her splash the contents of the cup. Strangely, I tasted the sugared milk, and there was definitely something else in the drink, probably laudanum." His eyes remained closed as he relayed this information.

"That's helpful to have our theory confirmed. What happened next?"

"That was all I saw from the nightgown, then I moved to the cloak. I saw Miss Chadwick. She was smiling and seemed not only to know the person whose memory I was seeing but was glad to see them."

Tilda found that reaction to be odd. Why would Miss Chadwick smile at her kidnapper? Unless the cloak held someone else's memories. "Any idea whose memory it was?"

"No, but it was a man, based on the hand. He caressed Miss Chadwick's cheek, and I felt an overwhelming sense of love and affection for Miss Chadwick."

"Love?" Tilda asked sharply. "I think we need to find out who that cloak belongs to. What about the hand? Did it match the one that wrote the ransom notes?"

"I don't think so, but I can't be sure." He exhaled. "The pain has made it difficult to recall the memory as crisply as usual. But the cloak must belong to the kidnapper. We can tie it to both women, and Lady Priscilla was wearing it when she was found."

"And it *doesn't* belong to her," Tilda said darkly. "Yes, I think we must conclude the kidnapper was in possession of this cloak and that he felt love for Miss Chadwick."

"Since she smiled at him, it's possible she returned his affection," Hadrian noted.

"It seems Miss Chadwick, like her friend, Lady Priscilla, may have had her own suitor. Perhaps *they* had planned to elope with her father's money." Tilda shook her head. "But that doesn't explain Lady Priscilla's abduction." She let out an angry huff. "Every time we take a step forward, I feel as though we're pushed back."

"Every step is important, even if we haven't made great forward progress yet," Hadrian assured her. "I wonder if Lady Priscilla knows about Miss Chadwick's admirer. We should ask."

"Good idea," Tilda said, relaxing. "Thank you. You're right, and I should not be frustrated. We'll speak with Lady Priscilla tomorrow. Is that all you saw?"

"No, that vision faded and was replaced with something far more unsettling. Miss Chadwick was dead, her eyes open and unseeing. She lay on a wooden floor. The wounds to her chest were new and bleeding. With that memory, I felt horrible sorrow, a grief that could not be consoled."

"It makes sense that someone who felt love for Miss Chadwick would be devastated by her death."

"Yes, so it must have been the same person's memories. I lost consciousness when the dark emotions overcame me." He frowned deeply, then it turned into a grimace. He put his bare hand to his head.

"Is that more memories than you've ever seen in close proximity?" Tilda asked. "I think so, when we include the two you experienced at Alnwick House. You've never collapsed before—clearly it was too many in such a short period."

"Yes, and I suspect it was because of the intensity of the emotions I felt from the memory with the cloak," Hadrian said.

Tilda tried to make sense of whose memory Hadrian had seen. "What you describe doesn't sound like the memory of someone who killed her, unless he'd done so in a fit of rage and experienced immediate regret."

"That's what I was thinking. I just—" He exhaled. "I can't think about it now. My head hurts so very much."

"We're nearly to Ravenhurst House," Tilda said, glancing out the window. "I'm helping you up to your chamber where you will take a lavender bath, then retire immediately. You do *not* need to join Teague and me tomorrow."

He pushed up from the side of the coach with another grimace. "Of course I will. He needs me to accompany him to see Mr. Chadwick."

"You must rest. He can manage without you."

"It would be better if I were there," Hadrian insisted.

She crossed her arms over her chest. "I'm not allowing you to endanger your health."

Hadrian exhaled. "I surrender."

The coach stopped, and Leach opened the door almost immediately. He helped Tilda down then assisted Hadrian. She stayed close as Leach guided Hadrian to the pavement. The coachman kept hold of Hadrian's left side whilst Tilda clasped his right arm. Tilda felt a slight tremor moving through Hadrian, and her worry grew.

As soon as they reached the door, Collier, Hadrian's butler, opened it. He assessed the situation with deep concern.

"His lordship has a terrible headache," Tilda explained. "He needs a very warm bath with lavender. Can you see to that?"

"Certainly." He took himself off.

"I can make my way upstairs to my chamber," Hadrian said.

Tilda gave him an expectant look. "The same way you made your way out of Scotland Yard?"

"I recovered somewhat during the coach ride." Hadrian turned his head to Leach. "Go take care of the horses."

Instead of leaving, Leach looked to Tilda.

"Yes, go ahead," she said. "I can take care of his lordship." If not, Collier would no doubt help her.

Leach hesitated but ultimately said, "Feel better, my lord." He then departed the house, closing the door behind him.

Hadrian looked at Tilda, his lips pressed together. "Seems you're in charge now. Just as you were at Alnwick House earlier when you ordered the butler about. You're rather good at household management."

She arched a brow at him, then escorted him into the staircase hall, keeping tight hold of his right arm and bracing her arm along his middle back. "We're going to take the stairs very slowly. I want you to clasp the rail with your left hand, and I'll hold your other side. Don't argue with me."

"I wouldn't dream of it," he said perhaps a touch sardonically.

They climbed the stairs slowly, as Tilda had decreed, and when they reached the top, she looked right and left. "I've no idea which way to go."

"To the left."

She escorted him along the gallery that overlooked the hall below. His house was truly magnificent, but she was far more interested in the man she clung to. He seemed a little steadier on his feet, but he still leaned on her.

"This door here on the right." Hadrian gestured to the last door along the gallery.

Tilda pushed it open into a gorgeous sitting room decorated in blues and greens. There were two bookcases and a carved mahogany desk. If she wasn't in such a hurry to see Hadrian settled, she would have stopped to appreciate the handsome room.

They moved into his bedchamber, which was quite large and dominated by a mahogany four-poster bed cloaked in dark green velvet.

"I'll just sit." Hadrian looked toward a dark brown leather

chair situated near the hearth. Tilda helped him get there, and he sat down rather heavily.

Tilda set her reticule on a footstool and once again removed her gloves. She turned back to Hadrian and knelt before him to remove his shoes.

He smirked. "How wifely of you. And don't tell me not to flirt. We're not currently investigating."

"How can you flirt at a time like this?" She removed the second shoe and set it aside.

"This is not a crisis," Hadrian assured her. "I've experienced headaches like this before."

"I would argue you have not." Tilda did not care for his blasé attitude. "As you noted, you've never collapsed before."

He scooted forward in the chair and started to remove his coat. Tilda helped him, drawing the garment from his arms. She moved to set it on a bench at the end of his bed. When she returned, she saw that he'd loosened his neckcloth and unbuttoned his waistcoat.

His valet came in through another doorway, his features pinched. "Good heavens, my lord, what trouble have you gotten yourself into?"

"This is nothing but a headache, Sharp," Hadrian replied. "You remember Miss Wren."

Tilda had met most of Hadrian's household during their second investigation together, when he'd been suspected of murder. She'd interviewed several of his retainers, including Sharp.

He was solidly built and when she'd first seen him, Tilda had presumed he was a groom. Except he'd been impeccably garbed, as he was now. He had light brown hair and warm hazel eyes along with a pleasing countenance often made brilliant with his smile.

"Another headache, my lord?" Sharp asked. "Or have the lice finally taken up residence?"

"Headache," Hadrian replied with a smirk. "Though you are welcome to inspect my scalp if it will give you solace."

"The footmen are bringing up water presently for your bath, as directed by Miss Wren," Sharp said briskly. "I will prepare things in the dressing chamber." He looked to Tilda. "Have you any other instructions, Miss Wren?"

"Er, no."

Sharp inclined his head and retreated from the room.

She put her hand on her hip and faced Hadrian. "Why does everyone keep asking me what to do?"

"As I said, you're in charge," Hadrian smiled. "I don't mind."

Tilda groaned. "Stop flirting."

She stood there a moment, knowing she should leave but unable to make herself do so. "How will I know you'll be all right?" she whispered.

Hadrian clasped her hand and pulled her toward him. "Sit."

"Where?" She glanced around, and he pulled her onto his lap.

"This is hardly appropriate," she murmured.

He looked her in the eye. "And you think being in my chamber somehow is?"

She pursed her lips. "No. I should go."

"I don't want you to," he said softly. "Not yet." He leaned his head back against the chair.

Worry surpassed everything else she was feeling. She put her hands on his temples and massaged her fingertips over his forehead.

He closed his eyes again, and his lips curved up. "That's nice."

She caressed the lines from his brow. "You gave me quite a fright."

"I think I frightened myself a little," he admitted.

She smoothed her hands down his cheeks and again stroked his cheekbones with her thumbs, then she slid her hands back over his ears and into his hair.

Hadrian opened his eyes. She was very close and at this proximity, she never failed to feel as though she were falling. Not in the way Hadrian had fallen at Scotland Yard, but the sensation that she was floating and gliding. He wrapped his right arm around her and clutched her side. His left hand rested on her thigh.

Tilda was exceedingly aware of him beneath her and of his embrace. "This is too familiar," she whispered.

"Our relationship is progressing, whether you want it to or not," he said, his eyes never leaving hers. His hand moved along her thigh, and Tilda gasped softly. He lifted his hand and stroked her cheek. "The emotions between us keep growing, as does our need for physical contact. Can you deny that?"

Holding her breath, she stared into his familiar, handsome—and beloved—face. "I cannot." She pressed her mouth to his.

The kiss was soft but not brief. Tilda felt each caress of his lips against hers in every fiber of her being. Finally, she lifted her head. "I must go. You need your bath and to rest."

"Yes," he agreed, sounding quite reluctant. "But I'm going to Chadwick's house tomorrow, and you can't stop me."

"You mustn't tax yourself. Please don't be foolish."

"I'll be fine. I promise I won't fatigue myself."

"You must also promise you will not use your ability," she said sternly.

He pouted briefly. "What if we need it?"

Tilda understood his desire to help, but not at the cost of his health and well-being. "Your gift has been incredibly useful, and I'm grateful for it. But if I could trade it away for you to be healthy and whole and not experience this recurring agony, I would do so. I'm very close to asking you to not use your ability when we investigate. We *don't* need it."

"Perhaps not, but how many times has it pointed us in the right direction?" he asked. "As you said, it's a gift. I will not turn away from it. I'm learning to manage it, and it's my hope that this pain will diminish over time."

Tilda worried it would not, but she didn't say so. "You should write to Captain Vale about what happened tonight."

"I will."

"One more thing, if your head still hurts in the morning, you must promise me you won't meet us."

He hesitated, then ultimately agreed. "I promise."

Tilda wasn't sure she believed him. "I'll be able to tell if you're in pain," she warned him.

"You think so?" he asked with a half-smile.

"I know you quite well, my lord," she said.

"Oh, now I'm 'my lord,'" he laughed, and then immediately winced.

*"Don't laugh."*

"Don't provoke me."

She stood from his lap, just in the nick of time too, for Sharp came back into the room. "The bath is ready, my lord. Will you be staying?" he asked Tilda plainly, without even the slightest bit of irony or judgment.

"No, but perhaps you could dispatch a note to my house later and let me know that his lordship has retired for the evening and is well?"

"I would be happy to," Sharp said.

Tilda picked up her reticule and looked back to the valet. "If his headache is still troubling him in the morning, he *must* stay abed." She sent a warning glance toward Hadrian.

"Certainly. If I detect his head is still hurting, I shall send word," Sharp vowed.

"Thank you." She turned her attention back to Hadrian. "I like your valet."

Hadrian smirked again, and his gaze seemed to smolder as he regarded her. "I wish you could stay," he whispered.

She tried to tamp down the rising heat inside her as well as her own strong desire to remain and care for him. He was in excellent hands, but it was hard for her to leave. She just wanted to be *with* him. Together, they were more than an investigative team.

But she couldn't stay. It wasn't her place to care for him in this way, and it certainly wasn't appropriate for her to even be in his bedchamber as she was. Not unless they were wed. Right now, in this moment, that held a singular appeal.

That shocking realization encouraged her to go. "Good night, Hadrian."

"Good night, Tilda. I'll see you in the morning."

"Perhaps." She narrowed her eyes at him briefly before turning on her heel and leaving.

She made her way back downstairs to the entrance hall where Collier awaited.

"We'll take good care of him, miss," he said. "You needn't worry."

"I'll try not to. I know he's in the best hands. Please make sure he gets an appropriate amount of rest. We have inquiries to make tomorrow, and I don't want him coming along if he's still unwell."

"Of course not," Collier said in agreement. There was a glint of admiration in his eyes as he regarded her. "We appreciate you taking care of him. He's lucky to have you."

Or was she lucky to have him?

She'd never wanted a partner in her work, let alone a romantic one. Yet, here they were. She couldn't deny what he'd said upstairs was true. They *had* grown closer, and they would continue to do so unless they stopped spending time together completely.

Tilda could not see or accept that happening. Which meant she had to determine what came next. Whether she wanted to acknowledge it publicly or not, they were courting. Furthermore, the idea of marriage was not as improbable or undesirable as she'd once believed.

She was going to need some time to become used to that change.

# CHAPTER 14

*T*ilda was waiting for Detective Inspector Teague when he arrived the following morning. Her thoughts were on Hadrian, as they'd been all night.

Sharp had been kind enough to send her a note last night and another this morning to inform her that Hadrian was doing well. He'd awakened claiming to feel normal, however Sharp had indicated his doubt to Tilda along with a description of Hadrian. He had dark circles beneath his eyes, and Sharp was concerned he hadn't slept well. The valet had closed the note with a promise to keep a close eye on Hadrian and keep Tilda informed.

Tilda briefly wondered what the Ravenhurst House staff thought of her and Hadrian's relationship, since she was so involved with caring for him. They'd not only seemed perfectly accepting of her behavior last night, they'd deferred to her. She wasn't sure what to make of that.

"How is Ravenhurst?" Teague asked as they settled into the growler he'd hired to convey them to Alnwick House in Upper Brook Street.

"Better," she replied. "I received word from Ravenhurst House. He's being well cared for."

"Will he be joining us later at the Chadwicks'?" Teague asked.

"I don't think so." At least she hoped not, given what Sharp had written that morning. Tilda eyed a worn notebook on the seat next to Teague. "Were you able to obtain Inspector Lea's notes from K Division?"

"I was, in fact." Teague picked up the notebook. "Wycombe collected this a short while ago. Apparently, Inspector Lea left several to K Division when he retired. This is the one that contains his notes about the Spring-heeled Jack attacks."

"I'm so pleased Wycombe was able to obtain them. Have you read the contents?"

"Not in detail, but I did read that Lea watched an experiment at the London Hospital which demonstrated that blue flames are not proof of a supernatural creature. Anyone can chemically create blue fire." Teague's eyes gleamed with excitement. "It's extraordinary. In the experiment, a man blew through a small tube that contained spirits of wine as well as sulfur, and he held a lit match at the end. The result is blue flame."

Tilda smiled. "How simple. I knew there was an explanation." She looked forward to reading the notebook herself. "I'd love to see how that works in practice."

"I would too," Teague said eagerly. "I'm keen to try the experiment later at Scotland Yard if you'd like to join me and Wycombe."

"I most certainly would." Tilda couldn't help thinking Hadrian would enjoy that too. Perhaps she'd see if he was feeling well enough to come. Except she probably shouldn't. He ought to rest until he was fully recovered.

As they turned into Upper Brook Street, Teague shifted his attention to the window and twitched with surprise. "That looks to be Ravenhurst's coach."

Tilda craned her neck to see out the window. It was indeed Hadrian's coach. He was not supposed to be here. In fact, even if he'd been well, this interview was to be conducted by just her and

Teague. Hadrian wasn't supposed to join them until the Chadwicks, at which time Tilda planned to wait with Leach.

Tilda barely waited for the growler to stop before bounding out and marching to Hadrian's coach.

Leach stepped down to the pavement to meet her. "My apologies, Miss Wren, I tried to convince him not to come. Everyone did."

Tilda groaned softly with frustration. "I suppose the earl gets to do whatever he wants."

Leach moved to open the door, and Hadrian was there, ready to step out. He looked tired. Tilda hadn't ever seen such dark purple swathes beneath his eyes.

"You shouldn't be here." Tilda wished he'd continue to rest.

Hadrian moved onto the pavement. "I promised I wouldn't come if I still had a headache, and I don't."

She narrowed her eyes at him and studied his forehead as if she could discern whether he was in pain or not. She had to concede; he did not visually appear to be hurting, but then again, if he were, he was likely trying very hard not to show it.

"Tilda, if you were in my position, would you really have been able to stay home?" he asked softly.

He had her there. "You must promise not to use your skill," she whispered, since Teague was standing not far behind her. "Do you swear?"

"I do," he said earnestly, his gaze holding hers.

She exhaled and stepped back, pivoting to welcome Teague into their conversation. "It appears Ravenhurst is feeling fit."

Teague smiled. "Glad to hear it. Though, we weren't expecting you here at Alnwick House."

"I thought it might be helpful for me to distract the duke and duchess so the two of you could speak with Lady Priscilla alone. You can't very well question her about Vincent Chadwick in front of her parents." Hadrian smiled briefly. "I suppose you *could*, but I would rather you not be responsible for exposing Lady Priscilla's secret epistolary affair."

"This is an excellent point, and I'm glad you thought of it," Teague said. "Let's go in, and afterward, we'll tell you about Inspector Lea's notes."

Hadrian's brows shot up. "You found them?"

Teague held up the notebook, which he carried, along with the letters, in his left hand. "Wycombe fetched them this morning."

"Lea wrote about an experiment he witnessed to create blue flame," Tilda explained. "We're going to recreate it this afternoon."

"Now, I'm especially glad I joined you." Hadrian smiled.

Tilda walked beside him as they approached the door and murmured, "Me too."

Teague stepped aside for Hadrian to knock.

The butler shortly opened the door and swept his gaze over each of them. "You've returned."

"Yes," Hadrian replied. "We've come to inquire after Lady Priscilla's welfare and ask her a few more questions, if she's feeling up to it. The duke is expecting us."

"He mentioned you might call." The butler opened the door wide and gestured them inside. "We'll go up to the drawing room." He led them upstairs to the room overlooking Upper Brook Street.

There was no one present, but the butler said he would fetch the duke and duchess along with Lady Priscilla. Whilst they waited, Teague shared the specifics of the information regarding the blue flame replication in Lea's notes. Hadrian listened raptly.

"I'd like to read the notes myself," Hadrian said, and Tilda knew he wanted to handle them in the hope of seeing one of Lea's memories. Except Lea was dead now, so that was unlikely.

Still, he might see someone else's memory that could be helpful. Not today, though. She wouldn't permit it.

The duke came into the drawing room alone. He also appeared tired. The flesh beneath his eyes was darker than Hadrian's.

"I'm afraid Lady Priscilla will remain abed all day, but she has consented to speak with you." The duke did not appear pleased by that. "She very much wants to help capture her kidnapper, so her mother and I will allow you a very short visit. The duchess is with her, and when she says the interview is over, you will leave at once."

Tilda was glad Lady Priscilla wanted to help them since it seemed her parents did not seem to care whether they caught the kidnapper.

"We deeply appreciate Lady Priscilla's help," Teague said. "Please pardon Miss Wren and me whilst we go speak with her. Lord Ravenhurst will remain with you."

As they made their way to Lady Priscilla's chamber, Teague glanced at Tilda. "How are we to persuade Her Grace to leave?"

"I'm not sure, but I'll try to think of something," Tilda replied.

They reached the bedchamber, and Lady Priscilla was sitting up in the bed. Her hair looked as if it had been washed and now hung in a plait against her shoulder. She wore fresh clothing, of course, and looked much better than she had last night. Her cheeks were pink and her features were smooth rather than distressed. Her Grace sat in a chair beside the bed. She pursed her lips slightly at Tilda and Teague.

"Thank you for agreeing to see us again this morning." Tilda stood near the bed, and Teague remained slightly behind her. She smiled at Lady Priscilla. "I hope you're feeling better today and that you were able to get some rest. You certainly look well."

Lady Priscilla smiled. "I am, and it's lovely to be in my own bed."

"We were hoping to ask you a few questions about your suitor." Tilda sent a meaningful look toward Lady Priscilla, then turned her attention to the duchess. "Would it be possible for us to speak with Lady Priscilla alone?"

Her Grace appeared reluctant, her brow creasing. "I think it's best if I stay." She fixed her gaze on her daughter.

Lady Priscilla clasped her hands in her lap. "It's all right, Mama."

"But I don't want to leave you."

"It's only for a few minutes," Lady Priscilla said.

"I don't know why I have to leave." Her Grace's lips pursed again as she rose from the chair and moved closer to her daughter.

"I don't want you to hear anything more about what happened, Mama." Lady Priscilla briefly touched her mother's hand. "It's too upsetting for you."

"All right. I won't be gone long." Her Grace walked—very slowly—from the room.

Teague mostly closed the door, leaving it slightly ajar.

Tilda moved closer to Lady Priscilla, and Teague joined her farther down the bedside, leaving some space between them. Perhaps he was trying to make Lady Priscilla more comfortable by not crowding her.

"Thank you for ensuring your mother left," Tilda said.

Lady Priscilla's shoulder lifted. "Well, you looked at me strangely, and I thought that's what you wanted."

"It was," Tilda confirmed with a nod. "You see, we wanted to speak with you about your *previous* suitor, Mr. Vincent Chadwick."

"Oh, my poor Vincent!" Lady Priscilla's jewel-like green-blue eyes widened as her features tightened with worry. "He must be so worried about me."

"I'm sure he'll be relieved when he learns you've returned," Tilda said.

"How will he know?" Lady Priscilla asked.

"As it happens, we are calling at the Chadwicks' residence

next. We'll be happy to inform him." Indeed, Tilda was looking forward to seeing Vincent's reaction to the news, but she doubted she'd be allowed inside.

Lady Priscilla smiled and shrugged her shoulders. "Thank you! I wish there was time for me to write him a note, but I wouldn't want my mother to know."

"She's not aware of your correspondence?" Tilda asked, though she knew the truth. Lady Priscilla never would have hidden the letters if she wasn't trying to keep them secret.

"Not at all." Lady Priscilla lowered her voice to a dark whisper. "My father is dead set against our courtship, but I love Vincent."

"I saw him recently," Tilda said. "He loves you too."

Lady Priscilla flushed and pressed her hands to her face as she smiled widely. "Did he say so? Where did you see him? Did he return from Richmond?"

"Yes, we saw him in Belgrave Square." Tilda wasn't going to say why, and she glanced at Teague to make sure he wouldn't either. He gave her a subtle nod.

"How did you find out about me and Vincent," Lady Priscilla asked skeptically.

"We discovered the letters he wrote you."

"You did?" Lady Priscilla blinked in surprise, then darted a look toward the corner where Tilda had found them. "How? I thought I hid them so well."

"Your maid might have encouraged me to look behind the wallpaper." Tilda glanced at the corner.

Lady Priscilla sighed. "I thought she suspected something, but we didn't discuss it. I was afraid she would tell my parents."

"As far as I know, she didn't," Tilda said. "In one of the letters, Vincent mentioned elopement. Did you have plans to do that?"

Lady Priscilla shook her head. "We both knew it could never happen, but we did dream about it in a fantastical way." She paused, then smiled again. "I'm going to tell my mother I want to call on Delia. That will allow me to see Vincent too."

Tilda exchanged a look with Teague. Lady Priscilla obviously didn't know that Delia was dead, and Tilda wasn't going to tell her.

"When did you and Vincent meet?" Tilda asked.

"When Delia and I became friends just before the Season started." She smiled warmly, her cheeks flushing a delicate rose pink. "Vincent and I immediately got on well together. I found him so dashing."

Tilda wanted to ask if Lady Priscilla was aware of Delia Chadwick also having a suitor or someone with whom she was romantically involved. However, Tilda couldn't think of a reason why she would do so without revealing to Lady Priscilla what had happened to Miss Chadwick.

"Have you thought of anything else that happened during your captivity?" Teague asked.

"No," Lady Priscilla replied.

Teague went on. "What about when you were taken from your bed? You said you saw blue flame. Do you remember seeing anything in the kidnapper's mouth before the flame ignited?"

She thought for a moment, her features creasing. "No. It all happened so fast. There was a smell, now that you mention it. It was like the wine my father drinks. Perhaps Spring-heeled Jack was drunk."

"Perhaps," Teague said with a nod. "Thank you, Lady Priscilla. We'll leave you to rest now."

Tilda felt sorry for the young woman. She would be denied the man she loved, and she was soon to learn that her dear friend had also been kidnapped but had not found her way home.

"You mentioned your friend, Miss Chadwick." Tilda had an idea for how to broach the topic of her friend without divulging what happened. "It sounds as though you are close. I know from her brother's letters that she was acting as a courier between the two of you."

"Yes, Delia is such a lovely person. It's been wonderful to have our first Seasons together."

"Did she also have a suitor?" Tilda was careful to ask as if Delia were still alive .

Lady Priscilla's auburn brows drew together. "No, though there was a time a few weeks ago when I thought she might have. There was something different about her. She seemed almost... giddy. But she swore there wasn't anyone. I decided I was hoping there might be so that we would fall in love and be married around the same time."

"Thank you, Lady Priscilla." Tilda gave her a warm smile. "Please take good care."

Tilda and Teague turned and left. Her Grace stood just outside the doorway.

Teague inclined his head. "Thank you, Your Grace. We'll try not to bother you again, but I can't promise we won't need to speak with Lady Priscilla in the future."

"I hope you catch this horrible Spring-heeled Jack, before he can terrorize someone else's family."

"That is our goal," Teague assured her. "And your daughter's assistance could be what helps us reach it."

He and Tilda returned to the drawing room.

The duke eyed them with impatience. "I hope you obtained everything you needed."

"We did—for now," Teague said. "As I told Her Grace, we are committed to catching Spring-heeled Jack before he kidnaps another young lady. If we uncover new evidence and need to speak with your daughter again, we hope you won't mind us calling."

"I'm sure you want to see the kidnapper captured," Hadrian said in a nearly cajoling tone.

"Of course," the duke replied. He inclined his head toward

Teague. "You may return and speak with Priscilla if it becomes necessary."

They left the house and made their way toward Hadrian's coach.

"How did it go with Lady Priscilla?" Hadrian asked, stopping and turning toward them. "Were you able to speak with her alone?"

"We were," Tilda said. "We learned she and Vincent Chadwick had no real plans to elope."

Teague eyed Tilda with curiosity. "Why did you ask her about Miss Chadwick having a suitor?"

Tilda noted Hadrian darting a glance at her. She'd planned to tell him about that exchange since they couldn't discuss the memory Hadrian had seen in front of Teague.

"I was grasping for information—or a suspect of some kind," Tilda said with a mildly sheepish tone. "Since Lady Priscilla had a secret romantic relationship, I was rather hoping Miss Chadwick might have one too."

Teague chuckled. "I don't blame you for asking. And Lady Priscilla did suspect it, even though she was wrong." He sobered. "We've learned very little of use. Wycombe and Constable Mercer have conducted several inquiries with Miss Chadwick's friends— from the list you gave me—over the past few days, and no one has been able to provide anything helpful. I believe they concluded the list this morning."

"Perhaps they'll have something to report at Scotland Yard," Tilda suggested.

"We should be on our way." Teague looked to Hadrian. "Do you mind if I ride with you? I didn't ask the growler driver to wait."

"Not at all."

When they were settled in Hadrian's coach and moving, Tilda let out a wistful sigh. "I feel bad for Lady Priscilla. She still loves Vincent and wants to see him." She glanced over at Hadrian. "She plans to ask her mother if she can visit with Delia so that she could perhaps see Vincent too."

Hadrian grimaced. "She doesn't know Miss Chadwick is dead?"

Tilda shook her head. "It will be a blow. I'm curious to see how Vincent Chadwick will react when he learns Lady Priscilla is safely returned."

"Does that mean you're going to come into the Chadwicks' with us?" Hadrian asked.

"I don't think Chadwick will allow it," Teague said. "And I'd rather you not try, because he may not agree to speak with any of us."

Tilda frowned, then blew out a frustrated breath. "I'll wait in the coach."

"You can take the time to read through Lea's notes," Teague suggested.

"Excellent idea." Tilda was quite mollified by that.

When they arrived at the Chadwicks', Teague climbed out first. Hadrian briefly clasped Tilda's hand. "Don't worry. I know what to ask. You've taught me well."

"Yes, but will you refrain from touching anything or anyone if I'm not there?"

He put his hand over his heart. "I give you my solemn vow I will not remove my gloves."

Hadrian departed the coach. Tilda didn't doubt him, for she knew him to be a man of his word.

## CHAPTER 15

Hadrian stood in a small sitting room in the Chadwicks' house with Detective Inspector Teague as they waited for the elder Mr. Chadwick to join them. The house was eerily quiet and somber with its black hangings and aura of grief.

"How do you do this?" Hadrian asked quietly.

"What do you mean?" Teague asked.

"I imagine you must speak to many people who are in mourning as you investigate deaths."

"I can't say I've gotten used to it," Teague said. "Thankfully, the vast majority of our work doesn't involve death, but other crimes. Most often, we investigate theft and fraud." He gave Hadrian a wry look. "I would say most of the murders I deal with these days somehow involve you and Miss Wren."

"It's not lost on us that our investigations somehow inevitably lead to murder."

"Don't let that get out," Teague warned with an edge of humor. "No one will want to hire Miss Wren anymore."

"I'm not sure they do now." Hadrian tried and failed to keep the scorn from his voice.

"This will pass." Teague's tone held a confidence Hadrian didn't feel. "People need only be reminded of her assistance with the apprehension of the Levitation Killers, and she may well yet catch this kidnapper. I would not bet against Miss Wren."

*That* Hadrian agreed with wholeheartedly. "Neither would I." The article Clement was purportedly writing about Tilda couldn't be published soon enough.

Chadwick walked into the sitting room. He wore a black armband around his upper left arm. "I hope you've come to tell me that you caught my daughter's killer."

Teague inclined his head. "Not yet, but we're collecting evidence which is bringing us closer." To Hadrian, that seemed optimistic to say the least. "We were hoping to speak with Mrs. Chadwick about anything that might have gone missing from Miss Chadwick's wardrobe when she was abducted."

"Specifically, we're interested in a dark gray cloak and a pair of black boots with three buttons along the sides," Hadrian said.

"I don't know the first thing about what my daughter wears— wore." Chadwick sniffed. "I can tell you she was dressed in the finest. Mrs. Chadwick has gone up to her room, but perhaps Bannet can help you, if she can stop blubbering long enough to be of use."

Hadrian and Teague exchanged a glance of concern as Chadwick retreated from the room. He returned a moment later.

"The butler's gone to fetch the maid." Chadwick moved to stand near the hearth where the small portrait of his daughter sat on the mantel. "I saw the warning in the *Daily News* today. Though no name was mentioned, may I assume the kidnapping victim who was returned is Lady Priscilla?"

"That's correct," Teague confirmed.

Chadwick's face instantly changed as anger and anguish carved lines around his eyes and mouth. "How are they so fortunate? Why was their daughter returned and ours was not?" He glowered at Teague. "The only difference is I was foolish enough to hire Miss Wren, who then involved you, Detective Inspector. I'm glad His Grace heeded my advice."

"Your advice?" Teague asked.

Chadwick held his head up proudly. "I sent him word yesterday afternoon, cautioning him not tell anyone if he received another note and to just pay the ransom. I wish to God I'd done the same."

"We don't know if that's why your daughter wasn't returned," Teague said evenly. "Believe what you must, but we will continue our investigation to determine the truth of what happened."

Chadwick's face turned red, but before he could respond, the butler returned with Bannet. She did indeed look as if she had been crying. Her face was quite red, as were her eyes, and she sniffed as she regarded them with apprehension.

"Compose yourself, Bannet," Chadwick barked. "They want to ask you about some of Delia's clothing—a cloak and a pair of boots."

Hadrian repeated the descriptions of both to the maid.

Her brow furrowed. "The cloak is not familiar. However, Miss Chadwick does have a pair of boots such as you're describing. I noticed only yesterday that they're missing. They're from last Season and had been stored in the back of a cupboard. I'm sorry I didn't tell you before."

Chadwick glared at Bannet. "You worthless chit." He turned his gaze on Teague. "How do you know about these boots?"

"Lady Priscilla was returned wearing them," Teague replied.

"They're Delia's," Chadwick said, his eyes a bit wild. "I want them back. My wife will want them back."

"Of course," Teague said gently. "Though we cannot release them to you until after we've solved this case. They are an important piece of evidence."

"They are *Delia's* boots," Chadwick said fiercely, but his tone also held an unmistakable note of despair. Hadrian was angry with the man for his treatment of poor Bannet, but he was in the throes of unimaginable grief.

Teague regarded him kindly. "We'll return them as soon as possible. I understand your agitation."

"How could you?" Chadwick asked bitterly.

Teague looked to Bannet. "Did you notice anything else missing?"

"I didn't," Bannet replied. She sent a sad glance toward Chadwick who was now staring at his daughter's portrait. "And I looked carefully after I discovered the boots were missing."

"Can you think of anything that might have been unusual in the days or even weeks before Miss Chadwick was kidnapped, such as a…romantic entanglement?" Teague asked.

Hadrian wondered if Teague was also grasping since he was asking the same question that Tilda said she'd asked Lady Priscilla earlier. Or, was he hoping to uncover something since Lady Priscilla had suspected her friend might have had a suitor?

Bannet hesitated. Her eyes darted again toward Chadwick, and her neck flushed. She clasped her hands together tightly. It seemed to Hadrian she was withholding something. Perhaps she was worried about revealing whatever it was in front of her employer. He disliked causing the young woman discomfort, but they needed information.

Hadrian began to think Teague—and Tilda—was on to something. He gave the maid a smile of encouragement. "If you can think of anything, no matter how small, it might be helpful to us."

Chadwick crossed his arms and glowered at the maid. "Out with it, Bannet."

She attempted to square her shoulders but ended up slumping. "Miss Chadwick's behavior changed a bit a couple of months before she was taken. She seemed excited about something, but when I questioned her about it, she was secretive. There were some afternoons she would visit with a friend, and when she came home, she was distracted. She seemed almost…rapturous. I asked her about it a second time, and she told me to mind my own business."

"As you should," Chadwick snapped at her. "What are you insinuating?"

Bannet turned ashen. "Nothing, Mr. Chadwick. I'm merely sharing what his lordship asked me to."

Teague regarded her with fervent curiosity. "What do you think was happening?"

"It seemed she may have had…a secret admirer." Bannet sounded uncertain, and her posture was of someone who appeared ready to flee.

Hadrian and Teague exchanged looks of surprise—and excitement. Hopefully, this was a useful clue.

Chadwick unfolded his arms and took a step toward the maid. "I don't like what you're implying, Bannet. Delia is gone. I can't believe you would suggest she was carrying on with someone secretly. I'd already been wondering why we would keep you on since Delia is no longer with us, but this settles the matter. Whether you're lying or you kept something about Delia from us, you have failed in your duties. Your employment here is terminated immediately. Pack your things and go."

"Now?" she asked, her lip trembling.

"Yes." Chadwick's gaze was hard, his tone sharp as a blade. "And I don't wish to see you again."

Hadrian couldn't stand by and watch the man berate the poor maid, let alone sack her. He felt terrible for the young woman. It was obvious that she was trying very hard not to cry. "Mr. Chadwick, I hardly think it's necessary to dismiss Bannet immediately. She is grieving too."

"This is none of your affair, my lord. You've stuck your nose in enough." Chadwick looked to Bannet. "Why are you still here?"

The maid spun on her heel and fled the room.

Hadrian clenched his jaw in anger.

"You're not to share anything Bannet just told you," Chadwick demanded. "None of that could be true, though I can't imagine why the maid would concoct such a tale. Delia was a good girl. Now please go, and don't return. I have no patience to speak with you again." He stalked angrily from the room.

Teague exhaled. "That was unfortunate, but we learned something. Lady Priscilla may have been right."

"We now have two people—independent of one another—who've suspected Miss Chadwick of having an admirer or a suitor," Hadrian said. Tilda would be thrilled to have a clue.

"We just need to find out who." Teague narrowed his eyes with purpose.

"Perhaps Vincent Chadwick might know." Hadrian hoped so.

"Let's find out." Teague led Hadrian back to the entrance hall where the butler was waiting. His features seemed taut.

"We were hoping to speak with Mr. Vincent Chadwick today," Teague said. "May we see him?"

The butler glanced toward the staircase hall, then moved closer to the door. "Mr. Chadwick would not appreciate me allowing you to stay."

"Speaking with Vincent could very well save a future kidnapping victim," Hadrian said. "Surely Mr. Chadwick would support that."

"Is this about Lady Priscilla?" the butler asked. "Is she...?"

Hadrian was surprised by the butler's comment and shot a look toward Teague, who appeared to have the same reaction.

"She's home safe," Teague assured the butler, who visibly relaxed upon hearing the news. "What do you know of her?"

"I'm so glad to hear she's all right." Indeed, the man looked most relieved. "We—the staff, I mean—know she and Vincent wished to court." He kept his voice low and kept glancing toward the staircase hall. "Vincent still loves her very much and would give anything to marry her, but His Grace has been clear that will never happen. If you wait outside, I'll see if Vincent will come out and speak with you. I can't promise anything."

Teague thanked him before he and Hadrian left. When they reached the pavement, Tilda opened the door of the coach and leaned out. "That didn't take very long."

"Probably because we didn't get a chance to speak with Vincent," Hadrian said. "The butler is trying to send him outside."

"Why couldn't you speak with him in the house?" Tilda asked.

"We didn't get a chance," Teague replied. "Chadwick was too busy sacking Bannet before throwing us out."

Tilda gasped. "What happened with Bannet?"

Hadrian related what Bannet had told them and Chadwick's reaction.

"How awful," Tilda said with sympathy. "The poor maid. But she suspected Miss Chadwick may have had an admirer? That's two separate people thinking the same thing!" Her excitement was palpable.

Before Hadrian could reply, Vincent walked up the stairs from the lower ground floor and met them on the pavement. He glanced back at the house. "I don't want to be seen out here with you, so let us walk," he said quickly.

Hadrian helped Tilda from the coach, and she held his arm as they strolled alongside Vincent. Teague strode on his other side.

"I'm so relieved to hear Priscilla is all right." Vincent smiled briefly. "Simpson—the butler—told me."

Tilda sent him a kind smile. "She wanted me to tell you that she loves you and hopes to see you soon."

Vincent's face split into a wide grin, but it faded as quickly as it had appeared. "I don't know how that will be possible, since we're in mourning."

"I'm afraid Lady Priscilla is not aware of that," Tilda explained gently. "She mentioned to me that she wanted to ask her mother if she could call on Delia in the hope that she could also see you. She does not yet know that Delia is gone."

Gasping, Vincent went pale. "My dearest love. She will take the news poorly. I wish I could be the one to tell her so I may comfort her. She and Delia were dear friends. It's their friendship that brought Priscilla and I together."

"Were you aware of your sister engaging in a romantic liaison with someone?" Teague asked.

Vincent frowned. "Not at all. Why do you ask?"

"Her maid seemed to suspect she might, though your sister would not confirm it to her," Teague explained. "When Bannet mentioned her suspicion to us earlier, your father gave her the boot."

"Poor Bannet." Vincent shook his head. "Is there anything I can do to help? I'll do anything to find the man who killed my sister and kidnapped Priscilla." His features drew tight as his eyes burned with rage.

"Not at the moment," Teague said. "But we may have more questions."

Vincent looked to Tilda. "If you see Priscilla again, please tell her I love her too." He turned and continued walking around the square.

Hadrian, Tilda, and Teague returned to Hadrian's coach, arriving as Bannet, carrying a valise, appeared at the top of the stairs where Vincent had emerged a short while ago. Hadrian approached the maid. "I'm so sorry for what's happened. Do you have somewhere to go?"

She shook her head.

"I'd like to help you, if I may," Hadrian offered. "I can provide you a place to stay until you find a new position."

The maid stared up at him in surprise, then cast her gaze toward the ground. "No one will hire me because Mr. Chadwick refused to give me a reference."

Hadrian heard Tilda make a sound of disgust.

"I'll provide you with one," Hadrian said, taking her valise.

The maid looked as if she were trying not to cry. "That is too kind of you, my lord."

Hadrian gestured to his coach. "Come, we'll take you to Ravenhurst House now."

They moved toward the coach where Leach waited. He took the valise from Hadrian and went to the back of the coach to secure it.

"I'll catch a cab to Scotland Yard, and you can meet me there," Teague said as he reached into the coach to grab Lea's notebook.

Hadrian nodded. "Sorry for the delay."

Teague's gaze warmed. "No apology necessary. You're a good man, my lord."

"You really ought to be calling me Ravenhurst by now. Or Raven, as many of my colleagues in the Lords do."

After Teague departed, Hadrian helped Bannet into the coach and then Tilda. The maid looked uncomfortable sitting across from them on the rear-facing seat. She clasped her gloved hands in her lap, and Hadrian noticed a handkerchief between them.

After several minutes, Tilda addressed the maid gently. "I'm sorry about what happened. Have you worked for the Chadwicks long?"

"Over a decade." Bannet sniffed. "I practically grew up with Miss Chadwick. I felt so fortunate to become her maid when she was old enough to have one." Tears rolled down her cheeks, and she dabbed at them whilst turning her face away, as if she didn't want them to see her grief.

"It's all right," Hadrian said softly. "You don't need to hide from us."

Bannet pressed the handkerchief to her eyes. "Thank you, my lord. Truly. I didn't know what I was going to do. I still can't believe you're going to help me." She began to cry again. "I'm sorry."

"There's no need to apologize, Bannet," Tilda assured her. "You're safe now."

When the maid's shoulders began to shake as she cried even harder, Hadrian wondered if she was thinking of Miss Chadwick and how she would never be safe again. He looked over at Tilda who was watching Bannet with a sad expression.

Perhaps sensing his gaze, Tilda turned her head. "You are the best of men, Hadrian," she whispered.

He didn't know if that was true but hearing that from her meant everything to him.

# CHAPTER 16

*A*fter taking Bannet to Ravenhurst House, Tilda and Hadrian made haste to Scotland Yard. Hadrian turned his head to Tilda, seated beside him in the coach. "Thank you for escorting Bannet inside and helping me introduce her to the housekeeper. I think that helped settle her."

Tilda felt sorry for the maid. Bannet was devastated over the loss of Miss Chadwick, and now she'd lost her employment as well. "I thought my presence would put her more at ease. In truth, I wanted to ask if she knows the identity of Miss Chadwick's secret admirer, but I just couldn't whilst she's so upset." Tilda was desperate to know, however. "Hopefully, she'll feel better later or tomorrow, and you can ask her." Her gaze lifted to Hadrian's head. "How is your head?"

"Improved from this morning." As soon as the words left his mouth, he grimaced comically.

Tilda shook her head at him. "It did hurt this morning!"

He actually blushed. "Only a little, but it's completely fine now. In fact, I feel well enough that if Teague hadn't taken Lea's notebook, I would have tried to experience a memory from it."

"Well, I'm glad he did," Tilda said. "I don't think you should overdo it today, even if you are feeling better. Plenty of time for that tomorrow. I'm sure we can come up with a reason to review the notebook."

"Did you learn anything new from it?" Hadrian asked.

"Inspector Lea interviewed the property master of the Pavilion Theatre who offered a different manner of producing the blue flame that they sometimes used on stage. It requires more ingredients because a sponge is soaked with spirits of wine, then a certain kind of acid, depending on the desired color of the flame, is dropped onto the sponge. If I were Spring-heeled Jack, I should think the tube method would be easier, especially when trying to create a quick, seamless effect."

"I don't know why I didn't think of a theatre trick," Hadrian said. "Perhaps Spring-heeled Jack works in a theatre. He also has a costume."

Tilda snapped her gaze to his. "What about the scent of greasepaint you detected from that cloak? The garment could have come from a theatre."

Hadrian grinned. "I finally feel as if we've deduced something helpful."

"I hope so. I look forward to hearing Teague's thoughts even though we can't tell him about the greasepaint." She sent Hadrian a covert glance. "Do you ever think about revealing your ability to Teague?"

"Not at all." He twitched beside her. "I wouldn't want it to become widely known."

Tilda lightly touched his arm. "I didn't mean to agitate you. I won't ever tell anyone. I do think you could trust Teague, but I understand if you don't want him to know."

"Thank you. It isn't about trust." He clenched his jaw briefly. "It's just…private."

"Of course."

"I *am* slightly concerned someone will notice my odd behavior." He turned his head toward her, his mouth curling into a half-smile. "I think I might borrow Wycombe's migraine explanation."

"I fully support that and will follow your lead should you wish to use it."

They fell quiet for a few moments as they rumbled toward Scotland Yard.

"Have you given any more thought to attending dinner at Ravenhurst House tomorrow night?" Hadrian asked.

"Truthfully, no. I've been too engrossed in the case. Sorry. Remind me, which of your sisters is coming?"

"Beatrice—she's two years older than me. They live in Wimbledon as her husband, Courtenay, prefers to keep more horses than he would be able to in London. He can be insufferable on occasion, and I confess your brilliant company will dull his presence."

Tilda laughed. "Then I suppose I must come, and I will." She met his gaze intently. "So long as no one else is kidnapped before then."

"Of course." He smiled widely. "I'm very glad you're coming. I look forward to introducing you to my sister."

"And how will you do that?" Tilda asked. "I hope you don't want to tell her about our private courtship as you did your mother."

His brows rose slightly as his eyes glittered. "I want to tell *everyone*, but no, I won't tell my sister." He brushed something from his knee. "I've been thinking about the romances between Lady Priscilla and Vincent and Delia and her mystery gentleman. It's too bad none of them were able to show their love for one another out in the open. It's a burden to disguise one's true emotions."

Was he speaking for himself? "Is that how you feel?" she asked quietly.

"Not burdened, no. But I would dearly love for everyone everywhere to know how much I love you." The smile he gave her could have lit the darkest night.

Tilda was suddenly overcome with emotion, as she'd been last night when Hadrian collapsed. She hadn't thought about wanting to display or share her love with anyone but Hadrian. But as her affection for him deepened, it was possible or even likely that she wouldn't be able to conceal it.

"I'm afraid my feelings were too exposed last night," she said. "I can only imagine what Teague thinks, let alone your staff, although they seemed surprisingly comfortable with my presence in your household."

Hadrian chuckled. "They were ready to let you run it."

They arrived at Scotland Yard, and the desk clerk directed them to the courtyard behind the building. Teague was there with three constables. They'd set up a table with tubing, matches, several strips of lamp wick sitting in a shallow vessel filled with a clear liquid, and a bottle that was certainly spirits of wine.

"You've arrived just in time," Teague said. "We just finished cutting the lamp wick. I sent these constables to fetch the various items, and of course, they want to observe. Poor Wycombe was not pleased about having to miss this to go to the magistrate's court." Teague sighed. "Alas, it couldn't be helped."

"I'm trying to understand how Spring-heeled Jack would produce this trick quickly," Tilda said.

"We thought of that as we talked this through before we obtained the necessary supplies," Teague said. "One of the constables suggested he might use a wick to hold the alcohol. Then it would slide into the tube. The remaining question is how the wick stays in the tube as Spring-heeled Jack carries it around in his pocket or wherever."

"The cap we found at Lady Priscilla's would work!" Tilda darted her gaze to Hadrian. "That would fit on the end of a tube, wouldn't it?"

He grinned. "Absolutely."

"Excellent deduction, Miss Wren." Teague looked from her to

Hadrian and then to the constables. "Who would like to conduct the experiment?"

Everyone volunteered. Teague laughed. "We'll see Miss Wren go first since she so brilliantly thought of the mysterious brass cap."

Stepping to the table, Tilda removed her gloves and set them at one end. "I take one of the wicks and insert it into a tube?" She pinched one of the damp wicks and slid it into one of the metal tubes. "I can see why you'd want caps on the end of this when you carry it around in your pocket as you plan to frighten someone."

One of the constables chuckled.

Tilda ruminated on how someone might accomplish this so as not to draw attention to the fact that it was, indeed, a trick. "Let us puzzle out how this would work. I would pluck the tube from my pocket, take one cap off and perhaps drop it back into my pocket. Then I'd withdraw a matchbook—perhaps from another pocket." She picked up a match from the table with her right hand whilst clutching the tube in her left. "I would have to hold the book or box along with the tube in one hand whilst I struck the match. And I would need to pull the other cap off and hold it in my hand with the lit match." She mimicked the movements as she said them but did not light the match because doing so would have tipped the tube, and the wick would have fallen out. "I put the match in front of the tube, and blow. I see how he dropped the cap at Lady Priscilla's," she finished wryly.

"We must investigate that cap more closely now that we know what it is," Teague said.

"I'd prefer not to juggle the tube with the spirits of wine and the match." Tilda looked at Hadrian. "Would you mind producing the fire for me?"

"It would be my pleasure." Hadrian plucked up the matchbook. "Ready?"

She lifted the tube to her mouth. "Ready."

He lit the match and held it in front of the tube. Tilda blew through it, and the flame grew larger and turned blue.

Everyone gasped. This was followed quickly with laughter and applause.

"Spectacular!" Teague smiled broadly. "Our very own Spring-heeled Jane!"

Once the laughter died down, everyone took turns producing the blue flame. The last constable endeavored to manage the tube and the match as they imagined Spring-heeled Jack might have done. He received the loudest applause yet and took a bow.

"It really is a performance." Tilda turned to Teague. "I meant to tell you that Lea's notebook included a record of his interview with the property master at the Pavilion Theatre." She explained how one might use acid to create different colors of flame. "Ravenhurst and I discussed the possibility of Spring-heeled Jack working for a theatre. He does wear a costume, after all."

"That's not a bad theory. Let's go to my office to look at that brass cap." Teague led them upstairs where he went straight to his desk. He cleared a space on top of it before unlocking a drawer and removing the cap they'd found in Lady Priscilla's bedchamber.

Teague placed it on the desk and moved a lamp to provide better illumination. Tilda withdrew her magnifying glass from her reticule.

She bent over the desk and looked at the cap. "I'm not sure what to look for. It appears to be a simple cap. We can suppose it's part of the device Spring-heeled Jack uses to create his blue flamed breath, but we can't know for sure. Furthermore, how would a device and a cap like this even be produced?"

Hadrian picked up the cap to inspect it. He still wore his gloves and hadn't removed them for the experiment either. Because if he did, he risked seeing someone's memory and he was being careful, just as he'd promised. Tilda smiled to herself.

"May I?" Hadrian glanced at Tilda's magnifying glass.

She handed him the instrument, and he held it in front of his eye as he pulled the cap close. "This has file marks along the edge, and it's somewhat crudely made. I don't see a maker's mark. I wonder if this is the sort of prop a mechanist at a theatre would create."

"Excellent observation, Raven." Teague put his hands on his hips as he narrowed his eyes in thought. "Though, I don't know how we'll find Spring-heeled Jack amongst all the theatres in London. If he even works at a theatre."

"We should start with any theatres the Chadwicks or Alnwicks frequented," Tilda suggested.

"Good idea," Teague said as Hadrian set the cap back on the desk. "When Wycombe returns from the magistrate's court, we'll go to Alnwick House and to Belgrave Square to determine their theatre habits."

Tilda had a sudden thought. "Do you have a newspaper?" she asked Teague.

The detective inspector gestured to the corner of his desk. "Those are this morning's dailies."

Tilda picked up the first one and turned to the theatrical column. She smiled and peered over the top of the paper at Hadrian. "Would you like to attend the theatre tonight? The Brittania is advertising a play with fire effects." She arched her brows.

Hadrian bowed. "I should be delighted to attend the theatre with you."

Teague eyed her with admiration. "Brilliant. You can question the property master afterward and ask if he's able to make a device like the one we've just experimented with. Hopefully you won't have any trouble gaining access."

"I'm sure the Earl of Ravenhurst will be able to speak with whomever he likes following the performance." She gave Hadrian a sly smile, and he laughed.

"That's why you invited me."

"Come now, that's not the *only* reason," Teague said with a chuckle.

Tilda wasn't going to ask what he meant by that. She'd been afraid Teague would discover there was more between her and Hadrian than their professional relationship. As Hadrian had pointed out, hiding their...romance was becoming difficult. It was also frustrating as she found herself wanting to lean on him, depend on him, and just...be with him more and more.

But a formal courtship was tantamount to agreeing to marry him, and the idea of becoming a countess, even *his* countess, was absurd and more than a little terrifying.

"Shall we reconvene in the morning?" Teague locked the cap away in his desk.

"Yes." Tilda tucked her magnifying glass back into her reticule. "Good luck with your inquiries."

"Thank you. I look forward to hearing what you learn at the theatre."

Tilda and Hadrian departed Teague's office and made their way from the building. When they were outside on the way to the coach, she looked over at Hadrian. "You should wear one of your costumes tonight from when we were working in the City." They'd been in disguise, and Hadrian had posed as her working-class brother.

"You *don't* want me to be the Earl of Ravenhurst?"

"I'm not sure I want to draw attention to us," Tilda explained. "I think you ought to be Mr. Becket again and become the earl if we think it's necessary." He'd gone by his surname before during their investigations.

"We're still hiding then," he said with a sigh.

"This is work, not a social event." Tilda rather wished it could be the latter. A night at the theatre—a real night—with Hadrian would be delightful. "We won't be hiding when I come to dinner at Ravenhurst House tomorrow."

Hadrian eyed her cautiously, but with hope. "Does that mean

you've changed your mind, and I can introduce you as the woman I'm courting?"

They'd reached the coach, so Tilda didn't answer. Hadrian directed Leach to take them to her grandmother's house, then they climbed inside.

Tilda set her reticule in her lap and kept her gaze focused on it. "I don't think I'm quite ready to make our courtship formal. That feels very…final. Even so, I wonder if it's becoming too hard to separate our work from our social relationship. You can't seem to stop flirting with me whilst we're investigating, and I confess I'm becoming less immune." She stole a glance at him and saw that he was grinning.

"That is most welcome," he said. "May I take that as an invitation to flirt with you more often?"

"*Hadrian.*" Tilda rolled her eyes. "I'm struggling with what to do. I love you. I want to be with you. But I don't know how that can work."

Hadrian took her hand and looked into her eyes. "My darling, it *will* work *because* we love each other."

"Are you truly prepared for people who will not accept me?" Tilda wasn't sure if she was.

"Yes. Those people don't matter to me." He brought her hand to his lips and kissed her wrist. "You do."

A delicious shiver danced up Tilda's arm. "I don't know that I'm ready for that. It's bad enough that Chadwick maligned my reputation. In fact, I worry that will reflect poorly on you."

Hadrian released her hand and cupped her face with his palms. "*I don't care.*" He kissed her, and she leaned into him.

After a moment, she pulled away. "Perhaps it would be best if we brought my grandmother as a chaperone tonight. I think I'd feel better if we don't risk anyone's reputation."

"Your grandmother would be absolutely delighted, and so would I. Yes, let's bring her with us. We'll have great fun."

"You're so thoughtful," Tilda said, overcome with how much

she cared for this man and how she'd never imagined she would feel such emotions. "We'll need to return Grandmama to the coach with Leach after the performance before we interview the prop master."

Hadrian nodded. "What time does the play start?"

"The newspaper said seven."

"That doesn't give us much time to dress and have dinner," Hadrian said with a frown.

Tilda laughed. "Spoken like a true peer. Remember, you aren't dressing for a Society event. Just replace your waistcoat and coat, and you can have dinner with us."

"How can I refuse a *second* invitation from you in the same day?" He grinned again. "I find I cannot. Indeed, even if you invited me to spend the night in a gloomy cemetery, I would not decline."

"A cemetery?"

He shrugged. "It was all I could think of that would be distasteful."

"I actually like cemeteries," Tilda admitted.

"But they're so sad."

"They're also full of love and remembrance, of dignity and respect," Tilda argued. "I used to sit with my father at his grave nearly every day after he died."

Hadrian put his arm around her and pulled her close. He pressed a kiss to her temple. "I shall never think of cemeteries as gloomy again."

They arrived at her grandmother's house, and Tilda turned to face him. "My grandmother still doesn't know we're privately courting. Our visit to the theatre is entirely for investigative purposes."

Hadrian looked nonplussed. "Isn't that precisely what it is?"

"Yes. Mostly." Tilda felt her face heat.

Leaning close, Hadrian whispered, "When you're ready for our formal courtship, I will take you to the grandest theatre, and we'll sit in the most prominent box. Everyone in London will know how I feel about you."

His words made her shiver—and not in entirely the best way. What he described was thrilling and terrifying. For if that came to pass, there would be no turning back.

~

Mrs. Wren was delighted that Hadrian had dined with them that night and even more thrilled to be invited to the theatre. Hadrian had spent as much time watching her and Tilda enjoying the performance as he had watching it himself.

The fire effects had been impressive, and the crowd had reacted with boisterous awe and rapture. A night at the Brittania was quite different than a night in a West End theatre. Hadrian was surprised to find they could eat and drink during the performance.

When the final play—there had been three in total with musical performances between them—concluded, they escorted Mrs. Wren back to Hadrian's coach, where Leach would wait with her whilst Hadrian and Tilda questioned the property master about the flame effects. Mrs. Wren understood they had investigative work to complete and told them to take as long as they needed.

"Let's find the stage door," Tilda suggested. "That would be at the side or back of the building."

Hadrian escorted her to a narrow side street that was little more than an alley. They made their way through the shadows to the back of the theatre. "I'm glad I'm with you," Hadrian said. "Sometimes I think about you investigating these cases without my assistance, and I confess it makes me agitated."

"But I'm not investigating these without you." Tilda gave him a brief smile.

"I know that, but if not for a chance of fate in which we encountered one another outside your grandfather's cousin's house those many months ago now, you would be."

"We were bound to meet during the course of that investigation," Tilda said. "It's fortuitous, however, that we met earlier on."

"Do you even understand what I'm trying to say?" Hadrian asked with equal parts frustration and humor. "I would worry about you doing things like this on your own. I haven't ever asked, but did you conduct investigations of this nature before we met?"

"If you mean murders, no. However, I did occasionally go out at night and watch for errant husbands who were being unfaithful. I always took my father's pistol."

Hadrian grimaced as he held up his hand. "Never mind, I don't want to know."

"I'm fine," she said with a laugh. "I'm here, aren't I?"

They arrived at the back of the theatre, where a door marked "stage" was illuminated by gaslight. Hadrian knocked and very shortly a squat fellow appeared. He wore a cap and squinted at them. He opened his mouth, then snapped it closed as he surveyed Hadrian.

"Good evening," Hadrian said. "I'm Becket. My friend, Miss Wren, and I were greatly impressed by the fire effects in tonight's performance, and we hoped to speak with the man responsible."

"Jesson'd be happy to speak with ye," the young man said with a quick smile. He invited them inside then closed the door. "'E's our prop master and mechanist. Follow me, if ye will."

They made their way through a labyrinth of corridors until they reached a small office. Through a doorway at the back, Hadrian saw into a large workroom which held a great many tools and props. A man a few years older than Hadrian sat at a desk and turned to face them as they entered.

"Jesson, this be Mr. Becket and his friend, Miss Wren," the doorkeeper said. "They want to talk to ye about the fire."

Jesson stood. He was a large man with broad shoulders and legs as thick as tree trunks. His presence immediately dominated the small office. It occurred to Hadrian that he would make a particularly fierce Spring-heeled-Jack.

The prop master inclined his head toward Hadrian. He had an extremely wide forehead and an almost unbelievably sharp, square jawline. "Happy to speak with ye." He spoke in a distinctly East End manner like the doorkeeper.

When the doorkeeper didn't immediately depart, Jesson waved him way. "Off with ye, Melvin." He turned his attention to Hadrian and Tilda as the doorkeeper trudged off. "You enjoyed the show?" Jesson asked.

"Very much," Tilda said with a smile. "We were hoping you might share how you created some of those effects."

"Well, I can't give too much away now," Jesson replied with a chuckle.

"I'm particularly interested in how the one character seemed to make flame spring from their fingertips," Tilda said.

Jesson nodded. "Aye, that's a neat trick." He went to a table against the wall opposite the desk and picked up a wire contraption. "This is what the actor wore." The prop master held it to the ends of his first two fingers. "Goes on here, but I can't wear it because me hand's too big. I made it just for him." He gestured to material at the end of the device. "The cotton here is soaked with spirits of wine, then the actor lights it with a stationery taper that's cleverly concealed onstage."

"I see," Tilda said enthusiastically. "It ignites far enough away from his fingers that it doesn't burn him."

"That's the idea," Jesson replied. "We don't use much of the spirits and it burns out fast."

"Genius," Hadrian said with a grin. "Do you often create devices for the effects on stage?"

"That's a big part of me job." Jesson stood straight, and Hadrian had to look slightly up at him.

Tilda held her hand out. "May I try it?"

Jesson handed her the device. "It'll be too big for ye, but go on."

She turned the item over in her hands. "I'd be afraid I'd burn myself," she said with a nervous laugh.

"The seamstress would sew that to the end of a glove," Jesson explained. "Some actors are afraid at first, but they learn the trick and overcome their fear. You would too," he added with a wink.

It was ironic that Jesson mentioned actors, for Hadrian could tell Tilda was acting. She was so good at assuming a role when they made inquiries. Sometimes she did it to put people at ease and other times she was trying to obtain certain information with a role she was playing.

Tilda looked toward Hadrian and offered him the contraption. He considered removing his glove to potentially experience a memory, but he'd promised Tilda he wouldn't. Furthermore, it was unlikely doing so would aid their case. Still, he wanted to look at the device and took it from her.

"Now, the gloves would be wool or leather—that's important," Jesson went on. "The costume designer and I work together to make sure costumes and equipment are safe. We always use wool or leather for anything to do with fire."

"Not oilskin?" Hadrian asked.

Jesson laughed. "Bloody 'ell, no. The oil used to treat the fabric is flammable. We would never want an actor to wear that if 'e were handling flame."

Hadrian glanced at Tilda. "Good to know."

Perhaps Spring-heeled Jack hadn't been wearing oilskin at all but leather. It wasn't as if they could know for sure. They only had eyewitness accounts, not confirmation of the material.

"How do you conceive of these effects?" Tilda asked.

Jesson lifted a shoulder. "Sometimes it's clear what we need to do." He gestured toward the workroom. "Other times, I go into me workshop and experiment. Occasionally, I consult with other property masters. Nicholas Larkin over at the Albion is the best on the Strand."

Tilda walked toward the workshop and peered inside. "Have you ever crafted something that would make it look as though a person were breathing flame?"

"Breathing? No." Jesson responded. "Probably use a tube with a material soaked in spirits of wine. The actor'd blow through the tube and whoosh! Fire!" He gestured with his hands like an explosion and cackled.

Hadrian quashed a smile but exchanged a glance with Tilda.

"What about exaggerated movements, such as jumping high or long distances?" Tilda asked.

"Believe it or not, lighting is the best for most effects," Jesson explained. "And sound. When we use them together, they distract whilst we move someone or something in what appears to be a fantastical way. For jumping, I've used springs in boots. That helps sell the effect. But, truly, ye need the lighting to increase the drama."

So long as they were inquiring about all of Spring-heeled Jack's extraordinary traits, Hadrian asked, "How would you make someone's eyes glow red?" Though Spring-heeled Jack hadn't done that yet in his new incarnation, it had been reported thirty years ago, and he was curious.

Jesson narrowed his eyes briefly. "Sounds like ye're asking about Spring-heeled Jack. Ye think 'e's a fraud?"

"We're investigating Spring-heeled Jack and the kidnappings he's committed," Tilda replied. "I doubt very much he breathes fire or has red eyes or claws."

"I agree with ye, but then I know how someone could make it look like that, so I'm more skeptical than most." His expression turned grim for a moment. "Me wife's terrified he's back. She was a wee thing when he was rampaging about, and the stories scared her something fierce." Jesson looked at Hadrian. "Are ye with the police? Pardon me for saying, but ye don't seem like a constable to me and ye don't sound like one."

"We work *with* the Met, not for it," Tilda said.

"I'm glad if I can 'elp," Jesson said. "To make eyes glow, ye'd use lighting. When we want to give someone on stage an eerie appearance, we might flash a colored light across their face. If I wanted me eyes to look red, I would use a bull's-eye lantern with a red slide. I'd hold it up like so." He lifted his hand to his face. "It would make me eyes reflect red. I don't know if it would be convincing, especially outside a theatre where we'd use light and costuming to disguise the lantern. But in a moment of fear or panic, someone might be fooled into thinking a person had red eyes."

Tilda smiled. "That is an excellent and satisfying explanation. You mentioned Larkin at the Albion as someone who is good at effects. Do—"

"Not good," Jesson corrected gently. "The best."

"Is there anyone else who's nearly as good?"

"Wilmer at the Imperial, and perhaps Harris at the Theatre Royal Drury Lane, but 'e's pompous, and I wouldn't ask 'im anything." Jesson wrinkled his nose.

"Thank you, Mr. Jesson," Tilda said. "You've been most helpful."

"I hope ye catch the bloke," he said. "It was one thing for 'im to go about frightening young ladies, but to kidnap and kill 'em—" He shook his head. "'Orrible business."

"Agreed," Hadrian said. "Thank you, Mr. Jesson." He put his hand on the small of Tilda's back as she turned, then escorted her from the prop master's office. Looking about, he frowned slightly. "Now, we have to find our way out of here."

"I think it's this way." Tilda led him along a corridor.

They turned a corner and came upon a space with several wooden pegs affixed to the wall from which hung a variety of costumes.

Hadrian froze. The smell of greasepaint permeated his senses, and the scent along with seeing the costumes reminded him of the memory he saw from the cloak.

He turned to Tilda. "This looks like the vision I saw from the cloak at Scotland Yard before I collapsed." He gestured around. "There were costumes hanging on the wall like this and the smell of greasepaint."

Tilda's gaze took on a sheen of excitement. "This theatre, exactly?"

"I don't think so. The wall in the memory was dark blue." He looked at her with enthusiasm. "I'm confident the kidnapper is somehow involved with a theatre."

"This is excellent," Tilda said happily. "I hope Teague and Sergeant Wycombe were able to ascertain the theatre habits of the Alnwicks and Chadwicks. If so, that would help us narrow down where to investigate, because, as Teague said, there are simply too many theatres in London."

Hadrian finally felt a modicum of satisfaction since they'd started this case. "This has been a fruitful excursion. Jesson's explanations were most informative."

"Indeed. It has me thinking the kidnapper could be someone like him. A property master or mechanist certainly has the necessary skills and knowledge."

"I know you don't mean Jesson in particular, but I confess that when I saw his size, I thought he'd make a fearsome Spring-heeled Jack." Hadrian chuckled.

"He would, but is he light enough on his feet to make a convincing leap?" Tilda mused. "Not that Mr. Jesson is under investigation at this time."

"Should he be?" Hadrian hoped not. He'd rather liked the man.

"If we find any clues that link him to Miss Chadwick or Lady Priscilla, yes. We'll see what Teague and Wycombe are able to learn with regard to the Alnwicks' and Chadwicks' theatre connections." She cocked her head. "I found the costuming information interesting. I suspect the Spring-heeled Jack of thirty years ago might have been wearing leather, even though it was described as oilskin."

"Agreed. That would have been safer for him if he was doing tricks with fire."

"Let's find our way out," Tilda said, moving to another corridor that ultimately took them back to the rear stage door. The doorkeeper was still there.

The doorkeeper grinned at them, revealing a gap next to his top front teeth. "Did you learn all the secrets?"

"Not all, but it was most illuminating," Hadrian replied. "Thank you for introducing us to Mr. Jesson."

"'Appy to be of help." He opened the door for them, and Hadrian quickly escorted Tilda to the front of the theatre. The air was quieter as the crowd that had departed the theatre following the performances was now gone.

When they reached Hoxton Street where the coach was parked, Leach jumped down to greet them.

"Is all well?" Hadrian asked.

Leach nodded. "Quite. Haven't heard a peep from Mrs. Wren. How did things go inside?"

"Excellent," Hadrian replied. "This was a very productive evening, as well as most agreeable." He smiled at Tilda. "Did you enjoy the play?"

"I did. In fact, for a short time, I forgot we were here to make inquiries. I've only ever seen a few plays, and I liked it more than I remembered. I know my grandmother had a wonderful time."

"Glad to hear it," Leach said as he opened the door to the coach.

Hadrian helped Tilda inside, then followed her into the coach. Right away, he heard soft snores coming from the rear-facing seat. Mrs. Wren rested against the side of the coach, a blanket covering her lower half. She appeared to be asleep.

Tilda turned her head toward Hadrian and put her finger to her lips. Hadrian nodded with a faint smile.

They began moving, and though Hadrian always wanted to talk with Tilda, he found he was enjoying the silence with her too. He reached for her hand, but she pulled away from him and inclined her head toward her grandmother, her eyes communicating that they weren't alone.

Hadrian shrugged and mouthed, "She's sleeping."

Tilda pursed her lips slightly and glanced at her grandmother. When she looked back at Hadrian, her brow puckered a moment. Finally, she took his hand. He squeezed her gently and smiled. They rode all the way back to Marylebone like that, and when they arrived, he released her with reluctance.

Leach opened the door and Hadrian climbed down as Tilda woke her grandmother.

"Oh," Mrs. Wren said sheepishly. "I must have fallen asleep. Dear me. Did you have success?" she asked as Hadrian helped her from the coach.

"I'd say so," Hadrian replied.

She looked up at him. "See you in the morning."

He nodded. "Sleep well. Good night, Mrs. Wren," he said to her grandmother.

Tilda took her grandmother's arm, and they walked toward the house. Vaughn had the door open for them before they reached the stoop.

"Seems as though you had a pleasant evening, my lord," Leach said.

"We did." Hadrian smiled the whole way home.

He could become used to many nights like this. Indeed, he would be overjoyed to have them for the rest of his life.

## CHAPTER 17

The next morning, as Hadrian and Tilda rode together to Scotland Yard, she was glad he didn't try to hold her hand again. Not because she didn't enjoy it, but their intimacy, for lack of a better word, was becoming too regular and too... normal.

What would happen if they decided they ought to remain friends and professional associates and nothing more? She wondered if they'd already moved too far past where things would become awkward if they didn't forge a romantic future together. It was likely their friendship and professional association would perish.

Tilda wanted to think about that even less than she wanted to think about how she could possibly agree to a public courtship, let alone marriage. She couldn't even manage to get a private courtship right. They were supposed to be quietly determining if they would suit, but what did that even mean?

They knew they got along well together. They had similar values. They certainly shared a primary interest in investigating. But what did they share aside from their investigations? How could she know if she would fit into Hadrian's world? She supposed she'd tried a few times—once at an event at Northumberland House for an investigation and a couple of teas with his mother.

However, those hadn't been attempts to enter his world on a permanent basis. As his wife. She wasn't sure she could do that, and she was even less sure she'd be accepted. Though, how could she know if she didn't try?

This was why it was important that she attend dinner with his family tonight. If it went well, perhaps she would feel more at ease about the direction in which they were headed.

"You're pensive this morning," Hadrian noted. "Are you thinking about what we discovered last night or anticipating what we'll learn from Teague this morning?"

"Both," Tilda lied. She didn't want to discuss what she'd really been thinking about. "It finally feels as though we're gaining some momentum with this case."

Hadrian grinned at her, and her belly did a flip. "Finally."

They arrived at Scotland Yard and departed the coach. As they walked toward the building, they encountered Sergeant Wycombe. Tall and slender, he looked as though he could be younger than Hadrian but was actually a couple of years older.

The sergeant's small blue eyes greeted them warmly. "Good morning, my lord, Miss Wren. Are you here to see Detective Inspector Teague?"

"We are," Tilda replied. "And you?"

He walked with them to the door of the building. "Yes. I assume you heard about the Spring-heeled Jack sighting last night off the Strand?"

As Hadrian opened the door, Tilda stopped short and turned to face Wycombe. "What was that?"

"You *haven't* heard." Wycombe's eyes gleamed with anticipation. "I suppose it hasn't made it into the newspapers yet. My apologies. I'll tell you about it on our way up to Teague's office."

They continued into the building and made their way toward the stairs.

"Spring-heeled Jack appeared outside a chandler just around the corner from the Strand," Wycombe said. "The theatres had just got out, so there was a crowd of people."

"What happened?" Hadrian asked as they started up the stairs.

Tilda's pulse raced. Was the kidnapper now committing attacks in public to mimic what had been done thirty years earlier?

"Witnesses say he appeared out of nowhere and breathed blue flame before he leapt up one story of the building in a single bound." Wycombe kept turning his head periodically as he spoke. "They described his cloak spreading like wings, and when he landed on the ledge, there was another flash of blue flame followed by a bright white flash. Then he vanished."

"Sounds like quite a spectacle," Tilda remarked at the top of the stairs. "Spring-heeled Jack just disappeared without attacking or kidnapping anyone?"

"That's right." Wycombe led them to Teague's office.

"What was the purpose?" Tilda asked rhetorically.

"Sounds like the sort of thing he did when he first appeared thirty years ago—in the instances where he didn't attack anyone," Hadrian suggested as they arrived at Teague's office.

"Perhaps this wasn't the kidnapper but an impostor." Tilda stepped into the office and Teague rose from behind his desk.

"Good morning," Teague said. "Are you discussing Spring-heeled Jack's spectacle last night?" He moved around the desk toward the seating area.

"Yes, and that's precisely what I just called it." Tilda sat in one of the chairs.

Hadrian looked to Wycombe. "You said it was just off the Strand?"

The sergeant nodded. "A side street."

"Did this happen near a theatre?" Tilda asked.

"Around the corner from one," Wycombe replied.

Tilda turned her gaze to Teague as he sat in the other chair opposite her. "What do you think this means?"

The detective inspector shrugged. "I'm not sure. I'll be going straight there to make inquiries after we discuss our discoveries from yesterday."

Tilda desperately wanted to accompany him. "Would you mind if we came with you?"

"Not at all," Teague replied. "I'm keen to hear what you learned—if anything—at the Brittania last night. Wycombe and I spoke with both His Grace and Vincent Chadwick about attending the theatre. The elder Mr. Chadwick refused to see us."

"Not surprising," Tilda said. "I'm glad the younger Mr. Chadwick was able to help. What did you learn?"

"Vincent said they attend the theatre quite often," Wycombe said. "Their favorite theatre is the Adelphi, but he noted that Miss Chadwick preferred attending the Albion of late. The Alnwicks are not regular patrons like the Chadwicks. His Grace couldn't name any particular theatre they preferred."

"What of your inquiries?" Teague asked.

Tilda related what they'd learned from Mr. Jesson about the use of a leather costume with flame effects and how property masters like him were skilled in making various devices to create effects. Of course, she couldn't tell him about Hadrian's vision that confirmed the kidnapper had something to do with the theatre.

Instead, she said, "Ravenhurst and I have a strong suspicion the kidnapper has some association with a theatre, and perhaps the Chadwicks' frequent attendance supports that. I'm very interested in making inquiries at the Albion and the Adelphi."

"In that case, it might be best if we divide ourselves today in order to accomplish more." Teague braced his elbows on his thighs as he leaned forward in his chair. "Would you mind visiting the theatres this afternoon instead of accompanying me and Wycombe?"

"Not at all. I'd be happy to." Tilda tamped down a slight sense of disappointment—she couldn't do everything. Not when another kidnapping could be imminent, and they needed to move quickly to apprehend Spring-heeled Jack. Furthermore, it wasn't as if she didn't want to conduct the inquiries at the theatres. In fact, it made sense for her and Hadrian to do so after their discoveries last night at the Brittania.

Teague abruptly stood and returned to his desk where he unlocked the evidence drawer. He withdrew something small and approached Tilda. "You should take this cap with you as you make your inquiries. You probably should have had it last night. My apologies." He placed the cap in Tilda's outstretched palm. "Perhaps we could meet later this afternoon to discuss our findings, if we've finished with our respective inquiries."

Hadrian grimaced faintly, and Tilda presumed he was thinking of his dinner. He would need to be home to dress and prepare—the things he'd suggested doing last night before going to the theatre. Tilda would not begrudge him those activities today.

If she was truly going to try to fit into his world, she needed to respect the work that went into it. If she couldn't do that, there was no point in having any kind of courtship, private or otherwise.

After tucking the cap into a small inner pocket inside her reticule, she gave Teague an apologetic look. "I'm afraid his lordship and I have an engagement this evening, so tomorrow morning would be preferable." She was aware of Hadrian sending her a small, secretive smile of both appreciation and something far stronger. The glint in his blue eyes sparked a sense of yearning within her.

Teague clapped his hands on his knees and rose. "Tomorrow morning will be soon enough."

Tilda and Hadrian departed and made their way downstairs.

"I want to start at the Albion," Tilda said as they stepped outside. "I confess I wish we could also investigate the Spring-heeled Jack spectacle."

"I'm curious about that too. However, Teague is right that we will accomplish more apart. At least there hasn't been another kidnapping. Perhaps Spring-heeled Jack is done with that and has moved on to performing."

"I hope there won't be another kidnapping, but we don't yet know if this Spring-heeled Jack who was seen last night is even the same person," Tilda cautioned. "I wonder how he made himself appear to jump a full story. There has to be some explanation of stagecraft, just as there was for the blue flame and the red eyes. Springs in his boots would have helped, but I doubt they would be enough to achieve that height. Jesson indicated lighting was the best form of trickery, but how would he manage that outside a theatre?"

"There's bound to be some evidence as to how he achieved the feat," Hadrian said. "We could certainly return to the Brittania today and query Mr. Jesson about how that might have been accomplished."

Tilda nodded. "We could also ask the property master at one of the theatres we visit today. They may be able to tell us."

"Good idea." They arrived at the coach, and Hadrian directed Leach to drive them to the Albion Theatre off the Strand.

Once they were on their way, Hadrian turned his head toward Tilda. "Thank you for telling Teague we aren't able to meet this afternoon. I wouldn't have been able to accompany you, and I appreciate you making sure I'm included."

"I couldn't have gone either," she said. "What I said is true—we have an engagement, and I must prepare."

He smiled. "I'm looking forward to seeing you socially this evening, and your grandmother. I'll send Leach to fetch you."

Tilda wasn't surprised by the offer. He often sent Leach to

drive her places when he couldn't accompany her. "That's very kind of you."

"Leach would berate me if I didn't ask him. In truth, he'd probably just do it anyway."

Tilda laughed. "You make it seem as if your retainers are becoming loyal to me." She thought of how the butler and his valet had deferred to her the other night.

"They like you very much, which is not surprising. In fact, if they *didn't* feel that way, I might find them wanting."

"They are *your* loyal people in *your* household," Tilda said. "You can't put me before them."

His eyes held hers with a steady promise. "My dear, I can put you before everyone. Indeed, there is nothing I want more."

Tilda shivered. His sentiment was lovely but also overwhelming. It almost made her feel as if she were on a pedestal, which is how she'd thought of her father. And she'd learned that loving someone that much came with a terrible potential for heartache and loss. She never wanted to endure that again—nor did she want Hadrian to. He'd already suffered the death of his brother.

Did that mean she never intended to love anyone again? It was already too late for that. She loved Hadrian quite fiercely.

She hadn't sought or chosen love, but it had found her. She just needed the courage to fully embrace it.

# CHAPTER 18

$\mathcal{A}$fter a short gathering in the drawing room at Ravenhurst House that evening, Hadrian's mother led everyone to the dining room. She was accompanied by Mrs. Wren.

As the ranking person in attendance, Hadrian ought to have gone first, but this was a family dinner, and he did not stand on such ceremony. In fact, he escorted Tilda last, allowing his sister Beatrice and her husband, the Viscount Courtenay, to precede them.

He'd left the menu entirely to his cook, Mrs. Rowe, and had no doubt it would be spectacular as usual. However, he had chosen the wine for each course and determined the seating arrangement. He sat at the head, of course, and Tilda sat at his right, whilst his sister was on his left. Next to her sat Tilda's grandmother, and Hadrian's mother was at the opposite end of the table from him. The final seat, to Tilda's right, belonged to his brother-in-law, Courtenay.

Hadrian might have preferred to seat Tilda next to her grandmother, but he knew his mother would have found fault with that. She was an enthusiastic proponent of ensuring guests had the chance to meet someone new. But Hadrian refused to place Tilda anywhere other than right beside him.

As they took their seats at the table, he couldn't help admiring Tilda's appearance this evening. He so rarely saw her dressed in such a manner. She wore the dark green gown she'd acquired for a dinner they'd attended at a medium's house during an investigation a few months ago. The color was perfect on her, and Hadrian found himself wanting to gift her with emeralds to wear at her ears and throat. Except, he didn't think she ever wore earrings. Emerald combs then. Her maid, Clara, had arranged Tilda's reddish-blonde hair into a flawlessly elegant style that would support such adornment.

But would Tilda even want to wear emeralds? She was used to simplicity and usefulness.

Hadrian had chosen a dry sherry to accompany the soup course with Tilda's grandmother in mind, for he knew she enjoyed sherry. He watched for her reaction when she sipped it and was gratified when her features lit with appreciation.

"I'm pleased you could join us this evening, Mrs. Wren." Hadrian's mother's blue eyes fixed first on Tilda's grandmother and then on Tilda. "And you, Miss Wren."

"We were delighted to receive the invitation," Tilda's grandmother replied. She looked down the table at Hadrian. "You must compliment your cook on this oxtail soup. It's delicious. And the wine is perfect."

"I will inform Mrs. Rowe," Hadrian said warmly. "I chose the wine with you in mind, so I'm very glad you like it."

Mrs. Wren smiled. "That was most thoughtful of you."

After a few moments of silence, Courtenay glanced sideways at Tilda. He was in his middle thirties and sported a rather robust pair of sideburns that cloaked his round face. "Is it true you're a private detective and that you investigate cases with my brother-in-law?" He asked the question as if the answer was in doubt when, in fact, Hadrian and Tilda's professional relationship was quite established. Perhaps he hadn't been paying attention when this had been mentioned in his presence.

"Yes," Tilda confirmed before taking a sip of soup.

Courtenay squinted at Hadrian. "How do you find time to do such things, and what do you *do* exactly?"

Hadrian set his spoon down. "We make inquiries of people who provide information about the case that we're working on. We investigate different persons associated with whatever we're looking for, and—"

"What is that exactly?" Courtenay asked, cutting him off. "I seem to recall Miss Wren had something to do with those murderous mediums a few months ago, which I find incredibly hard to believe." He tossed another glance at Tilda. "What could you possibly know about investigating a murder?"

"Courtenay, don't interrupt," Beatrice whispered toward her husband.

Hadrian kept a rein on his rising impatience. "She actually *solves* murders."

Tilda sent Hadrian an appreciative look tinged with humor. Did she find Courtenay amusing? Hadrian supposed that was better than if she found him annoying.

"I know as much as any other detective," Tilda replied serenely. "Perhaps more than some, since my father worked for the Met and taught me everything he knew about investigating and solving crime. I grew up believing in discovering the truth, and I possess a strong sense of justice. It's my calling to help those in need and ensure the safety of our society and community."

Mrs. Wren gazed at her granddaughter with unabashed pride. "It's most admirable."

"It's odd," Courtenay murmured. "Though, Miss Wren, I suppose you're in a position where you must have employment, and perhaps this was all you could think to do."

Beatrice sent her husband a pointed look, but he didn't seem to notice. Or if he did, he had no idea that she was losing patience as Hadrian was.

"I'm not the sort who can be idle." Tilda gave Courtenay an enigmatic smile. "Nor do I take pleasure in many of the more feminine pursuits, such as needlework or cooking. I find I prefer an enterprise that is much more invigorating for my mind. And yes, as it happens, being a private detective ensures my grand-mother and our household staff are well cared for."

"Still strange, if you ask me." Courtenay swept his gaze back to Hadrian. "Raven, you know people have been talking about this fetish you have for working with Miss Wren for some time now. I think everyone expected it to be a temporary distraction for you. Don't you think it's gone on long enough?"

Beatrice sucked in an audible breath, and Hadrian noted her nostrils flaring. She pursed her lips at Courtenay.

Hadrian had picked up his spoon to have more soup and now gripped it tightly as he tamped down his anger and kept the barest hold on civility. "On the contrary, I should like our association to continue indefinitely." He gave his brother-in-law a placid smile as he reminded himself that Courtenay was not actively trying to stir up trouble. He was merely fatuously obtuse. He often said things that were on his mind without thinking of how they would be received by his audience. Beatrice was a saint, for she managed to tolerate his boorishness and only intervened when he egregiously overstepped. If she did not, she'd likely be haranguing him endlessly.

The footman removed the soup and replaced it with the next course, a poached salmon.

Courtenay sent Tilda a pitying look. "I don't imagine there are a great many people wanting to hire you. You can't have much business."

Beatrice opened her mouth, but their mother spoke before she could.

"Courtenay, you must behave," their mother said crossly. She didn't have the patience for his thickheadedness, and Hadrian was surprised she'd endured his questions and comments this long. "I hired Miss Wren to investigate something for me. She's incredibly skilled. Now, do find something else to converse about."

"I do, of course, want to discuss yesterday's Ascot." Courtenay didn't look at all bothered by his mother-in-law's reproof. Rather, he grinned as he looked about the table. "I still can't believe Blue Gown did it—the Derby *and* the Ascot! Surprised you weren't there yesterday, Raven."

Courtenay didn't wait for Hadrian to reply, but then he hadn't asked a question. As he was now on the topic of horse racing, Tilda was safe from his obnoxious questions.

Whilst Hadrian listened to his brother-in-law drone on about his favorite topic, he noticed Tilda's grandmother's face turning red. Suddenly, Tilda jumped up from the table and rushed around to her grandmother's chair. Mrs. Wren leaned forward as Tilda massaged her back and bent her head to whisper in her ear. Nodding, Mrs. Wren tried to cough. Tilda then struck her back several times. At last, Mrs. Wren took a gasping breath. Tilda looked to the footman standing nearby and quietly asked him to bring a glass of water.

Courtenay had stopped talking to stare at Mrs. Wren.

Beatrice turned toward Mrs. Wren and looked at Tilda, her golden-brown eyes wide with concern. "Is there anything I can do?"

Tilda smiled softly. "I think she had a fish bone caught in her throat. It's happened before. Grandmama is rather sensitive to such things."

The footman brought a glass of water and handed it to Tilda, who put it to her grandmother's lips. "Can you take a tiny sip and see if it goes down?" Tilda murmured.

Her grandmother took a small sip and swallowed, then

inhaled deeply and leaned back against the chair. She smiled at Tilda and as she worked to bring her breathing under control.

Tilda continued to rub her grandmother's back as she fixed on Courtenay. "You were just telling us about Blue Gown's sire." She behaved as if nothing untoward had happened, *and* she'd kept the thread of Courtenay's rather boring monologue.

When Tilda finally stepped away from her grandmother, Hadrian noticed his mother lightly touched her forearm as she passed by her chair. She appeared to murmur, "Well done."

Tilda inclined her head and returned to her seat. They finished the fish course whilst Courtenay worked to put them to sleep.

The next course was a roast saddle of lamb with mint sauce and roast potatoes, one of Mrs. Rowe's specialties. The accompanying wine was a claret.

Beatrice's eyes gleamed with appreciation as she swept up her glass. She looked to Hadrian. "Is this my favorite from '63?"

"It is." Their father had maintained a respectable wine cellar, and Hadrian had aimed to do the same.

Beatrice held up her glass. "To Miss Wren and her various and wonderful skills, and to Mrs. Wren. I'm very pleased to meet you both this evening."

"Hear, hear," Hadrian said, lifting his glass.

They all toasted and drank. Everyone ate in silence for a few moments, then Beatrice looked over at Tilda. "I've never cared much for needlework either, but I do it when necessary."

"The irony in that is you're awfully good at it," their mother said.

Beatrice laughed. "Regrettably, yes. I much prefer riding." She looked at Tilda. "That's why Courtenay and I live in Wimbledon. It allows us to keep more horses, and we have space to ride. The country estate is just so far from London. Do you ride?"

"No," Tilda replied. "I've never felt the need to learn. Living in the city as I do, I have many ways in which to move about."

"That is true, but you might consider it for recreation." Beatrice wanted everyone to love horses and riding as much as she did. She'd always been exceptionally disappointed that her sisters preferred reading and music. "It's most invigorating. You mentioned preferring to activate your mind, and I feel the same. One of the things I like most about riding is I can think without interruption as the wind rushes over me and the ground passes beneath me. I can lose myself in thought. It's most restorative."

"That does sound intriguing," Tilda admitted. "Though, I'm not sure I'd want to lose myself in my thoughts whilst riding a horse. I'm afraid I would find myself on the ground."

Beatrice smiled. "Not with practice, you wouldn't. Something tells me once you put your mind to something, you make a success of it."

"Except for needlework," Mrs. Wren said, sending her granddaughter a warmly teasing look. "I'm afraid she's not successful at that."

"Is that because she tried and failed, or because she didn't really want to put her mind to it in the first place?" Beatrice asked with a faint smile.

Tilda had just swallowed a piece of lamb and put her hand to her mouth briefly. Hadrian could see she was smiling. She swallowed and nodded at Beatrice. "The latter, actually. I honestly can't say if I'd be good with needles, since I haven't tried, nor do I plan to."

"Nor do you need to, dear," Mrs. Wren said. "You manage the household beautifully. It's quite a feat, since we've more than doubled the size of our staff in recent months."

"Should we look forward to being invited to dinner at your house then?" Courtenay asked with a laugh.

Hadrian knew his brother-in-law was trying to be amusing, but in the context of his other oblivious questions and comments, he could be taken as rude.

Thankfully, Tilda's expression held mild amusement. "You never know."

"Where did you find your new retainers?" Beatrice asked. "I find myself in need of a new maid. Mine has decided to marry."

Tilda set her silver down and reached for her wineglass. "Surprisingly, I've found them through some of the investigations we've worked on. In fact, we know of a lady's maid who is searching for a new position." She looked to Hadrian. "Isn't that right?"

Hadrian nodded. "She's here now—temporarily—because I was going to offer her a position as a maid at Ravenhurst House. But I was rather hoping she'd find employment as a lady's maid, since that was her most recent position."

Mrs. Wren told Beatrice about their maid, Clara, and how she'd come to them after having worked for one of Tilda's clients.

Meanwhile, Tilda leaned slightly toward Hadrian and whispered, "Should you tell your sister that Bannet worked for a murder victim?"

"What's that you say?" Courtenay asked with a tone of alarm. "Are you discussing *murder*?"

All eyes at the table snapped to Courtenay.

"Beatrice, we should tell you that the maid, Bannet, was most recently lady's maid to Miss Delia Chadwick," Hadrian explained.

Hadrian's mother frowned deeply. "That poor young woman who was kidnapped and murdered."

"Yes," Tilda replied evenly. "Bannet is devastated, as you can understand. We hope that, wherever she goes to work, people will be kind with her."

"That would be quite bizarre." Courtenay forked a large piece of lamb into his mouth.

Beatrice's light brown brows drew together. "Such a tragedy. That poor girl and her family."

Their mother nodded. "I met Miss Chadwick just before the Season started at a tea hosted by the Duchess of Alnwick. Miss

Chadwick was rather quiet, but that's because she stuttered, and her mother seemed to encourage her silence. I saw her again recently, not long before she so tragically died, and she was much improved. She spoke quite smoothly. It's always so sad to see a flower blooming, then snipped too soon."

Hadrian blinked at his mother's rather florid words before taking a drink of claret.

They finished the course, and as the footman came around to pick up the plates, Courtenay snatched up his wine glass very quickly. "I'm not quite finished with this yet." His movement was uncontrolled, and some of the claret sloshed onto Tilda's sleeve. Hadrian was unaccountably outraged. He loved that gown, and he knew she didn't possess a great many fashionable garments.

Beatrice gasped softly. "Courtenay, you must be more careful."

Courtenay waved his free hand. "You know how clumsy I am. 'Tis a shame I lost that wine, though."

Tilda turned her head toward the footman who'd moved close. She spoke softly as she used her napkin to dry her sleeve. "May I have another napkin?"

The footman hastened to provide her with the replacement and took the soiled napkins when she was finished. Tilda readjusted herself and sent a warm smile to Beatrice across the table. "I understand you have four children. What are their ages?"

Beatrice launched into a lengthy description of her children, whom she loved dearly.

As the sorbet was served, Tilda listened intently and seemed genuinely interested in each of them. Hadrian couldn't help thinking she could be their aunt.

He realized he had no idea what Tilda even thought of children. Some people didn't care for them. Seeing his sisters with their children had encouraged Hadrian to want to experience fatherhood, but even more, he'd felt it was his duty to provide an heir. Now that he'd fallen in love with Tilda, he imagined miniature versions of her with her keen intellect and brilliant curiosity. She would make a fine mother.

They finished dinner in relative peace. Courtenay only put his foot in it once or twice more, and as with his prior offenses, Tilda handled each with aplomb.

Instead of remaining in the dining room to drink port, for Hadrian didn't particularly want to spend time alone with Courtenay, he suggested they all adjourn to the drawing room.

Hadrian made sure to sit beside Tilda on a settee with room for only the two of them. "Thank you for putting up with Courtenay," he whispered. "Perhaps I should have warned you, but he truly doesn't mean any ill. I will say he outdid himself tonight with his comments."

"He strikes me as the sort of person who perhaps can't think or see past himself," Tilda said diplomatically.

"That's a fair description. Sometimes I wonder what my sister saw in him when she agreed to their marriage, but they share a passion for horses, and perhaps that's enough." Hadrian leaned closer to her. "Have you been able to turn your thoughts away from the investigation this evening? I find it's lingering in the back of my mind."

"Surprisingly, yes," Tilda replied. "That doesn't mean I'm not looking forward to tomorrow. It was very disappointing not to be able to speak with anyone at the Albion Theatre this afternoon."

They had gone there first, but everyone they wanted to speak with had not yet arrived. They could have returned later, but they hadn't time, so tomorrow it would be.

They were, however, able to speak with the property manager at the Adelphi Theatre. As with Mr. Jesson of the Britannia, he'd discussed some of the things he made for special effects. He was not as forthcoming as Jesson, however, citing secrecy and preserving the "magic of theatrical display." He'd been a very serious sort.

Tilda's eyes glinted with anticipation as she regarded Hadrian. "I can't decide which I'm most looking forward to tomorrow: returning to the Albion or hearing what Teague discovered from his investigation into Spring-heeled Jack's performance last night."

Hadrian grinned, sharing her excitement. "I feel the same."

He caught his mother watching them. "We should stop whispering," he said to Tilda. "It's being noted, and it's probably rude."

Tilda arched a brow at him. "Only 'probably?'"

Hadrian laughed.

A short while later, Tilda and her grandmother departed. Hadrian's mother, sister, and brother-in-law prepared to leave as well.

Hadrian pulled his mother aside for a moment. "I hope tonight changed your opinion somewhat of Miss Wren."

"Is that why you invited her and her grandmother?" she asked. "I should have realized. You know I think highly of her as an investigator, but I confess I *am* seeing her in a different light. I just don't know if she's up to being a countess."

"You saw how she comported herself at dinner." Hadrian kept his voice even despite wanting to shout Tilda's charms from every rooftop. "She managed an obnoxious guest, an infirmity, *and* a wardrobe mishap. Plus, she was engaging and perfectly mannered."

"I can't argue with any of that, but I also can't forget that she works for a living and is expected to support a household with her income." His mother's brow puckered briefly. "Whilst I may support her professional endeavors, that doesn't mean I want my son's wife to be a common private detective."

"There is nothing at all common about Tilda." Hadrian worked to maintain an evenness and warmth to his tone. "Mother, you're going to have to relinquish some of your ingrained expectations. The world today is not the world you knew as a young woman entering into marriage."

Her brows pitched together as she regarded him with something akin to alarm. "Your advocacy of her is quite passionate. Is there anything I need to know?"

"I have no news to share as of yet, but if I'm fortunate, I will. Soon. I hope you'll be as happy for me as I hope to be." Provided Tilda agreed to marriage.

"I will be very happy indeed when you take a wife." She looked a bit uneasy, and Hadrian chose to ignore that. "I only hope you know what you're doing."

"Have I disappointed you yet?" he asked.

She smiled and patted his arm. "No, you have not. Good night, dear."

Hadrian bid her, his sister, and Courtenay good evening. His mother was coming around, and he was certain Beatrice was quite in favor of Tilda. They'd got on very well.

Now, he could only hope that Tilda would also be convinced that they belonged together.

# CHAPTER 19

The next morning, Tilda walked into the parlor to await Hadrian's arrival.

Her grandmother looked up from reading the newspaper, her gaze fixing on Tilda over the top of her spectacles. "Off to make more inquiries?"

"We are." Tilda drew on her gloves.

"I'm glad you were able to set all that aside last night. That was such a lovely dinner, except for Lord Courtenay." Grandmama sniffed. "I found him rather insufferable."

Tilda chuckled. "Yes, Grandmama, you said as much in the coach last night." Leach had driven them home after dinner.

"It bears repeating," Grandmama said with a shrug. "I may do so yet again. You handled him very well, as you did everything that transpired. I'm terribly sorry about that fish bone."

"I'm relieved it wasn't truly stuck." Tilda gave her a reassuring smile. Occasionally, her grandmother would feel a fish bone going down her throat and start coughing uncontrollably. In most instances, the bone wasn't actually stuck; it had just tickled on the way down.

"I'm glad you were there to help ease my discomfort. And Lady Courtenay was so very kind too. She seemed to like you."

"I liked her too." Tilda had enjoyed her conversation with Hadrian's sister.

Grandmama regarded her for a moment with a twinkle in her eyes. "I hope you don't mind my saying so, but you would make a very fine countess."

"You may be alone in that sentiment," Tilda said wryly. She went to stand before the mirror hanging over the mantel to adjust her hat.

"Nonsense, I'm sure I'm not the only person who thinks that. You must agree."

Tilda could see her grandmother's expectant expression in the reflection of the mirror. She seemed eager and confident, as if she thought she knew something. Or perhaps she only suspected something.

Tilda turned from the mirror and took a few steps toward her grandmother. "What are you hoping I'll say? That someone else has said I'll make a good countess too, or that *I* think I will?"

Grandmama pursed her lips, then threw her hands up. "I saw you and his lordship holding hands in the coach the other night when I pretended to be asleep."

"You *pretended* to be asleep?" Heat rose up Tilda's neck, and she hoped she wouldn't flush bright red.

"I was asleep at first," Grandmama explained. "However, I woke up at some point and noticed you holding hands. And, well, I didn't want to interrupt." She smiled. "It was incredibly sweet. It appears to me the two of you may be falling in love. Don't protest." She shook her hand at Tilda before letting it fall to her lap. "I've watched you over the last several months as you've grown closer. You can deny it, but you won't just be lying to me, you'll be lying to yourself as well."

Tilda blew out a breath. There could be no better time to confess. Furthermore, if she didn't say something now, her grandmother would be upset and hurt that Tilda had kept the truth from her.

"As it happens, Hadrian and I have *very recently* formed a romantic attachment. We are exploring a private courtship. I haven't wanted to say anything because I'm not sure how this will proceed."

Her grandmother's eyes lit with joy, and she pressed her hands to her cheeks as they flushed. "I'm so happy for you."

"I'm glad, but you mustn't interfere. Please, Grandmama. I do love Hadrian, and he loves me, but I just don't know if I want to be a countess. It's a great deal to consider. I would have to abandon my career, and I don't want to do that. And what would happen to you?" Tilda couldn't abandon her either. "I can't leave you here by yourself in this household."

"Oh, we could manage all that," her grandmother said without concern. "But you're right, it is a great deal to consider. You must be sure this is what you want."

Tilda felt an incredible relief, as if a stone had been removed from around her neck. "Thank you, Grandmama. It means so much to me that you would say that."

Her grandmother's eyes clouded. "I hope you don't feel pressured to make a decision. I don't want to contribute to that. I'm delighted for you, because you know how much I love you, and you know I would like to see you settled before I'm gone. I have to say that I've fallen in love with Lord Ravenhurst too, though not in the same way you have, of course."

Tilda couldn't help laughing.

"He's a wonderful man, and the two of you are wonderful together," her grandmother went on. "I will support you no matter what you choose."

Tilda went to her grandmother and bent down to hug her tightly. "Thank you, Grandmama," She felt surprisingly emotional.

"It's really too bad he's an earl," her grandmother said. "It would make things much easier if he weren't."

Tilda laughed again as she stepped away, basking in the mirth in her grandmother's eyes. "Since he *is* an earl, I'll have to make do." She glanced out the window and realized Hadrian's coach was outside, then heard Vaughn open the door. "He's here." Tilda leaned down and kissed her grandmother's cheek. "I love you, Grandmama," she whispered.

"I love you too, dear," she whispered back.

Hadrian stepped into the parlor as Tilda walked toward him. "Good morning, Mrs. Wren."

"Good morning, my lord. I must thank you again for last night. It was simply delightful, and I'm dreadfully sorry I almost ruined everything with that salmon, most of all because it was thoroughly delicious."

"You brightened the entire evening," Hadrian said with a kind smile. "You are welcome anytime."

Hadrian escorted Tilda through the entrance hall and outside. As Tilda stepped into the coach, she put the conversation with her grandmother from her mind. She would tell Hadrian about it another time. At this moment, she wanted to concentrate on the investigation.

To that end, Tilda spoke before Hadrian could bring up last night's dinner. "I have the brass cap with me in case you'd like to touch it with your bare hand. Though, I understand if you'd rather wait until after our visit to the Albion, in case your ability is needed there." Yesterday, he hadn't used his power because they hadn't even gone backstage at the Albion, and the Adelphi hadn't offered an opportunity.

She fixed him with an intent stare. "I don't want you to become overwhelmed today."

"Nor do I. I think waiting to handle the cap until after we visit the Albion is a good idea." He held her gaze as he smiled softly. "I hope you enjoyed yourself last night, despite my brother-in-law."

Tilda should have known she wouldn't be able to avoid the topic. "It was very nice. The meal was wonderful. My grandmother couldn't stop talking about the charlotte russe."

Hadrian chuckled. "Mrs. Rowe loves strawberry season. I had fresh jam on my scone this morning. There is truly nothing finer." His features grew serious. "I do hope you enjoyed yourself and aren't just saying so. Courtenay was incredibly obnoxious, bordering on rude."

"I liked your sister." Tilda preferred to ignore his brother-in-law.

"Did she persuade you to try riding a horse?" Hadrian asked with interest. He'd offered to teach her at one point, and Tilda tried to remember how she'd responded. Perhaps she'd said she'd think about it.

"Is it required that I ride horses if our courtship is to progress?" She was joking. Mostly.

"Not at all. But I agree with my sister. I think you might actually enjoy riding, and I also know you can accomplish anything to which you dedicate your energy." He held up his hand briefly. "But I have no expectations. My offer stands and always will, if you decide you would like to ride."

"I'd prefer to learn to drive, actually."

Hadrian regarded her with a hopeful sparkle in his eye. "I could arrange that too."

Tilda began to think about driving—perhaps a small pony carriage. She'd no interest in anything as fussy as a park phaeton. But keeping livestock was terribly expensive. She would have to rent a space in a mews stable, as well as hire a groom to look after the animals as well as the vehicle to keep it in good working order. As if she could afford any of that. Not now, but perhaps someday…

In the end, it was likely easier to continue as she was, provided she *did* continue as she was: an unmarried spinster, private detective, living independently. That had been her dream, and now it was realized. She might not be able to afford a pony carriage, but she earned enough to not fear they would end up in a workhouse.

However, fate had cast something else in her path instead. Something she'd never expected—the temptation to partner and, because she was a woman, be dependent upon someone else. Perhaps that was where some of her reticence came from. She was struggling to relinquish the independence she'd fought so hard to achieve.

"What are you pondering?" Hadrian studied her intently.

"That I might like to learn to drive and have my own vehicle. Would you be in favor of that?"

"I'm not sure my opinion matters." His tone was diplomatic and perhaps a bit uncertain. "Unless you're asking me in the context of a future in which we're together."

Tilda exhaled. "We must stop dancing around this question of our future. You know I am considering things."

"Yes, I do," he said solemnly. "That's one of the reasons I wanted you to come to dinner last night. To meet more of my family and decide if being my wife is a space you can occupy."

"If last night was all there was to being your countess, I would be delighted. However, we both know it's more than that, and I don't even know how we can have a proper courtship. It's not as if I have invitations where we will attend events together."

"We don't have to do that." Hadrian smiled. "I'm not enamored of balls or soirees or any of those Society occasions. There are certain things I *should* attend from time to time, due to my position, but a quiet night at home with you would be far preferable to just about anything else." He held her gaze, and Tilda began to imagine such nights…

The coach stopped, jolting Tilda from her reverie. She smiled at him. "Time to go to work."

They were soon seated in Detective Inspector Teague's office.

"Is Wycombe joining us?" Tilda asked.

"No." Teague had pulled his desk chair over to sit with them. The morning had been a bit chilly, and a fire burned behind the grate.

Tilda perched on the edge of her chair. "I'm most anxious to hear what you learned yesterday."

Teague's expression darkened. "First, I should tell you that Spring-heeled Jack was sighted again last night. This time in Covent Garden."

"What trickery did he perform?" Tilda asked. "Did he leap even higher?"

"There was no leaping, at least not that I've heard," Teague replied. "He accosted a young woman and breathed blue flame in her face. She also reported that his eyes glowed red, but she fainted afterward, so her testimony on that fact may not be entirely reliable. Other people in the vicinity did not report the glowing eyes, but they saw the blue flame, including her brother, who'd been walking beside her."

Hadrian's features dimmed with concern. "Did Jack grab her or hurt her in any way?"

Teague shook his head. "It was another performance, though I still don't understand the purpose."

Tilda couldn't fathom it either. "And there aren't any reports of a kidnapping?"

"Not that we've heard. We must hope that if it happens, it will be reported." Teague's eyes narrowed. "I have to think that since Jack's been seen the last two nights, he doesn't have anyone in captivity, but who can say?"

"I maintain this Spring-heeled Jack could be an impostor," Tilda said.

"Agreed," Teague said firmly. "Let me tell you about the evidence I collected yesterday about his performance near the Strand. Spring-heeled Jack jumped up to the first story of a three-story building with a projecting stone band above the frontage. I went up to the first-floor window, where the chandler's owner lives. Leaning out, I saw an abrasion on the stone where it appears Jack landed. I also found several short fibers which I concluded to be hemp."

"He used a rope," Tilda said.

Teague nodded. "It appears so. One of the other residents in the building said they heard something on the roof, so we investigated that as well. There was a footprint in the soot near a chimney, indicating someone had been up there quite recently. There were also marks on the parapet. I surmised a pulley block might have rested there, but I found no evidence of such a device. Whatever Jack used to hoist himself up and make it appear as though he were flying was immediately removed."

Hadrian frowned. "How disappointing. But it sounds as though you collected enough evidence to prove Jack's astonishing leap was no supernatural feat."

"I believe so." Teague cocked his head to the side. "The noise that was heard on the roof came before he made the jump. It seems he had help up there."

Tilda's nostrils flared as she leaned forward slightly. "He has an accomplice?"

"We must consider the possibility, at least when it comes to the performance he staged two nights ago. We're still questioning people who live in the building and those around it. I also found a bit of fine white powder residue on the cobblestones where witnesses reported seeing the bright flash." He clapped his palms against his thighs and regarded Tilda and Hadrian. "What did you learn at the theatres?"

"Not as much as we would have liked," Tilda replied with disappointment. "There was nobody at the Albion when we arrived, so we continued to the Adelphi. We spoke with the property master there, but he was not as generous with information as Mr. Jesson."

She and Hadrian together explained the man's guardedness.

Tilda concluded by saying they would be returning to the Albion when they finished their discussion.

"Will you report back after you've visited the Albion?" Teague asked.

Tilda rose, and everyone else stood with her. "We will."

They were interrupted by the arrival of a constable and a woman dressed in the latest fashion, which Tilda was only aware of after coming to know Hadrian and seeing how his mother dressed. The woman's gown was made of rich, plum silk decorated with silver braid. Her chestnut-brown hair was artfully styled, and a matching hat sat atop her curls whilst a veil of netted silver tulle angled over her forehead.

The constable introduced her as Mrs. Redmayne. "Detective Inspector Teague, she's come to report her daughter has been kidnapped."

Tilda's heart began to pound as her body quickened with both fear and anticipation. She was horrified this had happened again but relished the chance to catch the culprit.

"Please sit down, Mrs. Redmayne." Teague looked to the constable and asked him to find Sergeant Wycombe. "Tell him to join me here."

Tilda and Hadrian moved from the seating area so that Mrs. Redmayne could take one of the chairs.

Teague sat back down to face her. "I'm very sorry to hear about your daughter, Mrs. Redmayne. When did you discover her missing?"

"Her maid found her bed empty this morning with this note." She reached into her reticule and pulled out a piece of folded parchment which she handed to Teague, her hand shaking.

After scanning it quickly, Teague gave Tilda and Hadrian a subtle nod. Tilda knew that to mean the letter was the same as the others.

Teague eyed the woman with concern and gratitude. "Thank

you for bringing this, Mrs. Redmayne. I will ensure your daughter returns home safely."

"My husband didn't want to notify you because he thinks Florence will be killed, like that poor Chadwick girl." Mrs. Redmayne sniffed and removed a handkerchief from her reticule which she used to dab at her nose. "I told him Florence could just as easily be returned like Lady Priscilla was. I'm not convinced paying the ransom will help at all. They did that for Miss Chadwick and look what happened. I just want my daughter back, Detective Inspector."

The longing and worry in her voice tore at Tilda's heart. "Was your daughter friends with Lady Priscilla and Miss Chadwick?"

Snapping her attention to Tilda, Mrs. Redmayne narrowed her eyes slightly. "Who are you?"

"I'm Ravenhurst," Hadrian said calmly. "This is my associate, Miss Wren."

Mrs. Redmayne sucked in her breath. "I remember your name from the newspaper. I don't want you involved." Her voice was frigid as she looked Tilda up and down, then turned herself back toward Teague in a thoroughly cutting dismissal.

Tilda felt as if her breath had been knocked from her.

"Miss Wren and Lord Ravenhurst were just leaving, Mrs. Redmayne." Teague sent Tilda an apologetic glance.

Pivoting, Tilda turned and left the office, her legs wooden. She heard Hadrian follow. They said nothing until they reached the coach where Hadrian confirmed with Leach that they would go to the Albion Theatre next.

When they were settled inside, Hadrian turned his full attention on her. "I'm sorry, Tilda. Mrs. Redmayne is upset about the loss of her daughter. You shouldn't take it badly."

"She has every right to be upset. I don't blame her for not wanting my help." She kept her eyes trained forward as they moved away from Scotland Yard. "Honestly, there's no reason for us to continue with this investigation. We're not working for anyone, and we haven't been hired by the Met to assist Teague. I should just go home and take another case that would actually earn money. I've had several inquiries about finding lost and stolen items. Perhaps that would be for the best." She straightened her back against the squab.

Hadrian took her hand, and with his other hand, tipped her face toward him. "That is not what's best. I know you, and you can't walk away from this. Whether you're paid to investigate has nothing to do with it. Your sense of justice and discovering the truth will always win out."

Emotion swirled in Tilda. This was the comfort she hadn't realized she'd wanted. He understood her completely. "You know me too well. Aside from my tenacity, I owe it to Delia Chadwick to find her killer. I know you'll tell me I wasn't responsible, but I can't help feeling I let her down."

His gaze held hers. "You didn't. We'll find her killer together—and bring him to justice."

# CHAPTER 20

Hadrian didn't like the shadows in Tilda's eyes or the stiffness in her step as they moved from the coach to the stage entrance of the Albion Theatre on the Strand near Catherine Street. She was understandably upset about the encounter with Mrs. Redmayne. Helping was in Tilda's nature and to be told she wasn't wanted, especially in a capacity in which she excelled, was devastating.

The urge to continue to soothe her was great, but knowing Tilda, she wanted to focus on the investigation. "Who do you plan to speak with first?" he asked as they arrived at the stage door.

"Whoever is available. I suppose I'll ask for the property master." Tilda tried the door, and it opened.

"We don't need to knock?" Hadrian asked.

"I find I'm in the mood for begging forgiveness rather than seeking permission." Her gaze was cool, but he knew it wasn't directed at him.

Hadrian followed her inside and secured the door behind them. "Do you plan to just look around for someone?"

"That is my intent, yes." She led him along a corridor at the back of the theatre, and they came upon an open doorway to a large work room. Props and mechanisms along with supplies sat on shelves lining the walls, and a large worktable occupied the center of the room. A man perched on a stool at one end, his attention focused on a fixture he was repairing.

"Good afternoon," Tilda said.

The man looked up—through a pair of spectacles—and fixed on them with curiosity. Nearing fifty, he had dark curly hair tinged with gray, particularly at the temples. "Afternoon. Can I help you?"

"I hope so," Tilda said crisply. "I'm Miss Wren, and this is my investigative associate, Lord Ravenhurst. Are you the property master?"

The man nodded as he set down the device he'd been inspecting. He removed his spectacles and set them on the table. "I'm Larkin. Pardon me, but I can't imagine why you're here." His gaze lingered on Hadrian. "You can't be here fetching something for another theatre."

"No," Hadrian confirmed. "We'd like to ask you about your job and the props you make, particularly for special effects."

"You're investigators?" Larkin asked.

"Yes," Tilda replied. "Specifically, we're interested in how you create fire effects for the stage."

Larkin grinned. "You're asking about one of my favorite things. Creating special effects is my specialty, as anyone will tell you, and I'm always looking for new ways to awe the audience. There are many ways we create fire." He stood from the worktable, revealing he was on the shorter side and possessed a somewhat slight build. He limped to one of the shelves, and Hadrian wondered if he had an injury or ailment.

"These are some of the devices I've created for fire effects." Larkin gestured to a shelf holding several items, including one that looked very like what they suspected Spring-heeled Jack carried, except it was larger.

Tilda noticed it too as she went directly to it and pointed at the device. "What is this for?"

"Ah, that provided a wonderful effect in which we needed a dragon to breathe fire on stage. The actor in the dragon costume blew through this tube, which was stuffed with cotton soaked in spirts of wine with strontium salt added to make the flame red. Spectacular!" Larkin's enthusiasm for his work was evident. He went on to describe what some of the other devices accomplished.

"You designed and created all these?" Hadrian asked.

"I did indeed," Larkin said proudly.

"You've been doing this a long time," Tilda remarked.

"Been here at the Albion twenty years this autumn."

"Why did you think we might be from another theatre?" Tilda asked.

"I often sell props and devices like these to other theatres, especially the smaller ones. Even some from outside London. They can't afford to hire a mechanist to assist with their props. It's cheaper to just buy or even rent what they need from me or someone like me."

Tilda exchanged a look with Hadrian, and he was fairly certain she was wondering if that was how Spring-heeled Jack had obtained his device. She withdrew the cap from her reticule and held it in her palm for Larkin's inspection. "Does this brass cap look familiar to you? Might it be something you would create, perhaps to fit onto the end of a device used to create fire?"

"May I?" Larkin raised his hand to pick up the cap.

"Certainly." Tilda gave him the item.

Larkin studied it closely. "This is definitely something I would create. In fact, I'm fairly sure I crafted this one."

From the corner of his eye, Hadrian saw Tilda's reaction. Her chest swelled as she took in a breath, and her nostrils flared gently.

"Where did you find it?" Larkin gave the cap back to Tilda.

"It's associated with a kidnapping we're investigating."

Larkin's dark gray-brown eyes rounded. "Kidnapping? This isn't to do with that horrible Spring-heeled Jack impostor, is it?"

"You think he's an impostor?" Tilda asked.

"Of course." Larkin's tone said that, to him at least, this was obvious. "I can't believe that same creature has resurfaced thirty years later. If he even existed then. It's a stage performance moved to the streets to sow chaos and terror. Whoever is assuming the identity now is doing so to ensure his crimes gain notoriety."

"I think so too," Tilda said. "Do you know who might have purchased this cap from you?" She tucked it back into her reticule.

He shrugged. "I've sold so many different things to people that I couldn't say."

"Do you have receipts for those sales?" Tilda asked. "We'd be happy to look through them. I don't wish to trouble you unduly." She smiled.

"The treasurer has them. Though, it's possible someone simply took it from my workshop. Various stage workers and actors regularly come in here and take things—typically for something they're doing with a performance here at the theatre but not always." He frowned slightly.

"Do you know where we may find the treasurer?" Hadrian asked.

"He won't be in yet, unfortunately. You can try again closer to the performance this evening."

"We'll do that," Tilda said. "What of the costumer? Might they be here?"

"That'd be Maud Brimley," Larkin replied. "She's downstairs. Go back along the corridor past the stage door and the stairs are at the end."

"Thank you again," Hadrian said as Tilda turned to leave. He followed her from the property master's room, and they made their way toward the stairs. "That was helpful."

"Somewhat. I was really hoping he could tell us who obtained that cap from him." She let out a disappointed sigh.

"Isn't it suspicious that he made that cap and Delia Chadwick was fond of attending this theatre of late?" Hadrian asked.

"Not necessarily. Jesson said Larkin was the best prop mechanist in London, so I'm not surprised that Spring-heeled Jack may have wanted to use his fire-creating device. That supports our theory that the kidnapper is a member of the theatre community. He'd have to be to know that about Larkin."

"That certainly makes sense to me," Hadrian said.

They descended the staircase, but halfway down, Tilda paused and turned to him. The space was dimly lit, so her face was in shadow. "I'd intended to just ask the costumer about the ease of making a light-colored leather costume, but since the brass cap has a connection to this theatre, I plan to ask if she's made such a costume."

"Good idea. It will also be helpful to know her process for creating costumes. I wonder if she also fulfills orders from other theatres as Larkin does."

"Agreed." Tilda's tone held determination, and Hadrian was relieved to see her focused and even energized by the investigation.

They found the sewing room easily. A young woman with pale blonde hair stood at a table cutting fabric.

Tilda approached her. "Good afternoon, are you Maud Brimley?"

The woman shook her head and pointed to a doorway with her scissors. "Maud's in there, but she won't like ye disturbing 'er when she's drawing."

"I'm afraid we must." Tilda walked to the doorway, and Hadrian trailed her, hoping Mrs. Brimley wouldn't be difficult.

Tilda stepped just over the threshold of a small room. A

woman with a blue cap covering most of her sable hair sat at a table sketching a costume design. She did not look up. "Sarah, I've told you not to bother me when I'm working."

"My name is Miss Wren," Tilda said. "And this is my associate, Lord Ravenhurst."

Mrs. Brimley lifted her head. She appeared to be in her forties with a jutting chin and sculpted cheekbones. Her mahogany eyes fixed on Hadrian. "My lord. What brings you down here?" Her expression was a mix of curiosity, awe, and bemusement.

Since she addressed him, Hadrian answered. "Miss Wren and I would like to ask you about the costumes you make." He inclined his head toward her sketch. "I see you design them too."

"Certainly. Any good costumer along the Strand does so." She behaved as though she would be affronted if he suggested otherwise.

"Have you ever had occasion to design or create white or light-colored coveralls, perhaps made of leather?" Tilda asked.

Mrs. Brimley's eyes narrowed slightly as she set her pencil down. "I have. Just a few weeks ago, in fact."

Hadrian experienced a rush of excitement and knew Tilda had to feel the same.

"What about gloves with claws?" Hadrian asked. "Do you make any costumes like that, perhaps for animals?" He thought of the dragon costume Larkin had mentioned.

"Oh, yes, I've designed many animal costumes, and I did create a pair of gloves with claws recently too." She stared at them, her brow creasing. "Why are you asking about these things?"

"We are conducting an investigation, and these items were used in a crime," Tilda replied. "Who did you make these costumes for? And was there a mask, perhaps with horns that looked rather devilish?"

"Yes, there was a mask as well, but I don't remember who it was for, if I even knew."

Tilda's brows drew together. "You wouldn't have met this person? How would you fit them for the costume?"

"Occasionally I don't, but it's rare. I receive written orders for a costume, even if I've already discussed it with the manager. The treasurer insists on this process so that everything is accounted for. If I don't receive a written order, I'm not to make it." She twisted her lips into a brief frown. "It's a bit annoying sometimes."

"I don't understand why you wouldn't fit someone in person," Tilda said. "On what occasions did that happen and why?"

Mrs. Brimley shrugged. "Sometimes the actor has a wife or sister who makes adjustments. And sometimes, I make a costume for another theatre, and they have a seamstress who finishes it."

Hadrian could see Tilda's frustration that Mrs. Brimley hadn't met the person who'd ordered these items. But perhaps they could discover their name another way. "Did you receive a written order for these items?"

"I recall they were two separate orders—the leather suit was one, and the mask and gloves were another—but I don't know where they came from. I don't keep the orders." Mrs. Brimley waved her hand. "The treasurer files them somewhere because I refuse to clutter my workshop with such nonsense."

"Do any of the theatre's current or upcoming plays require those costume pieces?" Tilda asked.

The furrows in Mrs. Brimley's brow deepened suddenly, and her gaze darkened. "No, and now that I think of those pieces together, it sounds like Spring-heeled Jack." She put her hand to her mouth. "What have I done?"

"You are not to blame for anything Spring-heeled Jack has done," Hadrian assured her.

Mrs. Brimley stood abruptly and went into the main sewing room where the other woman—Sarah, presumably—was still cutting fabric. Stalking to the corner, Mrs. Brimley opened a cabinet and withdrew a folded piece of a very light yellow, bordering on ivory, leather. She held it out. "This is what's left of what I used. Does that help you?"

"It could, yes." Tilda smiled at the woman as she took the leather. "Do you mind if I keep this?" It could be useful evidence to Teague. Mrs. Brimley nodded, and Tilda thanked her. "Can you think of anything else about these orders, such as exactly when you received them?"

Wiping her hand across her brow, Mrs. Brimley's face creased with anguish. "I'm not certain, but more than a fortnight ago." She turned to the other woman. "Sarah, when did we get the orders for the leather coveralls and the mask and the gloves with the claws?"

Sarah cocked her head. "Three weeks ago. Thereabouts. The order for the coveralls was first, then the gloves came a few days after we finished that."

"Do you remember who they were for?" Mrs. Brimley asked, cringing.

"I don't recall, but it was an actor, I think." Sarah shrugged. "Not sure what it was for. I remember the orders had the same handwriting. I read 'em all what come in, and these weren't written by the manager or the stage manager. Sometimes we get orders from actors or other people or even other theatres, though those are usually marked somehow so the treasurer knows how to do the accounting."

"Were these marked in any specific way?" Tilda asked hopefully.

"I don't think so?" Sarah replied.

"You could ask the treasurer," Mrs. Brimley said. "Though, he's not usually here until later."

"We'll do that, thank you." Tilda smiled in gratitude. She withdrew two of her business cards from her reticule and handed one to each woman. "I'd be interested in hearing if you recall anything further—anything at all, no matter how small or seemingly unimportant."

Mrs. Brimley clutched the card as she looked to Tilda, then Hadrian. "I hate to think we made something that has been used for such evil."

"Evil?" Sarah gasped. "What evil?"

"Spring-heeled Jack." Mrs. Brimley launched into an explanation of the inquiries they'd made, and Hadrian inclined his head toward the door as he met Tilda's gaze.

Tilda nodded almost imperceptibly, then quickly preceded him back to the staircase. When they reached the top, she turned to wait for him to join her. Holding up the leather Mrs. Brimley had given her, Tilda arched her brows at him. "Do you want to do your thing here or in the coach?"

"The coach, I think."

Tilda led him back to the stage door, and they quickly returned to his coach. "We're going to remain here for a few minutes, Leach," Tilda said. "We may go back into the theatre."

Leach nodded. "Very good."

When they were in the coach, Hadrian removed his gloves. Tilda placed the leather in his palm, and Hadrian thought of the person who'd ordered the coveralls to be made. Who were they?

The coach vanished, and Hadrian was once again in Maud Brimley's small design room. The memory he saw was of a person sitting at her table—he recognized it because of a pair of drawings. But they'd been set aside, and the person was focused on a piece of paper.

*Leather coveralls made of the lightest leather possible*
*To fit a man of five feet, eleven inches with a waist*
*of thirty-two inches*

There were more measurements but no name. At the bottom, it read:

*Complete by 1 June and leave at stage right.*

But none of that was as astonishing as what Hadrian noticed. The handwriting matched that of Spring-heeled Jack's ransom notes. Hadrian's hand shook briefly, and he blinked. The memory faded.

He turned his head to Tilda who regarded him expectantly. He couldn't help smiling. "We have him."

~

Tilda held her breath. The excitement in Hadrian's expression drove her heart to pound madly. "What did you see?"

"The order for the coveralls. It was written by the same hand as the ransom notes."

"The kidnapper ordered them!" They indeed had him. "What's his name?"

"Er, the order didn't say." Hadrian grimaced.

Disappointment rushed through Tilda, and she frowned. "Then how could you say we have him?"

"I spoke too soon," Hadrian said apologetically. "We don't have his identity. *But* we do know he obtained costuming and likely his fire-making device from the Albion Theatre."

At least they'd discovered that much. "That's great, actually." It just wasn't what she'd expected based on Hadrian's exclamation. She took the leather from him and set it on her lap with her reticule.

"The order asked for the coveralls to be ready by the first of June and to leave it at stage right," Hadrian continued.

"We must go back inside and investigate that," Tilda said. "Perhaps we can find the manager if he's in. He may know who ordered them."

Hadrian opened the door and helped her from the coach. "We won't be long," he said to Leach before escorting Tilda back toward the stage door.

They managed to find the right side of the stage. A couple of dozen or so pegs dotted the wall and held a variety of costumes. "I see why the costume was left here."

Hadrian stepped toward the pegs. "The wall is blue." His voice sounded as though he'd found a treasure.

Then Tilda recalled that he'd seen a blue wall in his memory from the cloak at Scotland Yard. "Is this the same place you saw in your memory?"

"Yes." He removed his glove, but Tilda grabbed his hand.

"I don't think that's wise. There are too many pegs here, and it's entirely possible, if not likely, that one can remove a costume without touching the peg." She looked at him intently. "The risk of not learning something useful is too great compared with the certainty of pain—or worse."

He scowled faintly then rubbed his temple. "You're right."

"And you're already in at least a bit of pain after the leather," Tilda noted.

"You know me so well." He cracked a faint smile.

Tilda released his hand. "Your ability has already helped us— now we know the cloak came from this theatre. That's a third connection. Let's find the manager."

Mr. Fenton was in his office. He was clearly irritated by their interruption until Hadrian introduced himself.

Brightening, the manager stood, his dark brown mustache twitching as he smiled almost obsequiously. "Good afternoon, my lord. How can I be of service?"

"We are investigating some costuming items that were crafted here—coveralls made of a pale brown or yellow-ivory leather, a horned mask, and gloves with claws. We spoke with Mrs. Brimley and Sarah downstairs. Neither recalls who ordered them." Hadrian gave him his most arrogant stare. "It's imperative we find this person."

Tilda quashed a smile. Sometimes it was incredibly useful for him to bring the full weight of his earldom.

The manager blanched. "Er, I don't know who that was. Those items are not currently in use here. That information would be on the order form, which you'd need to speak with the treasurer about. I'm terribly sorry, but he's not here just now."

"I'm sure you could allow us into his office," Hadrian said, his gaze cool and expectant.

Now color rushed up Mr. Fenton's neck and flushed his cheeks. "I don't have the key, I'm afraid. But if you come back this evening, either before or after the performance, you will surely catch him. Or the proprietor will be here, and he has a key."

"What about a list of employees?" Tilda asked. The kidnapper had used Larkin and Brimley to outfit himself, and he'd taken the cloak from here. It made sense that he may indeed work at the Albion Theatre. He at least had *some* connection. She thought of what Larkin had said about Jack—a stage performance moved to the streets. Perhaps Jack was an actor. Sarah had indicated that actors submitted costuming requests.

Now, Mr. Fenton looked distinctly uncomfortable. "I don't have that list either. You'd need to obtain that from the proprietor or the treasurer also."

Hadrian's brows snapped together, and his mouth hardened. "Don't you have a list of who's working on your current plays?"

"The playbill is posted outside the theatre," Mr. Fenton said. "But that won't include all the employees. For instance, we don't list people who work temporarily to build scenery or sew costumes, and we don't include temporary actors who may be called upon if we need a new understudy. We've a few of those right now—there's the fellow who teaches dancing and another who gives elocution lessons."

Tilda froze. "Did you say elocution?" Mr. Fenton nodded. "And he's an actor?"

"Yes, but if you ask me his name, I'm afraid I don't remember." He glanced at Hadrian. "I'm very sorry, my lord. I do hope you'll return this evening. Here, let me provide you with one of our boxes. We've just one left available for tonight, but it has an excellent perspective." Mr. Fenton went to his desk and pulled a ticket from the top drawer which he handed to Hadrian.

"Thank you." Hadrian tucked the ticket into his coat and turned from the manager, escorting Tilda back outside. "Should we go to the proprietor's house or the treasurer's?"

"That may not be necessary." Tilda walked very quickly toward the coach—much faster than her usual pace. "We must return to Ravenhurst House to speak with Bannet." They reached the coach, and she looked up at Hadrian with unchecked anticipation. "She and this elocution tutor who is also an actor may be the keys to the entire case."

# CHAPTER 21

The moment Leach closed the door to the coach, Hadrian turned to Tilda, his eyes sparkling with unconcealed anticipation as he smiled at her in admiration. "What brilliance have you uncovered?"

Tilda laughed. "I don't know if it's brilliant yet, but it's something to go on, anyway. Do you recall at dinner last night when your mother mentioned Delia Chadwick stuttered at the start of the Season but that she'd seemed to overcome the impediment when she saw her recently?"

Furrowing his brow, Hadrian shook his head. "I'm afraid I don't. I was rather focused on keeping my brother-in-law from being an insufferable clod."

"Well, *I* remember, and she's not the only person to mention Miss Chadwick's stutter. Harper, Lady Priscilla's maid, also noted it. When Mr. Fenton mentioned that one of their temporary actors taught elocution, I immediately thought of Delia Chadwick."

Hadrian gasped. "Do you think she took lessons from this actor?" His brow furrowed. "Elocution wasn't on her list of activities, nor did her parents provide the name of a tutor."

"Which is why this may not lead anywhere." Tilda didn't want to allow hope to overtake her. "We could ask the Chadwicks, but I don't think that would go very well, especially if they withheld that information for some reason. Thankfully, Bannet can help us, and she's at Ravenhurst House." Tilda smiled.

"*Blast.*" Hadrian grimaced. "I'm afraid Bannet *isn't* at Ravenhurst House. I was so distracted by your excitement that I didn't put that together before we climbed into the coach." He knocked on the roof so Leach would stop.

"Where is she?" Tilda asked.

"Likely already in Wimbledon at my sister's house—or nearly there," Hadrian explained. "Beatrice spent last night at our mother's, then called this morning to meet Bannet. They got on very well, and Beatrice offered her the position of lady's maid."

The coach had stopped, and Leach opened the door. "Change in destination?"

Tilda looked at Hadrian. "Must we take the train to Wimbledon?"

"I'd rather not deal with the schedule since we need to return to the Albion later." Hadrian turned his attention to Leach. "To Sorrel Cottage. With haste."

"Right away, my lord." Leach closed the door and they were quickly moving again.

Hadrian suddenly kissed Tilda. The connection of their lips was fleeting but lovely. It was also surprising.

"Why did you do that?" she asked.

"Because sometimes I'm overcome with admiration and love for you." Hadrian grinned. "I can't quite believe I'm fortunate enough to have met someone I adore as I do you."

Tilda blushed profusely and wished she could just not. But no one had ever said such things to her before, let alone with such sincerity and joy. It was almost intimidating. "Thank you," she murmured.

Hadrian took her hand. "I didn't mean to make you uncomfortable."

"You didn't. At least not in a bad way. I'm still becoming acclimated to…us. Is your sister's house really a cottage?"

"Compared to Courtenay's pile in Staffordshire, yes."

Tilda wasn't going to ask for clarification. That might lead to discussion of Hadrian's country estate, which she didn't know much about, other than it was located in Hampshire. The idea that she could possibly be lady of such a place seemed utterly impossible. She wouldn't know the first thing. And that should be the end of any consideration she might have of becoming Lady Ravenhurst.

She pushed her anxious thoughts away in favor of focusing on their investigation, which seemed to finally be moving forward. It was too bad they had to drive all the way to Wimbledon, but it would be worth it if Bannet could confirm whether Delia Chadwick had been engaged in elocution lessons.

Better still, if Bannet could confirm he was also an actor *and* provide his name, Tilda felt confident they would rescue Miss Redmayne. They only need find him and determine if he had Miss Redmayne in his captivity.

But why had this actor kidnapped three young women? Was his motive as simple as wanting money? In Tilda's experience, that was often enough to motivate someone. That didn't, however, explain why he'd killed Miss Chadwick and not Lady Priscilla.

Was this actor also the Spring-heeled Jack leaping upon buildings and accosting women? What was the purpose of that? Perhaps he was simply enthralled with his work and thrived on having an audience.

Tilda grew more anxious as they left London and even more so as they approached Wimbledon. She'd never been there and tried to enjoy the sights rather than fixate on the upcoming interview.

At last, they turned into a narrow drive, and Hadrian said they'd arrived at the house, which was clearly set back from the road as Tilda could not yet see it. They passed a large green field on the right, and the house came into view as they drove by a stand of trees.

It was as much a "cottage" as Tilda's grandmother's house was a church. "The roof isn't even thatched," Tilda said sardonically. It was, in fact, an Italianate villa with an octagonal belvedere rising above the slate roof in the front right corner. Tilda was certain it provided gorgeous, sweeping views of the commons and surrounding countryside.

Hadrian laughed. "I suppose not. Courtenay built this after he wed my sister and wanted it to feel somewhat like a country estate without all the space and upkeep of one."

"I wouldn't know if he accomplished that," Tilda murmured.

The coach came to a stop in front of the house, and Leach opened the door a moment later. Hadrian stepped out, then assisted Tilda to the gravel drive.

They walked to the front door and were shortly greeted by the butler, a bright-faced middle-aged man with a shiny pate. He smiled upon seeing Hadrian. "Good afternoon, my lord. Were we expecting you?" He opened the door wide, encouraging them to step into the entrance hall.

"No, Armitage, I'm afraid I've arrived unannounced and without invitation," Hadrian replied. "We've come to speak with my sister's new maid, Bannet. Allow me to introduce my associate, Miss Wren."

Tilda noted he did not identify her as his friend. Perhaps he wanted to be clear that this was not a social call. She appreciated that.

"Why don't you wait in the sitting room?" Armitage gestured to the room on the left of the entrance hall. "I'll fetch Lady Courtenay." The butler disappeared, and Tilda entered the sitting room with Hadrian.

"Why isn't he fetching Bannet?" she asked.

"I'm sure he wants to make sure it's all right with Beatrice that we speak with her maid."

Tilda grumbled faintly. "I suppose."

Hadrian smiled. "I know you're anxious. I am too."

Beatrice arrived a moment later. "Hadrian, I'm surprised to see you here. Did Bannet leave something at Ravenhurst House? You didn't have to deliver it personally."

"That is not why we've come," Hadrian said. "We must speak to her about an urgent matter regarding Miss Chadwick."

"Of course. I've asked Bannet to come here," Beatrice said, glancing behind her. "She should arrive momentarily. Do you mind if I stay whilst you speak with her? The poor thing is in delicate shape. She's told me a little of what happened, and I'm devastated for her. Absolutely awful of Chadwick to toss her out like that."

Hadrian glanced at Tilda. "I explained the unfortunate situation of Chadwick's treatment of Bannet."

"Yes, it was perfectly horrid," Tilda said to Beatrice.

The viscount sailed into the room just then. "My goodness, you *are* here. I thought Armitage must be mistaken. What brings you all the way out to our charming little cottage?" His gaze settled on Tilda. "And with you too, Miss Wren."

"Just a small inquiry we need to make," Hadrian said tightly. Tilda could tell he didn't want to elaborate to his brother-in-law.

"An investigative inquiry? Now, don't harass Beatrice's new maid," he said in an almost scolding tone. "She hasn't even settled in yet."

Tilda wasn't able to remain quiet. "We would never harass her. Indeed, we're hoping she can help us catch the kidnapper."

Courtenay's eyes rounded, and he clapped his hands together. "Well, that will be most diverting!" He went to sit in an over-stuffed blue damask chair and watched them expectantly as if he were waiting for a performance to start.

Hadrian looked to Tilda with apology, and she responded with an infinitesimal nod. Courtenay could listen, but the moment he interjected, Tilda would have no compunction about asking him to leave.

Beatrice also sent Tilda an apologetic glance as she perched in another chair. "You're welcome to sit."

"I would rather stand for now," Tilda replied. "We've been sitting all the way from London."

Bannet entered, clutching her hands nervously. "My lord, Miss Wren."

Tilda smiled warmly at the maid. "Good afternoon, Bannet. I trust your journey here was pleasant. I'm delighted you found a new position so quickly—and a very good one at that."

"I can't tell you how grateful I am to you and his lordship." Tears welled in Bannet's eyes as she regarded them, but she blinked them away before they could fall. Still, she dashed a fingertip over one eye.

"We've come to ask you about Miss Chadwick again," Tilda said gently. "Hopefully, this will be the last time we bother you."

"I don't know what else I can say." Bannet wrung her hands. "I'd rather put all that behind me and focus on my new position here."

Tilda tamped down a short burst of frustration. Of course the maid didn't want to speak of this anymore. It had been a traumatic experience. "I do understand, however another young woman has been abducted, and we must find the kidnapper before it's too late. I have a simple question—did Miss Chadwick receive elocution lessons?"

Bannet's jaw fell open, and she pressed her hand to her mouth. It was too late for her to mask her reaction, but she tried anyway. "I don't—I don't know."

"Bannet, you must tell us the truth," Hadrian said, using a firm but kind tone. "We know Miss Chadwick had a stutter and that it improved over the Season. How was that accomplished if not with elocution lessons?"

"I'm sorry, my lord!" Bannet began to cry, her shoulders shaking as emotion poured out of her. Beatrice leapt up and went to her, putting her arm around the maid.

"Now see here, Bannet, you must collect yourself," Courtenay said. "You can't fall to pieces like that. Just answer Raven's questions, for heaven's sake." He didn't appear angry but discomfited, as if Bannet's outburst was somehow a problem for him.

Beatrice sent her husband an irritated look. "She can't help herself. Have some compassion. She's suffered an ordeal and it isn't over yet." Beatrice turned her attention to Bannet. "There now, it's all right. Just tell my brother and Miss Wren what you know. You'll be helping them save another young woman. That's a noble endeavor, is it not?"

The maid nodded as she sniffed and worked to draw in air. After a few moments, her shoulders stopped quivering, and she dried her face with a handkerchief she took from the pocket of her apron.

"Yes, Miss Chadwick had an elocution tutor," Bannet said, her voice scratchy from her crying. "I'm sorry I didn't tell you before, but we weren't allowed to discuss it outside the household. Mr. and Mrs. Chadwick didn't want anyone to know about Delia's stutter. They worried it would hurt her marriage prospects."

"Surely that wasn't a concern after she was killed," Hadrian said. He apologized as Bannet's shoulders began to shake again.

"Why didn't you tell us about this after Mr. Chadwick dismissed you?" Tilda asked.

Bannet took a moment to compose herself. When she looked up at Tilda finally, her eyes were wet. "Miss Chadwick *was* having an affair—with her elocution tutor. I knew about it, but she swore me to secrecy. I promised on her life that I wouldn't tell anyone. How could I tell you, especially after she died?" A sob escaped Bannet, and she briefly pressed her handkerchief to her mouth as she fought to take a breath. Doing so, she calmed herself before breaking down again. "I tried to direct you toward their affair the other day without telling you outright. I'm sorry, Miss Wren. And your lordship." She sniffed and wiped her eyes.

"It's all right," Beatrice soothed. "You were trying to keep your promise to Miss Chadwick. But now, we need you to help save someone else. You want to do that, don't you?"

Bannet nodded.

Tilda wanted to hug Beatrice. Instead, she fixed on Bannet. "Do you know if the elocution tutor was also an actor?"

"Yes." Bannet blinked.

"Do you know the man's name?" Tilda held her breath.

"Oscar Mobray."

At last, they had a name. "Do you know where Mr. Mobray lives or where we might find him?"

"I know he performed at the Albion—that's where the Chadwicks made his acquaintance and hired him as her elocution tutor. I'm not sure where he lived." Bannet's face puckered as she appeared to think for a moment. "I do recall hearing Miss Chadwick talk to him about something to do with Savoy Street. That was during their last meeting before she was kidnapped." Bannet's expression became forlorn once more, and her lip began to quiver. "What does Mr. Mobray have to do with Miss Chadwick's kidnapping and murder?"

Tilda didn't want to upset Bannet anymore today. "We don't know for sure yet."

"He was always very kind," Bannet said. "I could see he and Miss Chadwick cared very much for one another. I wondered what Mr. Mobray thought about what happened to her."

"I have one last question," Hadrian said, surprising Tilda. "Can you describe what Mr. Mobray looks like?"

Bannet nodded. "He's tall, though not as tall as you. I suppose he possesses an attractive form. Miss Chadwick certainly thought so." She blushed faintly. "His hair is the color of wheat with curls that seem unjust for a man. His eyes were dark and sparkled with mirth—he was most charming from what I saw of him, which wasn't much. But I'm sure it was his dazzling smile that captivated Miss Chadwick. He looked like someone who would almost certainly beguile his audiences."

"Thank you, Bannet," Tilda said. "You've been incredibly helpful."

"Apologies for our intrusion," Hadrian said to his sister before glancing toward Courtenay.

The viscount stood. "Well, that was most exhilarating." He looked at Bannet. "Your loyalty to Miss Chadwick is commendable. My wife has made a fine decision in bringing you into the household." He turned his head toward Hadrian. "Raven." He barely spared a glance for Tilda. "Miss Wren." Then he strode from the room.

"You may go back up to your room, Bannet," Beatrice said softly. "And I meant what I said earlier—you will have a warm bath, and you will not begin your duties until the morning."

The maid nodded, then dipped a curtsey to Hadrian before fleeing the room.

"I'm sorry you had to drive all the way out here," Beatrice said. "You're more than welcome to stay for dinner. Hadrian, the children would love to see their favorite uncle." She glanced over her shoulder. "Don't tell Courtenay," she whispered with a smile. "His brothers are too dour."

Tilda had no trouble seeing Hadrian as a favorite uncle. Still, she wondered what he did to earn the title. If they were not in such a hurry to find Oscar Mobray, she would have actually been delighted to meet the Courtenay children and even stay for dinner.

Good heavens, what was happening to her? This was not what she'd foreseen for herself! But why not? Was it because they were members of the peerage? No, it was the large, extensive family— something Tilda didn't have any experience with. She had no siblings, and for a very long time now, it had just been her and her grandmother.

"Whilst we appreciate the invitation, we must be on our way back to London," Hadrian said with regret but also a touch of eagerness. "We've a murderer to apprehend."

Beatrice nodded. "Of course. How silly of me. I do wish you the very best of luck. You must come another time." She looked to Tilda. "It was lovely to see you again so soon, Miss Wren."

"Likewise, my lady. I mean, Beatrice." Last night after dinner, she'd asked Tilda to call her by her Christian name.

Tilda and Hadrian took their leave. "Should we go to Savoy Street or Scotland Yard?" Hadrian asked.

"Straight to Scotland Yard." Tilda glanced at him as they approached the coach. "We've no idea if Mobray lives in Savoy Street or what could be waiting for us there. We should go with Teague and whoever else he wants to bring."

Leach had been standing next to the vehicle and opened the door. "Did I hear you say Scotland Yard?"

Hadrian nodded. "Once again, with the greatest haste."

"As fast as I can, my lord."

"Thank you, Leach." Hadrian helped Tilda inside.

They settled into the coach and discussed Bannet's revelations. "It's a tragedy Chadwick wouldn't allow anyone to tell us about Mobray," Hadrian said. "We would have made the theatre connection much sooner. I imagine he'll blame himself something awful." He looked over at Tilda. "He'll owe you an apology."

"I don't expect one," Tilda replied. "I'm only sorry things ended as they did for his daughter. And how did they exactly? If she and Mobray were in love as Bannet indicated, how on earth did Delia Chadwick end up dead?"

"Perhaps Mobray was pretending to be in love with her and only wanted the ransom money?" Hadrian shook his head. "No, I sensed the love he had for her—and the distress he felt after she was dead. It doesn't make sense, unless he killed her in a rage and immediately regretted it."

"Or she was killed by someone else," Tilda suggested darkly.

"Mobray had to have had an accomplice for his performance at the chandler's," Hadrian said. "Perhaps he had one all along."

"That's what I'm beginning to think." Tilda considered their next steps. "If we can confirm that Mobray is the actor from the Albion who also works as an elocution tutor, then we can tie him to the theatre where Spring-heeled Jack obtained his costume, the fire-creating device, *and* the gray cloak Lady Priscilla was wearing."

"We already know he's associated with the Albion." Hadrian spoke with great animation. "Whoever took that cloak from the blue wall loved Miss Chadwick—and Bannet just confirmed that to be Mobray."

Tilda frowned slightly. "*We* know that, but we can't *prove* his connection to the theatre yet. We *can* tell Teague our suspicion that Mobray, who we can also say we know was Miss Chadwick's elocution tutor, works as an actor at the Albion where we discovered Spring-heeled Jack obtained his costume and fire-breathing tool, as well as the gray cloak—and perhaps even the dress he supplied to Miss Chadwick. It makes sense now that it fit her so well."

"Indeed. Her kidnapper knew her and thus knew her size."

"Once we obtain the list of employees from the theatre and find Mobray on it, we can show Teague that he works there," Tilda said. "But I don't want to wait for that. We have enough to find him and question him. The only problem is we don't know where he lives."

"It seems Miss Chadwick was in on the kidnapping, doesn't it?" Hadrian asked.

"It does, which makes her death even more perplexing. Did she somehow put their enterprise at risk?"

"That would make sense," Hadrian said. "Perhaps Mobray saw no choice but to kill her and was sad that it ended that way."

Tilda's mind was whirring. "We know Miss Chadwick and Mobray were in love. Presumably, they planned to elope together. Was the ransom for them? That was a great deal of money to ask for."

"Miss Chadwick likely knew her father could afford it," Hadrian said wryly. "But why kidnap Lady Priscilla? That's an even greater sum."

"I suppose they became greedy." Tilda exhaled. "Even after what we've learned, this case is still confounding."

Hadrian removed his gloves. "My head is feeling better from earlier at the theatre. I want to handle the cap. Perhaps that will give us some answers about Oscar Mobray."

Tilda fished the cap from her reticule. "Be careful." She dropped it into his palm and watched as he closed his hand around the item.

He stared past her, his eyes glassy. Tilda realized she was holding her breath again and blew it out.

A moment later, Hadrian blinked. "I saw a man I don't recognize. Something about his appearance was off. I think this was sometime in the past, perhaps twenty years ago, based on what he was wearing."

This was not the first time Hadrian had seen a vision from many years earlier. "What did the man look like?"

"Blond hair, conventionally attractive, in his early or mid-twenties. He seemed aloof, and the memory carried a sense of outrage. No, stronger than that. Fury."

"But you know it was from twenty or so years ago."

Hadrian pursed his lips. "I shouldn't assume a time period based on someone's garments. You may recall that when we met, your wardrobe was entirely outdated."

Tilda smiled. "You're smart not to make assumptions. I nearly did. What if the man was wearing a costume for a play?" She arched a brow. "Was his blond hair curly as Bannet described?"

"Definitely not."

"Probably not Mobray then," Tilda said with disappointment. "I was hoping you were seeing his accomplice's memory."

"It's someone who has touched this cap," Hadrian said.

"If Mobray is the kidnapper—"

"We know he is," Hadrian insisted.

Tilda appreciated his fervor. "Yes, but until we have proof, I prefer not to speak definitively. If Mobray is the kidnapper, it's likely he obtained this cap from the Albion. We know Larkin made it."

Hadrian's brow furrowed, and he massaged his forehead. "Could Larkin be his accomplice?"

"Do you need lavender?" Tilda asked.

"No, I'm fine. My head is just a little sore." He exhaled.

Tilda returned to their discussion of Larkin as the accomplice. "Given Larkin's limp and build, I don't know how he could pull Mobray up the side of a building and get away quickly. I suppose we must consider him, but Jesson seems a likelier candidate. And there are plenty of other property masters we have yet to meet. It's a needle in a bloody haystack." She pressed her lips together with determination. "Let us hope Savoy Street has something helpful to reveal."

## CHAPTER 22

Detective Inspector Teague was fortunately at Scotland Yard when Hadrian and Tilda arrived. Hadrian mostly listened as Tilda informed Teague of everything they'd learned at the Albion and from Bannet. Teague was especially thrilled with their discovery of Oscar Mobray as Miss Chadwick's elocution tutor and lover, as well as the likelihood that he was also the kidnapper and an actor at the Albion.

Teague was as keen as they were to confirm that connection. He took the leather from Maud Brimley as evidence and promptly locked it in his drawer.

"Since the evening performance is already underway at the Albion, I suggest we go to Savoy Street," Tilda said. "It's probably too much to hope we find luck there, but I think we're due."

Teague flashed a brief smile. "We are, indeed. Yes, let's investigate Savoy Street." He looked at Hadrian. "Do you mind if I ride with you whilst I dispatch Wycombe, Mercer, and others in the police van?"

"You have a standing invitation to ride with me," Hadrian replied.

After Teague spoke with Wycombe and instructed him to

gather Mercer and the others and meet them at Savoy Street with the van, he, Hadrian, and Tilda made their way to Hadrian's coach.

Hadrian addressed Leach. "We're going to Savoy Street, but we don't know exactly where or even what we're looking for. Why don't you pull to the side and park the coach once we're there?"

"Yes, my lord." Leach held the door as they entered the coach.

As soon as they began moving, Teague slapped his hand against his thigh. "Your information was so engaging and helpful that I forgot to tell you what we learned today—it pales in comparison. We have a description of the man who assisted Spring-heeled Jack with his leap the other night."

Tilda and Hadrian exchanged an eager look. "I imagine he's large to have pulled Mobray up," Tilda said.

"In fact, he is," Teague replied with a nod. "A neighbor saw a very tall—well over six feet he said—broad-shouldered man carrying several items, including a rope, from the chandler's building the night of the performance."

Hadrian and Tilda shared another look, but Hadrian spoke this time. "That could be Jesson."

"The prop master at the Brittania?" Teague asked.

"Yes," Tilda replied. "Though the cap definitely came from Larkin at the Albion, and I didn't have the sense that Jesson would need to purchase such items from Larkin."

"It's possible he did—so that the cap wouldn't be traced to him," Teague suggested.

They arrived in Savoy Street and Leach parked the coach. When they were all on the pavement, Teague turned to Leach. "The police van will be along shortly. Please stop the driver and direct him to pull in front of you. Tell Wycombe I said to wait until I fetch him."

Leach nodded. "Let me know if there's anything else I can do."

Savoy Street wasn't terribly long, running from the Strand

almost to the Thames embankment. Tilda took Hadrian's arm, and Teague walked on her other side.

The Queen's Chapel of the Savoy was on the right up ahead. Tilda glanced at the opposite side of the street from the church and nearly tripped. "There's a tobacconist."

Hadrian sucked in a breath. "Perhaps Mobray lives there."

"Because Lady Priscilla's garments smelled of tobacco," Teague said anxiously.

It was good the cloak and nightgown had carried the scent of tobacco, or Hadrian and Tilda would have had to explain why they suspected Mobray lived in that building. They crossed the street. The tobacconist was still open.

"I'll ask if Mobray lives upstairs," Teague said. He hurried into the shop.

Hadrian tipped his head back and surveyed the stone façade of the building. The shopfront was painted black with gold lettering that read FINE TOBACCO AND CIGARS. A simple cornice sat at the top, and he idly wondered if Mobray practiced leaping up to it from the pavement.

"Mobray may be up there now," Tilda whispered. "I should have brought my father's pistol."

"I have mine, and Teague has his," Hadrian said.

Teague came from the shop, his eyes gleaming with anticipation. "Mobray lives upstairs on the second floor in the back. The shopkeeper lives on the first floor. He hasn't noticed anything odd in recent days or weeks."

"Anyone who consistently visits Mobray?" Tilda asked.

"No," Teague shook his head. "But I want to question him more thoroughly after we apprehend Mobray. I'm in a hurry to get upstairs." He looked up the street. "There's the van. I see Leach intercepting them. I'll run and inform Wycombe that we're going upstairs and to follow us." He started to go then looked back at them. "Do not go up there without me."

Hadrian was fairly certain he heard Tilda mutter something. "We won't let Mobray escape," he assured her.

A few moments later, Teague had returned, and he led them into the building. There was a door to the right, that presumably led to the shop. A gas sconce flickered in the stairwell.

They started up the stairs, trying to move quietly. By the time they reached the first floor, Wycombe, Mercer, and another constable had caught up to them.

Another sconce lit the stairs up to the second floor. It did a poor job of illuminating the landing, but it was better than darkness.

Teague moved onto the landing then turned and motioned for Hadrian and Tilda to step aside. Then he gestured for Wycombe and Mercer to join him.

Hadrian could feel Tilda's tension beside him as Teague and the others went to the doorway to the rear rooms. Teague knocked. The air thickened as they waited. There was no response.

Teague knocked again. "Mr. Mobray?"

The waiting, though only a few moments, became interminable. Still there was no response.

Turning his head, to Wycombe, Teague nodded. He tried to open the door, but it appeared to be bolted. Wycombe, who was the largest of the three of them, took Teague's place and pushed at the door with his shoulder. The door opened, and Tilda took a step forward.

Hadrian grasped her forearm. "Wait," he whispered. What if Mobray was just inside? He released her as the three men went into the room.

"I can't stand this waiting," Tilda muttered.

Fortunately, it wasn't too long before Wycombe came back out, his features a mask of disappointment. "Mobray's gone. Looks as though he left in a hurry. You can come in."

Tilda strode behind Wycombe into Mobray's lodgings.

Entering the open doorway, Hadrian agreed with the assessment that he'd departed quickly.

The main room—there was another visible behind the first—contained a seating area with a worn, blue velvet chair and a mismatched faded settee in what was likely once a garish red and yellow. A glazed bookcase stood against the wall opposite the main doorway, its doors open with most of its contents remaining. A man in a hurry would not pack many books, as they would be too heavy to carry. Hadrian recognized the desk that sat to the left of the bookcase. It bore a lantern and the book Hadrian had seen in a memory. The mirror he'd seen wasn't there.

He walked to the desk, removing his gloves and tucking them into his pocket. Picking up the book, the name on the spine returned to him before he read it: Enfield. He flipped open the cover and read the title, *The Speaker, or, Miscellaneous Pieces Selected from the Best English Writers*. It was a book on elocution. He should have thought to determine what Enfield had written. Discovering the title of this book might have led them in this direction sooner.

Before he could draw Tilda's attention to what he'd found, the room changed. It was full daylight, not the approaching twilight of the present moment. He stood in this very room near the table by the window carrying a cup of what smelled like tea. He looked across the sitting room where there was a cupboard. The door was ajar, and in the shadows inside of it, Hadrian barely made out a hand.

He wasn't able to investigate it further as he moved through a doorway into the bedchamber. It was a bedchamber with an iron bedstead along with a washstand and dresser. A woman lay in the bed, her eyes closed as her dark hair caressed her bare shoulders.

The memory-holder approached the bed, and the woman opened her eyes. It was Delia Chadwick. Her lips curled into a happy smile. If Hadrian was experiencing Mobray's memory, he could again confirm the man felt deep love for Delia. Why had he killed her then?

The effort to make sense of the memory brought a stab of pain through his temples. His vision clouded, and he was once more holding the elocution book, not a teacup. He'd returned to the present.

His inability to investigate the cupboard and what he'd seen troubled him. Pivoting, he moved toward the cupboard.

Tilda intercepted him, her gaze darting to the book he still held. "What's that?"

He handed it to her lest he see another memory, which he wasn't opposed to, but he needed a moment's respite. "I found it on the desk. It's the book I saw with the silver filigree mirror on top of it. It's a book about elocution." He grimaced, regretting his inaction with the author's name.

Tilda's brows shot up. "Did you see a memory when you picked it up? You look unfocused."

"Yes. I think it belonged to Mobray. He was carrying tea into the bedchamber where Delia was awaiting him in bed. But there's something about this cupboard." He moved toward it and opened the doors.

A gasp shot from Tilda's mouth. The cupboard was the length of the main room, perhaps eight feet in length. It was about four feet high. Inside, there was a thin pallet.

"In the memory, this door was ajar and I was sure I saw a hand in the shadows. I think this is where he kept Lady Priscilla and Miss Redmayne." Hadrian crouched down and reached inside and touched the pallet.

He saw the same interior, but there was a woman inside—a blonde, her hair coming loose around her faced. Her eyes were closed and she was pale. The memory-holder pulled her from the cupboard, lifting her into his arms. The young woman's lips parted, and Hadrian could tell she was alive. *Thank God.*

"Do you think they were kept in there?" The question broke

through the memory, and the vision disappeared. Pain seared Hadrian's scalp and brow.

"Perhaps." Tilda knelt next to Hadrian. "Are you all right?" she whispered.

He pressed his hand to his head, dislodging his hat. Tilda caught it.

"I'm fine." He grimaced.

"Go sit down." She handed him his hat, then crawled into the cupboard, whilst Hadrian managed to stand. "There's a chamber pot in here, and some dishes." She retreated into the room, her nose wrinkling. "And blonde hairs." She held them between her bare fingers—she must have also removed her gloves—and handed them to Teague.

"Miss Redmayne has blonde hair." Teague frowned, then addressed Wycombe and Mercer. "We need to collect every single item in here for evidence. Wycombe, fetch the other constables from the door downstairs and the van. Instruct the driver to move the van in front of the building so we can easily transport evidence."

Wycombe departed, and Mercer returned to the bedchamber.

Despite the pain in his head, Hadrian wanted to touch the pallet again. He wanted to see Miss Redmayne's memory. Perhaps it would tell them something about where she was. "I'll help you pull this out." He ignored Tilda frowning at him.

Hadrian bent to grab one end of the pallet, and Teague grasped the other. As Hadrian pulled, he was overcome by another memory. He couldn't see anything but light filtering under the cupboard doors. The smell of the chamber pot was overwhelming. The worst part, however, was the sense of terror. He felt cold and clammy. The pain in his head intensified.

"*Hadrian.*" Tilda said his name with alarm as she took his end of the pallet.

He relinquished his hold and managed to stagger to one of

two chairs at an oak table near the window where he flopped down. Tilda and Teague set the pallet in the middle of the floor.

"You all right, Ravenhurst?" Teague asked with concern.

"I fear I'm coming down with a migraine. Carry on. I just need a moment to collect myself." He mustered a faint smile as Tilda came toward him.

"You are *not* all right," she whispered as she surreptitiously withdrew the vial of lavender from her reticule.

His pulse beat a frenetic rhythm, and he gritted his teeth against the pain in his head.

She handed him the vial and kept her voice low. "How many memories have you experienced since we arrived?"

He considered fibbing so she wouldn't worry, but he wasn't ever going to lie to her. "Three."

Tilda looked over her shoulder at Teague who was inspecting the pallet. "I'm concerned your repeated unsteadiness will be noted by Teague."

Hadrian smoothed the lavender oil into his temples. "I said I had a migraine."

"I'm picking up a great deal of hair from this pallet," Teague said. "Blonde and also auburn—not as red as my hair."

"That could be Lady Priscilla's," Tilda replied. "It appears Mobray kept his kidnapping victims in the cupboard." She shuddered.

"But not Miss Chadwick," Teague said. "I haven't found any dark brown hair."

"He didn't keep her there because he'd planned to run away with her," Tilda explained. "That is, *if* Bannet was telling us the truth about Mobray and Miss Chadwick being in love, and I've no reason to doubt her."

"Why did he flee now?" Teague asked with frustration. "And where has he taken Miss Redmayne?"

Tilda looked at Hadrian in question, and he replied with a

subtle shake of his head. None of the memories he'd seen had answered those questions, unfortunately.

Wycombe returned with the other constables as Hadrian handed the vial of lavender oil back to Tilda. She slipped it back into her reticle.

Teague directed the constables to take the pallet down to the van.

"We should post handbills asking for information about Oscar Mobray," Wycombe said. "With a reward."

"Who's to offer the reward?" Teague asked.

"I'm sure one of the fathers would," Wycombe replied. "I'll ask Redmayne first."

"I'll offer it," Hadrian said. "How much do you need?"

Teague blinked at him. "That's very generous of you. Are you sure?"

"Absolutely. How much?"

Wycombe exchanged a look with Teague. "I'd say a hundred pounds?"

Teague nodded. "That should be sufficient. Thank you, Ravenhurst." He turned his attention to Wycombe. "We need a photograph of Oscar Mobray, if possible. Go to the Albion and see if they have one—assuming you're able to confirm he worked there. I would think they'd have his photograph if he did. Then find a printer that can make these handbills immediately."

"I'll pay for that too," Hadrian offered. "Including whatever it takes for the printer to work through the night."

Tilda smiled at him and mouthed, "Thank you."

"And if the theatre doesn't have a photograph of Mobray?" Wycombe asked, his brow creasing faintly.

"We have a description from Miss Chadwick's maid," Tilda said. She provided it to Wycombe who recorded it in his notebook.

Wycombe nodded as he tucked his notebook away. "I'll find you here later or at Scotland Yard."

"Probably Scotland Yard by the time you're finished." Teague held up his hand. "Actually, no. When we finish here, we'll go to the Albion. I want to question everyone there about Mobray as soon as the performance is finished."

"Excellent. See you there." Wycombe departed with haste.

Teague addressed Hadrian and Tilda. "You should go home. We'll reconvene at Scotland Yard tomorrow. Though, you don't need to be involved any longer—unless you want to be."

"I do," Tilda replied crisply. "I can't rest until Miss Redmayne is found. I'm especially worried for her safety now that she's been moved."

"I understand. Let's meet at half one tomorrow. I think we could all use a morning at church."

Hadrian knew Tilda must want to join them with their inquiries at the Albion, but Hadrian didn't think he could. Before he could suggest she go, Constable Mercer walked toward them from the bedchamber. "I found these in a drawer next to the bed." He handed Teague a stack of pamphlets.

Teague read, "*Spring-heeled Jack and the Terror of London.*'" He flipped through the flimsy parchment. "It looks as though he collected every volume of the story about Spring-heeled Jack. These have been well-read—there are pencil marks on some pages, and several corners are folded down."

The urge to handle the penny dreadfuls was great, but Hadrian didn't think it was wise, nor did he think Tilda would allow him to do so. He glanced at her, and sure enough, she gave him a stern look.

Tilda, however, accepted Teague's offer to study them. She went to the table and sat across from Hadrian, going through each one meticulously. "Based on the marks and folded corners, Mobray seems very interested in the vigilante aspect of this Spring-heeled Jack character. That could explain why he decided to dress up as this legend, except it doesn't fit Mobray's role as a kidnapper."

She gasped softly as she neared the end. "He did love Miss Chadwick." She held up one of the volumes and showed a page where the name Delia Mobray was written alongside Mr. and Mrs. Oscar Mobray.

"Or at least wanted to marry her for her money," Teague said cynically.

Tilda finished her review then handed them back to Teague. She looked at Hadrian. "We should get you home in case your migraine worsens."

"What about assisting with inquiries at the Albion?" Hadrian asked. "Surely you want to accompany Teague on that endeavor."

"I would," Tilda said hesitantly. "But I need to see you home. Teague doesn't need me."

He might not, but that didn't negate Tilda wanting to go and Teague likely appreciating her help.

"Take care of Ravenhurst," Teague said. "I'll see you tomorrow and provide a thorough update."

Hadrian stood and was glad not to feel too wobbly. He escorted Tilda from Mobray's rooms and down to the ground floor. When they stepped outside, he took a deep breath of the evening air.

The sun had set, and gaslight illuminated the narrow street. The headstones in the churchyard on the opposite side of the street gave a maudlin impression, or perhaps Hadrian was simply feeling the weight of not finding Mobray as well as the pain in his head.

"I'm sorry to pull you away from the investigation," Hadrian said. "You could go back and meet them at the Albion to help with their inquiries. Leach would be happy to convey you."

"I'll consider it." Her tone did nothing to indicate which way she was leaning.

They arrived at the coach, and Leach could tell things had not turned out as they'd expected. Tilda explained about Mobray having fled.

"That poor young woman is still missing then?" Leach frowned but then gave Tilda an encouraging nod. "You'll find her."

"To Marylebone," Hadrian said.

"Actually, to Ravenhurst House," Tilda said. "Then, you'll be driving me to the Albion to assist Detective Inspector Teague with inquiries there."

Leach nodded. "Happy to."

They settled in the coach and Hadrian angled toward her on the seat. "Do you want to hear what I saw with the pallet?"

"Of course." Her features and her tone gentled. "Your collapse the other day frightened me. I'm concerned what could happen if you experience too many memories."

"The intensity of them seems to matter more than the duration or quantity. The ones at Scotland Yard were deeply upsetting and had more of an emotional impact. The last one in Mobray's rooms was like that. I couldn't really *see* anything—it was the memory of one of the young women who was being held captive. I could only make out the light at the bottom of the cupboard, and I felt horrendous fear. It still lingers in my chest." He shifted uncomfortably on the seat.

Tilda moved closer to his side and splayed her palm against his chest. "Here?"

Hadrian lamented the fact that she'd put her gloves back on. Her bare hand would have been even nicer. "Yes."

She pressed against him firmly, and her touch settled him.

"That was the second vision I saw touching the pallet." Hadrian explained about the memory in which the man pulled an unconscious blonde from the cupboard. "I can't say for certain it was Miss Redmayne, as I have not seen a likeness of her."

"I think we can assume it was." Tilda tucked her hand beneath his waistcoat so that only his shirt and her glove separated their bare flesh. "Your heart is still beating a bit too quickly."

He arched a brow at her. "It wasn't until you touched me like that."

She gave him a faux scolding stare. "You can't help but flirt with me."

"You're the one touching me," he argued playfully. "I'm not flirting, I swear." He put his bare hand over hers on his chest. "I'm explaining my body's reaction to your proximity and care. I simply can't help the extraordinary effect you have on me."

Withdrawing her hand, she turned on the seat and pressed her back against the squab, though she still sat close enough to him that their thighs grazed one another. "It's difficult to indulge in feelings of happiness and pleasure when Miss Redmayne remains missing."

"I know." Hadrian clasped her hand. "We're going to find her."

"I hope you're right." She was quiet a moment, then turned her head to look at him. "You mentioned feeling fear. That reminded me of the first memory you saw when we took this case."

"From the first ransom note the Chadwicks received," Hadrian said. "I felt fear from that note. We decided it was the emotion of Mr. or Mrs. Chadwick, since they'd touched the letter."

"Yes, but what if it wasn't? If Mobray is the kidnapper, and he felt sadness after Miss Chadwick died, is it possible he also felt fear?"

"What do you think that would mean?" Hadrian asked.

Tilda exhaled. "I don't know. I'd dearly love to find his accomplice."

"Perhaps you will at the Albion," Hadrian said. "I'm incredibly disappointed I can't go with you. And I'm disappointed I couldn't touch those penny dreadfuls."

"You will." Tilda gave him a sly smile. "I purposely didn't show them to you so that you'd have an excuse to look at them tomorrow—if you're improved. You must take a lavender bath and perhaps douse more than just your pillow with lavender oil."

He laughed softly and pain flashed in his temple. "What do you recommend?"

"Why not a lavender-soaked turban?"

Hadrian couldn't help laughing again, then held up his hand. "Stop. It hurts." He continued to laugh.

She laid her hand on his arm. "I'm sorry!" She giggled. "Now I can't stop picturing you in a turban."

They'd sobered long before they reached his house, each falling into a contemplative silence. At least, that was what Hadrian had done and assumed Tilda had done the same.

The coach stopped, and Hadrian pressed a kiss to Tilda's wrist. "Good luck tonight."

"You take good care, please." She caressed his cheek. "I'll see you tomorrow."

Hadrian climbed from the coach and wished he wasn't going into the house alone.

# CHAPTER 23

The following morning as Tilda and her grandmother prepared to attend service at St. Marylebone, Teague arrived. Tilda had just descended the stairs and heard him speaking to Vaughn in the entrance hall. As she walked in, the detective inspector removed his hat. His expression was grim.

"Has something happened?" Tilda asked with alarm. Last night at the Albion, they'd questioned everyone they could find, including the proprietor and the treasurer. The two had confirmed Mobray's employment and provided a photograph of the actor which Wycombe had used to create the handbill. Constables had worked through the night posting them all over, particularly near the Strand and theatres throughout London.

"The Redmaynes received another ransom note this morning. I'd like us to meet at Scotland Yard to discuss. I've sent Sergeant Wycombe to fetch his lordship."

Tilda's grandmother arrived in the entrance hall, and Teague bid her good morning. "Good morning, Detective Inspector, though I'm not sure you look as though you truly think it's 'good.'" She turned her attention to Tilda. "Why do I have the feeling I'm going to church alone again?"

"I'm sorry, Grandmama. There's been an urgent development in the case. If someone's life wasn't in danger, I would accompany you to the service."

Her grandmother's eyes rounded. "You must go, dear. I understand. Please take good care."

"Can we at least drop you off at the church?" Teague offered with a smile. "I've asked the cab to wait, and it's no trouble at all."

"Thank you, Detective Inspector," Tilda's grandmother replied with a grateful smile. "You are most kind."

Tilda escorted her grandmother outside as Vaughn held the door. Teague assisted her into the cab and directed the driver to St. Marylebone. Tilda sat beside her grandmother, then Teague joined them.

"Are you close to solving the case?" Tilda's grandmother asked.

"Not as close as I'd like," Teague replied.

"We're making progress." Tilda sent Teague an encouraging smile. "Those handbills will likely generate some leads to finding Mobray."

Teague crossed his arms. "We've had several people come to Scotland Yard already, but none of them have provided anything useful. They're just interested in collecting Ravenhurst's hundred pounds."

Tilda's grandmother's brow puckered. "Why would they get Ravenhurst's money?"

Tilda explained the reward.

"I'm not at all surprised to hear of his generosity." She smiled widely at Tilda.

As they neared the church, Tilda's grandmother asked when she could expect Tilda home. Tilda arched a brow at Teague. He shrugged almost imperceptibly to communicate that he couldn't say.

"I won't be late, Grandmama. Will you walk home with Mr. Lambert?" He was their neighbor, and when Tilda didn't attend church with her grandmother, they typically walked to the church and back together.

"Oh, yes, don't worry about me." Grandmama patted Tilda's hand. "You go and save this young lady. She's counting on you." She gave Tilda a confident nod as the coach stopped.

Teague stepped out and helped Tilda's grandmother to the pavement. They were soon on their way to Scotland Yard.

Tilda tried not to think of what her grandmother had said—that Florence Redmayne was counting on her. Delia Chadwick had been too, and Tilda had utterly failed her.

She would not let that happen again.

"Your grandmother doesn't worry about you in your chosen career?" Teague asked with a curious glint in his dark gaze.

"Not overmuch. She doesn't particularly like when I go out at night. Or alone."

"Does that ever happen?" Teague gestured toward her. "Going out alone, I mean. Seems to me, you're always in Ravenhurst's company."

"Usually."

Teague smirked. "Do you have plans to employ him? I've heard he could use the funds."

Tilda knew Teague was being sarcastic and smiled. "Hadrian gives his time and expertise free of charge, which is quite noble." Too late, she realized she'd used his Christian name, though Teague hadn't seemed to notice.

"He is most principled," Teague said. "I confess, I've been surprised that he continues to work with you, particularly when he went to the City with you for that case several weeks ago. I would think his other commitments would prevent such... dedication."

Teague glanced out the window, and Tilda couldn't tell if he was merely being conversational or if he had genuine curiosity about the time they spent together. In truth, Tilda often wondered herself if other parts of Hadrian's life were suffering because of their investigations.

"He probably keeps up with everything," Teague mused without waiting for her to respond, which gave her the impression he was simply conversing. "That may explain his recent exhaustion. He seems to have a bit of trouble staying upright of late." He said this with a smile.

"Yes, he works hard," Tilda murmured. "And he has the occasional migraine."

"I was sorry to hear that. I hope they're not too troublesome."

Eager to not only change the topic but to hear about the latest note, Tilda asked, "How did you learn about the ransom note this morning?"

"The Redmaynes brought it to us. Rather, Mrs. Redmayne did, and her husband accompanied her—reluctantly. She's adamant that the Met remain involved, and I'm glad." His brow darkened, and his expression looked more like it had when he'd first arrived at Tilda's grandmother's. "The note was horrible. It was nothing like the others."

Tilda was surprised to hear that. "That's odd, as is the timing of the delivery today. In the other two kidnapping instances, the notes arrived on the second day after the women were taken. Today is only the first."

Teague nodded. "I noticed the same thing. I immediately wondered if it had been written by someone else, but I compared it to the other notes, and the handwriting matches."

"How was it different from the others?"

"I didn't bring it, as I wanted to keep it locked in my evidence drawer, but you can review it when we arrive at Scotland Yard. It was very explicit with threats to Miss Redmayne if the ransom is not delivered tonight at Cremorne Gardens."

Pleasure gardens? "Why such a public place?"

"I agree that it's strange," Teague said. "Redmayne is to leave the ransom in a small bag beneath a specific bench along a path leading toward the river from the main performance area. The bench will be marked with a red ribbon tied around one leg."

"Do you have a plan to deliver the ransom and catch Mobray?"

Teague stroked his knuckles along his jaw. "The start of one, but that's why I want everyone to gather in my office. We need a thorough scheme, and we need plenty of people on hand."

Did he expect Tilda and Hadrian to participate? She couldn't imagine Teague's superiors would endorse that, even if they weren't compensated. And the Met hadn't yet paid Tilda for her work as the City of London Police had.

"I'm surprised you're including us," Tilda said. "I appreciate it."

Teague met her gaze with a flash of sympathy. "I know what it's like to feel as if you've failed. Let me tell you, however, that you have *not*. I also understand your need to see this to the end."

"Thank you," Tilda replied softly. Teague was a believer in justice and truth, much like her father had been. "You and my father would have got on well, you know."

"It's my privilege to work with his daughter. However, I can't officially work with you on this," he said carefully. "I'm sure you understand what I'm saying."

"Of course. You can't pay me." She chuckled. "I know you would if you could. Furthermore, my presence is likely not appreciated by many in the Met."

"Something I hope they're able to overcome someday," Teague grumbled.

They arrived at Scotland Yard and entered Teague's office just after Hadrian and Wycombe. Hadrian stood near one of the chairs and met Tilda's eyes with a smile that didn't lift his lips.

How could she know he was smiling at her when his mouth didn't move? She just did. They shared a private communication now, and she wasn't quite sure how it had happened. Not that it mattered, for the connection made her happier than she could have imagined.

Tilda moved toward him as Teague went to his desk and opened the evidence drawer. "This was delivered to the Redmaynes' this morning just before nine o'clock. Someone knocked and when the butler opened the door, the note was sitting just over the threshold beneath a small rock, which was likely meant to be a paperweight."

"No one saw who delivered it?" Tilda asked.

"The butler reported seeing an errand boy dashing off, but that is all," Teague replied with a slight frown. "Not terribly helpful." He held the note up to read it.

*Redmayne,*

*It's time to pay. Deliver twenty thousand pounds in bank notes in a bag to Cremorne Gardens tonight before eight o'clock. Leave the bag beneath a bench on a path leading from the performance area to the river. The bench will be marked with a red ribbon tied around one leg. Do NOT solicit help. I will know, and I will hurt your daughter far worse than Miss Chadwick. She will be unrecognizable in death.*

*Spring-heeled Jack*

Tilda shivered. "That is chilling, and not at all like the tone of the other notes. You say they were written by the same hand?"

"Come see for yourself." Teague cleared a space on top of his desk and set the note he'd been reading down. He then placed the others from the evidence drawer beside it.

Tilda, Hadrian, and Wycombe gathered around the desk to inspect the notes. "The handwriting appears to be the same," Wycombe said.

"May I?" Hadrian asked Teague who nodded in reply.

Before Hadrian, who'd removed his gloves, could pick up the note, Tilda did so. She didn't want him touching it. It was too risky, for they were all standing together with their collective focus on the note. Wycombe and certainly Teague would notice Hadrian's eyes unfocusing.

Even worse, what if Hadrian collapsed again? He couldn't very well have *another* migraine this morning.

Though Teague's notice had seemed off-hand, what if he became truly aware of Hadrian's episodes and began to question what was happening with him?

Tilda held the note up so she and Hadrian could look at it together. In fact, she positioned it to shield her mouth from Teague and Wycombe. "It's too risky," she barely whispered as she gave him an urgent look, then darted her gaze toward Teague.

Hadrian's nostrils flared and his eyes sparked with surprise. He turned his attention to the note she held. "This looks like the same hand to me."

After returning the note to the desk, Tilda sent Hadrian a look of apology. She then addressed everyone. "The specific threat to Miss Redmayne sounds angry." The phrase, "it's time to pay," also read strangely to her, but perhaps that was only because Mobray hadn't used it before.

"Yes, the tone seems angry to me as well," Teague said. "And the fact that he sent it sooner than the others indicates he may be losing patience, which makes sense. Perhaps he fled his lodgings because he knows we've identified him."

Wycombe glanced at everyone. "I'm surprised he didn't flee London altogether. One would think the other two ransoms would be more than enough."

Teague narrowed his eyes briefly. "Indeed, but Mobray seems committed, and we can hope that will be his downfall. We'll have plenty of police at Cremorne Gardens this evening. Everyone will be in plain, dark clothing. Married constables will bring their wives, and we'll employ some of the women who work as searchers to act as companions to the unwed constables. We don't want any single men milling about, which may draw Mobray's attention."

"Would you like us to be there?" Hadrian asked.

"You won't be part of the official operation since Mrs. Redmayne explicitly stated she didn't want you involved." Teague grimaced apologetically. "However, who am I to stop you from attending Cremorne Gardens on a lovely June evening?" He shrugged before returning to discussion of his plan. "We'll drop a bag filled with counterfeit bills."

Wycombe cocked his head, his brow furrowing with uncertainty. "Is Redmayne in favor of this scheme?"

"No." Teague flattened his lips briefly. "Regardless, we will carry on as planned."

"Don't you need Mr. Redmayne to be there?" Tilda asked. "The note said he should come alone, which could mean Mobray will be watching for him."

"Yes, but if he refuses to participate, we'll use someone who bears at least a passing resemblance to Redmayne." Teague shrugged. "What else can we do?"

"Nothing," Tilda replied.

A knock on the door drew them all to turn their attention in that direction. Teague went to answer the summons. "Mr. Redmayne. Come in." He opened the door wider.

Redmayne appeared to be in his late forties or early fifties with blond hair and of middling height. Fine lines fanned from his mouth and eyes, and deep furrows marred his brow.

"I came to tell you I've changed my mind about this evening," Redmayne said gruffly. His gaze drifted toward the rest of them gathered near the desk. "Did I interrupt something?"

"Just making plans for tonight," Teague said. "We'll be certain everything goes smoothly. Though it's Sunday, we have called many of our constables in."

Redmayne's eyes rounded briefly, and he appeared almost

panicked. "There can't be too many of you! Spring-heeled Jack mustn't be aware of your presence."

"No one will be in uniform," Teague assured him. "Your presence would be most helpful as we believe he'll be looking for you since the note instructed you to come."

"*Alone*," Redmayne grumbled bitterly. "I will—*very reluctantly*—go along with your scheme."

Teague took a breath. "Thank you, Mr. Redmayne. I will deliver the counterfeit ransom for you to take with you tonight. I'd like to accompany your coachman on the seat, so that I'm with you from the moment you leave your house."

"Fine," Redmayne grumbled. His gaze once again strayed toward Tilda and Hadrian.

Tilda wondered if Mrs. Redmayne had told her husband of their presence. Regardless, Tilda thought it best that they leave. She sent a look toward Hadrian and inclined her head slightly toward the door.

Hadrian bobbed his head the barest amount. "We'll take our leave of you, Detective Inspector."

Teague thanked them for their assistance, and they departed. At the base of the stairs, Hadrian paused and glanced back up toward Teague's office. "Redmayne seemed familiar to me. We've probably met."

"I hope so, because if not, he was probably looking in our direction because Mrs. Redmayne told him about us." Tilda scowled faintly. "I suppose both those things could be true."

Offering Tilda his arm with a flourish, Hadrian gave her a dazzling smile. "Would you care to visit Cremorne Gardens with me this evening, Miss Wren?"

She smiled, absurdly flattered by his flirtation. "How can I resist an invitation such as that? Though you may be tempted to dress in your finery, you must wear something drab."

Hadrian laughed as he escorted her to the door where a constable opened it for them with a nod of his head. Stepping outside, Hadrian cocked his head. "Something from my City of London disguise wardrobe?"

"Yes, those garments are more than sufficient. I suppose I must wear one of my old gowns again," she said with a sigh.

"When we met, you were loath to surrender those gowns," Hadrian noted with a chuckle.

"They've served me well, and I don't like to replace clothing unless it's absolutely necessary. I know it's important for me to dress like a successful detective, so new costumes became necessary." She gave him a sheepish look. "I confess I don't enjoy wearing my older gowns anymore. These new ones are more comfortable. However, the old ones are useful for disguises, so I've kept them."

They arrived at the coach, and Leach opened the door for them.

Once they were settled inside, Tilda continued to think of her wardrobe. "If I became a countess, would I need to constantly buy the latest fashions?" She grimaced. "I don't know if I could ever be that wasteful."

"If you become my countess, you don't have to do anything you don't want to." He sent her a quelling glance. "And before you say that may not be possible, I promise you right now that we will always find a way." He made the vow with such conviction that Tilda wanted to believe him. But she knew Society would not bend to his will, even if he was the Earl of Ravenhurst.

They rode in silence for a moment before Hadrian turned toward her. "You were very concerned about me touching the ransom note. Why did you think it was too risky?"

"Because Teague has noted you feeling poorly—first with the collapse the other day, and then last night at Mobray's lodgings with your alleged migraine."

Hadrian's eyes darkened with apprehension. "Has he said something to you?"

"Rather off-handedly, in the context of how busy you must be since you manage to find time to investigate with me in addition to all your other duties." She met his gaze with a bit of concern. "I confess, I've been wondering why you haven't been going to Westminster as much."

"I go when there's something critical on the agenda or if I need to speak, but in all honesty, there are plenty of days I don't need to be there." He lifted a shoulder. "I'm not in the cabinet, nor do I have any designs to be. You don't think Teague suspects anything is wrong with me?"

"I don't think so. But then, nothing *is* wrong with you."

He sent her a sideways glance. "You know what I mean. I can't think of anyone who wouldn't find my…skill to be *wrong*."

Tilda blinked at him. "I didn't. Nor did your mother."

"You two don't count. You both care for me."

"I didn't know you very well when I discerned you were hiding something from me," Tilda said.

"You didn't care for me immediately?" Hadrian touched his chest in mock dismay. "I'm wounded, for I began to fall for you not too long after we met."

Tilda snapped her gaze to his. "Did you really?"

He chuckled softly. "You needn't sound so surprised. Is it any wonder I would be attracted to the most brilliant and captivating woman I've ever met?"

Thankfully, she didn't blush. Perhaps she was becoming accustomed to his flattery and flirtation. "My rule about not flirting during our investigations really has no teeth, does it?"

This provoked an all-out laugh from Hadrian. "Apparently not. My apologies."

"We should turn our attention to tonight's scheme. Teague is right that everything must go smoothly."

"Agreed. I will fetch you just before seven." He clasped her hand. "I'm sorry to disrupt your grandmother's evening again. You're spending a great deal of time away from home on this investigation."

"That is almost always the case." Tilda looked at their joined hands and thought of her grandmother and how she was now aware of their courtship. She ought to tell Hadrian, but they were nearly to her grandmother's house.

She would tell him that evening, for as much as she'd hoped to keep their secret courtship moving slowly, it seemed that was not to be. Unless something within the investigation prevented her from discussing it with him. She hoped not, for they really did need this to go smoothly. Spring-heeled Jack's new reign of terror was about to come to an end.

~

"At what point did your grandmother call your bluff?" Hadrian asked with a laugh as he and Tilda were on their way to Cremorne Gardens that evening.

"I didn't want her to worry." Tilda explained that she'd told her grandmother Hadrian was escorting her to Cremorne Gardens. "However, she took one look at my costume and concluded—correctly—that we were working, and that this was not a social occasion."

"You may have to start including her in your investigations," Hadrian said. "She's developing an excellent skill for deduction. I wonder if that's something that happens to all of us who are fortunate to be in your orbit."

Tilda rolled her eyes, and he laughed, for he was trying to provoke her humor.

"She wouldn't have believed this was a social excursion, anyway." Hadrian froze briefly. Unless… "Did you tell her about our courtship?"

"I didn't have to, as it happens." She slid him a sideways glance. "She was not asleep the other night in the coach after the theatre."

"I see." Hadrian tried to recall what had happened in the coach whilst Mrs. Wren had been "sleeping." Had they kissed? No, he would never have done that with Tilda's grandmother occupying the coach with them. Then he remembered. "She saw us holding hands."

"I'm afraid I had to tell her the truth."

Hadrian wasn't sure he liked her choice of words. "Did you not want to?"

"I'd hoped to wait until after the investigation was finished, but I'm glad I didn't." She smiled. "Grandmama was most supportive and advised me not to rush into anything. I appreciated her saying that, for I expected her to be so overjoyed that she would want to make wedding plans immediately."

Hadrian found no fault with that. "Was she not happy?"

"She absolutely was." Tilda laughed. "Her greatest wish is for me to be wed. She worries about who will care for me when she's gone. Rather, I think she's concerned that I will need someone to care for."

Hadrian laughed with her. "The latter is the greater concern, I think. Though, I don't think you'll have any trouble finding someone to care for. You simply can't help yourself."

"In any case, Grandmama is delighted for she adores you. And she knows this is a secret courtship. For now."

Those words—*for now*—he liked. And the adoration of Mrs. Wren made him quite happy.

They arrived at the gardens, and Leach held the door as they departed the coach. The coachman's dark eyes shone with anticipation. "I'll be keeping a close eye on the entrance, just as you instructed, my lord. If I see that menace, Spring-heeled Jack, I'll follow him inside." In the event something like that happened, a groom had accompanied them and would drive the coach if necessary.

"Excellent, Leach." Hadrian inclined his head before escorting Tilda toward the pay-box where he would pay their admission. A massive gaslit star illuminated the area.

The evening was warm, heralding that summer would soon be upon them. He took in Tilda's old blue gown with its over-full skirt. It was the same she'd worn to the theatre the other night. Whilst it may be out of fashion, the color was lovely and she radiated beauty and confidence. Hadrian decided she would look alluring even if she wore rags.

After Hadrian paid the entrance fee, they walked into the gardens. Tilda sent him an excited smile. "I've never been anywhere like this. I can hardly conceive of all there is to do."

"I came here often a decade or so ago. My friends and I would watch the circus acts or whatever special performance was playing. We mostly drank too much wine and flirted with young ladies."

"That sounds rather carefree."

It was, and Hadrian knew that was a far cry from what Tilda had needed to do at the same age. She'd already been managing her grandmother's household. "We'll come back another time this summer when we're not focused on an investigation. We'll dine in one of the supper boxes and dance around the pagoda."

She sent him a faint grimace. "You know I don't dance. Surely that should disqualify me from becoming a countess."

Hadrian paused along the path and regarded her with concern. "Are you looking for reasons to deny my suit?"

"I don't have to look for them, Hadrian," she said quietly. "They are right there staring us in the face. But that doesn't mean I'm going to deny you. It only means I'm nervous and still deciding."

"Good." Hadrian started walking once more as he patted her hand that clutched his right arm. "There are many reasons you would be an excellent countess, and I counter that those are also staring us in the face." He sent her a confident look, and she laughed.

They arrived in the central part of the gardens where the pagoda was located. It was surrounded by a huge dance floor that could support thousands of people on any given night. An orchestra played from the pagoda.

"We've plenty of time until eight, if you'd like to explore the gardens a bit," Hadrian suggested.

"All right," Tilda replied. "So long as we don't move too far away from this area. I wouldn't mind going down a few paths to see if we can find the bench marked with the ribbon."

Making their way about, they recognized constables and pretended not to. They even saw Teague at one point and simply strolled right by him. On the third path they took from the main area, they found the bench. Mr. Redmayne had already dropped the bag in place.

Hadrian glanced about surreptitiously and located one of the constables who'd been assigned to watch over the bag. He and his wife sat together on another bench across the path and appeared to be having a romantic evening. Hadrian hoped he and Tilda might have an assignment like that someday.

When the eight o'clock hour passed, they were back in the main area. Hadrian found his pulse was moving more quickly. "Any time now," he murmured.

"Raven? Is that you?" A male voice called from several feet in front of them. The man walked toward them, coming from the supper boxes, with three other young gentlemen.

Hadrian recognized him as he grew near and had to swallow a curse. The young, relatively new MP, Cecil Blyth, was boisterous and nearly always talking—mostly about inconsequential gossip rather than pertinent business. He was just about the last person Hadrian would have wanted to recognize him tonight. It was most frustrating, as Hadrian had gone to great trouble to blend into the crowd. Was his costume not drab enough?

"It *is* you," Blyth said loudly. He turned his head toward his friends. "This is the Earl of Ravenhurst. I told you I know important people," he taunted with a laugh.

"Are you sure, Blyth?" one of them asked as he joined them. He swept his gaze over Hadrian. "Doesn't look like an earl to me."

Blyth's brow furrowed with confusion. "He doesn't usually dress like this." He tried to fix his gaze on Hadrian, but he was quite foxed. "Why *are* you dressed like a shopkeeper or perhaps an undertaker?" The other men sniggered.

The third of the four men brushed up against Blyth and spoke in an overloud whisper. "The earl might be here seeking female *entertainment*." He shot Tilda a suggestive leer before elbowing Blyth.

Hadrian opened his mouth to verbally eviscerate the young man, but Tilda clutched his arm tightly. "Let us be on our way," she murmured.

"No, Raven isn't that type, as far as I know." Blyth took a step forward and narrowed his eyes at Tilda as he regarded her intently. Hadrian was about to tell him to take himself off when the young MP's face lit. "I know who this is! This is that notorious lady detective he's always gadding about with."

Hadrian fought the urge to push Blyth to the ground. "You must pardon us."

"Are you here in disguise so no one knows you're together?" Blyth asked, his eyes rounding. "No! You're on a case. Are you catching a thief? Perhaps a murderer?" He looked around at his friends who were now all staring eagerly and curiously at Tilda and Hadrian, clearly titillated by the encounter.

Fortunately, they were spared further awkwardness by a bright white flash to their right.

"Bloody hell!" someone yelled near them, and Hadrian realized it was one of the young men, who'd spun around toward the flash.

"It's Spring-heeled Jack!" someone called.

Some people ran forward to get closer whilst many ran away from the flash. Tilda, of course raced toward the spectacle, and Hadrian followed.

"There!" Tilda pointed to a dark, flowing cape. His white leather costume was clearly visible beneath the cloak as was the matching mask that covered Mobray's face. "We've got him!"

Mobray lifted his arm in a dramatic fashion, then a giant blue flame leapt from his mouth. But something went wrong. The flame did not extinguish. The hood of the cloak glowed blue.

"Oh my god, he's on fire," Tilda breathed.

# CHAPTER 24

For a bare moment, Hadrian could do nothing but
gape in horror.

People screamed and nearly everyone fled the area. Those
that didn't were the disguised police and perhaps a few other
curious onlookers. Spring-heeled Jack—rather, Mobray—spun
around and tried to throw his cloak off. But the garment was
entirely aflame.

"Water!" Hadrian yelled and others joined the chorus.

A few men raced forward and threw their wine on Mobray,
which only fed the flames. Mobray screamed.

Tilda waved her hands. "Don't throw your wine!"

By the time someone brought a pitcher of water, Mobray was
on the ground and no longer moving. Parts of his leather
costume were singed away. More pitchers followed, and when
the flames were doused, Teague moved close to Mobray. He bent
down into the steam rising from Mobray's body.

"Is he dead?" Hadrian whispered.

"I don't know, but I can't imagine he'll survive that." Tilda
strode forward to join Teague, as did several other constables
along with Sergeant Wycombe.

Teague crouched down next to Mobray. "Where is Miss Redmayne?"

"Is he breathing?" Tilda asked.

"It's difficult to tell since we can't see his face. And I don't want to touch him yet to remove the mask."

Tilda's expression took on a sheen of distaste that was akin to horror. "You may want to wait for the surgeon to remove the mask. It's likely stuck to his charred flesh."

Hadrian shuddered. What a horrible demise.

"I think you can touch him now," Wycombe said. "I will if you don't want to. Just to see if he's conscious."

Teague wore gloves, and he tentatively pushed at Mobray's shoulder. "Mobray, can you hear me?"

The body didn't move.

"Damn." Teague rose. "How in the bloody hell will we find Miss Redmayne now?"

"The accomplice," Tilda said. "There has to be one. How could Mobray have done all this alone? We know he had help with the performance at the chandler's."

Teague nodded. "We need to put all resources into finding this man."

Mr. Redmayne approached them, striding quickly in the company of an inspector from A Division. "I just heard there was a spectacle with that monster." He stopped short when he saw the body on the ground. "Good God, is that him?"

"I'm afraid so," Teague replied darkly.

"What happened?" Mr. Redmayne stared at the body in shock.

"I'd say his trick to breathe blue fire went badly." Teague stepped toward Redmayne. "He appears to be dead."

"How will you find Florence now?" Redmayne swayed, and the A Division inspector grasped his arm to steady him. The furious father fixed his gaze on Teague. "You swore this would work!"

"No one could have predicted this would happen," Teague

said. "But we are not without other means to find your daughter. You should go home. We're doing everything we can to rescue Miss Redmayne."

"This is a travesty," Redmayne cried.

"Please go with him," Teague said to the A Division inspector.

As they left, Teague turned wearily to Constable Mercer. "Fetch the ransom bag unless someone else already grabbed it." He looked about, his gaze settling on the couple who'd been assigned to the bench. Neither of them held the bag.

Tilda grasped Hadrian's hand. "They don't have it." She started toward the path where the bench was located.

Hadrian followed her, his spine tingling. He could tell she thought something was wrong. Tilda had a heightened sense for when things weren't right, and Hadrian had the same for when she was in prime investigative mode.

The constable who'd gone to fetch the bag came running back. "It's gone, sir!"

Teague dashed toward them, continuing past them to the path. Tilda and Hadrian hurried after him. Indeed, the bag was no longer under the bench.

"Did anyone else pick it up?" Teague asked loudly of the remaining constables and others here working for the police.

No one replied.

Hadrian set his hand on his hip. "What if Mobray's accomplice took the ransom?"

"That's entirely possible," Tilda said.

"Or it could've been taken by anyone." Teague's brows pitched together. "I hate having counterfeit notes in circulation, but I fear if we publish a notice about it, we risk alerting the accomplice that we were involved with the ransom."

"You can't do that whilst Miss Redmayne is still missing," Hadrian said with concern.

"Exactly." Teague growled with frustration. "I would at least like to publish a notice asking anyone who was here tonight to come forward if they witnessed Spring-heeled Jack's spectacle. I'm sure all the papers will be going to print late tonight after what's happened here with Spring-heeled Jack."

"We can stop and speak with Clement if you'd like," Tilda offered.

"I would appreciate that, thank you. I'll be here for some time searching for evidence and interviewing people."

"What about Mobray's body?" Hadrian asked.

"I dispatched Wycombe to fetch the coroner. I suppose we should at least make sure he's dead." Teague turned, and they walked back to the main area.

Teague went to the body again and knelt, removing his glove. Hadrian and Tilda followed him and watched as he carefully pulled down the edge of Mobray's glove to reveal the man's wrist. Teague felt for Mobray's pulse. After a long moment, he shook his head.

"I want to take him back to Scotland Yard, rather than the parish mortuary," Teague said. "We need to ensure the body remains secure. Spring-heeled Jack was notorious, and I wouldn't put it past someone to try to steal in to see him."

"What can we do besides speak with Clement?" Tilda asked.

"I don't know yet. You're welcome to come back in the morning. I want to do a thorough investigation when we have daylight. Or you could look for the accomplice, though we don't have much to go on—just a vague physical description." He nodded toward them. "You should be on your way to speak with Clement before it's too late."

"See you in the morning, then," Tilda said.

Hadrian offered her his arm, and together they took a last look at Mobray before walking toward the King's Road entrance where they'd come in.

"You're unsettled," Hadrian said. "Your curiosity was heightened when the bag was discovered missing."

"This kidnapping is just different from the others. Delia

Chadwick was connected to Mobray, and Lady Priscilla was connected to Delia Chadwick. How is Miss Redmayne connected to any of them? Why did her second note arrive early carrying a different, more vicious tone? And why did Spring-heeled Jack conduct a performance tonight when he was meant to pick up the ransom? All eyes were on him, and he clearly didn't have the bag in his possession, which means he hadn't yet picked up the ransom."

"Perhaps the accomplice fetched it for him," Hadrian suggested.

"That's *exactly* what I'm thinking."

Hadrian smiled briefly. "You've taught me well."

They reached the pay-box which now displayed a sign that read CLOSED. Across the street, Leach waited for them next to the coach. Hadrian could see the coachman's anxiety from here.

"I heard Spring-heeled Jack caught fire," Leach said as they approached. "Is that true?"

Hadrian related what happened, and the coachman grimaced. "Have you no way to find Miss Redmayne now?"

"We know there is an accomplice," Tilda replied. "We need to find him, but we only know that he's very tall and broad."

"You also know he's acquainted with this Mobray fellow," Leach said.

Tilda smiled. "You're right, Leach. Perhaps you should be making inquiries along with us."

Leach stood a little taller, and Hadrian stifled a smile. "Happy to help in whatever way I can. To Marylebone now?"

"Actually no," Tilda said. "To the offices of the *Daily News*."

Leach nodded as he opened the door to the coach. "Right away."

Inside, Tilda blew out a long breath and closed her eyes. Hadrian watched her for a few minutes, then removed his glove to take her hand. "We'll find her."

Tilda opened her eyes. "I want to share your optimism." She

sounded weary. "This has been the most difficult investigation I've ever conducted. I can't help feeling as if we're thwarted at every turn."

Hadrian squeezed her hand gently. "We've been foiled before only to emerge victorious. I know you, Matilda Wren, and you do not give up. We will prevail. You don't know how to do anything else."

Tilda smiled at him. "How do you know exactly the right thing to say?" She squared her shoulders and steeled her features. "We *will* find Miss Redmayne. Anything else is unacceptable."

"There's London's best and most brilliant detective," he said softly. "And the woman I love with all my heart." He bent his head to kiss her and was thoroughly enraptured when she kissed him back.

Still, he sensed the unease in her—perhaps because he felt it too. They would do everything in their power to find Miss Redmayne. But Hadrian also knew that sometimes, even if you tried very hard and exhausted every effort, the results were not what you hoped for.

Tilda and Hadrian arrived early at Cremorne Gardens the following morning to join Teague and his crew to search for clues and conduct interviews. They'd been able to speak with Clement last night, as well as the night editor.

Clement had eagerly recorded their account of what had happened with Spring-heeled Jack. Hadrian had encouraged him to include a few lines describing Tilda's brilliance as a private detective since he'd yet to publish his article about her. This had caused Clement to blanch.

However, Tilda had instructed Clement not to name her or Hadrian as the witnesses for the account he was publishing. She'd told him to refer to them as "anonymous bystanders." Clement had reluctantly agreed.

Then, in the coach, Hadrian had asked why she didn't want Clement to name them. She'd pointed out that they'd so far avoided newspaper coverage of their investigations together, and she thought it best that they maintained that privacy as long as possible. Hadrian had seemed disappointed, but he hadn't argued.

This morning's *Daily News* included a request for anyone who'd attended the gardens Sunday evening to visit the nearest Metropolitan Police Station to answer questions. The entire Met was focused on finding Florence Redmayne.

Unfortunately, the *Daily News* also contained a succinct front-page article about what happened at Cremorne Gardens, and despite Tilda's efforts to keep their names from publication, it mentioned the Earl of Ravenhurst being present in the company of his "lady detective friend." Clement's name was not on the article, so Tilda could at least be grateful he hadn't written it.

Tilda tried not to think of what the article could mean for her reputation—or Hadrian's.

Teague greeted them with a stern expression. "Detective Inspector Williamson is here this morning."

Williamson was the lead detective inspector and generally seen as the head of the Detective Branch at Scotland Yard. "Should we go?" Tilda asked, though she didn't want to and would be upset if they must.

"I don't think so." Teague glanced toward the pagoda where Williamson stood with a few other men. "Let's see what happens. I appreciate you taking care of the announcement in the *Daily News* today. We've already had several people come by to report what they saw. Unfortunately, nothing has been helpful yet—no one saw where Mobray came from."

"Sorry to hear that," Hadrian said. "My coachman was watching the King's Road entrance, and he didn't see anyone in a cloak enter. They would have stood out because it was a warm evening."

"That's good to know. It's possible Mobray came in another entrance, even from the river." Teague pivoted and gestured toward a tree. "The most substantial thing we've found so far is the apparatus Mobray clearly planned to use to leap away from the area. I can also confirm his boots contain springs. Furthermore, we found the device he used to breathe the blue flame. Interestingly, it was markedly larger than the one he used before—the cap we have is much too small to fit the one he used last night." He started toward the tree, and Tilda fell into step with him.

"That would explain the exceptionally large flame." Tilda realized Hadrian was not with them. She turned her head to see him tuck something into his pocket then he hurried to catch up with them. "It may also be the reason the trick ended in disaster—the fire was too big and managed to reach the flammable hood of the cloak covering his head."

Teague nodded. "That's my conclusion as well. The surgeon who came to Scotland Yard last night found greasepaint on the hood of the cloak and said that made it catch fire more easily. Bad luck for Mobray."

They walked to the tree where Sergeant Wycombe was writing notes about the contraption they'd found. Teague explained that a rope and pulley had been installed, likely earlier in the day yesterday, and Mobray had been wearing a harness he would have hooked onto the device in order to "leap" away.

"From the tree, he could have jumped to a narrower path that leads to the river. We believe he was going to escape that way."

Tilda studied the contraption in the tree for a moment before glancing at Teague. "Did you find a boat he may have taken earlier in the evening that he might have planned to use to escape?"

"We did not. Perhaps his accomplice, assuming he was here

last night, fled the scene after what happened." Teague lifted a shoulder with a sigh—his frustration was again evident. "It's all we can come up with for now."

"What can we do to help?" Tilda asked.

"Actually, I think perhaps we should leave," Hadrian said, stirring Tilda's curiosity about what he'd stashed in his pocket. "We're not officially affiliated with this case, and I don't think we want to provoke Williamson's ire." He looked to Teague. "You can always send for us if you need our assistance."

"That's probably the best course," Teague said. "We still have many interviews to conduct with the employees."

Tilda didn't really want to leave, but she suspected Hadrian had a good reason for suggesting they should. She wished Teague luck and departed with Hadrian.

As they walked back toward the King's Road, she glanced toward his pocket. "What did you take?" She realized as she asked the question that Hadrian's hand had been bare when she'd seen him put the item in his coat. He must have donned the glove on his way to join them at the tree. "You saw a memory."

Hadrian pulled the item from his pocket and held it up between his thumb and forefinger. "I found one of the caps from the device Mobray used last night. It's exactly like the other one, only larger."

Tilda took it from him with a gasp. "What did you see?"

They stopped in the path and Hadrian faced her with an eager smile. "A newspaper article about Frederick Redmayne from 1842. It was about his newly acquired patent for the Redmayne Gas Governor, a pressure-regulating valve placed between the gas main and the burner. I don't know whose memory it was, but the person holding the newspaper was enraged."

"Did you see a hand?"

"Unfortunately, no. However, it can't be Mobray's memory since he's dead."

"You're right—this can't be Mobray," Tilda agreed. "Perhaps it belongs to the accomplice. Do we think Larkin made this cap as well?"

"Possibly." Hadrian cocked his head. "Even likely. But that doesn't mean it's his memory. We've no idea who else may have handled it. You may be right that it's the accomplice."

"We need to interview Redmayne," Tilda said with steely determination. "This is the connection we've been looking for—someone who touched this cap, perhaps the accomplice who aided him here last night."

"Now you see why I wanted to leave," Hadrian said as they continued toward the entrance.

"I do and also why you took the cap without telling Teague. He will need this evidence, however." She sent him a grimace. "In fact, you should have given it to him immediately, especially since you already saw a very useful memory."

"I thought about that, but what if I need to use it again?" He shook his head firmly. "I don't want to risk not finding Miss Redmayne because I relinquished this cap too soon. Besides, they have the actual device that was used. They don't need this cap to prove anything."

Tilda stopped again as a very large man walked through the entrance toward them. He glanced about, perhaps nervously, his gaze settling on Tilda and Hadrian briefly before darting away. Hadrian had stopped beside her, and she grabbed his hand.

"What's wrong?" he asked.

"Look at that man. He's huge."

"He is—" Hadrian sent her a round-eyed look. "*Yes.*"

Tilda cleared her throat. "Excuse me, are you here to help with the investigation regarding last night's tragedy?" she asked.

The large man paused, his dark gaze moving anxiously. "I'm looking for Detective Inspector Teague."

His name had been on the handbills about Mobray. "We can take you to him," Tilda said as excitement thrummed through her. "What's your name?"

"Dowd."

Tilda gestured the way they'd come. "He's this way." They began to walk. Hadrian moved to Dowd's other side. "I'm Miss Wren, and this is Lord Ravenhurst."

Dowd paused and looked over at Hadrian. "Your lordship?"

Hadrian smiled pleasantly. "Yes. I don't suppose you have information about Oscar Mobray? We've been assisting with the investigations into the kidnappings perpetrated by Spring-heeled Jack."

The giant hesitated, his brow creasing as he regarded Hadrian. "I knew Oscar Mobray and that he dressed up as Spring-heeled Jack."

Tilda remained quiet. She didn't want to interrupt Dowd whilst he was revealing things to Hadrian.

Hadrian didn't move his gaze from Dowd. "How did you know Mobray?"

"We worked together a few years ago at the Anchor Theatre in Whitechapel," Dowd said. "I'm a stagehand, and I work at different theatres. We saw each other from time to time. Recently, he asked for my help with a stunt. He said he wanted to take advantage of Spring-heeled Jack reappearing and put on a performance."

"When was that?" Hadrian asked.

"A week or so ago." Dowd shifted his weight and shot a glance down the path toward where the police and others were gathered. "He offered me twenty pounds, and I never say no to a job. I helped him leap onto a building near the Strand."

Hadrian nodded. "The chandler shop? You operated the pulley?"

"That's right."

"Pardon me." Tilda moved around to stand next to Hadrian. She was unable to keep quiet any longer. "Were you aware that Spring-heeled Jack had been accused of kidnapping young women when you agreed to help Mobray?"

Dowd swallowed. "I did. I asked him if he was involved with that, but he swore he wasn't." The stagehand shrugged. "Mobray was always a decent bloke. I didn't have any reason to think he was lying."

"And now you do?" Hadrian asked.

"Things changed after we completed the stunt." Dowd scrubbed his hand over his jaw. "We took the supplies we'd used back to the Albion Theatre—that's where Mobray had borrowed them from. Mobray changed out of his costume, which he also stashed at the Albion, and we went to a pub so he could buy me an ale."

Tilda considered asking Dowd to pause until they could speak with Teague, but she was too eager to hear the rest. "What changed?"

"We drank several ales. Mobray was never very good with drink. He became upset, kept talking about his lost love, 'Delia.'"

"Delia Chadwick?" Hadrian asked urgently.

"He didn't say her surname, just 'Delia.' But I thought the name sounded familiar. He said they were supposed to elope but something bad had happened. That's when I recalled her name from the newspaper and that she'd been killed. I asked him if she was the same Delia. He started to sob, made a bloody fool of himself." Dowd's shoulders twitched, and his features creased with discomfort. "He swore he didn't kill her, that he was her rescuer. He said he'd saved Delia from her father and freed her so they could marry."

"That almost sounds like he kidnapped her," Tilda said gently. And yet, if Mobray saw himself as Delia's protector, that certainly aligned with his perception of Spring-heeled Jack as some sort of hero.

Dowd nodded. "I thought so too. He blubbered about how Delia hadn't deserved what happened, that she was just trying to be happy. I asked again if he had anything to do with the kidnappings or the murder of Delia Chadwick. This time he admitted he'd taken her but explained they'd planned it together. They were going to elope with the money they ransomed from her father." He grimaced as he paused his story briefly. "That sounded awfully cold to me."

Tilda exchanged a grim look with Hadrian. "Did he explain how Delia ended up dead? It doesn't sound as if he wanted that."

"He only repeated that it wasn't his fault. In fact, he was insistent about it. He even grabbed me and made me look into his eyes as he swore he didn't kill her. He was crazed."

"I don't suppose you asked him who did kill her?" Tilda asked.

"Of course I did, but he ignored my question. He started sobbing again and said they never should have taken Lady Priscilla, that he hadn't wanted to. If they hadn't, Delia would be alive."

Tilda was desperate to know why. "What happened after he kidnapped Lady Priscilla?"

"He wouldn't say, and I was beginning to lose track of his story. He was a mess, and it was getting harder to understand him with his sobbing and his drunkenness. After a while, he calmed and said he needed to make sure the ransom money was given to those in need, as Spring-heeled Jack would do. Then he gave me another two hundred pounds—he had the banknotes on him—and begged me not to repeat what he'd told me." Dowd looked at them with sorrow. "I'd decided to leave London with the money he gave me, but then I saw the handbills yesterday and I knew I had to come forward. I was working up the courage, and then I read in this morning's paper that Mobray had died." He sniffed. "If I'd gone to Scotland Yard yesterday, perhaps Mobray would still be alive."

"Perhaps," Tilda said kindly. Even if he was, it was possible he would be hanged for his crimes. "You mentioned Mobray said 'they' shouldn't have taken Lady Priscilla. Was he working with someone?"

"I think so, but I didn't ask. He'd stopped answering my questions and was just blubbering by then." Dowd's mouth pulled into a solemn frown. "Poor bloke."

"I wonder if the other person killed Delia," Hadrian said.

"He has to be," Dowd said somewhat passionately. "I know Mobray, and he wouldn't hurt anyone."

"I apologize, but you'll need to repeat all that to Detective Inspector Teague," Tilda said. "We'll take you to him."

They walked Dowd to the performance area but stayed at the periphery. Tilda went to fetch Teague whilst Hadrian remained with Dowd.

Teague appeared surprised when she approached. "I thought you left."

"On our way out, we ran into Mobray's accomplice." She glanced toward where Dowd and Hadrian stood together beneath a tree.

"He just showed up here?" Teague asked as he pivoted toward Hadrian and Dowd.

"He saw the handbills about Mobray. However, he's not the accomplice for the kidnappings," Tilda added quickly.

Teague turned back toward her. "What do you mean?"

"He only helped with the stunt near the Strand the other night. I'll let him explain the rest." She walked with Teague and introduced him to Dowd.

"We're going to be on our way," Tilda said.

"Is there nothing to follow up on?" Teague flicked a glance at Dowd.

Tilda shook her head. "Not really, though some things are clearer. We need to find Mobray's true accomplice. Ravenhurst and I are going to call on Redmayne. I'm troubled by the vicious, personal tone of the note he received yesterday. There must be some connection between him and Mobray or his accomplice, whoever that is." That was as much as Tilda could reveal to Teague.

"That bothers me too," Teague replied. "Let me know what

you find out." He turned to Dowd. "Now, tell me everything you told them—and more if you can think of it."

Hadrian escorted Tilda back toward the entrance. "Chadwick is going to be devastated when he learns his daughter was part of the kidnapping and ransom scheme."

"Yes." Tilda felt very bad for him, despite his treatment of her. "I hope we can find out what happened to her. Why did she end up dead? And why did Mobray regret kidnapping Lady Priscilla?"

"Now that we are all but certain there's an accomplice, hopefully he'll be able to answer those questions," Hadrian said. "We just have to find him."

Tilda nodded. "After your vision with the cap, I believe Redmayne may very well hold the key to finding his daughter."

# CHAPTER 25

*H*adrian knocked on the door of the Redmaynes' house with purpose. The summons was quickly answered by a butler in his late thirties with prematurely whitening hair and piercing gray eyes. His sharp nose was beak-like, and his long, thin legs also put the notion of a bird into Hadrian's mind.

"Good morning," he said evenly. "I'm Ravenhurst, and this is my associate, Miss Wren. It's urgent we speak with Mr. Redmayne regarding his missing daughter."

The butler's eyes widened. "Do come in. Mr. Redmayne will be eager to see you. I'll show you to the drawing room." He led them upstairs to a lavishly decorated room absolutely stuffed with curiosities ranging from far eastern art to a large pair of antlers affixed to the gleaming mahogany paneling over the sculpted stone fireplace.

The butler left them to fetch Mr. Redmayne.

"What an eccentric room," Tilda murmured. "Do you suppose he collected all these things from his travels?"

"Perhaps. Or he's doing his best to show he has means."

"Ah, that makes sense." Tilda regarded him with a shrewd glint. "You're looking at things like a true detective now."

Hadrian chuckled. "It's hard not to in my present company. And I wouldn't have it any other way," he added. He glanced about the room, taking in the various items. His gaze froze on a photograph sitting on a table. The subject was a young man dressed in garments that would have been fashionable more than twenty years earlier.

He quickly went to pick up the photograph. Because he still wore his gloves, he did not feel or see anything, nor did he need to for he recognized the man. *"Tilda."*

She came toward him. "What is it?"

Satisfaction rushed through him as he met her gaze. "This is the man from the memory I saw from the smaller cap we found at Lady Priscilla's. Redmayne is the younger man."

"More proof of a connection between Redmayne and Spring-heeled Jack. Mobray could not have been the only kidnapper."

Redmayne strode into the room, and Hadrian set the photograph down. He moved toward the man, whose blond hair was disheveled.

"Have you found Florence?" he asked desperately, the flesh beneath his eyes was dark and puffy.

"No, but we've come to ask you some questions that will help us do so," Tilda replied.

Redmayne waved his hand. "I can't do that right now. I'm on my way out."

Tilda's brows shot up, and Hadrian shared her surprise. "What could be more important than finding your daughter?" she asked.

Hadrian noted the edge of suspicion in her tone.

"How can your questions possibly help find Florence?" Redmayne asked sharply. "I need to go."

"Why?" Tilda cocked her head. "Do you know something we

don't? We want to ask you about your patent for the Redmayne Gas Governor. Did that earn you any enemies?"

Redmayne's brows snapped together, and his eyes somehow grew even more wild. "Why would you ask about something that happened over twenty-five years ago? I don't have enemies. I'm well-liked and respected." He glanced toward the door in agitation.

Hadrian could see how badly the man wanted to go. But why? Shouldn't he want to do everything he could to help them find his daughter? Unless...

"You don't have *any* enemies?" Tilda persisted.

A stocky man in a somber suit and wearing a highly distressed expression crept over the threshold of the drawing room. He looked nervously toward Redmayne and coughed. "Mr. Redmayne," he said with just enough volume to be heard.

Redmayne pivoted, and the stocky man came toward him carrying a black case. He wordlessly handed it to Redmayne, then quickly retreated from the room.

Hadrian's pulse picked up. "What's in the case?"

"None of your business."

"I think it's a ransom," Tilda said calmly. "Did you receive another note from the other kidnapper?"

Eyes rounding, Redmayne sputtered. "How do you know?"

"Because we're aware you had an enemy regarding this patent. You're either not telling us for some reason, or perhaps you simply don't recall. As you said, it was many years ago. But I'm begging you right now, on your daughter's life, you must try to remember," Tilda demanded urgently.

Redmayne swiped his free hand through his hair, indicating how it came to be in its current state. "There was a man...we had a falling out over the patent. He wasn't my *enemy*. None of that matters now. I must leave *immediately*."

"Show us the note." Tilda's voice was cold and determined.

"You cannot just walk into whatever the kidnapper has planned for you—for your safety and your daughter's."

Hadrian could see she was not going to suffer the man's attempts at concealment. He would prevent Redmayne from leaving if he had to.

After a long moment in which he was clearly conflicted, Redmayne set the case down. He fished a folded piece of parchment from his coat and held it out to Hadrian, his hand shaking.

Tilda intercepted it, which Hadrian expected. He would have time later to touch it with his bare hand.

"How was this delivered?" she asked.

"It was left on the front step. The same as yesterday's note."

Tilda unfolded the paper and held it so Hadrian could read the note along with her.

*It was very foolish of you to try to pay me with counterfeit bills! I know the Met was there, as well as those pesky detectives. I warned you to come alone! Never forget, I have your precious daughter or you will spend your days in misery lamenting your choices.*

*You have one more chance to see her alive again. Bring the ransom to the old railway construction store in the alley across from the railway depot in Nine Elms by noon—and no fakery this time! Come alone or Florence will pay the price for your arrogance.*

*Spring-heeled Jack*

Hadrian glanced at Tilda. "The handwriting is the same as yesterday's note which matches all the ransom notes. That seems to indicate Mobray was never the author of the notes." He needed to think back to the memories he saw initially. Perhaps he could recall something that would help them find this kidnapper and thus Miss Redmayne.

Tilda nodded. "You're right. Though, this and yesterday's note are very different from the others. As soon as we discovered Mobray was the man behind Spring-heeled Jack, things began to fall apart. Mobray fled and the notes changed."

"And Mobray died," Hadrian said.

She pivoted toward Hadrian. "Mobray was an actor. He *performed* as Spring-heeled Jack. We know his costume was made by Maud Brimley, his devices likely came from Larkin, and he apparently stored his supplies at the Albion. Neither Mrs. Brimley nor Larkin seemed to know anything about the kidnappings or Spring-heeled Jack and were shocked at the connection of their costumes and devices to him, but what if they *were* involved?"

Facing Redmayne once more, Tilda refolded the note. "You said you had a falling out with someone over the patent. Was that person heavily involved with the invention?"

"Why would you ask?" Redmayne's neck flushed red. He appeared uncomfortable.

"Whoever wrote this note has your daughter, and they know you well enough to find you arrogant and to realize your daughter is 'precious' to you. They also have no problem seeing you suffer for the rest of your life." Tilda paused briefly, then raised her voice. "Who did you fall out with over the patent?"

As Redmayne hesitated, Hadrian recalled the emotions he'd sensed from the ransom note that had been left on Lady Priscilla's pillow. There had been fury and bitterness. Perhaps that had come from someone who'd lost something valuable, such as patent rights to something that had earned Redmayne a fortune.

Hadrian kept a tight rein on his patience, but only barely. "Answer the question, Redmayne. Your daughter's life hangs in the balance."

Redmayne flinched and his face flushed scarlet. "I worked on the gas regulator with a man named Lawrence. He was brilliant and could devise just about anything. But I had the appropriate contacts, and my family had the money we needed to support the work we were doing."

Hadrian recalled the newspaper article he'd seen in the memory earlier. There'd been no mention of a man named Lawrence. "So, you cut Lawrence out of the patent? I'd say that would make an enemy out of anyone seeing as how you've profited."

Tilda turned her head toward Hadrian. "I know who we're looking for. Larkin is the only person who makes sense. He *made* these devices for Spring-heeled Jack. Redmayne just said his former partner could create anything, and Larkin is the right age." She looked at Redmayne. "Did he have a limp?"

Redmayne shook his head. "Not then. But I suppose he could have one now."

"Is Nicholas his given name?"

"*Yes*," Redmayne answered almost breathlessly.

"What time is it?" Tilda asked Hadrian.

"Half eleven."

Tilda took a deep breath as she turned her attention to Redmayne. "Pick up the ransom, Mr. Redmayne. We're driving you to Nine Elms where we'll drop you off near the old railway construction store but not directly in front of it in case Larkin is watching. Do you have a footman we can send to Cremorne Gardens?" She glanced at Hadrian. "We must notify Teague so he can meet us there."

"But I was told to come alone!" Redmayne cried.

"You will not," Tilda said calmly. "Larkin—or Lawrence—has been waiting over a quarter century to exact his revenge. I don't believe he has any intention of allowing you or your daughter to go free. In fact, I wager he's been planning to snare and kill you both whilst stealing a large portion of your fortune. What greater revenge could there be?"

Redmayne paled. *"Good God."*

Tilda fixed a stern stare on Redmayne "Listen closely, Mr. Redmayne. You're going to do exactly as we say. This is our one chance to save your daughter, and I'm not going to let it slip away."

~

"We're going to take this ransom to Larkin," Tilda said.

Redmayne stared at her. "That's what I wanted to do."

"But you're not going alone. We'll explain the plan on the way there. Right now, I need to send a message to Detective Inspector Teague." She strode to an ornate desk and opened drawers until she found parchment and pencil. Turning her head toward Hadrian, she asked him to fetch a footman to deliver the note to Scotland Yard.

"Not to Cremorne Gardens?" Hadrian asked.

"I don't want to miss Teague if he's left. I think it's better to send this to Scotland Yard—the constable at the desk will know what to do." She quickly drafted the note, and a few moments later, sent it off with a young footman under express instructions to deliver it as soon as possible to a constable or sergeant and to indicate it was urgent.

The footman dashed off, and Tilda preceded Hadrian and Redmayne from the room. Outside, Tilda told Redmayne to wait in the coach whilst they spoke with Leach.

Redmayne's face flushed as he clutched the ransom to his chest. "We can't tarry!"

"We'll leave presently," Hadrian assured him with scant patience.

Scowling, Redmayne stepped into the coach.

Hadrian spoke in a low tone to Leach. "We don't have time to explain everything now, but we're taking Redmayne to deliver the ransom to the other kidnapper—it's Larkin, the property manager at the Albion Theatre."

Leach's brows shot up. "You're going to give him the ransom?"

"Hopefully not," Tilda replied. "I believe this is a trap, and I want to turn the tables and entrap Larkin." She explained where they were going in Nine Elms. "Stop the coach a short distance from the alley, and we'll let Redmayne out. Then you'll drive past the alley and park the coach. The three of us will depart—provided you're able to find someone to watch the horses—and quickly make our way to the old railway construction store where we'll steal inside and thwart Larkin's plan."

"Will the Met be there?" Leach asked.

"Not immediately, but we've dispatched a message for Teague to meet us there," Tilda said. "However, we must be prepared for the likelihood that he won't arrive in time to help us."

"You must bring your Tranter, my lord," Leach said, referring to Hadrian's revolver that was now stored in a compartment beneath the forward-facing seat in the coach.

Hadrian nodded, then turned his head to Tilda.

Before he could speak, she held up her hand. "I know what you're going to ask. No, I didn't bring my father's Adams this morning, as I didn't think it would be necessary, and yes, I need a smaller pistol, which we will purchase after this case is solved."

"We also have the pistol in my box, my lord," Leach said. "We'll be ready."

"Thank you." Hadrian clapped his hand on Leach's shoulder before helping Tilda into the coach.

They settled on the forward-facing seat—Redmayne had possessed the wisdom to sit on the rear-facing seat as the guest—and Hadrian removed his revolver from the compartment.

Redmayne goggled at him. "You're bringing a pistol?"

"Larkin either murdered someone or assisted in murdering someone," Tilda replied sharply. "Of course we are."

Slumping against the seat, Redmayne rested his arm on the case holding the ransom beside him. "I can hardly fathom Lawrence being capable of such malfeasance. He always possessed such a charming demeanor."

Tilda had thought so too during their interview at the Albion. "Was that before or after you excluded him from a patent for a device he helped invent?"

Redmayne winced. "He was angry, but I only saw him once after that."

"I would have avoided him too," Hadrian said sardonically. "Why would you cut him out of something he rightfully deserved?"

"I was young and desperate to make a name for myself as my father had done. He was instrumental in the construction of gas works and expanding gaslight throughout London." Redmayne exhaled with perhaps a note of self-recrimination. "I'm not proud of what I did."

"Perhaps you should offer to make amends when you see Larkin, or Lawrence, shortly—assuming he's waiting there for you," Tilda suggested.

"Isn't that what I'm doing with this ransom?" Redmayne asked bitterly. "It isn't even as much as he asked for. I couldn't obtain that much. As it is, this will ruin me." He straightened his spine, and his eyes looked damp. "But I would pay twice this to have Florence back."

Tilda was glad to hear that. She couldn't decide if Redmayne was callously ruthless or a man who'd made a mistake.

Hadrian narrowed his eyes at Redmayne briefly. "How would you do that if you couldn't even come up with the full amount?"

"I was going to borrow money, but there wasn't time." He blinked as his shoulders twitched, making him appear quite nervous.

"What had you planned to do if the kidnapper counted the money and saw you were short?" Hadrian asked with a frown.

Redmayne's shoulders slumped. "I don't know. This was the best I could come up with."

"It doesn't matter now," Tilda said crisply. "When we arrive, we will drop you off before the alley and you'll walk to the old construction store. You'll go inside, and we won't be far behind you. If your daughter is there, you'll deliver the ransom. If she's not, you must try to leave."

"Try?" Redmayne's voice cracked on the single syllable.

"Larkin may have already killed someone, and it seems you and your daughter were his ultimate targets. I won't lie and tell you that there's no danger."

Redmayne stiffened as he notched up his chin. "I don't care. I'll risk anything to rescue Florence."

"We could also wait for Detective Inspector Teague to arrive," Hadrian said.

"No!" Redmayne shouted. "I can't miss the appointed time."

Hadrian sent Tilda a look of concern. She replied with a subtle nod. It was a dangerous scheme, particularly since they'd no idea what they were walking into, but it was all they had.

They traveled in silence for some time. Once they crossed the Vauxhall Bridge, the tension in the coach thickened.

"Are you ready?" Tilda asked the man as he picked up the case and set it in his lap.

"We won't let anything happen to you or to your daughter," Hadrian gave the man a reassuring look as the coach stopped.

Hadrian opened the door, and Redmayne took a deep breath that seemed to catch in his throat. He stepped out of the coach, and Hadrian pulled the door closed.

Leach drove past the alley and parked the coach. Hadrian quickly stepped out and helped Tilda to the pavement. Leach found a boy to watch the horses and paid him a few pennies before joining them. He carried the pistol he kept beneath his seat.

Nine Elms was dominated by the railway depot on the opposite side of the road. The area was a warren of streets, with a gas works and brewery nearby. The scent of coal and river mud clung to the morning air.

They hurried to the alley and quickly found the old store that Larkin had described in the note. It was utterly derelict with its boarded-up windows and crumbling brick façade. There was a single door at the front and a larger, boarded-up entrance to the right side of the building that was likely used to move supplies in and out.

"We should go to the back and hope there's a rear entrance," Hadrian said.

He led them around the building, and Tilda's eye was drawn to the black iron gas pipe that ran along the brickwork. It was old and rough-looking, but the fittings where it met the wall were bright and recently worked.

Not wanting to call out and be overheard, Tilda reached forward and grasped Hadrian's sleeve. He stopped and turned his head to look at her. She pointed at the shiny pipe fittings. Hadrian frowned then moved closer to inspect the pipe where it entered the building.

The report of a pistol startled Tilda, and she saw Hadrian flinch. He took off toward the back of the building. Tilda ran after him and heard Leach following behind her.

Fortunately, there was a rear door. Hadrian drew his revolver from inside his coat and, with a quick glance back at them, rushed inside. Tilda paused so that Leach came abreast of her. He also had his weapon ready. How she wished she was armed as well.

She gestured for Leach to go in after Hadrian, then she followed. They stepped into a large open space that was almost the entire first floor, save an antechamber at the front of the building. There was a loft, with a ladder leading up to it. Dozens of candles burned everywhere, including the loft. A stack of bricks leaned against one wall, and some rusted chains were piled in a corner.

Given all the light, it was easy to see Larkin standing on the right of the large room where Miss Redmayne was seated against the wall, her hands and ankles bound, and a gag tied around her mouth. She sobbed as she tried to scoot closer to her father who was lying on the flagstone floor, blood seeping from his hip where he'd apparently been shot. He clutched the wound as he reached for his daughter.

Larkin held the ransom bag in one hand and a revolver in the other. He'd pivoted toward them but was still also angled so he could see the Redmaynes.

Hadrian raised his Tranter and pointed it at Larkin. "Drop your weapon and surrender, Larkin. Or Lawrence." He cocked the pistol. "The Met will be here presently."

Tilda stood slightly behind Hadrian, and Leach moved up on her left, his pistol also raised. Pulse racing, Tilda inhaled sharply to fill her lungs, only to smell something alarming. "I smell gas!"

Suddenly, there was another shot.

Tilda instantly looked toward Hadrian, but he didn't falter. Leach, however, dropped to the floor. Tilda rushed to his aid as Hadrian fired his revolver, then ran forward, presumably after Larkin.

"Hadrian, don't!" Tilda cried. "There's gas. I believe Larkin plans for this building to explode."

"He told me he removed the regulator," Redmayne called out. He groaned. "Please, you must get Florence out of here!"

Hadrian raced back, his features dark and furious. "Larkin will escape."

"Unfortunately." Tilda had only seen Hadrian look like that once before—when she'd nearly been killed in the not-too-distant past, and Leach had killed the man threatening her.

Leach!

Tilda focused on the coachman who appeared to have been shot in the leg. Blood streamed from just above his left knee. "Oh, Leach. We must get you out of here."

"If you can help me up, I think I can walk if I lean on you." He clenched his jaw.

"Hadrian!" Tilda called.

He rushed to her side and frowned down at Leach. "You'll be all right. I'll ensure you have the finest physician."

"Help him stand," Tilda said. "Then I can assist him out of the building."

"You must help Florence!" Redmayne shouted. "The building is going to explode as soon as there's enough gas in the air. That could be any moment!"

Indeed, the smell of gas was becoming stronger by the second.

"Can't you blow the candles out?" Leach suggested. "The gas won't ignite then."

Hadrian put his arms under the coachman's shoulders and lifted him to stand. Leach grunted as Tilda sidled close to him. He put his arm around her to steady himself.

"Too many candles," Hadrian said. "We've no idea how many are up in that loft. Better to get you all out of here. You walk out with Tilda and I'm going to help Redmayne. Go out the front so you can move as far away as possible."

Leach nodded, and Tilda met Hadrian's gaze for the barest moment. "Please be careful," she said urgently. "And quick!"

Tilda helped Leach walk out the front. They moved as fast as they could, but it was still slow due to Leach's wound. He groaned every few steps, and Tilda kept darting nervous glances at Hadrian helping the Redmaynes. He'd first removed Miss Redmayne's gag and was now working on her bindings.

When she was free, she wrapped her arms around her father. Her sobbing grew louder. Hadrian told her there would be plenty of time for that after they escaped the building.

Tilda didn't see what happened next, for she and Leach had reached the antechamber. A few steps later, they were outside. She took several deep breaths, as did Leach. The coachman slowed his pace slightly.

"You can't slow down," Tilda urged him. "We must get as far away as possible. Keep going, Leach. You can do it."

He picked up his speed once more, and Tilda resisted the urge to look back to see if Hadrian and the Redmaynes were out. They were going to make it.

Halfway down the alley, Tilda felt a deep concussion in her chest. It knocked her down, taking Leach to the cobblestones with her. An all-encompassing sound followed—a rolling boom that seemed to wash over them like a wave on the shore, or how she imagined that to be. The boom echoed around them, intensifying the sound. Tilda absorbed it in every fiber of her being.

She felt a rush of heat behind them, and all she could think was that Hadrian and the Redmaynes had to have escaped. But she couldn't get up or even turn to look.

Debris fell from the sky like an angry storm—bits and chunks of brick and grit and timber. Tilda squeezed her eyes shut and put her arms over her head.

The world went dark.

# CHAPTER 26

The blast threw Hadrian several feet, and he landed hard on the cobblestones. He'd managed to get the Redmaynes out—he and Miss Redmayne had practically carried her father between them. They'd managed to clear the building by more than a dozen yards before Hadrian felt the ominous shudder in his gut followed by the percussive roar that had thrown him.

He was struck by falling debris, a piece of which felt hot on his back, despite his clothing. His own memory of Spring-heeled Jack burning overwhelmed him. Panicked, he moved quickly to dislodge whatever had hit him.

It was difficult to see amidst the grit in the air. The alley was obscured by a dark cloud. Hadrian tried to breathe and coughed. How he prayed Tilda and Leach had escaped the alley before the blast. He needed to assist the Redmaynes to safety.

"Redmayne!" Hadrian called. "Miss Redmayne!"

"Here," came a feminine reply. "Papa?"

Hadrian waved his arms through the dusty air and moved slowly. "Miss Redmayne?"

"I'm here."

A hand grasped Hadrian's calf. He looked down and made out Miss Redmayne's form. "Can you walk?"

"I think so," she replied. "I can't see my father."

"We'll find him. Let's get you to your feet." Hadrian crouched down and offered her his hand. She rolled to her side and he rose, pulling her up. She clasped his wrist with her other hand until she was standing on her own.

She coughed. "Papa! Where are you?"

"*Hadrian?*"

Hadrian recognized that voice. Why was Tilda still in the bloody alley? His heart hammered anew as fear ignited in his chest. "Tilda! Where are you?"

"About halfway down the alley. Are you all right?"

"Yes. We need to find Redmayne." Hadrian squeezed Miss Redmayne's hand. "Is Leach with you?"

"Yes," she replied, her voice a ghost in the cloud from the debris and the smoke from the fire. "He's fine."

"Make your way out of the alley," Hadrian called. "We'll come to you."

"Please hurry, Hadrian!" The worry and fear in her tone echoed his own.

He waved his free hand again, desperately trying to see through the haze. At last, it began to clear a little—enough that he could finally make out Redmayne's form. "There, Miss Redmayne." He pointed toward her father.

Together, they worked to turn him over.

"*Papa!* Can you hear me?" Poor Miss Redmayne sounded nearly hysterical.

Redmayne coughed, and his daughter threw herself over him as she sobbed anew.

"We must move out of the alley," Hadrian urged them. "Mr. Redmayne, we must get you up."

Miss Redmayne turned her head to look up at Hadrian. "I

don't think I can help bear his weight. Something hit my head and I don't feel particularly steady."

*Damn.* "Tilda! Send help when you can!" he shouted as loud as he could, hoping she wasn't too far away to hear him amid all the chaos.

"Miss Redmayne, can you walk on your own?" Hadrian asked.

"I can try." She tried to stand and wobbled so that she tilted heavily to the side, and Hadrian had to catch her.

"I'll help you out of the alley first," Hadrian said, pulling her up once more.

"No, I can't leave my father!" She turned to look down at Redmayne who appeared to be opening his eyes.

"Go, Florence," he croaked. "Please, I need you to be safe. For your mother."

Hadrian swept Florence into his arms. "This will be faster." He took off at a near run toward Nine Elms Lane. As he neared the opening to the alley, the air cleared considerably but was still filled with dust and smoke.

He saw Tilda standing near a police van! Teague had arrived. In fact, the detective inspector rushed toward him along with Sergeant Wycombe and two constables.

Teague's dark auburn brows were pulled tight over his eyes. "What can we do?"

Hadrian set Miss Redmayne on her feet and looked to one of the constables. "Can you help her to the van or perhaps to my coach? She's been struck in the head by debris and is also likely weak from her captivity, so she's not steady on her feet." The constable moved to take her, putting his arm rather awkwardly around her waist.

"We've a cab coming to transport anyone needing medical attention," Teague said. "And the fire brigade should be here shortly." He turned to the constable. "Take her over there with Leach, for now." He gestured to the railway yard across the lane.

Leach was indeed seated on the ground, propped against the side of a small, brick building.

The constable nodded and tried to escort her across the street. She would not move, however. Her gaze fixed on Hadrian. "You must rescue my father!"

"I will," Hadrian promised. The poor girl had been through so much. She was covered with soot so that her hair didn't even appear blonde just now. "But you must move to the other side of the street where the air is clearer. Your father would want you to do that."

She nodded though she appeared defeated. The constable guided her across the street.

"Where's Redmayne?" Teague asked, drawing Hadrian's attention back to the matter at hand—rescuing Redmayne.

"In the alley, about fifteen or twenty yards from the building that exploded," Hadrian replied as he pivoted to return to the alley. "Come, I'll show you."

Teague put his hand up, blocking Hadrian's forward movement. "No. You've done enough. Go and let Miss Wren tend to you. She's frantic." He clapped Hadrian's shoulder before dashing into the smoke with Wycombe and the other constable.

Hadrian didn't have to walk to Tilda, for she met him halfway. She slipped her arms around him though they were both covered in grime. He held her tightly and, as she put her head against his chest, he took a long, deep breath of cleaner air.

She lifted her head and looked up at him. "I thought I'd lost you."

"I worried the same." He kissed her forehead, heedless of the soot—or anyone who might be watching. "How is Leach?"

"In some pain, but the wound doesn't seem too terrible. The bleeding has slowed a great deal, but a constable is still keeping pressure on it. I should go take over now that you're here so the constable can do his job." She glanced up and down Nine Elms

Lane. "People are starting to gather, and they'll need to be kept at bay."

"Teague said there's a cab on the way that will transport the Redmaynes. We can take Leach in the coach." He froze a moment then looked down the lane to where they'd parked the coach. It wasn't there but Hadrian saw it a bit farther down. "The horses were likely spooked by the blast."

"Leach concluded the same, but it seems the boy was able to keep them from bolting," Tilda said.

Relieved, Hadrian started across the street. Tilda clung tightly to his arm as if she couldn't bear to be away from him. That was more than acceptable to him, for he did not want to be away from her either just now. Or perhaps ever.

"You'll drive?" she asked.

He nodded. "You can sit in the coach and take care of Leach, if you don't mind."

"Not at all. I feel absolutely terrible about what happened to him."

"I'll wager if given the choice, he'd do it again. He's quite committed to supporting your work."

"That doesn't mean he should want to get shot," she murmured.

Hadrian chuckled. "I don't think he wants that specifically."

They reached Leach who looked up with a weary smile. "How do I look, my lord?"

"Perhaps slightly less blackened than me," Hadrian estimated. "How's the leg?"

"It'll heal." Leach summoned a smile for him, and Hadrian felt a rush of affection for his dedicated coachman.

"We'll get you home and send for a physician," Hadrian promised.

"Dr. Giles," Tilda suggested.

The mention of Dr. Giles reminded him of Tilda's recently wounded shoulder. His attention snapped to that part of her. "How are you? You only just had the stitches out last week."

"I fell due to the blast, but it seems fine." She moved her shoulder. "A bit stiff, but it has been periodically. Dr. Giles said that could last another few days."

"Still, I want him to look at it," Hadrian said with concern.

The fire brigade arrived, and things became even more chaotic. Teague, Wycombe, and the constable emerged from the alley carrying Redmayne. They brought him to the cab which had just pulled up in front of where Hadrian and Tilda stood with Leach and Miss Redmayne.

Teague and the others carefully set Redmayne into the cab. Miss Redmayne said she would care for him on the way home and thanked them all.

"I'll come by later," Teague said. "Both to check on Mr. Redmayne and to conduct an interview with you about your kidnapping. I'm sorry to bother you with it, but it's essential we record what happened whilst it's fresh in your memory."

"I understand. I hope you catch him. He's horrible."

"*Catch him?*" Teague turned his head and goggled at Tilda and Hadrian. "What happened?"

"There's much to explain," Tilda said. "Starting with the identity of the second kidnapper—Nicholas Larkin, the property manager at the Albion Theatre. Though that is an alias. He was originally known as Lawrence. He and Redmayne worked together a quarter century ago, and Redmayne excluded him from a patent for a device that Lawrence helped invent."

Teague gaped at them. "Kidnapping Miss Redmayne was an act of vengeance? That's completely different from the kidnapping of Lady Priscilla, and we now know Miss Chadwick wasn't kidnapped at all. How did Larkin manage to escape?"

"He'd flooded the building with gas and lit candles everywhere so that when the level of gas was high enough, it would ignite and cause the blast," Hadrian explained. "We barely rescued the Redmaynes and Leach, who Larkin shot when I threatened to shoot him if he didn't surrender."

"Damn." Teague shook his head then exhaled. "We'll find Larkin. We know who he is now."

"He has Redmayne's ransom," Tilda said. "And likely the ransoms from Chadwick and His Grace. It's possible he's fleeing London or even England as we speak."

"We'll catch him," Teague vowed, his eyes glittering with dark promise. "You go on home now. Leach needs a physician. I can't thank you all enough. I'll come by and check on you later as well."

"Come to Ravenhurst House," Tilda said. "I'll be there for some time, I'm sure." She glanced at Hadrian as if to confirm that was acceptable.

It was beyond acceptable. Having Tilda at Ravenhurst House fulfilled his wildest dreams, even if it was only for a while.

Teague nodded. "Do you need help moving Leach to your coach?"

"We can manage," Hadrian replied. "You've much to do here."

As Teague left to deal with the chaos of the growing crowd, Hadrian helped Leach up. The coachman was able to lean on him heavily and limp to the coach.

"Sorry it's a bit farther away now," Hadrian said.

"I'm just glad the horses are all right." Leach sent him a grateful glance. "I was worried until I saw they were safe."

"I'll give the boy a shilling." Hadrian helped Leach into the coach first, and Tilda stepped in after him.

Hadrian thanked the boy, gave him the shilling, and then climbed onto the seat. As his body settled for the first time since the blast, he became aware of aches and pains. Yes, he'd send for Dr. Giles as soon as they arrived at Ravenhurst House. He was extremely grateful they were all whole.

~

*H*adrian set Leach up in a guest room on the second floor despite the coachman's protestations. The servants' quarters wouldn't do for his recovery, and he certainly couldn't return to his lodgings in the mews.

Fortunately, Dr. Giles had arrived quickly and proclaimed the bullet had gone through a fleshy part of Leach's leg above the knee. He required stitches and would need to stay off his feet for several days. Dr. Giles would be back the following day to monitor for infection.

Whilst it was not a horrible wound, it was more serious than what Tilda had recently sustained. Or what Hadrian had recovered from when he'd been shot during another of their investigations. The bullet had grazed his biceps. He'd also been hit by pottery shrapnel as Tilda had, but only the top of his ear had been nicked and no hint of injury remained. They'd been very lucky.

Whilst Dr. Giles had tended to Leach, Hadrian cleaned up at his valet's insistence. Tilda had also relented to the housekeeper and allowed one of the maids to help her tidy. Still, her garments were covered in soot. At least her beautiful reddish-blonde hair was still the appropriate color since she'd been wearing her hat. Poor Miss Redmayne had not been so lucky, and her locks looked nearly black. She had, however, been wearing a day dress and boots at least, which was better than if she'd still been in her nightgown.

Hadrian realized her gown did not fit as well as the one Miss Chadwick had been wearing when she'd been found. This made sense, for Mobray had supplied a garment for the woman he loved and knew well. Whereas, Miss Redmayne had been provided a gown that did not match her frame, for she was unknown to Mobray—and to Larkin.

It was mid-afternoon before they met in the drawing room.

The housekeeper brought sandwiches and tea, and they ate ravenously for a few minutes.

"I'm glad Mrs. Kenworth put a cloth over the chair," Tilda said. "I wouldn't want to soil your furniture. I really need to go home and change my clothing. And have a bath." She smiled almost dreamily.

Hadrian chuckled. "A bath would not come amiss."

"At least *you* have fresh garments." She peered at him over the rim of her teacup before taking a sip.

"Sharp insisted. He said he was going to finish the job the blast started and just burn what was left of the clothing."

"There was a sizeable hole in the back of your coat," Tilda said with a grimace. "You weren't burned?"

He shook his head. "I felt a stinging sensation and was able to remove the debris. Dr. Giles gave me a thorough review, and I'm fine aside from a host of aches and pains. What did he say of your shoulder?"

"It's unharmed. I also have a few pains, but I would guess yours are worse, given your proximity to the blast." She met his gaze with relief and something warmer that filled Hadrian with joy. "I'm so happy you were not in the building."

Collier appeared in the doorway with Teague. "Detective Inspector Teague is here."

"Thank you, Collier." Hadrian had asked the butler to show Teague up as soon as he arrived. "Would you care for something to eat?" he asked Teague as he walked to the table.

"That would be most welcome." Teague removed his hat, and Collier rushed to take it from him.

"I'll have Sharp tidy this up," Collier said. "It will be waiting for you downstairs."

"Thank you." Teague seemed surprised. "That is most kind of you." The butler departed, and Teague gave Hadrian a sardonic look. "I'm sure you don't want my filthy hat on any of your furniture, and I don't blame you."

"In fact, I'm sitting on a cloth," Tilda said with a smile. She poured tea for Teague. "Did you already visit the Redmaynes?"

She and Hadrian hoped he had, so Teague could tell them what he'd learned from Miss Redmayne.

"I have. Poor Redmayne is in rough shape." Teague sipped his tea. "He's quite weak after being shot and suffering from the proximity of the blast." He eyed Hadrian. "I'm surprised you aren't worse off."

"Redmayne was already wounded, and Miss Redmayne was in a weakened state," Hadrian said. "I'm not without aches and pains, however. Something hit me in the back, and it's quite sore."

"It also ruined his coat," Tilda said softly but with humor.

"And how are you, Miss Wren?" Teague asked. "Your shoulder was wounded not that long ago."

"I'm quite well, thank you, and Leach will recover nicely."

"Glad to hear it." Teague ate a sandwich, and Hadrian exchanged a look with Tilda. They silently agreed they would let him eat. When he was finished, he took another drink of tea. "Unfortunately, Miss Redmayne did not see her captor until she arrived in the old construction store. She'd been blindfolded since the last time she awoke, which she estimated to be this morning.

"She suspected there might be two kidnappers, but not because she heard them speak. In describing her captivity, she recalled the sound of normal footfalls until last night when the person she heard outside the cupboard seemed to have had a limp."

"That would indicate Larkin," Tilda said. "How extraordinary that she noticed the distinction. What did she say about her abduction?"

"That it was Spring-heeled Jack," Teague replied. "He was masked and breathed blue flame at her. She described having a cloth soaked in chloroform pressed to her mouth as Lady Priscilla did."

"Wasn't she taken in a nightgown?" Hadrian asked. "I wondered how she came to be garbed in different clothing."

"She said when she awakened in the cupboard, there were undergarments and a gown for her to wear. She also commented that they smelled as though someone else had worn them. I took them as evidence, and I can also report that the neckline of the gown had greasepaint on the edge." Teague picked up a butter biscuit. "I believe the items came from a theatre—probably the Albion."

"I wonder why she was given a gown and Lady Priscilla was not," Tilda said. "I understand now why Miss Chadwick wasn't in her nightgown—she was not a captive."

"Perhaps Miss Redmayne was given something to wear since she was moved?" Hadrian suggested. "I fear we may never be able to answer all the questions we have."

"I've been thinking about the device Mobray used last night," Tilda said. "It was larger than the others and produced a bigger, more impressive flame which ended up leading to Mobray's death. It's possible Larkin made a device that would produce a flame that was *too* large—uncontrollable even."

Teague swallowed the biscuit he'd popped into his mouth and leaned toward her slightly. "You think Larkin schemed for Mobray to burn to death?"

Tilda looked from Teague to Hadrian and back again. "I'm trying to work out how Mobray fit into Larkin's plan for revenge. The two men had very different objectives for kidnapping these women. Mobray took Delia Chadwick so they could elope. Dowd indicated that Mobray hadn't wanted to kidnap Lady Priscilla, so it seems that was Larkin's idea. But what was his motive? We know he wanted to kidnap Miss Redmayne to exact revenge against her father."

Teague's brow creased as he appeared to grow pensive. "Is it possible Mobray was Larkins's tool this entire time?"

"I think so," Hadrian said. "Mobray had the interest in Spring-heeled Jack. Perhaps Larkin suggested they revive the legend so Mobray could 'rescue' Miss Chadwick."

"That's diabolical." Tilda sent Hadrian a shrewd look of appreciation. "It's also an excellent theory. Hopefully, we'll catch Larkin and learn the truth." She sipped her tea.

"It's a very good thing you decided to call on Redmayne this morning," Teague said.

"We were fortunate enough to arrive just before his secretary, or whoever that was, handed Mr. Redmayne a case." She glanced at Hadrian. "Redmayne was horribly agitated and kept insisting he needed to leave immediately. We deduced the case held the ransom and asked him if that was true."

Teague's brows arched. "He didn't prevaricate?"

"We didn't give him a chance to," Hadrian replied. "We explained his daughter's life was in danger and that if he was going to deliver the ransom personally, his would be too. That's when he showed us the note he'd received."

"His butler gave it to me when I was there earlier," Teague said. "Larkin sounded as though he truly hated him."

"Did Redmayne fully explain why?" Tilda asked.

"He tried, but the laudanum took effect and he lost consciousness. I was hoping you could fill in what I don't know."

Tilda and Hadrian explained the background shared by Larkin and Redmayne. Teague shook his head. "No one deserves what Redmayne has gone through, but he certainly invited Larkin's rage."

"Larkin is a dangerous man," Hadrian said, voicing the concern that had clung to the back of his mind since the man had limped to his escape. "He's already waited over a quarter century to exact revenge against Redmayne. And he failed. Redmayne lives."

"But he has Redmayne's fortune," Tilda pointed out. "Redmayne told us he's all but ruined. Perhaps that will satisfy Larkin."

"I don't think so," Teague said, with a shake of his head and a dark expression. "He shot Redmayne—not to kill him but to wound him so he couldn't escape or help his daughter to escape. He planned for them to die together in that blast. He's a ruthless murderer. I, for one, will not rest until we catch him."

"Neither will I." Hadrian lifted his teacup toward Teague. "We should do this with brandy or whisky, but tea will have to do for now."

Teague held up his teacup, and both men drank.

Tilda sipped her tea as well. "I don't want to be left out. I've already stated my express need to capture the man if only to satisfy my curiosity." She'd made the comment with a bit of levity, but her features grew quite sober. "I agree he's dangerous. The Redmaynes will need to be careful."

"As will you," Teague said, spearing Tilda with a worried stare before transferring it to Hadrian. "Every police department in the kingdom will be looking for Larkin. Or Lawrence, or whatever alias he may choose to adopt next. We hope to obtain a photograph of him from the theatre as we did with Mobray, though I'm not as optimistic since Larkin is not an actor."

"You really think he won't flee England and set himself up somewhere else?" Hadrian asked. "I would."

"I don't think he's in his right mind," Tilda said. "He won't like that he failed. He could very well wish to finish what he started."

"And perhaps take the two of you down in the process." Teague looked at them intently. "I want you to be exceedingly careful. I wonder if you ought to leave London for a while."

"I can't do that," Tilda responded almost sharply. "I don't have a country estate I can jaunt off to." She glanced at Hadrian who arched a brow at her. He knew what she meant, but he hoped that she might want to "jaunt off" with him.

"The good news to come out of this at least is that this version of Spring-heeled Jack is dead," Teague said with satisfaction. "The denizens of London can breathe a sigh of relief."

"Until the next impostor appears," Tilda said wryly. "Though I'm sure the newspapers will wring as much as possible from these horrible events."

"Are you worried at all that they'll focus on the latest Society gossip: Lord Ravenhurst and his lady detective?" Teague asked. "Your names already appeared together in the newspaper as being present at last night's spectacle at Cremorne Gardens, and your presence at the blast today was noted."

"I'm not worried." Hadrian could tell that Tilda was, however. She was working to keep her features placid in reaction to Teague's query, but Hadrian detected the tension beneath the calm.

"I wondered if your…association might change after this," Teague said carefully. "I hope the three of us will continue working together as we are able, but I'll understand if something happens that would preclude your ability to conduct investigations."

Tilda folded her hands in her lap. "Nothing would do that, save my complete incapacity."

Teague smiled. "Good. Well, I'll be on my way. Thank you again for the refreshment and the company. It was most restorative to sit for a short while." He stood. "Back to it. I'll keep you apprised of the search for Larkin."

"Thank you, Detective Inspector." Tilda gave him a warm smile as he departed.

Tilda sat straight as if she were going to stand. "I should be going too. You said you've another coachman who can drive me home?"

"Perhaps I should come with you," Hadrian said with concern. He would not be able to stop thinking about Teague's warning. Hadrian didn't want Tilda to be alone. More accurately, he didn't want to be away from her.

"That isn't necessary." She narrowed her eyes at him, but there was a playful glint within them. "I can see you're worried about

Larkin coming for us. He may, but not today. He's likely hiding somewhere licking the wounds to his pride after his failure—assuming he even knows that the blast didn't kill anyone."

"You're probably right. Still, I'll call on you tomorrow."

She shook her head firmly. "You need to stay here and rest. *I* want to rest. Surely, we've both earned a day of respite."

"More than." Except Hadrian only wanted to repose with her.

Tilda stood. "Shall I let Collier know I'm ready to depart?"

"I'll ring for him." Hadrian began to rise and realized just how much his back hurt.

"I can do it." Tilda sent him a smile and waved him back down.

He watched as she went to the pull and called for the butler. It was as if she lived here. He could envision it. He could almost feel it. He wanted it more than anything.

But that wasn't going to happen tonight or even tomorrow. He needed to be patient and try very hard not to mope in the time they were apart. Good heavens, he was turning maudlin now. He supposed another near-death event such as happened today would do that to a man.

They parted a short while later. Hadrian tried very hard not to settle into a funk.

He failed most miserably.

"I can't tell you how happy I am you're taking a respite from investigating!"

Tilda's grandmother had said that no less than a dozen times in the past two days since she'd returned home from the blast caused by Nicholas Larkin, who was still missing. His photograph and names—the two they knew of—had been shared far and wide. The Duke of Alnwick was offering a reward of one thousand pounds to anyone whose information led to Larkin's apprehension.

Glancing up from the book she was reading in their cozy sitting room at the back of the house, Tilda smiled at her grandmother. "The respite is only for a few days."

"Still, it's overdue. You've been working far too much." Grandmama dipped her gaze to the newspaper she held. "Here's another account of the 'Nine Elms Blast.'" She lightly cleared her throat before reading aloud, "Lord Ravenhurst and his lady detective, Miss Wren, were the heroes of the day, saving Mr. Redmayne and Miss Redmayne from certain death!"

Grandmama set the paper in her lap. "Is that why you didn't

wish to walk to the grocer with me and Mrs. Acorn this morning?"

"I rarely do that," Tilda replied. But the truth was *yes*. Despite not having left the house since returning from Ravenhurst House two days ago, she was keenly aware of the newspaper articles and the gossip that was likely spreading all over London, particularly London *Society*.

She may have been redeemed, at least in the press, but to her, the case wasn't finished. Which also meant, at least to her, that it was unsuccessful. The disappearance of Larkin weighed heavy on her mind.

Which wasn't to say there weren't other things claiming her attention. The numerous articles about Hadrian and his "lady detective" were the printed version of a cacophony. Tilda kept recalling Teague's curiosity about how she and Hadrian would carry on.

Could they? Her reputation as a lady would not support it. And her reputation as a serious detective was perhaps suffering due to her notoriety as the earl's *frequent companion*.

In a word, she was trapped.

She hoped that by taking a *forced* respite from detective work, the gossip would calm, and she could go about her life as she had been. Except that meant she would still be in Hadrian's company, and the interest in them would once again rise to a fever pitch.

Engrossed in her thoughts, Tilda failed to hear that someone had arrived. Vaughn appeared in the doorway. "Miss Wren, Lady Ravenhurst is calling."

Grandmama's head snapped up from the newspaper. "Lady Ravenhurst?" Her rounded gaze shot to Tilda. "Did you know she was coming?"

"I would have mentioned it." Tilda felt an odd surge of anxiety.

Why was Hadrian's mother here? Tilda had received a note from him yesterday inquiring after her welfare. He'd signed it "yours," and Tilda still felt as if she were glowing from within. "Vaughn, please ask Mrs. Acorn to prepare tea."

Vaughn inclined his head. "Her ladyship is in the parlor." He departed in his slow, shuffling gait.

Rising, Tilda glanced down at her rather drab dark blue gown. It wasn't as ancient as some of her others, but it wasn't one of her new, more stylish garments either. She'd donned a light morning gown since she hadn't planned on going out. Or receiving.

Was this what it would be like to be a countess? She must dress every day to welcome whoever may decide to pay a call?

"Are you wondering whether you should change your clothes?" Tilda's grandmother asked kindly.

"I suppose I am, yes."

"Normally, I would say yes because a countess is calling. However, Lady Ravenhurst is a friend, perhaps even a close one given your relationship with her son, and she will understand that you are recovering from an ordeal." Grandmama's features softened with love. "You look fine, my dear. Better than fine— you are always beautiful and tidy."

Tilda tamped down a laugh. How could she find fault with tidy? "Thank you."

Gathering her courage, Tilda strode to the parlor and hoped all was well with Hadrian. "Good afternoon, my lady." She smiled brightly as she greeted Hadrian's mother.

Lady Ravenhurst wore a gorgeous sapphire silk gown, the skirt swept back into an elegant bustle trimmed with ivory ribbon. A small matching hat with a pearl pin sat precisely atop her beautifully styled gray-brown hair. Her blue eyes regarded Tilda and narrowed the faintest amount as if what she saw was lacking, but she quickly masked the reaction with a smile.

"Good afternoon, Miss Wren. I hope I'm not troubling you. I know this must be a trying time."

"I'm well, thank you." Tilda gestured for her to sit and perched in a chair as Lady Ravenhurst swanned to the settee. "Mrs. Acorn is bringing tea."

"I needn't stay for that, though it's kind of you to offer."

Tilda's stomach knotted. "Is everything well with you? And his lordship?" How strange that sounded. Tilda hadn't referred to him as "my lord" in months.

"Oh, yes. I saw Ravenhurst earlier—just before I came here, in fact. He's feeling much better than yesterday. He was quite sore."

She'd come from seeing Hadrian? Why did that make Tilda feel even more anxious, despite learning he was well? "I'm glad to hear he's recovering. Do you happen to know how Leach is faring?"

"The poor man." Lady Ravenhurst clucked her tongue. "Apparently, he's a bit surly, but the physician called this morning and said he's doing very well. He also indicated Leach's disposition should improve in a few days. It is my experience that an ill or wounded man is the worst of patients. It's best to leave them to their misery and await the arrival of their good humor along with their recovered health."

Tilda tried not to laugh but could not suppress a smile. In truth, she'd always liked Hadrian's mother, despite the difference in their classes and the fact that Lady Ravenhurst rarely let her forget that. It wasn't that she was ever rude. No, she was simply a dowager countess whilst Tilda was the daughter of a policeman —facts of which Lady Ravenhurst was acutely aware.

"I hope you won't find my call intrusive," Lady Ravenhurst began, finally moving to the purpose of her visit.

Tilda steeled herself.

"Having read all about your daring rescue with Ravenhurst and Leach, I wanted to ascertain your welfare." She paused and put forth a brief, somewhat strained smile which did nothing to ease Tilda's apprehension. "I also need to explain to you how things are now."

"And how is that?" Tilda was proud that her voice was steady.

She clasped her hands in her lap and crossed her ankles demurely.

"You must be aware of the other…items in the newspapers, which I have also read. You and Ravenhurst have been noted together quite publicly in multiple places. One could explain away your visit to the gardens since you were apparently conducting an investigation in disguise. And the same could be said for your excursion to Nine Elms. However, it's come to my attention this morning that you were also seen attending the theatre together along with your grandmother last week."

"That was also part of our investigation." Tilda was not certain where Lady Ravenhurst was going with her concerns.

"Be that as it may, I'm sure you see this is untenable. If you continue as you currently are, your reputation will not survive, and I'm afraid Ravenhurst's will also. He *must* maintain a certain standing in our circle and in the political world. He is the Earl of Ravenhurst."

"Yes, I'm aware." Tilda was both irritated and sad. She knew what the dowager was trying to say—it was the very thing Tilda had been consumed with before she'd arrived.

"You and Ravenhurst must decide on a path forward." That was *not* what Tilda had expected her to say. She'd been waiting to hear that Tilda must no longer work with Hadrian. Was Lady Ravenhurst saying she would support something other than their separation?

"You must marry or sever ties completely. You simply cannot continue as you are."

Marry! Tilda was momentarily stunned. It wasn't the most promising endorsement, but it was not at all what Tilda had expected. It seemed Hadrian's mother would accept them marrying.

But would the rest of Society?

Tilda's hesitation stemmed from her own desire for the independence she'd craved and earned but also from her fear that she would not be accepted as a countess because of her background. And because she would not—*could* not—surrender her career. Being a private detective was about more than earning a living. Obviously, she wouldn't need to concern herself with that if she was Hadrian's wife. She could not abandon her calling.

There were so many other things to consider too. Her grandmother and their household for one. How were they to manage without Tilda?

Then there was the question as to how Tilda could possibly assume the role of countess. She could perhaps run Ravenhurst House, but Ravenswood? She didn't know the first thing about managing a country estate. *She'd never even been to one.*

Courtship was supposed to answer those questions, wasn't it? Except they hadn't had a proper courtship at all. They'd been too focused on this case. *Tilda* had been too focused.

From the moment Miss Chadwick had been found murdered, Tilda had pushed everything aside and dedicated herself completely to uncovering Spring-heeled Jack. She and Hadrian had managed to grow closer, in spite of that, but they hadn't had a courtship. And now it might be too late for one.

"You're awfully quiet," Lady Ravenhurst observed.

"My apologies. I'm thinking about what you said. Hadrian has not proposed marriage." Not officially anyway. Too late, she realized she'd called him by his Christian name. His mother hadn't reacted, so it seemed she was both aware of and perhaps even at ease with their closeness.

"He clearly loves you, and what matters most to me is that he's happy. I have wanted him to marry for so long—not just for his duty to the earldom but because I love my son and wish for him to have a joyful marriage. I believe he will have that with you. Provided you stop endangering yourselves," Lady Ravenhurst added sternly.

"Your counsel is well taken," Tilda murmured. She couldn't quite believe what she was hearing.

"I've grown fond of you, Matilda. You prefer Tilda, don't you?"

"Only my mother calls me Matilda."

"Ah, yes. Your mother." The dowager pursed her lips briefly. She'd met Tilda's mother a few weeks earlier when she'd been visiting from Birmingham. They'd had tea with Grandmama at Lady Ravenhurst's house. Tilda's mother had made no secret about hoping for a match between Tilda and Hadrian.

At the time, Lady Ravenhurst had been rather unambiguous in her lack of support for the union. But it seemed she'd changed her mind.

"I imagine she would be delighted if you and my son decide to wed," Lady Ravenhurst continued. "But only the two of you can make that choice."

"I don't know the first thing about being a countess," Tilda whispered.

Lady Ravenhurst waved her hand as if she were swatting at a fly. "Nonsense. You comported yourself exceptionally well the other night at dinner, particularly with my blowhard son-in-law. I promise the other two possess better manners. You're a bright young woman, even brilliant to hear my son tell it, and I've no doubt you can master anything you set your mind to. I will stand by you every step of the way."

"You would?" Tilda blinked. "I confess I'm overwhelmed by your kindness. You've given me much to think about."

"Good. You must not make any decision lightly. I will endorse whatever you choose, even if it's not my son. I would much rather you step away now if you can't be completely certain you will be happy together." She fixed on Tilda with a sharp intensity. "And you must accept that your career cannot be primary any longer."

She didn't say she couldn't *have* a career. Tilda found that encouraging. "I will consider all you've said."

Mrs. Acorn came in then with the tea tray wearing a sunny

smile. "Welcome, Lady Ravenhurst. I've tea and lavender biscuits."

Lady Ravenhurst stood. "Lavender? I was about to depart, but I think I must have just one." She flashed a smile before removing her right glove and plucking a biscuit from the tray Mrs. Acorn held.

Tilda met Mrs. Acorn's gaze and inclined her head to the round table near the front window. Mrs. Acorn deposited the tray as Lady Ravenhurst sampled the biscuit.

"Delicious," Lady Ravenhurst said before putting the rest of the biscuit into her mouth and donning her glove. After swallowing, she said, "Please give my compliments to your cook."

That was Mrs. Acorn, but Tilda didn't say so. Their household was much smaller than probably anywhere Lady Ravenhurst had lived.

Tilda walked Hadrian's mother to the entrance hall. "Thank you for calling. I appreciate everything you said."

"I trust you'll make the right decision—whatever that is." She gave Tilda a warm smile.

Vaughn opened the door, and Lady Ravenhurst swept from the house.

Once the door was closed, Tilda turned. She stopped short as she saw Mrs. Acorn standing in the doorway to the parlor and Grandmama at the opposite side of the entrance hall, having come from the back of the house. They both eyed Tilda with barely concealed…glee.

Tilda gaped at them. "Were you listening?"

Mrs. Acorn lifted a shoulder. "I came up with the tea, but then I heard what her ladyship was saying, and I couldn't just walk in, could I?"

"So you decided to listen instead?"

"I fetched your grandmother first," the housekeeper explained. "I thought it best if she heard for herself instead of from me."

Blinking, Tilda found she could not be outraged. Instead, she laughed. They laughed too. Even Vaughn joined in.

"Did you listen too?" Tilda asked when she could catch her breath.

Vaugh shrugged. "You know my hearing isn't the best."

"I know it's better than you say it is." Tilda smiled as she shook her head. Then she walked to the parlor, and Mrs. Acorn stepped aside to let her pass.

Walking to the tea tray, Tilda picked up a biscuit and nibbled the edge. She perched on a chair as Mrs. Acorn and her grandmother came into the parlor.

"It wasn't enough to eavesdrop, now you want to discuss what you overheard?" Tilda asked.

"Don't you want to discuss it?" Grandmama came to sit at the table with Tilda. Mrs. Acorn joined them and poured the tea.

"Not particularly."

"Well, I'm here if you do," Grandmama said.

"As am I," Mrs. Acorn added.

"Thank you. I do appreciate the support."

Grandmama's features drew together into a serious and thoughtful expression. "Lady Ravenhurst laid things out rather clearly."

"She did." Tilda took another small bite of the biscuit.

"It's nice to hear his lordship loves you," Mrs. Acorn said with an encouraging smile.

"Tilda loves him too," Grandmama told her.

Tilda didn't mind her sharing that with Mrs. Acorn. The housekeeper was family to her. In many ways, she was closer to Tilda than her own mother.

"I know you want to hear what I plan to do, but I don't know yet. And I'm sorry, but when I do, Hadrian will be the first to know."

"As he should be, my dear," Grandmama said. "But if you need to discuss anything, to work things out, we're here for you." She glanced at Mrs. Acorn who nodded.

"Let's just drink tea and eat more of these delicious lavender biscuits please." Tilda smiled and hoped the tea would settle her stomach and her nerves.

It did neither.

~

Hadrian couldn't stand it anymore. He'd resisted calling on Tilda, telling himself he ought to wait for her to invite him. But that was absurd. He'd never stood on such ceremony before.

He'd endured two entire days without seeing her. And here it was, the third day without Tilda, and he simply couldn't bear it.

His coach stopped in Marylebone in front of her grandmother's house. He climbed out without waiting for his replacement coachman, Towson, to open the door.

Hadrian glanced toward the puzzled coachman. "Pardon, Towson. Sometimes, I'm overeager."

"As you like, my lord." Towson was a good twenty years Leach's junior, which made him a few years older than Hadrian. He was tall and wide with a mop of dark blond hair that, together with his full cheeks, gave him the appearance of someone who looked a few years younger than Hadrian.

"I'm not sure how long I'll be," Hadrian said. Towson inclined his head, then climbed back onto the seat to wait.

Vaughn opened the door before Hadrian reached the step. "Afternoon, my lord. I trust you're recuperating well from that horrible blast."

"I am indeed, thank you."

"What of your coachman, Mr. Leach?" Vaughn closed the door as Hadrian stepped into the entrance hall. "I quite like him."

"I'll tell him you said so." Hadrian removed his gloves and hat and handed them to the butler. "He's on the mend, thankfully, though he detests being abed."

"I appreciate that very well, my lord. I think I'd be up and about already, and there's nothing anyone could do about that." He nodded perfunctorily before setting Hadrian's accessories on a small table.

Hadrian smiled knowingly. "If I recall, that's precisely what you did after sustaining a concussion before you came to live here."

Vaughn inclined his head. "Just so, my lord. If you want to go into the parlor, I'll fetch Miss Wren." The butler ambled slowly toward the back of the house.

Hadrian walked into the parlor and noted, not for the first time, how comfortable he felt here. This wasn't his home, but the people here made it seem as though it could be. He hoped Tilda felt the same about Ravenhurst House or would come to. And what of Ravenswood? He feared she may not care for his ancestral pile. Tilda had spent her life in London. What if she disliked living in the country, even for just a part of the year?

He tried to see things from her perspective. What if the roles were reversed and Hadrian had to give up his household to wed Tilda? He'd no longer be an earl, but *Mr.* Wren. Shockingly, he didn't think he'd mind that.

How horrified his father would be. He'd instilled in Hadrian the privilege that came with being the Earl of Ravenhurst and the expectation that he must rise above those beneath him and lead. Hadrian had no problem with leading, but he understood his privilege and that was precisely why he would not rise above anyone. Who was he to do that based on happenstance of birth? Perhaps that was why Hadrian had no quarrel with becoming Mr. Wren.

"Hadrian." Tilda strolled into the room looking fresh and beautiful, her red-gold hair styled simply, and her slender form dressed in a plain but still fetching gown of dark moss-green. She smiled and appeared genuinely happy to see him. "I'm glad you've come. I was going to call on you today."

"Were you?" That made him ridiculously pleased. "How fortuitous that I've come."

Tilda sat in one of the chairs, and Hadrian tamped down his disappointment. He preferred when they sat together on the settee. Hadrian sat there anyway in case she decided to move.

"Is all well? How is Leach?" Tilda asked.

"Improving every day," Hadrian replied. "He misses driving, of course. And yes, all is well. Was there a reason you were going to call on me?"

She hesitated, and small lines formed between her brows. Hadrian had the sense something was wrong, and he tensed.

"I received a note a short while ago." She removed a folded piece of parchment from her pocket. "It arrived in an envelope marked in the same way as the second ransom notes that were mailed to the Chadwicks and the others."

Hadrian's blood froze as he took the paper from her. He willed his hands to be still as he opened it and read the contents.

Lord Ravenhurst and Miss Wren,

You have ruined my plans most egregiously, and there must be a consequence. As you know, I'm a very patient man. I will have my revenge.

Spring-heeled Jack

Hadrian looked up from the note and was surprised to see that Tilda did not look terribly concerned. The lines between her brows had smoothed away.

"I expected as much from Lawrence," she said.

"But this is a blatant threat." Hadrian frowned. "I don't like this at all."

"Nor do I, but we knew it was likely he'd seek vengeance again."

"Yes, however we don't know if it will be soon or in twenty-five years."

"I suspect he'll be too old in twenty-five years," Tilda noted with a sardonic smile.

Hadrian refolded the parchment. "This is not amusing. Have you shared this with Teague?"

Tilda shook her head. "Not yet. I wanted to tell you first. We can show it to him together. It is to both of us. I'm surprised he didn't send the same note to you."

"Perhaps he did, and I just haven't received it yet. It may have arrived since I left." Hadrian was suddenly very angry. And more than a little afraid. He couldn't bear if anything happened to Tilda."

"It's too bad it didn't arrive a little earlier, for then I could have shared it with Wycombe. He called to tell me that Lawrence has not returned to the Albion, and his lodgings have been abandoned. He also said the Redmaynes have retreated to the country to fully recuperate. Wycombe intimated that Teague had suggested they leave London for a time."

"Just as he said to us," Hadrian said. "And now that you've received that note, I think it's necessary. You and your grandmother can be my guests at Ravenswood."

"Don't you need to stay here for Parliament?" Tilda asked.

"I can take the train back and forth. Hampshire isn't terribly far."

"Is that an invitation, or are you making a demand?"

"I would never demand you do anything," he replied, though in this case he wanted to. "You have a standing invitation to any of my homes."

She stared at him. "Are there more than two?"

He realized this had never come up before. "Er, yes. There's a hunting lodge in Scotland as well as a lovely cottage in the Lake District."

"I'd no idea. Who takes care of them?"

"The lodge has a groundskeeper and a housekeeper. They're married actually. The cottage has a small contingent of servants."

She arched a brow in a thoroughly wry expression. "Is this a *cottage* like Lord Courtenay's?"

Hadrian chuckled then grimaced. "Somewhat larger, I'm afraid."

"I see," she murmured. "One wonders what else I don't know about you."

Probably a great many things, just as there were countless things he didn't yet know about her. But he was eager to. He'd never wanted to discover anything more than every single thing about Matilda Wren.

"I received a letter from Captain Vale in answer to my query about the effects of experiencing too many memories in a short period. As with nearly everything with this skill, it varies from person to person."

Tilda regarded him with concern—and tender care. "Did you tell him you lost consciousness, and you suspect it's due to the intensity of the emotions you're sensing?"

"Yes, and he was alarmed to hear it." He saw Tilda's eyes darken and the lines in her forehead deepened. He rushed to add, "But he wasn't overly concerned. Apparently, his son suffered in the same way the first few years after he obtained the ability." It was generally triggered by some kind of trauma to the head.

"Years?" Tilda's eyes widened. "I'm sorry to hear that."

"No sorrier than I," Hadrian said wryly. He did not look forward to years of such debilitating pain and having to closely monitor the use of his ability, particularly when they were in the midst of an investigation.

"Since we are speaking of letters, I also received a missive yesterday from Mrs. Chadwick," Tilda said.

Hadrian's brows rose sharply. "Did you?"

Tilda nodded. "She thanked me for discovering who kidnapped and killed their daughter. She also apologized for her husband's treatment of me, particularly the article he asked to be published about my mishandling of the case."

"You didn't mishandle a thing," Hadrian grumbled. "That was kind of her to take the time to write to you, especially given the suffering they must be experiencing."

"Yes, she mentioned her shock and grief that their daughter had conspired to fake her own kidnapping and steal their money in order to elope with her elocution tutor." Tilda shook her head. "It sounds like the plot of a penny dreadful, except it's true and very sad."

"I can't imagine how they must be feeling."

"Actually, she concluded the letter with a bit of good news," Tilda said. "Apparently, the Duke of Alnwick has consented to allow Vincent to court Lady Priscilla—after a suitable mourning period for his sister. Mrs. Chadwick hoped something good may come from everything that's happened."

"I will hope so," Hadrian said solemnly. "For all their sakes."

They fell silent, which didn't happen very often for they were typically involved in a case that required discussion and theorizing. "Have you chosen your next case?" he asked. "I'm eager to assist, but I suppose you wouldn't have a case if you decided to sojourn at Ravenswood."

Tilda frowned, and Hadrian's stomach churned. She stood and went to close the door, which only fed his anxiety. Returning, she sat on the settee but situated herself as far away from him as she could get, positioning herself so her back was against the arm. She twisted her upper body to face him.

"Hadrian, we can't have any more cases together. Not the way it's been."

Harian felt as though the earth were collapsing beneath him. "Why not?"

"The press coverage, and the gossip…it's been too much. It hurts me as a detective to be an unmarried woman working with an unmarried man. An earl, no less." She took a breath, and Hadrian didn't at all care for the sympathy in her eyes. "I fear our arrangement damages you even more. You need to marry and you have duties, which you've ignored whilst working with me, your 'lady detective.'"

"What are you saying?" His voiced sounded hollow. He *felt* hollow. "I can't *not* work beside you. You've completely changed my life. Can't you see I'm a private detective now too?" *Never mind how desperately I love you and can't bear to be apart from you.* He wanted to say the words, but fear and despair clogged his throat.

"I can, actually, and I'm so happy to hear you say that, for the one thing I really don't want to give up is our work together. However, there is only one way we can continue as we have."

Hadrian began to breathe a little more easily. "I'm glad to hear you say you don't want to stop working together. I can honestly tell you that being apart from you for even a pair of days is agony."

"Then perhaps you'll approve of my solution." She scooted toward him and clasped his hands. Her eyes met his, and her lips curled into the most beguiling smile he'd ever seen her wear.

"Hadrian, Lord Ravenhurst, will you consent to be my husband?"


**Don't miss the next thrilling book in the Raven & Wren series: A WHISPER OF FATE! Will they capture Nicholas Larkin/Lawrence? How will Hadrian answer Tilda's question? Join your favorite sleuthing duo as they travel to Ravenswood in Hampshire where old family secrets may reveal the key to Hadrian's bizarre power.**

Spring-heeled Jack is an urban legend from the Victorian period in the United Kingdom. He was sighted on many occasions and accused of attacking two young women in London in early 1838. Those attacks on Miss Jane Alsop and Miss Lucy Scales are included in this book. The details of their attacks are unchanged from the source material. In some cases, I chose one source's information over another. For instance, the attack on Miss Alsop happened either February 19 or 21. I chose the 19th.

James Lea investigated Miss Alsop's attack, and he also arrested the killer in the Red Barn Murder in 1827. I don't know whether he was alive or not in 1868, so I made the narrative decision for him to be deceased. Former investigator James Hopkins is entirely fictional.

I devised the various tricks that were employed to make Spring-heeled Jack appear as though he had red eyes or breathed blue flame. The springs in his boots seem to be something that was suspected.

Spring-heeled Jack began as a terrifying boogeyman in the mid-19th century. His legend was written into stories and plays throughout the 19th century, and over time he became an antihero or vigilante. The first instance of that characterization is in the 1863 story, *Spring-heel'd Jack, The Terror of London*, by Alfred Coates, which I reference in this book. Jack is recognized as a precursor to 20th century superheroes, particularly Batman.

I had never heard of Spring-heeled Jack until my daughter sent me a podcast about him. She thought it would be cool to include him in one of my Victorian mysteries, and she was right!

# ALSO BY DARCY BURKE

**Historical Mystery**

***Raven & Wren***

A Whisper of Death

A Whisper at Midnight

A Whisper and a Curse

A Whisper in the Shadows

A Whisper of Secrecy

A Whisper in Darkness

Only Murders in the Square

In the Midnight Hour

**Historical Romance**

If the Duke Dares

Because the Baron Broods

When the Viscount Seduces

As the Earl Likes

Until the Rake Surrenders

Since the Marquess Demands

What the Scoundrel Desires

How the Devil Sins

***The Phoenix Club***

Improper

Impassioned

Intolerable

Indecent

Impossible

Irresistible

Impeccable

Insatiable

***The Matchmaking Chronicles***

Yule Be My Duke

The Rigid Duke

The Bachelor Earl (also prequel to *The Untouchables*)

The Runaway Viscount

The Make-Believe Widow

***Marrywell Brides***

Beguiling the Duke

Romancing the Heiress

Matching the Marquess

***The Untouchables***

The Bachelor Earl (prequel)

The Forbidden Duke

The Duke of Daring

The Duke of Deception

The Duke of Desire

The Duke of Defiance

The Duke of Danger

The Duke of Ice

The Duke of Ruin

The Duke of Lies

The Duke of Seduction

The Duke of Kisses

The Duke of Distraction

***The Untouchables: The Spitfire Society***

Never Have I Ever with a Duke

A Duke is Never Enough

A Duke Will Never Do

***The Untouchables: The Pretenders***

A Secret Surrender

A Scandalous Bargain

A Rogue to Ruin

***Love is All Around***

*(A Regency Holiday Trilogy)*

The Red Hot Earl

The Gift of the Marquess

Joy to the Duke

***Wicked Dukes Club***

One Night for Seduction by Erica Ridley

One Night of Surrender by Darcy Burke

One Night of Passion by Erica Ridley

One Night of Scandal by Darcy Burke

One Night to Remember by Erica Ridley

One Night of Temptation by Darcy Burke

***Secrets and Scandals***

Her Wicked Ways

His Wicked Heart

To Seduce a Scoundrel

To Love a Thief (a novella)

Never Love a Scoundrel

Scoundrel Ever After

### *Legendary Rogues*

Lady of Desire

Romancing the Earl

Lord of Fortune

Captivating the Scoundrel

## Contemporary Romance

### *Ribbon Ridge*

Let Go (a prequel novella)

Get Lucky

Sparks Fly

Fall Hard

Can't Stop

Break Free

Hold Me

Turn On

So Right

This Love

Prefer to read in German, French, or Italian? Check out my website for
foreign language editions!

# ABOUT THE AUTHOR

Darcy Burke is the USA Today Bestselling Author of historical romance and mystery and contemporary romance. Darcy wrote her first book at age 11, a happily ever after about a swan addicted to magic and the female swan who loved him, with exceedingly poor illustrations. Join her Reader Club newsletter for the latest updates from Darcy.

A native Oregonian, Darcy lives on the edge of wine country with her guitar-strumming husband, incredibly talented artist daughter, and imaginative, Japanese-speaking son who will almost certainly out-write her one day (that may be tomorrow). They're a crazy cat family with two Bengal cats, a small, fame-seeking torbie named after a fruit, an older rescue Maine Coon with attitude to spare, an adorable former stray who wandered onto their deck and into their hearts, and two bonded boys (a Russian Blue and a Turkish Van) who used to belong to (separate) neighbors but chose them instead. You can find Darcy in her comfy writing chair balancing her laptop and a cat or three, attempting yoga, folding laundry (which she loves), or wildlife spotting and playing games with her family. She loves traveling to the UK and visiting her cousins in Denmark. Visit Darcy online at www.darcyburke.com and follow her on social media.

facebook.com/DarcyBurkeFans

instagram.com/darcyburkeauthor

pinterest.com/darcyburkewrites

goodreads.com/darcyburke

bookbub.com/authors/darcy-burke

amazon.com/author/darcyburke

tiktok.com/@darcyburkeauthor

bsky.app/profile/darcyburkeauthor.bsky.social

A small press bound by the belief that every voice matters.

Sign up for our newsletter to learn about new releases and more.

*Buy directly from us to save on ebooks, book bundles, and special editions.*

Follow us on social media:

facebook.com/oliverheberbooks
instagram.com/oliverheberbooks
tiktok.com/@oliverheberbooks
bsky.app/profile/oliverheberbooks.bsky.social
youtube.com/@OliverHeberBooksPublisher
oliverheberbooks.substack.com
amazon.com/oliverheberbooks